JANE EVANS

Based on the true story

of a Welsh woman's journey

from drover to the Crimea

CHRISTINE PURKIS

yLolfa

First impression: 2019
© Christine Purkis & Y Lolfa Cyf., 2019

Cover design: Olwen Fowler

ISBN: 978 1 912631 00 1

The publishers wish to acknowledge the support of
Cyngor Llyfrau Cymru

Published and printed in Wales
on paper from well-maintained forests by
Y Lolfa Cyf., Talybont, Ceredigion SY24 5HE
e-mail ylolfa@ylolfa.com
website www.ylolfa.com
tel 01970 832 304
fax 832 782

Prologue

*J*ANE EVANS KILLED *her mam. Her brothers told her so.
Split her front to back. Blood flooded the alcove-bed in the
kitchen, dripped down onto the floor and trickled between the
flagstones to the front step, where the dogs lapped it up.*

*Born to be different Jane was, arriving feet first, kicking and
struggling and bursting for breath. The bulk of her! A girl –
twice the size of her three brothers, so her Aunt Anni said; and
she should know, for she had brought them all into the world.*

*Her tad had returned to Caio from the Hereford horse fair in
the March of 1820 without a horse, but with an English wife
who had been working in service there, shocking the village
on both counts. Her name was Mary. Why could he not have
chosen a local girl? Eventually, after producing three fine sons,
and proving herself a resourceful, generous, hard working
woman without a superior bone in her body, her foreignness
was almost forgiven.*

Until the new arrival's head was wetted in the local inn.

*Tad had left Mam weak and pale, but with no thought of her
dying on him.*

'Congratulations, John Evans! Is the name chosen?'

'Jane. Jane Evans.'

*It took Mam six years to die, though she never regained her
strength after Jane's difficult birth. Thin as a skeleton she was.
In a wild wind, only the weight of her boots tethered her to
the earth. The loss of the mother the boys had known all their
lives was clearly Jane's fault. If they hadn't made certain Jane*

knew herself to be responsible, she might have grown up not knowing she was a murderess and that could never be right.

When Mam gave birth to William six years after Jane, the miracle was a double one: first, that she had had a baby, because no-one knew a baby was on the way – Mam least of all, or so she said; second, that William survived, a tiny scrap of flesh, skinny and long as a newborn lamb.

Mam did not live to hear him say 'Mam-mam-mam', though Jane taught him with great determination. The boys stuck together. William could not be blamed for Mam's death. It was Jane who had killed her.

CHAPTER 1

A Terrible Inheritance

WHY DOES EVERYONE hate me? I've done nothing!

Jane ran down the road holding her wooden clogs in one hand and her gathered skirt in the other. Mud squelched under her feet and splattered her legs. The ruts from the carts were deep. At this time of the year they were often black with tadpoles. She slowed to look. Wriggling, but still held in jellied water. Tiny flecks of life. Not a chance they had, born in a rut in the road. Sometimes she stopped, scooped them out in a pot and carried them to the stream at the bottom of Dipping Field. But not today.

Clouds pushed across the sky. The blue hills were clear as Heaven. Rooks circled above the trees on the Dinas, their voices rough and rasping. They were building their nests high: a good summer ahead, so Mam used to say. A cloud of white gulls in the far corner of Dipping Field meant Griffith was down there with the plough. He'd not notice her anyway, with his mind on the horses and the line of the furrow.

How Jane used to love watching Tad ploughing, pulling back the reins hard, the horses rearing up so you could see their hooves, huge as dinner plates. Everything started in Tad's shoulders: the plough followed in a wide arc as the horses moved on one spot, churning and trampling the earth. No pause. Heads down and they were off, slicing and turning the dark earth.

Difficult, Tad called his soil: claggy and heavy. But it was enough – just – to keep seven of them in bread. When they *were* seven. Five now. Mam underneath, Tad on top in one grave behind the chapel.

A line separated the green grass from purple scrub and rock on the far hillside. The slopes were dotted with black cattle and white sheep. Sheep looked after themselves most of the time, eating and fattening, dropping their lambs. Not like the pigs.

Griffith had calculated another week of waiting but he was always on the cautious side, with a belief in figures and averages and things that made Jane impatient.

The Evans farm, Tŷ Mawr, was set a long way back from the lane; a low long house, grey and gloomy with small windows and a thatched roof. Bright green moss was a sign that things had gone too far. Green is right for the fields, wrong for the roof, Tad would say. He had taken a pride in his thatch – unusual in those grey slate parts.

With a glance left and right, Jane slipped across the yard. Please let them not have come while I was at school, God.

In the farrowing pen, cut off from the other pigs, lay Morwenna – the White Maid. All the pigs were given names by Jane from the stories – for weren't they beautiful as the fairy princesses with their pink skin and hair like gold from the Dolaucothi Mines? There was no need for the boys to know their names. They would only scoff.

In the open section of the sty, pigs tore around in a frenzy. Pigs could never believe things were not going to be as they wanted. Jane fed them mornings and evenings, but they never gave up hope that she'd feed them any time if they screamed long enough. There was so much to admire in a pig.

Jane opened the sty door as far as she could before it stuck on the earth floor, and squeezed in. Morwenna lay in the mired straw, sleeping. Occasionally her ears twitched. Her lumpy side rose and fell. Jane checked her rear end. Nothing.

Let it be soon, God. Before the end of the week and make Griffith wrong. And let them all live and let her live too.

Distressing it was when a piglet slipped into the world dead already. Tiny and perfect and dead. Hard then to understand God's purpose.

Life was not fair or easy. Four boys and one girl: Griffith, Richard, David, then Jane and lastly William; growing to be like his brothers, which was hard to bear. He was Jane's baby. She'd nursed him and fed him and washed him and changed him all the long months when her mother was ill. He'd slept in the curve of her stomach – her protection, her protected.

To be left the only woman in a house of men is a terrible inheritance. So much was expected of her and no-one helped. Every day the mud was tramped in and left in clods on the floor, when all they had to do was take their boots off at the door. They'd lined them up for Mam in the porch. Why not for Jane? Never would they take their dishes to the pantry now; they'd get up from the table leaving everything.

Jane threw the dirty plates into the stone sink. No water. The handle of the well in the yard creaked and complained at every turn as the bucket filled. Now it was summer it wasn't so bad. In winter her hands stuck to the metal handle and the disc of ice was too hard to break. Even when she threw rocks down, they skittered over the surface and made no impact at all. Until the thaw came, Jane had to wipe the dishes clean with crusts of bread. Snow lingered on the mountain tops now and no place else.

The pigs were screaming again. Thinking of Morwenna made all the chores faster and easier. Griffith had promised

Jane she could keep two sows this year for breeding, and fatten the boars for market after gelding. They might make the spring drove to London if they fattened up in time. The more piglets, the better pleased Griffith would be and that would be good for everyone.

Dear God, don't let Morwenna squash them, like she did last year. Griffith had blamed her. Jane closed her eyes and pushed the thought away. It was a skill she had, chasing memories from her head. Oh, they were there, lurking, but she had the power to keep them on the very edges of her mind, without words and formless.

The potato sack was kept in the old pantry. She reached inside. Right down at the bottom, the potatoes she pulled out had long white feelers on them. Blind, thin and worm-like. She snapped them off quickly and tossed them into the pigs' bucket. The skins were wrinkled, the flesh soft.

The fire looked dead. She poked it. That would be terrible luck. Especially for Jane – Griffith would take his belt to her.

God, please make it alive.

She must feed it sweet kindling, coax it into life like she had her mam with the beef tea she never wanted to take. Jane would prop her up in the alcove bed with one arm and feed her with a spoon. Like a bird she was: light, with her bones barely covered by her flesh.

Jane blew gently. Ashes stirred and floated in the air. She breathed out again, a long slow breath. A red spark lit and faded away. She blew again, teasing with wisps of dry grass and bark. This time it ignited and slowly the fire spread and gained strength. A point always came when certainty was reached and then, and only then, Jane smothered the flames with logs and lifted the heavy pan onto the hook.

Her scratching stick she had left leaning against the sty. If she bent over the low wooden fence she could reach right behind Caer's ears. Ten months old Caer was now, almost the size of his mother. He loved that scratching so, standing in a trance and begging for more when she stopped.

A door slammed behind her. The footsteps on the cobbles were slow and clumpy: Aunt Anni, Tad's aunt, who had pulled her out feet first into the world; Jane's first and only friend. Aunt Anni didn't welcome 'demonstrations', as she called them: hugs, holding, touching. Once, when Jane was little, Aunt Anni like a mother cow had pushed her away hard when she was clambering on her lap. Jane fell backwards and cried from the spurning. She never tried again.

'Jane. There you are with your pigs.' Aunt Anni's smile was in her grey eyes. Her mouth had given up the effort now she was old and her cheeks sunk without the teeth to shape them. She was never seen without her bonnet, even in her bed: black and tied beneath her chin. She wore men's boots and was holding her skirts up, treading carefully to avoid the worst of the mud.

She pulled the corner of her shawl over her face.

'Step away, Jane. We can sit here in the sun.'

Outside the cowshed lay a block of stone. No-one knew what it was nor where it had come from. Too big for a gate post or marking stone, with no sign or inscription on it. Aunt Anni knew in her bones the stone was old and wise and had lain here much longer than the house or the farm or even the church, and Aunt Anni's bones were never wrong.

Aunt Anni spread her fingers gently on the stone when she sat.

'Come. Sit. Not too near. Ah, it's good to feel a little warmth on your bones.'

She raised her face towards the low sun. Her cheeks were as criss-crossed with tracks as the hills. Hair thick as pig's bristles sprouted from her chin and above her top lip.

Jane could wait no longer. Words spilled out like a river bursting a dam.

'They were mean as they always are. Gwendolyn and Pedr and the rest of them. All I was doing was walking down the street and they were hiding and jumped out at me and took my basket and threw it in the river. And now I don't have the basket to get the eggs, and Griffith will be so angry and...' Jane jabbed her stick into the ground. 'Why do they dislike me so?'

'Put that stick down, Jane.' Aunt Anni took Jane's empty hand and turned it palm up.

'Lord, Lord, Jane. What's to become of you?'

Jane shrugged.

'Well, I've not stopped for this. I bring news. The dogs are back.'

Now that was better news: an occasion in the inn to look forward to when the drovers returned – that would put everyone in a better mood.

'The corgis ran into the yard at noon, black with dirt and panting like the Devil. Two days, we always reckon before the men appear, though it might be one. Dogs don't stop at the Drover's Inn with their pockets full of money. I'm leaving you to tell the boys,' she said. 'Come by tomorrow.'

'I will, unless Morwenna....'

'Ah, Morwenna. I thought it would be another week yet?'

'But you can never be sure with birthing.'

'That is true Jane, and I know you will tell me as soon as there is something to tell.'

She looked at Jane with sudden seriousness. 'You do tell me everything, don't you, Jane? You would not keep anything from me.'

CHAPTER 2

A Fair Price

S ORE HEADS AND short tempers men have when their bellies are hollow. The way they were, you'd think Jane was responsible for every calamity: the weather, the falling price for the sheep, the mines closing. A desperate winter they had with the cold biting deep and staying until they had no food but the scrapings of oatmeal; no eggs now with the hen house empty in the barn. Occasionally David caught strange creatures: once he threw her a pine marten to cook. There's no meat on a pine marten.

Mr Morgan, their neighbour, came into the farmhouse one evening when Jane was in her bed. She heard his greeting. Drifting to sleep she was, when her name was mentioned. Griffith repeated it, like a question: 'Jane?'

She sat up, ears straining to catch every word.

'Times are worrisome, Griffith. I've a proposal. I'll take Jane off your hands with nothing. Fifteen is she? Thereabouts. A good age. You can't say that's not a fair offer. Your tad was a good friend to me, and your mam a good neighbour when my Alis passed on.'

Jane's heart banged against her ribs.

It took a while for Griffith to speak.

'She's young and you are not so young... It would be hard for us to manage without a woman.'

'I know it. It's for that reason I am here. You'll find yourself a woman the quicker, young Griffith, when the need is the greater. And until you do, I'm willing to let Jane come over every day to look after you all.'

Jane's whole body froze.

'It's a fair price I'm offering. It will see you out of your troubles.'

Those words cracked the ice. Jane leapt from the bed with her heart bursting like a bulrush. If only she could fill the air with fluff and drift away on the wind.

No, never, not Mr Morgan. That toothless old beast with his leery eyes and twiddling fingers. Never! Jane paced up and down, her hands clenched in knots. The kitchen door opened and closed on its latch. Griffith's tread on the stairs was heavy – as well it might be.

Married to Mr Morgan! Never.

The house fell still. A suffocating silence seeped in under doors and through windows. Right on the edge of the bed Jane sat, her feet in contact with the floor, the blanket round her shoulders.

Eventually she lay back, staring into the dark. Fully clothed, Mr Morgan was a horrible sight. Bare and fleshy and her husband, backing her onto the bed, his face coming nearer and nearer... Jane shook her head. Could this be her life? Put on earth for this? Never.

'I will run away somewhere else, somewhere I'll be lost to everyone here. Only God will know where I am.'

How could Griffith do this to her? He wasn't a bad person, though held in to himself so you never knew what he was thinking. But he was bad to *her*. They all were. Mr Morgan was their neighbour with fine breeding animals – a boar and a bull – known to them all for years. Years! That was the point. Hadn't Griffith himself said Mr Morgan was old and Jane young? How could anyone look at the man and not see how he was? Would Griffith not know how she hated the sight of him?

Jane sat up. No. He might not know. She hadn't told Griffith. Not straight. Not 'I hate the man', clear as that.

The next morning in the early grey of dawn, she raked the ash and built a new fire from the old embers. The kettle would be boiling by the time she returned with milk. She'd make *sucan blawd* just as Griffith liked it, scalding the milk for him. She'd make bruised oatmeal cake and buttermilk for mid-morning. He would have to understand this marriage was out of the question.

Griffith was the last to come in from the yard.

'I hate the man. I won't and you can't make me.'

Griffith would not look her in the eye. The others stole quietly away. They were all in on it.

'I have given my word, Jane. He's a good neighbour.'

'That does not mean I have to marry him.'

'It would be the end to our problems.'

'And the beginning of mine. What about me, Griffith?' Jane threw herself at his knees. 'Please Griffith, I'll do anything you ask of me.'

'This is what I am asking, Jane. Get off me.' He shook her away, but he didn't hurt her. At the door, he stopped.

'Not till next week, Jane. There are a few days to prepare.'

Jane ran outside. She stood in the middle of the yard not knowing where to go. I will not! This will not be! She ran towards the pigs. No. Back towards the barn. Not inside. Nowhere where walls pressed in on her. She had to keep moving. Pacing, a solution might appear, pumped up from her heart to her head. Why did you have to go and die, Mam? Why did you go and leave me to this, Tad? Mr Morgan coupled to your daughter. Your Jane. You'd not consider it in a thousand years. What can I do?

A few days to prepare. What did Griffith think she'd be doing? Mending her clothes, smoothing lanolin into the cracks in her hands, bathing her face in morning milk, putting a shine into her hair with an egg? She stopped. Aunt Anni. Aunt Anni. Griffith would listen to Tad's aunt as Tad had! A wiser woman did not exist in the world. Aunt Anni was her last hope. She told me I must keep nothing from her. She will help me. She will. I am too young. She will see it my way. I know it. Griffith will listen to her. He will. He must.

Jane raced down the lane, leaving Griffith unmoved as the block of cold stone in the yard of Tŷ Mawr. Right over the far side of the village Aunt Anni lived, not far as the crows fly but a distance for anything without wings. Down the main street in the village she ran, past St Cynwyl's church and the Inn opposite, over the bridge, past the chapel and the standing stone, right through the woods and up over two fields.

Cousin Isaac was sitting outside his cottage, knitting socks for the pigs.

'Jane! What brings you here?'

She could hardly speak for the rasping of her breath.

'Where's Aunt Anni?'

'You've missed her, Jane. She's off to Doctor Harris for a few days while I'm at home and can look after her hens.'

George, his five-year-old son – a skinny pale child with a pinched face but a thatch of black hair – was sorting kindling into piles at his feet. All was lost! Jane sank to the ground, beating her fists on the earth like a child.

'Jane, Jane. Whatever is it?' Isaac held her up and hugged her. She folded into him and sobbed.

'I can't. I won't. What can I do?'

He led her to the seat.

'George, go in to your mother and bring tea for Jane. Generous with the honey. Tell me what's happened, Jane.'

'Griffith is selling me. He has no money.'

Isaac nodded.

'Times are hard,' he said.

'Not so hard that you sell your sister to your horrible old neighbour.'

Isaac frowned. 'Who?'

'Mr Morgan!'

'To marry?'

Jane wiped her nose on the hem of her skirt. 'What else?'

Isaac whistled through his teeth. 'He's older than you, Jane – is that it?'

'He's old and I cannot bear to think of him.'

'The look of the man. Is that all there is?'

'No! It's the age of him *and* all the rest.'

Elisabeth, Isaac's wife, came out of the house with the tea. Skin pale as thin milk and clothes hanging loose on her body, she handed it to Jane and left without saying a word.

'You're fifteen now, aren't you, Jane? Though I can hardly believe my little cousin to be of the marrying age already.'

'Because I'm not!'

'A person does not have to marry for love now, Jane.' Isaac kicked at a chip of wood by his foot. 'Love might grow. It might not. But you have to learn to live your lives together.'

'No, I don't have to learn that. I'm not going to marry for love or any other reason. I don't want to be married at all.'

Isaac smiled.

'Don't laugh at me. I mean it.'

His face was serious at once. 'I wasn't laughing at you, Jane. And I know you mean it.'

'Now Aunt Anni is gone and she was the one person who could help me. What can I do?'

The sobs started again. *Self-pity is a waste of time!* The words were as clear as if Aunt Anni were right beside her.

Every question has an answer. Find it! Suddenly she sat up, clear and calm. Shaking her wild hair behind her shoulders, she stared Isaac straight in the eyes.

'Take me with you.'

Isaac stared back, trying to understand her words.

'Take me with you. On the drove. Why not?'

He shook his head, starting to laugh, when he thought better of it. 'Jane. No woman has ever been on a drove.'

'Take me with you.'

'I cannot.'

Jane hadn't finished her tea but she set down her cup, rose, and without another word set off back down the field.

There were places over the hills to run to: that's what she reasoned as she walked back to Tŷ Mawr. If Isaac would not take her on the drove, she would take herself. She needed no-one. Didn't she have legs and strength? If she took a few clothes, some rags for her needs, a cup maybe, some food – oatmeal bread would last an age. She would take it all and not leave the boys a single crumb.

William would feed the pigs. And she'd think the word 'pigs', not their names, and all would be well.

There was no-one in sight at Tŷ Mawr. Jane slipped inside, took the oatcakes from the griddle, ran upstairs and folded them into a shawl. No reason to look around. There was nothing she'd be sad to say goodbye to. Apart from William. And the pigs.

She kept to the hedge till she was well past sight of Mr Morgan's neighbouring Long House. At the fork in the road, her head down, she collided with William coming up from the village.

'Jane.'

She sprang away and, like a fool, started to run.

'Where are you going?'

She ran the faster without answering him. Why had she acted so stupid? If only she'd made something up! Now William would run back and fetch the boys, without thinking. Or if he did think, he would only think of himself: of how his life would be without her.

Breathless and berating herself, Jane laboured upwards, following the stream through the oak trees and mossy rocks to the open bracken on the sides of the hill. The path merged with narrow sheep tracks. An occasional startled sheep bounded out of its cover and fled.

Above the bracken, bare scree rose sharply to the crest. Her feet slipped and a bitter wind cut through her clothes.

'Jane! Jane!' Faint cries rose from far below. She turned, in a panic. Two of Mr Morgan's ponies were clear of the woods and making towards her. Griffith and David. Only a few feet further and she'd be at the summit and down the other side, finding a hiding place where they could not track her down. Holding her bundle in her teeth freed her hands to scrabble at the loose rock.

A small cairn of stones marked the summit. Beyond it – misery! – the ground fell sheer away. There was no place else to go. She sat heavily on the stony shelf, the wind throwing her hair across her face. A kestrel hovered only a few feet in front of her. Its rusty feathers trembled. Their eyes were level. The bird was far up, held on the thin air, and Jane still on the ground.

Below, the land folded into valleys as deep as the cracks on crusty bread. Sheep tracks cut curving green lines round the sides of the hill. Far ahead where the valleys opened, tiny limewashed houses just like Tŷ Mawr dotted the darker green. In the Bible in Revelation there was a grand story of a woman given the wings of the great eagle so that she could fly from a serpent into the wilderness, *into her place, where she is nourished for a time, and times, and half a time*. Next time. Next time.

Her legs dangled over the edge. The ponies were huffing up the hill behind her, hooves slipping on the scree. She stared straight ahead.

'Jane, don't!'

She turned, laughed. Griffith's dark eyes were pleading. The wind swept his fair hair back off his face, leaving his forehead white and flattening his cheeks.

'Did you think I'd throw myself off, Griffith? I'll not go that far.'

David would not look at her but sat on Mr Morgan's fat pony, staring off over the hills as though looking out for deer. Ever the hunter with his fox hair and keen green eyes, he pretended Jane was not his quarry.

She rode back in front of Griffith. The pony's flank was warm inside her thighs. No need to speak. Nothing to say.

Back home, William was poking the fire. He jumped up, his face caught between a smile and a frown.

Griffith followed her upstairs.

'You'll not leave the house again, Jane, till the day you are wed. I have put a bolt on the door. I don't like to do it. You are making a sacrifice for us all. Like the preacher said: *Present your bodies a living sacrifice, holy, acceptable unto God.*'

He closed the door behind him. The bolt slid across.

This is *not* acceptable to God. What kind of God would want a brother to sell his own sister to a monster? The house was silent. No visitors this night. Mr Morgan would be in his house up the lane. She shuddered, thinking of him sitting by the fire, his belly hanging, his trousers tight over his thighs and that ugly bulge he was forever rubbing and moving about. And the lips on him! Wet and hanging, with his tongue always resting there, fat and pink.

CHAPTER 3

Sharp and Quick

SEVEN OF THE longest days later, Jane crouched in the bracken at the side of the road. The ground fell steeply behind her to the cave where she had been hiding. Her head was down but if she straightened, her eyes were level with the dirt road. Sounds from the village drifted out of the thick fog like a wind, but far away, a fiercer wind was blowing in from the wilderness to the west, sweeping everything in front of it. Yet above Jane's head, the trees were still.

So many times she had watched the drove gather, she could see it now. A wondrous sight: those lines of white sheep and black cattle pouring off the hills like water, all funnelling onto the little hump bridge, spilling out into the field by the river. Old Jones would have his anvil out in the middle to fit the iron cues on the cattle. Young Jones by his side would be dipping the pigs' socks into his tar bucket. Such a shrieking and complaining and dancing in circles while the dogs nipped at their legs. Geese were easier to fit with their tar boots, and quieter because Old Jones could tuck them under his arm while his son held their beaks shut. The air would be churning with something about to happen; the sheep would be darting off when they saw an opportunity and the dogs kept busy. Only the cows would have their heads down, eating. A cow is not an excitable creature. And Isaac would be calm in the middle of the commotion. At his whistle, the whole drove would be away, moving in the same direction, quieter now, for their breath would be needed for the pull uphill from Caio.

Whoops and shouts were still distant but growing nearer.

The teller was leading the way. *'Heiptro Ho! Heiptro Ho!!'* The distant grumble grew to a rumble of hooves, the roar of hundreds of animals on the move. The drove was on its way and she would be part of it.

Where was William? The ground was vibrating. Her heart skipped in a panic until she calmed it. She could not, would not, wait. This was the moment, the opening and she must take it. She must pull herself up the path and join. The fog would give her invisibility. No-one must see her now.

The path was steep and slippery, her only help the dead bracken fronds. On the road above her they'd be by now. She fell forwards into the bracken.

Please God. Don't let me be seen.

She must not breathe, nor move a muscle. Someone was on her tail and she had not even begun. This was too cruel. If she let go of the bracken, she would fall.

'Jane!' William appeared above her. He scrambled down to a ledge below the level of the track. 'Give me your hand.'

He pulled, and she pulled with all her strength. Together they crouched in the bracken, their heads below the level of the road as the first geese waddled past, teetering on their spiked boots. A boy in a hat with a long stick followed them. Jane and William shrank back.

'Here.' He passed her a basket. 'Food.'

Jane crammed her mouth with stale bread. The night in the cave had left her hollow inside.

'Put these on.' William passed her clothes. The feel of the rough cloth, the smell, caught in her throat. 'A man won't be noticed. Be quick.'

'They're Tad's clothes. I won't wear Tad's clothes.' She pushed them back to William, pulling her shawl over her head. 'I'm Jane Evans. I'll go as Jane Evans. The fog will cover me.'

The pigs were passing, followed by the sheep. Men on ponies, boys with sticks, flanked either side; dogs too busy keeping the animals moving to notice them.

As the black cattle loomed like ghosts out of the mist, Jane and William jumped to their feet, ready. Four deep the cows were, walking slowly. Warmth from their bodies Jane felt on her cheeks. The suck and slurp of the mud mingled with their laboured breath.

'Go.'

William gave her a sharp push and the cattle surrounded Jane, moving her away.

She would be discovered – some time – but not yet.

Please God, make it long enough so it's impossible to send me back.

She was in the herd, part of the drove, her arms touched by the sides of the cows next to her. All she could see were the bony arched rumps in front and flicking tails. Occasionally a tail would stiffen and lift. Flops of green manure spattered the hem of her skirt. This fog was never going to last. Wrong time of year. Wrong kind of fog.

Terrible muddy it was, with the soil churned by all the animals in front of her. Behind her was the weight of breath and bodies, but she did not turn for fear of being seen. For the moment the fog was thick and she would keep low; but if her back ached beyond endurance and she *had* to straighten up and someone glimpsed a person in a shawl – nothing would be thought of it, surely? She'd be seen as someone travelling the same way as the drove, that's all. Unless that someone was Cousin Isaac. In charge, he'd be alert to everything.

Thinking about it made it so: her back an agony. A person cannot draw breath doubled up like that bent woman in the village who died when her ribs pressed into her hip bone, she was so crooked. It must have been a terrible thing to see nothing of the sky above for years, only the ground and your own feet. This was all Cousin Isaac's fault, clearly. If he had said yes, she would now be upright and walking with him and being useful as she could be.

Trees whispered over Jane's head, muffling the animals in its leaves as the droving track turned into the forest. In a flash of chestnut and coarse dark manes, the ponies were upon her, linking the front of the drove with Isaac at the back. She had no time to bury her face in her shawl. She held her breath. Nothing happened. They hadn't seen her, but her heart thumped with the closeness of discovery.

Keep your wits about you, Jane – or you'll be Mrs Morgan before you know it. She shuddered. Please, God, no. I'll do anything you ask me. Just keep me sharp and quick.

By the time the drove broke from the woods above Cilycwm, the sky was clear blue, the sun strong and the distant horizon clear. Jane bent below the height of the cows, though her back ached so. The roofs were visible along the village below – one long street with a church and inn in the middle and the school at one end. The drove would take a drink there, slow to a stop, and Jane would be found if she did not think quickly. Cilycwm folks always turned out to see the drove.

Before the fog lifted, the teller would have ridden into the village, blowing his horn and warning people to pen their animals if they did not want them tagging along on the drove. Right now, he'd be sitting outside the inn supping beer, keeping alert. As the first animals emerged from the wood, he'd finish his beer and ride off down the High Street.

'*Heiptro ho! Heiptro Ho!*'

The schoolteacher Mr Norris would no longer be able to keep the children at their slates when they heard him. The doors would open and out they'd stream to clamber onto the walls for a better view. Stools and rockers would be put out for the elderly. Jane could not go through the village, for certain. She'd be recognised by one of Elisabeth's family, who lived there, or Aunt Anni's friends, and taken back to her bed by nightfall to be wed in the morning.

She must break away and loop round the town, rejoining somewhere along the route. A line of scrubby hawthorn marked the gully, taking the water off the hills to the valley. If she could make it there, she could find safety.

She eyed the cow she was travelling next to. It eyed her back. She pushed its flank. She could slip out behind it but it refused to budge out of line. Never did cows do what you wanted them to. In fact, so stubborn they were, you could imagine they picked up your thoughts and did the opposite.

Four paces between herself and the runnel. The drove turned, cutting a diagonal line over the field, the animals moving more slowly now, lowering their heads to snatch at the grass. Now was the moment to take a breath, dash and pray.

She ran as never before, diving headlong into the gully. So small and shallow it was, there was nothing for it but to lie motionless with her forehead resting on a stone. She braced herself and held her breath, expecting to hear running feet, rough hands to seize her.

Nothing happened. The noise of the drove grew distant. Her breath escaped in relief. Face down in a stream of water, she was soaked through to the skin, but not discovered. Her whole body started to shake with laughter.

Lying motionless, she listened to the sparrows chirping in the hawthorn, the drone and whine of the insects. The boys would be on the benches outside the inn drinking, the ponies sucking from the water channels down the road. The innkeeper's face would be red from all the rushing about.

Isaac would ride along to Elisabeth's mother's house to pay his respects. Elisabeth's blind grandmother, shrunken to a tiny creature like a *bwca*, would sit bright as a bird with her head on one side, waiting for the sound of Isaac's pony on the cobbles.

The Cilycwm dogs were barking now, believing they were chasing the teller out of town towards the bridge. Surely she would be safe to move? She scrambled to her feet, wringing water from her clothes. The basket was a nuisance. If she wound the rags at her waist she could make a pouch and carry the oatcakes that way. She tossed the basket into the shrubs and began her descent.

All she had to do was follow the stream down to the point it merged with the river. The banks were higher there. If she kept close to the water, she could loiter down by the bridge behind a willow until they had passed.

At the first sound of feet on the bridge overhead, Jane held her breath. The pattering changed to a continuous thundering, which lasted so long she had to breathe again and again. The dogs yapped unendingly, as they always did. And there he was – Burr, Isaac's corgi, standing up on the bank right in her line of sight, barking, shrill and persistent. His little legs were planted firmly. There was going to be no budging him until he was taken seriously. A boy with a hat pulled low over his face appeared behind Burr, peering down under the bridge. She whipped her shawl over her face.

'What is it?' Isaac's voice she knew instantly.

'Just a girl by the river.'

Burr stood his ground until Isaac's whistle.

Close! Jane counted to fifty after the last of the drove had passed. Change of plan – she wasn't going to be *in* the drove any longer. She'd follow. At a distance. God must be on her side, she'd had such a narrow escape.

The climb was long and strenuous, though with the sun dropping behind the hill, the heat drained quickly from the day. With her head down, she watched for useful plants: docks, dandelions, hyssop and herb Robert, which she stowed in her rag pouch and down her shirt.

'Keep your eyes always alert, for God will provide,' Aunt Anni always told her.

Humming took her mind from her empty stomach, though when she asked herself whether she was really desperate for food, she had to answer she was not. She'd been hungrier than this many times.

As she climbed higher, purple rocks appeared on the far side of the valley over the hills. That's where she had sat, dangling her heels, above where the rooks circled on stiff wings. She had thought that the answer. It had not been. There had been no answer at all, nothing to be done. And then there was – there always is.

CHAPTER 4

No Place for a Woman

CYNGHORDY INN WAS a vast building with stables, barns, a cobbled yard and secure grazing fields and pens. From behind the barn, Jane watched Isaac lift his saddlebags from the pony, leaving Rhys to rub the pony down and feed him. He was one of the boys who worked for Mr Johns at the Big House in the village. Jane shrank back. To be spotted by Rhys – the most hateful boy she knew, with his loud mouth and sneering way – would be the worst of the worst.

The sky was streaked pink and the evening star glittered in the clear sky. The clatter of the hooves and the chatter of the boys died away. Being alone in the dark was a lonesome feeling. If she could have been with the animals, that would have been a comfort; better than being with the boys, for sure. One window lit with a yellowish flickering light was set in the wall further down. On tiptoe, Jane peeked over the sill. No-one looked in her direction.

Inside, a stone chimney took up the whole of one wall. The men gathered round the blaze: red-cheeked, hair plastered to their heads. It must have been hot in there, for who needs such a blaze in autumn? But cold out here.

The innkeeper – Davy, a friend of her tad's – came in from a side door, rolling a barrel of beer. Isaac walked over to him to shake his hand. Everyone knew Isaac, a man with a reputation as a fine dependable lead drover: that's what her brother Richard had told Jane when he thought to join the drove, before he changed his mind. No doubt he had considered the hard demands of the work, the distance he'd be from the girls in Caio, and the fact that the money offered would likely be less than he could earn by taking sheep to the glue factory in Bristol. Richard's temper would be no help on a drove.

Isaac's back was towards the men at the fire, but Jane noted the glance over his shoulder before passing the saddlebags to Davy, who nodded and took them away.

She could not stay here; cold, watching others enjoying themselves. The yard was deserted. The top half of the barn door was open. She pushed the bottom half and slipped inside. The straw and the ponies made the stable warm. Hay was piled high on one side. She clambered up. From her perch she could watch the sky darken through the top door, and the stars appear.

I shouldn't feel bad being alone because that's what I want to be. I'm not complaining, God. He was used to these silent conversations. Not only did He know everything, so no explanations were necessary, but He heard everything and He understood everything too. Still, when people are laughing and having a good time, you can't help thinking it would be good to be with them.

Though, truthfully, laughter was not her custom. It wasn't a thing to do on your own – unless you were face down in a ditch. It was safe here, being with the ponies, the huff of their breath, the stamp of their feet. She broke crumbs from the oatcake, trying not to think about the food they were eating in the inn.

What would they be doing at Tŷ Mawr now? Richard: drinking, no doubt. David: hiding away down at the Big House with Sarah, in her room at the top of the house.

29

A way he'd found to climb up onto the roof, leaping from the branches of the cedar that stood behind the stables, Sarah had told her. And William... oh, it was painful to think of him. Please don't let Griffith take it out on William, God. You must look after him.

And Griffith himself – Jane breathed hard. Bad she felt, leaving him to face the anger of Mr Morgan, with no-one to wash his clothes or cook the food, and now all those taxes to pay and no money.

'I wish I didn't have to make things so awkward for you, Griffith, but you made me do it. The truth is, this is all your own fault.'

Jane snapped awake as the barn door opened, shrinking into the shadow. Dawn, and she'd missed her chance to move before she was discovered. A pony snickered, nodding its head up and down, kicking the ground. Isaac's outline was unmistakable. A blanket flicked, the saddle creaked, the leather bags whacked the pony's flank and the bit clanked on its teeth. Isaac's voice was a low croon as he backed the pony into the yard. Hooves clattered on the cobbles.

Outside, the geese were beginning to protest, the pigs to grunt. Every second, the light grew stronger and the shadows slipped away. A run across the yard was impossible. Through the door, she could see the grazing fields. The men and the boys were up. The boy in the hat was inspecting a cow's hooves. Uriah was there, stooping down with a bowl by the side of their milking cow. The sheep were walking in agitated circles, heads up and ears startled.

There was only one way to go: jump out of the opening in the back of the barn, run past the privy and the back of the pens to the road. The opening was narrow but she could squeeze out sideways and turn on the ledge. Not much of a drop. She was on the point of jumping when Rhys came sauntering round the corner of the barn. He hawked and spat. Jane shrank back, flattening herself to the wall. What was he doing? She hadn't heard him pass. Should she check? Then she heard straining and uneven breathing. Dirty beast, with the privy only a few paces away.

He must be finishing, straightening and pulling up his trousers. His footsteps receded. This time she jumped on the count of three and raced to the trees. Behind the thickest spruce, she stood catching her breath. Two routes to choose from: left under the trees or straight up to the bare hills opposite. Up would be quicker.

Which way, God?

She was in His hands. She closed her eyes. Up it was.

Jane waited, poised, under the cover of thick hawthorns. The geese led the drove, necks stretched forwards, bodies quite a way behind, sheep, the pigs and now the cows. They were near enough to slip in unnoticed. She focused on a gap between two milkers. Their heads were down, and their milk-heavy udders swayed from side to side as they laboured up the hill. She felt the pace. When the first cow passed, she would steal in.

She was ready, weight forwards.

As she pushed between the nearest cows, she stumbled. They leapt, startled; tossing their heads, kicking up their hooves. Not a thing she could do before the kick landed on her arm with the force of a hammer blow, knocking her down into the ditch. Her scream was out before it could be stifled. She lay tight as a bud, her foot curled under her, hurting now worse than the arm for the way she had fallen on it. She held it as a precious thing broken when she did not mean it to be. From above, confusion raged: the dogs, the shouting and mooing of the disintegrated drove.

All over. Over. The word rolled round her head.

'You alright?'

She hugged herself the tighter. Her eyes were shut but she knew Isaac had leapt from his pony and started down the bank. She shrank from him, wriggling at speed so he would know she was not badly hurt.

'I fell. At the last moment. Tripped and fell.'

He would know her voice.

'Jane?'

She pushed herself up on her arm, her back to him.

Isaac shook his head. 'No, Jane.' His voice rose. 'I said no. I meant it. You must go home – now!'

Jane lowered her head. 'I won't and I can't.'

'Jane.' His voice was low and even. 'You have no choice. This is the end of the matter. Get back up here. The inn is still in sight. I will take you back there myself.'

'No.' Jane's mind was whirling. She spun round. 'God has spoken to me. This is God's will.'

As she said so, it was.

'He wants me to go. He has told me not to take no for an answer. Because His word is mightier than yours. I am to do God's work. This is His plan, not my own.'

Her heart was pounding, her cheeks on fire. She'd surprised herself; hadn't known before the words came to her mouth that it was God's work she was fulfilling. It was obvious now. Her duty. Her purpose. Everything had a different spirit to it. Her arm ached. Making a fuss was something beaten out of her long ago.

Isaac, a man of God as she knew, wavered under her stare. From this position, low in the ditch with Isaac on the bank above her, she must fill her words with great passion.

'He wants you to protect me. He has chosen you. Just like He has chosen me.'

Isaac looked down, looked away, tapped his boot with his stick, turned a full circle before speaking.

'Look at you, Jane... you're not equipped. No boots, nothing to keep out the weather. London is a long tough way away, Jane. A drove is no place for a woman at all.'

Jane did not falter. 'God can make all things possible. Place your trust in Him.' So certain she was now, the words came strong and fast.

Behind them the dogs were racing over the hill, scooping up the stray animals. Uriah rode up, jerking hard on his reins when he saw Jane. The pony reared; flecks of sweat fell on her shawl.

Isaac stretched out his hand to help her up the steep, muddy bank.

'Jane Evans is coming with us,' Isaac said slowly. 'She will ride with me.'

CHAPTER 5

Uprooted

IT *WAS* HIS plan. It had to be. This was why she was here. The dragging, guilty feelings of deserting the boys fell away. Griffith in particular was a Bible man. Once he was told, he would know there was nothing more important in this world than serving God's purpose, however awkward the effects might be. Richard might laugh and look at her with those sharp eyes and say, 'How convenient, Jane.' But she'd take no notice of him.

Could it be that even Mr Morgan was part of His plan? Certainly giving her something as hideous, as unthinkable as Mr Morgan, God must have known that Jane would run from him.

No-one was looking. Jane lifted her skirt where she sat. Her ankle had twisted. She squeezed the swelling flesh. If she moved her fingers over the skin in a firm yet gentle way, as Aunt Anni had taught her, she could feel the bone underneath and know if it was broken. Not this time, which was lucky.

'Go down, will you?'

As she moved the foot, pain shot up her leg. She would feel it when she put her weight on it – a nuisance, taking her mind from her head, which was light with God's intentions.

She rolled up her sleeve. The outline of the iron cattle cue was branded on her arm like a half moon. She pressed it; her fingers left white prints in the red. Nothing broken, though the truth was it throbbed, begging to be soothed. If she saw some comfrey or hyssop she would bind it tight to bring out the bruise.

Isaac was still talking to Uriah. Some of the boys had gathered round him, Rhys among them, with his black hair and bearded face. He scowled at Jane over his shoulder.

Quick as she could, Jane slipped down to retrieve her clog, which had tumbled down the bank and stopped short of the water by a clump of marsh grass. She scooped a handful of water to wash her face and stood on the flatter stones. Water cascaded over the swollen ankle, numbing and clean.

'Jane!' Isaac was up on the bank above her. His face was stern. 'You'll ride at the back, Jane, with me. I have told the others. We will stop at Tirabad and pray there.'

Jane scrambled back up the bank.

'Have you hurt your leg, Jane? You're limping.'

'No... not at all.'

He swung his leg over the saddle and jumped down.

'She's tough and stubborn, my Banon – but so are you.' He held the reins out to her.

Jane shook her head. 'I'll walk, Isaac. You will not be inconvenienced by me.'

Isaac's laugh was a bark. The sort of laugh that isn't a laugh at all. Not one that rises from seeing the comedy of life. Jane hung her head.

'Come on, Jane. Lift that head. Let me feel God's purpose in you.'

If that were a comment from one of her brothers, she would know it for a tease, but with Isaac... There were things she didn't know about Isaac.

Hitching her skirt up so it would not strain and rip, she was used to, though it left more of her legs showing than she liked. Astride the pony was a fair place to be, if she hadn't the pressure of Isaac toiling behind, muffled up in this heat. Brown paper he wrapped round his body on a drove to keep out the cold, Aunt Anni had told her. Heat you must learn to bear. Cold must be kept at bay. He was deep in his own thoughts now, which she couldn't guess at all with his face shadowed by that broad-brimmed hat.

Whenever Isaac was back home from a drove and came to visit Tŷ Mawr, he would sit for an age listening to Jane's chatter, and Jane listened to the stories he told. Last time they'd met, he had told her about the rumblings of another war – all the talk in London. Perhaps it was the war he was thinking about now, weighing him down. War was the English word, short and blunt, and it didn't sound good nor feel good in the mouth. The Welsh was better – *rhyfel*. Though that didn't sound like the terrible thing it was, taking the young men away. Most never came home. Like Mr Johns' brothers and his boy, though he only fought the yellow fever in Spain and lost to it. Terrible the pain in women's eyes and the sadness that spilled from them when they came to talk to Aunt Anni, reminding Jane of an urgent need to be elsewhere.

If a man ever returned, he was strange, like Old Mr Jenkin, who roared in his sleep and was never the same again. That's what was said in the village. Men were unknowable creatures altogether, with their need for excitement, for owning things, for fighting each other to be top of the pile.

Not her brothers though. David said he would never go to war. He wanted to go to America with Sarah. He'd do fine in America, which teemed with animals, so many you could reach out and catch them, no need for nets or traps or any effort at all. More fish than water in the rivers, with land there, and chances unimaginable in Wales.

Richard was too lazy.

Griffith had too much to do.

Besides, what need did they have of fighting when they had Jane? Ah, but now they didn't have Jane, so who would they kick out at and blame for every little thing that went wrong?

After a long, wearisome climb, the ground levelled out. Rounding the line of the hill, they came to a grey stone farmhouse. The teller had done his job. From the barns and outhouses came the loud protesting of the local animals, shut away to provide grazing for the visiting drove.

The dogs and men worked hard, corralling the animals into grazing fields, but Jane had nothing to do. Isaac unhooked his saddlebags and slung them over his shoulder. She slid down carefully from Banon onto her good leg and led the animal to the water trough, where she sucked noisily for so long it was a wonder she could hold that quantity inside. When Banon lifted her head at last, Jane led her to the barn. Three ponies were already pulling from the hay bale above their heads. At least she knew to remove the saddle and tack and rub the sweat straight away with straw.

Steam rose from the backs of the other ponies. She might as well wipe them off too. As she approached, clicking a low greeting, they shifted nervously.

'They're not used to a woman. Leave them, Jane. Come with me.' Isaac stood in the doorway with a pair of old boots in his hand.

'Try them. The farmer will sell them. They're his son's.'

'Won't he be needing them?'

'He's dead.'

'What happened to him?' Jane sat on a stone in the yard to pull a boot over her good foot.

'He died last year in the winter cold. I want a coat for you but I don't know where from.'

'Had the dead boy not a coat, then?' Conversation took her mind from the shooting pain as she forced her foot into the second boot.

'I could hardly ask that.'

Three men with fiddles walked into the yard.

'Isaac! Are you not coming in for the music?' one asked, tucking his fiddle under his chin and playing a trill of notes. His bow hand flicked to and fro faster than a dog shaking water from its fur.

'Later. I have some business first.'

The fiddlers ran off into the farm, nudging each other and stifling laughter.

The boots were tight even on her good foot. 'They're grand.'

'None of this is going to be easy. We need help. Come.'

The lane was dark and silent. From the distance came the soft rush of the river. Dark pines added a dourness to the place; paler fallen needles softened their footsteps. They walked on until they glimpsed flashes of silvered water.

The tiny church of Tirabad was set on the bank, as plain as a cottage. No porch, just a simple door, which Isaac pushed open. Inside, it was cold with moss and age. Isaac pulled a candle from his pocket, lighting it with his tinderbox. He tipped it until the wax dropped onto the floor, then he set it upright. Smoke curled up towards the cross from the tall orange flame.

Bird droppings mired one wall; a white and purple mound had formed on the stone floor. High above it, a deserted martin's nest clung to the rafters: a little cup of mud. There were none of the coloured windows or decoration of St Cynwyl's in Caio, just a stone font and a bare cross, the walls unadorned.

'We will pray until the flame dies, Jane. We must pray we are doing the right thing and that God will guide us, that this is as He wills it, and neither of us has misunderstood His purpose.'

A candle, even a short tallow one, burns very slowly. Praying next to Isaac, with a deep quiet all around in this chill, damp place, was not easy. Especially for one who usually prays wherever she is, whatever she might be doing, not on her knees. Kneeling is painful and soon you long to move. Even stretching a foot, or momentarily sitting back on your heels, marks you as a fidget. Isaac was so still.

Jane looked deep into the flame. Round the wick, before the orange, there's a clear part. That's the mystery. The space where many people see God. Not Jane, who worried the draught might extinguish the flame. You did not need to think of seeing Him for He was everywhere, and not such a mystery either. The truth was, He was *inside*, not out; a real comfort because everywhere you were, He was there too. When you wanted to talk to Him, it was like talking to yourself. You could ask Him any question you wanted and sometimes He'd make you think of the answers yourself. And sometimes not. He was a bit of a tease. People said He was unknowable, which was strange because she knew Him well enough. A special building made her no nearer to Him. And candles were a distraction. Hard it was, not to take a look at Isaac, knowing his eyes would be shut. Such a fine face he had with the colour so warm in this light; a great nose, and his chin was dark with the hair and the shadow. See! Now she was thinking about beards. But the candle was no help, for look at the way that thin thread of smoke curled away, blackening everything it touched.

Her hands were clasped in front of her, as Isaac's were. Filthy, her nails. And the skin all grimy. How ashamed Mam would be if she knew Jane had gone into God's house in such a state.

'God likes clean children,' she used to say.

On Saturdays Mam lugged the bath from the hook in the pantry to the open fire. The water scalded. Jane sobbed as Mam scoured her skin until she stood, dripping and bright red. She would not sit, however Mam pressed down on her shoulders. Hair washing, kept to the last, was agony. For hours Mam dragged a comb with metal teeth through her heavy brown tangles, humming through the hurt she was causing. Jane prayed to hear the words: 'All done. Fit for God's house.' Then her mother would pull Jane to her chest and rock her like a baby. Jane felt Mam's bones under the dress and her heart beating against her own. On Saturday nights Jane's hard pillow was so damp, she dreamed of dank caves seamed with gold.

Sin was dirt. And weren't they all sinners? That's what the preacher said in chapel. If there were no sinners, there would be nothing for God to do. God couldn't mind black under the fingernails. Tad's nails were always black. Mam said God could read your mind too: a comfort to know you were never really alone. But if God truly was a mind reader, you must be careful what you were thinking.

There was not even a pew here in Tirabad. Would the congregation just have to stand? If there was a congregation. Not a cottage had she seen on their walk. In their chapel, the Evans family sat near the back. Jane could never see the preacher for she was always behind Mr Jerrard, who sat in the pew in front and was a great block of a man. Once she had watched Mr Jerrard, hands bandaged, naked to the waist and glistening with sweat, boxing in the Drover's Inn. God would not like one of His congregation to be thinking of that fight, especially when meant to be listening to His Word.

The Bible stories were fine to listen to but while the preacher was talking, you might hope that Mighty Michael – Aunt Anni's neighbour, who sat in the back row at the side with his mother Old Ma Penny, and was twice her size – would rise to his feet, shouting terrible blasphemous words, stamping his wooden clogs and roaring. He could not help himself because, as Aunt Anni explained, he was born to be different. Tad and Griffith would take him outside and walk him round until he was quiet again. They brought him in for the singing. How he loved the singing, sitting quiet as a lamb and rocking with his mouth gaping, dribbling like a baby.

Such a glorious singing voice Tad had had, so powerful he'd shatter the mud nests in the rafters if he sang here, and all the birds would fly round in a panic. Standing with his legs apart, he was like the place where the rivers met and thundered on, twice as powerful. He held his hands behind his back to hide those fingernails. Once Jane had joined in. David stamped on her foot and Mr Jerrard turned round and stared. Men were the singers. Music was another thing for Jane to dream to, like the sermons. She could float away through the walls and over the hills to wherever she wanted, until the preacher banged that huge Bible down with a thump.

Their chapel in Caio was full of sound – not like here in Tirabad, a melancholy place so far from anywhere. Such a distance she was now from anything she knew. Halfway between the life she had left behind and the life which was to come. She was a thing that has been rooted in the ground, like a turnip, but pulled up. All her growing must be done from now on as she moved. A potato might be a better thought, for a potato does not wither in the same way as a turnip. It might wrinkle and grow soft with age, but strong white feelers grow out of the shrunken body in all directions, searching blindly but with great resolve.

The walk back to Spite Inn was black and moonless. Such a name, Spite Inn. She would change it at once if she lived here. A boisterous wind pulled at Jane's hair, wrapping her skirt round her legs.

Isaac flicked mud from his boot with his stick.

'Tomorrow and the next day will be your wilderness, Jane. It can be bleak and lonesome up on the Epynt. Let's hope it won't stretch to the forty days our Lord was tested.'

They walked in silence with only the whistle of the wind to be heard until music reached them, faint at first but growing louder with the undertones of song and men talking, laughing and drinking.

'It's not such a desolate place,' Jane said. '*We* are here.'

CHAPTER 6

Nothing to Ruin

T HE WINDOW WAS in the wrong place – at the foot of the bed when it should have been to the side. Men were shouting. Jane sat up, confused before she remembered. Spite Inn. The bed which should have been Isaac's.

'Take the offer while it's there. Worse is to come,' he'd said, turning away.

She jumped up, her leg crumpling in pain. The dead boy's empty boots stood ready on the floor by her clothes. Singing was what Aunt Anni recommended to David for the pain when his shoulder came out of its socket that time and his arm dangled the wrong way round in front of him. A great bonesetter was Aunt Anni, with such skill in her hands, people came from all over Wales with twisted limbs.

> *Rock of Ages*
> *Cleft for me*
> *Let me hide –*

On the high note she tugged at the boot on her injured foot and didn't stop till her heel touched the bottom. Cold sweat beaded her forehead.

'Jane!' Isaac shouted up the stairs.

She'd wanted to be ready before he called her. She had planned on saddling Banon, on holding the gate for the sheep, on being useful. Barely had she time for a few spoonfuls of oatmeal and sips of tea. Her intention had been to use the privy before she left and now she hadn't the chance. She was up on Banon and away.

The day was mild and blue. Once they'd laboured up the first hill, the sky was as wide and huge as she'd ever seen. All around, the land stretched away: vast, brownish green, undulating and without feature. The animals wound like a river over the land in front of Jane.

She clenched her muscles. Fine it was for the men, who were better equipped for a journey like this. All they had to do was point and stream like the animals, when and where they felt like it. She was near bursting point herself. It's not nice at all to have your mind on your needs so often. She shifted her weight, wriggled and sang hymns silently inside until there was no choice in the matter. She jumped, hobbled back past Isaac and squatted there in the path the animals had trampled. Banon's head was down, pulling at the tough grass while Jane squatted. Easy. Isaac said nothing as she passed him again.

Now her heart lifted and everything was wondrous: stony it might be with no depth of earth, but the long brown grass whispered secrets and laid sideways like corn in the field, but without the worry the grain would be ruined. Here there was nothing to ruin.

By the time Banon reached the first resting point, where the peaty soil was black, and the ground solid enough for the animals to drink, the first had drunk their fill and were grazing hungrily. The dogs lay under the lone marker tree, stretched out and asleep. Uriah and the boys rested alongside them, eating bread and cheese and swigging ale from their leather bottles. They were laughing raucously but as Jane dismounted, they grew silent. She attempted a smile, but they looked away. She would not join them but find a place by herself. Hungry she was, but would say nothing.

Not as hungry as that terrible winter when they had had nothing to eat at Tŷ Mawr. She had taken Cadwy, son of Morwenna, into the woods to hunt for acorns and buried things. There's nothing like the nose of a pig for finding edible treasures, even under snow. Richard had caught her with her pockets full, taken everything and beaten her for her deceitfulness, though she shouted she was going to make an acorn cake as a surprise and now he'd ruined everything.

And he'd said: 'Oh yes, Jane, of course you were.'

And her fury had been that she knew it wasn't true.

Isaac came over, holding out a flask. 'Water, Jane, from the spring at the inn. I know your thoughts on drink.'

She could have downed it all but stopped, wiping the mouthpiece on her sleeve before handing it back.

'Finish it, Jane. I'll drink beer. I've not your high principles.' He handed her bread and cheese. Was he teasing again?

He did not sit with her, but neither did he sit with the other men, choosing to eat as he walked round the animals. Jane sat near the pigs. One leaned his huge bulk against the stunted hawthorn tree and rubbed himself up and down against it. Watching a pig scratch was almost as good as scratching yourself: a kind of bliss. The other pigs were rooting and snuffling together behind the tree.

'What a fine bunch you are, aren't you? The size of you would put my fellows to shame. And look what you've got on your feet: stockings! Tar boots on the bottoms! All dressed up in your finest for the market, eh?'

She leaned forward and scratched one on its rump. Its skin was hot and tough. Nearby, a pig stood on its own,

45

snout resting almost on the ground and the tail straight. A bad sign. It limped forwards a few paces before slowly its legs folded beneath it as it flopped over with a giant grunt.

'Are you alright, fellow?'

Jane laid her hand on its side. The pig looked up at her but didn't move. Its eye was blue as a cornflower. If only she had the power to draw out the pain like Aunt Anni had; if she tried, the pain might flow up her own arm. Aunt Anni hadn't explained how to stop that happening. Should she say something to one of the others? It wasn't her business. Yet, why not?

She went over to where the boys were resting. Rhys, with the sparse black beard, was throwing mud balls at the sheep, laughing as he hit them.

'I don't know who I should tell...' Two of the boys exploded in laughter. One had a weasel face, another a hat pulled down low over his face. Boys together could be so stupid. Pedr, the third boy, she knew from school days – the cousin of Gwendolyn at the inn. Surely he would take her seriously?

'Me. Tell me.' The fourth boy, Rhys, leered up at her. The others sniggered.

'One of the pigs is lame.'

'Lame is it?'

'He's standing hunched and there's pain in his eyes.'

'Pain in his eyes, did you say?'

'I think someone should take a look.'

'Do you now?'

'I do.'

'When I need a woman to teach me my job, I'll let you know.' Rhys jumped up. 'I've urgent business.' He jerked his body forwards, taking hold of his balls through his trousers and jiggling them up and down in Jane's face. The weasel boy and the one with the hat were creased with laughter.

'I don't care about you. It's the pig I care about!'

Jane was stomping away when Pedr called after her:

'Jane Evans, won't they be missing you at Tŷ Mawr?'

'That's none of your business!' Jane whipped round. For a second she caught shock in Rhys' eyes. Had he not known who she was? He stared hard at Pedr before darting away into the grazing animals, knocking them out of his way with kicks and swipes of his stick.

If that stupid Rhys would take no notice, maybe she should tell Isaac, who was over the far side of the sheep. It was difficult to make him hear.

'Isaac!'

He raised his head. She waved and threaded her way over to him, scattering the animals.

'Careful, Jane. What is it?'

'There's a pig going lame.'

'Tell the boys.' He sounded irritated.

'I have, but...' She was talking now to his back.

He should take notice of her. She knew about pigs. She did. And Isaac knew she did.

Grey clouds built overhead through the afternoon and the colour drained out of the wild empty plain. She'd done her best. Why should she worry any more? But the poor creature walked like Richard after a skinful. If they did nothing about him now and made him walk, he would get worse. That pig had had no business setting off with them in the first place. It should have been noticed. Although, to be fair, he might have been injured on the journey. Perhaps his boots didn't fit him right, or he'd stumbled and hurt his leg.

Banon's saddle was hard. Terrible sore her legs were from the rubbing. She should have britches. She could have been in Tad's clothes right now if she'd known how it would be.

That was a foolish thing to send William away with them. But it's not possible to imagine what you don't know. You learn a thing backwards so you know it forwards. She looped her legs in front of her over the saddlebags. Bulky. Uncomfortable. Isaac's great Bible, wrapped in greased cloth, was tied to the pommel with no room for her leg between it and the saddlebags, whose straps were fastened tight. No guessing what was in them. Something of value, no doubt about that. Hadn't she seen Mr Johns himself on the porch of the Big House, passing packages and little bags to Isaac?

Taking eggs she was, to the Big House; their last precious eggs. Jane, her basket now empty, had just turned the corner for the shortcut across the front of the house when she saw them. She'd shrunk back behind the hedge. Mr Johns would not like anyone cutting across the front of the house.

'Deliver them safe, Isaac,' Mr Johns called.

'I will.'

'My contribution to the war effort.'

The clouds had gathered force, bunched up, advanced and spread out until now the whole wide sky was dark, cold and threatening. On a pony's back you were right in it. She must fix her mind on something, not let it drift around, and leave feelings that were nothing to do with this moment: tie her mind to the tail of the black cow labouring along in front of her.

Rain began to fall; slow at first, then fast, stinging her cheeks and dropping hard on her head.

'Cover yourself, Jane.' Isaac drew level with her. 'It's a hat you need, and a coat too. I'll ask at the inn. Prepare for a wet night with not much cover for us or the animals.'

Jane's backside was burning under her skirt. 'Will you not take a turn, Isaac? I'm ready for walking.'

'I'm fine, Jane.'

Jane waited four more strides.

'The thing is, Isaac. I'm not. I was wondering if there might be a chance of a pair of britches to be had?'

'I don't know about that, Jane.'

There in the driving rain they changed places. A rubbing boot was easier to bear than chafing thighs. Down on the ground you didn't feel the emptiness around you.

'Can you see the pigs from up there, Isaac?'

'I can.'

'Will you take a look at the one I was telling you about?'

There was a silence, then without a word, Isaac pulled the reins and kicked Banon into a gallop up the right-hand flank of the animals. Jane hurried after him, water dribbling down the inside of her shirt.

Isaac was on his knees when she reached him. The pig lay on its side, panting.

'I should have taken notice of you, Jane,' Isaac said, ripping off the pig's muddy, rusty boots. The tar bottoms were supposed to protect, but the trotters were a mess of raw flesh and blood.

The pig squealed once, lifted his head, then flopped back down with a groan. Jane hunkered down beside Isaac to scratch the pig's neck. 'You poor thing.'

Pedr and Uriah stood watching.

'Where is he?' Isaac's face was grim.

Pedr pointed to the other side of the stream where Rhys was busying himself, picking a bramble from a sheep's coat. Isaac strode over, shouting his name. Their words were lost in the rain but there is satisfaction in seeing someone who has treated you with such scorn hanging their head in shame.

Even greater would have been the pleasure of saying something to Isaac when he returned, but Jane could sense by his tight shoulders her words would not be welcome.

Isaac was so quick: lifting the pig's snout, slicing across its throat. Jane and the pig screamed together. Hot blood spurted out. There is so much blood in a pig. It leaked into the peaty puddles, merging with the rainbow film. Isaac wiped his blade on the grass.

'Where's that Rhys now?' His voice was angry. 'He's a way of disappearing when he's needed.'

Three men it took to heft the pig onto Banon's back. She danced in circles, rolling her eyes in panic. Death makes animals nervous.

'Keep her steady, Jane,' Isaac staggered with the back legs. Pedr and Uriah had the messy, bloody end.

Holding an animal against its will is not easy when you both know it is strong enough to pull free and race for the horizon. Jane blew gently on Banon's flared nostrils. Calming a horse was something she could do. She knew that from the time the bees swarmed onto Jessie, sending her racing across two fields, still dragging the harrow, leaping a hedge and rearing up when anyone approached her, long after the bees had vanished. It was Jane Tad called to settle her.

Pedr washed his hands in a peat puddle which the dogs lapped at as they tore at the bloodied grass. Uriah remounted and galloped to where the geese were grazing, throwing his hat into the air and shouting to rouse the men. Threats and sticks it took to tear the dogs away from their feast back to their job: moving the animals on.

Jane walked one side of Banon, Isaac the other.

'That's thirty shillings less for William Meredith back home. Or thereabouts. And he has five children and a sick mother to feed. I'll have the coat and hat in exchange for that pig, Jane, you'll see.'

Droving under a low sky in the driving rain was a test for sure. Hard to know if you were in the clouds, or on the earth. The horizon was brought so near you thought you could reach it in four paces, but it was never reached. Everyone was silenced and made miserable by it. Apart from the geese, flapping the water from their feathers when they stopped for a short rest, stretching their necks in a gloating way. Rain does not soak right through sheep's fleeces but they must be made heavier; a wonder that their legs did not bend. Jane's weight pulled her into the ground and her boots sank.

'Change your mind, Jane,' Isaac said, offering her Banon. 'We could move the pig.'

She shook her head.

'I forgot,' he smiled. 'You never change your mind.'

It was probably meant in a good way, but with cold water dripping off your nose, it was easier to doubt.

Weather never lasts long in one state. Just as you imagine you will dissolve into a puddle yourself and be sucked into the land, the rain will stop. The heavy clouds will lighten, the horizon will pull back, with luck the sun will be out and everything steaming. You knew it, but it was hard to believe it when you were in the wet part.

'It lasts as long as it lasts,' Aunt Anni would say.

And now she was in Jane's mind, puffing on her pipe, her boots on the flagstones and her old feet purple as heather; the nails like chicken's talons, curving over and yellow. 'It lasts as long as it lasts,' she'd said, one terrible cold winter, the worst anyone had ever known for snow and hunger. If you knew you must endure six weeks before it stopped strangling the life out of you, you could have hope, portion out what you had.

Isaac had not brought sufficient tobacco that winter, so Aunt Anni smoked herbs she had gathered in the summer and hung from the cottage beams. She spat into the fire.

'You could try the hens again, Jane.'

Hens would be the answer. Eggs whenever they wanted them and without that walk over the hill to Aunt Anni's, with the guilt each time she broke an egg into the pan for taking eggs away from Isaac's sick wife.

Mam had kept hens. Her old henhouse was rotting in the barn. One of the boys could mend it. Of course, the hens would have to be locked away at night for fear of foxes.

A broody hen Jane discovered behind Aunt Anni's soil box in the privy.

'Clever. But not clever enough,' Jane said, seizing her and tucking her under her arm.

'Take care of her, Jane.'

She did. By the next year the hens had multiplied and all were laying, but one day Young Arthur Jones rode up red-faced on his pony, shouting that Mrs Jenkin's waters had broken and she must come quick to help Aunt Anni. Jane went straight away, not thinking of the time it might take and the things that might happen.

A terrible damp cottage those poor Jenkins lived in, not something she'd noticed when Mam had died and William was taken there to share Mrs Jenkin's milk with her first baby. The one window at the front was small and grimed with soot from the blacksmith next door. Had Mrs Jenkin's thin legs not been so white, she'd never have seen her, sitting on the one stool in the room, her legs and that huge stomach gleaming in the flickering light.

'Jane Evans is to help.' Aunt Anni set her cloths, her glass bottles and her pouch on the table top.

'The girl will be put off for ever,' panted Mrs Jenkin.

Jane shook her head quickly. 'I won't be having children.'

Mrs Jenkin laughed, gasped, screamed terribly and bent her head to her stomach.

Distant thunder rumbled round the Epynt. Jane lifted her head to shake the drips from her nose and the sound from her ears.

The light was draining from the sky. There's that time in a journey where everything goes slow and silent, and then there's a quickening, a lifting of heads. The inn must be near, though you might not see it.

Jane leaned forward to get there the faster, but Mrs Jenkin's scream was still in her ears and now it was her own cries from that same terrible day, when Griffith pulled her from her sleep and pushed her so roughly down the stairs.

'What have I done?' she shouted.

'See for yourself!' he thundered.

The porch door was open. Glass and Fly were tied to the post. They didn't know how to greet her: ears flat, tails twitching between their legs, panting. Things were bad. Feathers on the ground stirred in the moonlight. More feathers further off. Dark, wet patches on the cobbles. A mangled body in the middle of the yard. All scattered, dead.

'Stupid dogs!' she'd shrieked at them; a terrible thing to do, for it was not their fault. 'Why didn't you bark? What do we keep you for?' She should not have done that. There's a horrible curling pain in thinking about something you wish you had not done.

But Griffith should not have beaten her for that. That was wrong. *He* should be curling inside at the thought of it.

'I have to do this, Jane. You have to learn. And I have to teach you.'

'You don't. Griffith, you do not.'

'I do.' He brought his belt down – thwack! – on her bare legs, right there in the scene of devastation.

CHAPTER 7

Skinny Piece of Nonsense

From out of the mist loomed the faint outline of a pine tree. The inn at last. The dogs knew it well, racing ahead with fresh energy, yapping and squealing; the collies with their tails like flags, the corgis' stumps quivering. A child's drawing of a building that inn was; no lodging for the men, only corrals for the animals. Where would she lie, Jane wondered, to be kept safe?

Isaac instructed Jane to go inside and dry by the fire. Rhys lingered, stepping forward to help with the pig, glancing towards Jane. She lingered to overhear what he had to say for himself.

'Shall I rub Banon down for you, Isaac?' he volunteered. 'I'm sorry I missed the pig going lame. I should have listened to Jane.'

'You should,' Isaac said, undoing the girth and removing the saddlebags. 'But thank you, Rhys. I like a man who can admit mistakes. Maybe you should say that to Jane.'

Isaac walked away with the leather bags over his shoulder. Jane stepped forward, ready to hear an apology. Rhys threw the most sneering look at her, pulled back his head and spat onto the cobbles. How could Isaac not see him for the wicked person he was?

Inside the inn, a fire roared in the hearth. Steam rising from wet clothes thickened the air. Soup was served in wooden bowls with hunks of bread. Smoke from the pipes had Jane choking. She sat on a wooden bench as the men drank and laughed. No-one spoke to her. Isaac was deep in conversation with Uriah on the far side of the fire. Her eyes were stinging and growing heavy. A sudden need to sleep, fall away, overpowered her. Not here. She'd never hear the end of it. She'd be fine outside with the animals.

The rain had stopped. In the doorway she met the innkeeper with an armful of logs. 'Where do you think you're going?'

'To sleep.'

'Outside is no place for a woman. You sleep inside when the men have gone.'

'No, I don't mean to put anyone to any trouble.'

He gave a sharp laugh. 'I'll have a word with Isaac.'

'No need,' Jane said quickly. 'He knows already. I can take care of myself.'

The innkeeper looked doubtful. 'The ground's wet. Have my coat. For the night, mind. I've only the one and I need it. Bitter it gets up here. When the snow's over the windows, we have to dig ourselves out like rabbits.'

He put down the logs to struggle out of the coat. 'Take it.'

The smell was so bad Jane could taste it, worse than the sheep; but a smell is something you quickly grow used to. Stiff with dirt, it was difficult to bend but warm with the heat of the innkeeper and for certain it was cool outside, though the air was sweet after the smoke. Sleeping with the pigs was natural enough. They were easy to find, pale bulks even under a moonless sky. Jane settled herself on the far side of a large boar for protection.

The power of gazing eyes is to be wondered at. No need to open her own. She knew someone was there.

'Jane.'

She didn't move. It was only Pedr.

'I won't hurt you, Jane.'

Inside, fear rose from her stomach. His voice was odd, his breathing more like panting.

Stay calm, Jane. Stay calm. 'Pedr, I want you to go away right now or I will scream.'

She opened one eye a crack. Pedr was rubbing his hand up and down the front of his britches. She turned away. His breath came fast and shallow. If she opened her mouth, her voice might only squeak.

'Have you seen Jane?' Isaac's distant voice cut the tightness in her limbs. She sat straight up.

'I'm here, Isaac.'

Pedr's body crumpled as though he'd been hit in the stomach. 'Don't tell on me, Jane,' he whimpered, backing away into the shadows.

Why did men love themselves so much? Led by that skinny piece of nonsense. Bloated, they acted all big and powerful, scaring the lights from you – and suddenly all shrivelled and snivelly and pitiful, acting like they couldn't help it. She'd not tell anyone because if she did, *she* would be seen as the trouble.

Isaac marched towards her, dark against the light from the inn door.

'Jane! I'll not have you out here. Get inside, as I told you!'

His voice was as harsh as she had ever heard it.

The boys were leaving as Jane walked back inside. Rhys stood talking to the innkeeper.

'Crossing at Erwood then?'

'Day after, tomorrow,' Rhys said, as Jane held out the innkeeper's coat.

'Keep your wits about you,' he said, still talking to Rhys.

'Hear that, Jane?' Rhys said. 'Keep your wits about you.'

Jane said nothing. She had no wish to talk to Rhys.

'Bad things sometimes happen at Erwood, don't they?' Rhys said to the innkeeper, though his eyes were on Jane. His speech was loud, slow from the drink in him. Best to ignore him completely. 'Bad things. And we don't want that, do we, Jane?'

'Come on now, man, be off with you.' The innkeeper led Rhys to the door.

'Don't take no notice of that one,' the innkeeper said, turning the last logs on the fire and smothering it with peat. 'That boy's a mouth on him and no mistake. I've bolted the door. You're safe in here. You're to take the closet room next to Isaac at the top of the stairs. There's no bed in it, but my wife's found a blanket. There's an old pair of britches she's left too, on Isaac's instructions. Big, mind. They were my wife's father's and he was a giant.'

The only way to reach her closet was by walking through Isaac's room. He said nothing and his silence was cold.

'Goodnight!' she called as she closed her door. He said nothing. The britches lay on the blanket. Great it felt slipping each leg inside. She could turn up the bottoms and if she kept her skirt bunched at her waist, that would hold them up and she'd be the warmer.

'The britches are fine, Isaac,' she called out. There was no reply, just a short hard breath as he extinguished his candle.

It's only when a thing is past that you have the time to think about it. And now she could not sleep for thinking of Pedr. Pitiful Pedr! And now Mighty Michael came bursting into her mind again.

Halfway over the stone style near Aunt Anni's cottage she was that day, when Mighty Michael popped up from behind the hedge. His eyes were open wide like he was as surprised to see her as she was to see him.

And here was a picture stuck in her head for ever. His britches round his ankles, with one hand he pumped, with the other he cupped a handful of pink hairy flesh. With whoops and shrieks as though riding a steer, he jerked back his head and laughed. Milky spume jetted suddenly into the air and fell on a stone at Jane's feet. He gave two convulsive groans as juice dribbled down into his cradling hand.

His head flopped forward then slowly up, his eyes empty, frightened. With a sudden bark, he grabbed his britches and started to slaver and cry. He doubled over himself, stumbling in his haste to get away.

'Michael. It doesn't matter,' Jane called after him. It didn't. Yet it left her out of sorts, like she was at the sight of the dogs eating foulness from behind a pig – so awful, she could not bear to watch, but trapped so she could not look away.

She never mentioned it to anyone.

A few days later, taking the eggs down to the Big House, Mr Johns was standing with a group of boys outside his stables. David was there – a surprise because she did not know he was one of Mr Johns' boys. Rhys, yes, of course; and his brothers, and sometimes the man with the withered arm and his friend with the red hair who organised the dog fights behind the Bear Inn in Llandovery.

She hurried past, not wanting to be seen, though they were too engrossed.

Sarah, taking the eggs, told Jane someone had been seen outside the nursery window, where the two little Johns girls were playing with their cousin.

'He was...' she giggled, 'you know...'

'What?' Jane said.

'Oh, Jane, you've a lot to learn,' Sarah said, handing her the empty basket.

Then she knew.

Later that same week when Jane was walking home from Aunt Anni's, she could not see which boys were up in the top field because it was so misty you could barely see your own hand in front of your face. Everything had the appearance of a vision. Ghosts in the clouds. A group of them came running down the hill, waving their arms. Best to see nothing.

But when Aunt Anni came through the rain later that evening to Tŷ Mawr to tell them that Mighty Michael had been found face down in a treacherous bog, Jane's heart nearly stopped. How he came to be there, how he came to fall, and how he could have died in a few inches of water was a mystery to everyone. Keeping silent with a voice screaming inside was a difficult thing to do.

They were all there at his funeral. She sobbed not for him, but for herself and the terrible weight of things in her head, all the wonderings about whether she was right or wrong not to tell someone – like Aunt Anni, who said Jane must not keep things from her. But when Jane mentioned that she thought it wrong that David had not been at the funeral – she had seen him riding off on Mr Morgan's pony with the man with the withered arm that very morning, after another night when he had not slept in his own bed but most probably was off with Sarah in the Big House – Aunt Anni had said, 'Don't be hasty to judge others, Jane. Nobody likes a tittle tattle', words that did not encourage someone to share their thoughts.

Jane was not a judge, she was not. David had his uses. After Tad died, he played the hero when things were black and the date for tithe was near. Everyone knew about the toll booth on the main road. Iniquitous, Richard called it; greedy faceless men in towns far away setting up tolls and charging farmers who had always used the road for free. They'd pay no toll when he and David walked the sheep to Llandovery. They'd use the back lanes – longer but free.

When Richard burst into Tŷ Mawr that evening, thunder was in the way he opened the door, hurling his coat angrily onto the settle.

'Blocked the back lane now. Barriers so no man can pass without some parasite demanding money. Worse than an honest highwayman.'

'How much did the sheep fetch?' Griffith asked calmly.

Richard's face was black. Jane shrank back into the shadows and prayed. 'This man came out with the dogs from hell. Little fellow he was, with the face of a toad. I showed him my empty pockets but he wouldn't let us pass. What could I do? I knocked him down.'

'What happened to the sheep?'

'You know sheep. All of a dither, going this way and that, and the road was full of men on ponies – clubs and sticks, they had. I dived into the ditch and David went running off, hollering and carrying on. That boy is fast, I tell you. Wily as a fox. They took after him, chasing over the hills. I kept low until the way was clear, and here I am.'

'Where are the sheep?' Griffith's voice was so level it set Jane's heart racing. Night after night, Griffith sat with his ledgers, calculating, his tongue poking out of the corner of his mouth, his brow like a ploughed field.

'Damn you, Griffith... I'll get the blasted sheep. They're marked, aren't they? What would you have done, eh? Paid the toll? With what? You have to fight, Griffith. If you lie down, they'll trample all over you.'

'And if you knock them down?' Griffith was icy. 'I'm off to look for David.'

Richard laughed. 'David! He'll be safe in the arms of some girl. No need to worry about David! He'll look after himself.'

Griffith called the dogs, and pointed at Jane in the dark corner, though she had not known he knew she was there.

'Not a word, Jane, or it will be the worse for you.' He slammed the door behind him.

She would have told Aunt Anni else. So hard it was, to know which promise was the most important to keep.

CHAPTER 8

Under Attack

T HE DROVE DISAPPEARED into the mist as they set off the next morning. Everything was grey with a fine wetness that wasn't rain yet weighed everything down, clothes and thoughts. Tiny silver droplets beaded Jane's clothes and tufts of spiked grass by the track. Coarse comments about the britches she had expected, but none came.

All day they moved slowly through a tunnel of mist, with everything ghostly and quiet. But as the track descended steeply to the valley, things became real: the animals slipping and sliding, bellowing, flapping and complaining. Jane's toes bunched in the toes of her boots, rubbing on the hard leather. The backs of her legs were tight and ached so. Now was a time when she would have accepted a ride on Banon with no argument, but Isaac was riding at the back of the drove and out of sight whilst she was with the pigs, her job to stop them darting back to where the going was easier, though she had a mind to do the same. All the time the light was fading, so you could not see the stones till you were tripping over them nor the dips till your feet were in them.

It was dark when they arrived at Erwood. Stars glittered above them and a half moon threw a faint blue shadow of Jane leading Banon across the dark yard to the stable.

A meagre portion of watery cabbage soup and coarse bread was provided inside the Erwood Inn, which was so thick with smoke Jane's eyes stung. Rubbing made them worse, till she could barely see Isaac coming towards her.

'There's a room prepared for us upstairs, Jane,' Isaac said. 'I explained we were cousins, that you were under my protection.'

'Isaac, I need no special consideration!'

'There's a straw pallet on the floor. Take the bed, Jane.'

Jane lay on the straw pallet facing the wall, holding her sore toes in her hands. Aunt Anni would have dabbed them with cider vinegar. If she had time the next morning before the crossing, she would stuff the toes of her boots with comfrey leaves; or if not comfrey, any leaves would be soothing.

The moon was bright in her eyes but she did not want to turn to face the room. Isaac must think her asleep. He would see the shape of her on the floor and his bed empty and he would know her for the selfless person she was, and no inconvenience to anyone.

The door opened. She heard his deep sigh, heard the door close and the two thuds of Isaac's boots on the floor and squeak of the bed until he settled. His breathing was deep and even in a minute, leaving her wide-eyed and restless.

Downstairs a door slammed. No! Light already and a river to cross! And Isaac gone. Jane ran to the door, pulling on her boots and fastening her britches.

The innkeeper stood at the bottom of the stairs in his long woollen underwear, passing the saddlebags to Isaac. Burr lay stretched on the porch, asleep to alert in a second. All the cockerels in Erwood were on their toes. Behind their crowing, the river rushed. The animals were stirring. The boys stumbled to the water butt to dunk their heads and shock headaches and muzziness away.

Isaac nodded to Jane and crossed the yard. Jane followed, wrapping her shawl round her against the chill.

Rhys was at the stable door with Uriah, eyes darting this way and that.

'I'll saddle her up, will I, Isaac?' Rhys said. Worse than ever he was, so eager to please.

Isaac nodded, stroking Banon's head as Rhys tightened the girth.

'I'll help you at the rear at the crossing, shall I, Isaac?' Rhys said.

'That would be grand. Jane, I'll send you over with the geese.'

Geese! The only creature on the drove she knew nothing about. There is nothing to fathom in a bird's beady eye, and their heads are too small for a thought of any interest. And could geese not swim? A point she made to Isaac.

'It's their boots, Jane,' he answered, turning away with the look of one who did not want conversation or discussion of any kind.

The sky was touched pink with the sunrise, the water pigeon-blue as it streamed over the pale rock slabs. Either side of the valley the hills and mountains rose: the Epynt was behind them, unknown forests ahead.

The teller crossed first, slipping and splashing, though the water reached only up to the pony's legs. He rode straight to a cottage on the far side to bang his whip on the door without dismounting. A man stumbled out, putting his arms into his coat sleeves as he marched to a boat tied in a creek. The teller set off up the far lane, his horn waking every dog in the neighbourhood. Their barking echoed round the valley.

Soon all the animals were making a noise, unaware of the cause. The moment they caught sight of the water, their hubbub increased to panic.

Such a thrill it was for a person who has never been in a boat before to ride the water in something sturdy and wide and flat. The geese stretched their necks and flapped their wings to steady themselves as they slapped their little tar boots down, honking wildly. Fortunately they were packed so tight that when the boat moved, they were kept upright by the sheer number of them. Hardly time for Jane to register the watery feeling under her feet, the rush and slap of the river, before they were over and she was shooing the outraged geese out onto the grass.

The noise behind was thunderous: a solid raft of animals all straining to keep their heads out of the water. First came the pigs: leaping, splashing, screaming; next the silent sheep with their heads flat on the surface and their ears pricked up; pushed over by the panicking cattle leaping clear of the water and surging forward. The ponies danced in the shallows, twisting and turning to keep the cattle in check. Isaac and Rhys kept busy with their whips. The dogs were the last to cross after fetching the stragglers, keeping clear of the dangerous flailing cattle.

There was no sound she could recall, but something alerted Jane to look over towards the far bank.

Three men on ponies appeared from under the trees. Isaac was riding Banon into the shallows, unaware of them behind him. Rhys saw them. He stooped and picked up something from the shore before stepping into the water, upriver from Isaac. Jane saw it all, she did. Clear as could be. Rhys lifted his arm and threw a stone right at Banon. A great big stone. Banon reared up, whinnying. A second stone sent Isaac crashing back into the shallow water. Quick as quick, Rhys leapt splashing to Banon. In a trice, the saddle flaps were up, the saddlebags were in his hands and he was leaping for the bank.

Isaac struggled to his feet, retrieving his hat, which was floating off downstream. He turned just as one of the men leapt straight from his pony onto Rhys, right on the edge of the water. The saddlebags went sailing through the air, caught by one of the two remaining men, who turned and galloped off up the bank. Rhys and the first man tussled at the water's edge. Pushing, wrestling – like play-fighting, with Rhys always on top. Just as Isaac reached them, Rhys fell back onto the stones on the bank with the loudest scream, holding his head. Isaac hesitated but Rhys waved him away. The other man ran for his horse. His foot was in the stirrup but Isaac was too quick for him. He caught his leg and dragged him back. Rhys was up in an instant, head forgotten, leaping towards Banon, who was still standing in the shallows, her head jerking up and down in a panic. He pulled Banon upstream and deeper, one hand holding his chest as though he'd been hurt. The second man, on his feet again, pushed Isaac back into the water. This time Isaac held onto the man's arm and pulled him with him.

Everything happened so quickly, and yet the details stretched out the action and slowed it. Uriah, almost on the slope on Jane's side of the river, turned back; kicking his pony, sending up great arcs of water, passing Rhys and Banon. Before reaching the shallows, Uriah sprang from his pony, keeping his hand clear of the water. He held a gun. He cocked it, pointing it towards the pair struggling in the water.

There was no doubting what Jane saw. Rhys, crouching behind Banon, watched Uriah. His eyes never left him as he, Rhys, slid a gun from his coat and also pointed it towards the pair in the river. The two shots were so close they were as one, with what sounded like a single echo. The man fighting Isaac fell back, arms beating the air as his head disappeared under the surface. Isaac looked up, stricken.

'I wasn't shooting at him!' Uriah cried, loud enough for Jane to hear. His face was shocked. 'I aimed to the side.'

When Jane looked back at Rhys, his gun was nowhere to be seen. He stood clear of Banon, his face horrified, the look exaggerated like it was not a true feeling. The silence beneath the bellowing of the animals was terrible.

Isaac dragged the man to the bank, shouting to Rhys, 'Help me, will you?'

Rhys stayed motionless as Uriah laboured through the water to Isaac.

The boys had gathered round Jane to watch. They had seen it too. No-one said anything. On the far bank, Isaac and Uriah were leaning over the man. Uriah straightened and took a step back, his hand over his mouth. Isaac took his arm, Uriah nodded, mounted his pony and splashed back into the water.

'Jane,' he called from halfway across. 'I'm to take you back.' His face was anguished. Were her skills needed at last?

'Is he not dead?' she asked, as he helped her up into the saddle in front of him.

'Not when I left him.'

'Am I to help?'

'Pray God you can, Jane,' Uriah gulped. 'I only fired to frighten him.'

Water swirled round Jane's boots.

'I know it, Uriah. I saw it all.'

Isaac's coat was spread over the man lying on the bank, his boots sticking out. His head rested on his hat, his face turned away. He'd a terrible head wound: a flap of flesh and the bone yellowish beneath it, the ear flipped over onto his neck. Blood pumped red as poppies onto his shirt collar.

Isaac said nothing. He placed his hand gently under the man's cheek and turned him slightly towards Jane.

David.

The silence was a terrible singing in her ears.

'How can it be you?' Jane shut her eyes tight. 'Let it not be you!' She opened them again. His blue lips moved faintly.

'Jane?'

She sank to her knees.

'Oh no, David!'

'Jane.'

'Were you coming after me?'

His eyes were glazing. His lids dropped, flickered once, then closed. His lips parted but no sound came.

'No, David! Don't die, please!' Jane took hold of his shoulders and shook.

'I'm so sorry, Jane.' Isaac took hold of her arm. She jerked free and threw herself onto David's body.

He was very still. The blood was seeping, not pumping. She took his hand. It was cold from the water and limp, and there was no beat under her fingers. She held it to her cheek. She spread his fingers out till they covered her whole face. Such rough skin he had.

'No, no, God – how could You let this happen?'

She flung his arm away, clenched her fists and lifted her face to the sky.

'This is so wrong!'

She turned back. His hair. His sweet hair. Dark now with the river but fine with a touch of the fox, Tad used to say. What would Mam say now if she knew this had happened?

'I'm sorry, Mam, I didn't take care of him,' Jane sobbed.

Isaac's hand was on her back. 'My cousin's child. I can't believe this!' He rubbed at his face, whispering the words to himself. 'A terrible accident. The only comfort is that he is with his mother now, Jane. With your mam and tad.'

'He should be safe at home. Not here like this.'

Isaac stooped to pull his coat over David's face.

'Don't! He won't like his face to be covered. He'll choke.'

Isaac gave Jane his hand to pull her to her feet. He steered her away to a river-smoothed stone at the water's edge, where they sat side by side.

'What was he doing here?' Jane cried. 'He shouldn't be here.' She looked straight into Isaac's face. 'He was coming to take me back! I've murdered him, haven't I?'

'No, Jane, no.'

'I have. This is my punishment. Oh God, what have I done?' Jane leapt up and started walking away, pulling at her hair.

Isaac caught her arm and turned her to face him. 'Listen to me, Jane. David was in with a bad lot. They were after the gold I'm taking to London. I don't know how they knew.'

Jane shook her head fiercely.

'David would never do that, Isaac.'

'Sit down, Jane, and listen to me. I didn't want you to know this, Jane, but I'd rather you knew than have you blame yourself.'

'And did they get your gold?'

Isaac shook his head with a wry smile. 'They'll have a shock when they open the saddlebags and find river stones!'

'David was killed for river stones?' Jane wailed.

'He never knew that, Jane, if that is any comfort,' Isaac said, standing and walking back to where David lay.

'Comfort!' She hurled the word after him in disbelief. 'There's no comfort of any kind to be had in any of this!'

The water swirled and tumbled over the boulders. Jane wept. She stopped. She wept again. I don't understand. How could You let this happen? Unless this is God's sign to me – am I to go home? Is that why You sent him?

She thought on. Or is this a test? Am I to go on? What do You want me to do?

Agony on agony. So complicated now when it had been so simple.

'Jane, you should take these. They are no use to him now.' Isaac stood behind her with David's hat and boots in his hands, and his coat over his arm. 'I know the boots you have are too small.'

A sudden calm came over her as she took them. Tall the boots were, of thick brown hide, and heavy. The toes curled up so the soles weren't flat to the ground. They were cracked round the top where his strides had creased them and were worn black and shiny inside.

She pulled them on. They were still warm. She put on the hat and wrapped the coat, sodden with river water, round her body as though climbing into David's skin.

'I have a plan, Jane.'

She stood quiet in David's boots. Isaac's eyes were sad but there was an urgency in his jaw. 'We could take David up to the new chapel at Llandeilo Graban. It's on our route. We have a cousin there. We could leave David in God's care and ask Cousin Frederick to take him home to Tŷ Mawr. He could tell Griffith that you are protected with me, and I will see you safe in London. Would you like them to know that, Jane?'

'I would. That is the right thing to do.'

David's boots were a good fit. She could walk on in these. His coat trailed in the mud.

'I've sent Rhys to the inn for something to wrap him in.'

Jane's blood ran cold.

'No, Isaac, not Rhys. He shot David. It was Rhys.'

Isaac shook his head. 'You are mistaken, Jane. It was Uriah. A terrible mistake. He had no thought of hurting him.'

'I saw it all. It was Rhys.'

'Jane, Jane.' Isaac knelt beside her and took her hand. 'It was Uriah. Not Rhys. He has no gun. I know that. And no reason at all. You are distressed, Jane, of course you are, and misjudge the situation. Understandable. But it was Uriah.'

'Rhys has a gun. I saw it.'

Isaac stood. 'Jane.' His voice was harder. 'Believe me. I have good reason to know Rhys has no gun. And what is more, no reason to shoot David at all.'

'To help you. To be in your favour. Ask the others! I was not the only one who saw it all!'

The stones cracked together as Uriah helped Isaac pick up David's body behind her, swaddling him in a blanket as Jane used to swaddle William, his arms and legs bound tight to his body. Mam must have wrapped baby David just the same. Someone had fetched a cart to pick him up.

Water slapped against the sides of the ferryboat as it drew near, a dull scrape as it ground into the shallows. Voices were low, respectful, as the cart was pushed onto the ferry.

'Jane.' Isaac's hand on her shoulder brought her back. 'Would you like to take David across the river?'

Shoals of tiny transparent fishes flitted through the shallows; almost water themselves, not there at all. At her first step, they vanished. Isaac stepped ahead onto the boat and held out his hand.

As the cart was wheeled down from the boat, the boys stood quiet with their hats in their hands.

'Ask them!' Jane said.

Rhys stood waiting with Banon's reins in his hand. Isaac motioned the boys to move aside with him.

'We saw nothing,' one boy said. 'We were too busy with the animals.'

'You did!' Jane said. 'You know you did. You were standing right by me. Bryn? Pedr? Someone?'

They hung their heads.

'They don't dare, Isaac. Can't you see it?'

Isaac breathed through his teeth. 'Right, Jane. If I search Rhys for a gun, would that satisfy you?'

Or course it wouldn't. He wouldn't have the gun now!

Isaac walked over to Rhys, who shrugged and held out his arms. Isaac patted him up and down, then shook his head. She couldn't bear to look at him.

The chapel was opposite Cousin Frederick's farm at Llandeilo Graban. Uriah went on with the drove to Painswick. Cousin Frederick would take David's body back to Tŷ Mawr the next day. Isaac and Frederick carried David up the chapel steps, head first. Such care they took, laying him on the wooden trestles like a mother putting down the babe who has fallen asleep in her arms. Jane kept her mouth tight. Where should she look?

'We'll leave you with David, Jane,' Isaac said.

The door closed behind her and a deep silence filled the chapel. The plaster walls were fresh; the windows tall and clean. Light fell on the cloth where David's head must be, though his feet were in evening shadow.

Silence is awfully lonesome and so heavy in the company of a dead brother.

It could be anyone lying there. Not David at all.

She parted the material. His forehead was smeared with rust, flat as stone. His eyes were closed, his nose fine and chill-looking without the breath to warm it. She lifted a lock of his hair. She kissed him. The last time and the first. He smelt of river water with a tang of blood.

That night in the cot bed in her cousin's house, Jane fell instantly into a deep dark place but rose so fast she was panting and almost lifted out of the bed.

From the window, she could see the chapel. Bigger and more solid it appeared now with the moon behind it, just the lane between herself and the steps. The lane too was silvered like a river. You would not expect to see anything stirring at this time of night. A fox, maybe, or a badger, or an owl hunting. Not ponies. Not ponies with men on their backs. Two of them came trotting along the road. There, and gone, rising and falling behind the hedge. At this time, in the dead of the night.

CHAPTER 9

Thinking Is a Waste of Time

JANE FELT NOTHING. Everything in the world was different now. It was as if David's boots, like David himself, were no longer on this earth. His soul was rising like bread dough with the yeast. More like smoke from the wood fire. Dough reached its peak and fell over itself; smoke went on curling until it disappeared from sight. It would be like that.

He would be buried behind the chapel next to Mam and Tad, near Ma Penny and Mighty Michael. Would Jane be mentioned? They'd have received the message. How important was Jane – alive – next to David – dead? Sitting round the kitchen table at Tŷ Mawr, they'd be. A drink was the custom, a bite to eat maybe. The talk might turn to her. Aunt Anni would tell them it was for the best, that Jane would be safe with Isaac.

If David had not been coming after her, had no-one considered it? Had they just let her go without a second thought? A sudden pain rose in Jane's throat, a mix of a cry and a cough. She choked and choked, bending over with her hands flat on her knees, heaving for breath.

'Jane? Whatever is the matter?' Isaac thumped hard on her back. He turned her round to face him and hugged her.

'Let it out, Jane. If God hadn't intended us to shed tears, He'd not have given us the pain to suffer. And remember, Jane, suffering brings you closer to God and to all humankind.'

'I'm so close to you, Isaac, I've slobbered over your coat.'

Three trees marked a farm in Paincastle as a safe night-grazing place. Jane was to stay there, Isaac in the inn in the village. The shoeing was taking place on the grass outside.

A barrel-chested man in a leather jerkin was leading a cow down to the blacksmith, whose anvil had been set in the field like Old Jones back in Caio. A great action this feller had: muzzle in one hand, one horn in the other, hooking his leg round the animal's front leg. With a kick and a twist it crashed under him and he was astride before it could holler. So hard the cow slammed down, its horn stuck into the ground.

The feller stretched the cow's neck while the blacksmith was busy shoeing another animal. The cow continued to bellow, its dark tongue quivering in its open mouth. An ugly sight. Once David had pinned Jane's forearm to the table at Tŷ Mawr and scraped it with a cow's tongue her Mam was about to cook. He scraped till the blood oozed. Such a mean laughing look he had in his eyes. Jane had screamed. Mam shooed David away, took the tongue and slit it down the centre. When she folded back the skin, there was another tongue inside, the same shape but red and smooth. A tight circle Mam made of it and boiled it for hours, so the whole house stank and the windows ran with tonguey tears.

Of all the men, it had to be Rhys who brought the pigs to the field – Rhys, who knew nothing at all about them. He'd seen her. She knew by the speed he turned his head away. The behaviour of a guilty man. She knew what she had seen. A gun. Without question! Doubting herself would be the most terrible betrayal.

She jumped over the low fence, throwing the crumbs from the pockets of David's coat onto the ground for the pigs.

The weasel-faced lad came sauntering over to join her.

'You've a way with the pigs.' His voice was slow but his eyes were quick, never still in one place.

'I have. I like them.'

'They're intelligent – pigs.'

'That's why they like me.'

The boy smiled. His teeth were broken and flinty.

'That Rhys is no good with pigs,' he said, glancing at her.

'He's no good at all.'

'Your brother, was it?' the weasel boy said.

Jane nodded.

'Bad business.' There was truthfulness in his voice, but with men you could never be sure.

'It was.'

The boy stretched up, easing his muscles to the very tips of his fingers.

'My name's David too, but they call me Dai. There'll be wrestling and fiddlers later. Bit of singing maybe. Will you be up for it?'

Jane shrugged. 'I don't know whether to think about it or try not to.'

'Thinking's a waste of time, I reckon.' The boy picked up his hat and moved away.

He might be right, for certainly thinking was getting her nowhere at all.

She did not know what she did want, but knew what she did not – fiddlers, music, the company of other people. While everyone else drifted towards the inn, Jane turned back to walk along the road. The trouble was that walking lifted thoughts from deep inside. Perhaps she should lie still somewhere.

A carriage rumbled down the road behind her. She stood flat to the hedge as it passed. The man inside stared straight ahead. The door had a fancy crest on it – a flash of a blue and silver shield, and it was gone. A coach like that in these parts was rare, but everywhere, hidden away in the folds of the hills, were big houses and carriages and the kind of people who went to church not chapel, who paid for gravestones and stone angels to stand guard over them for eternity.

The animals were in the fields. The boys would not come near her after what had happened. She was the safer because of it. Not a good thought to climb the stairs and lie down with on the narrow truckle bed, narrow as the cart that took David to Tŷ Mawr. The wheels would rumble and jerk over the ruts in the road. Terrible uncomfortable it would be. Why could he not have had a ride in a carriage with springs, like the one that had passed her?

Mr Johns had a carriage. And now she was thinking about that Sunday when the carriage had overtaken them, walking back from the chapel. Three little faces had peeped out from under Mrs Johns' skirts, like chicks under a hen. The two Johns daughters Jane had seen before, but not the other: a face bone-white and sickly.

A girl – a stranger – was walking down the hill behind the carriage, taking quick steps to keep up with it. She'd a straw bonnet on which was yellow with age, but a white cap under it. Her hands were clasped together tight across her chest and she looked down, all modest. The boys didn't look away as she trotted past and Richard did not spit as he usually did when the Johns' carriage overtook them. The hem of the girl's skirt was ragged and her feet were in clogs.

As soon as she was past the boys, she lifted her head and smiled at Jane. Her teeth were crooked as the tombstones in the churchyard.

Jane saw her a second time when she was sent to the Big House with eggs from Aunt Anni.

'They've a cousin from Chester who is not well,' her aunt said. 'It's only eggs she can keep down now, so I hear.'

'I saw her in the carriage,' Jane said. 'Such a peaky look to her.'

The Big House stood in the lushest, greenest grass imaginable. Wondrous trees grew tall as giants with so much space around them. Two soft dogs with gold hair ran barking to greet Jane. Their tails wagged, their eyes were a welcome. Jane scratched their heads as they sniffed around her skirts.

The back door was open and the girl with the tombstone teeth waiting. Free of the bonnet and cap, her brown hair was coiled round her ears like snail shells.

'These are for the sick one.' Jane gave her the eggs. 'From my Aunt Anni.'

'Would you like some milk?' The girl showed Jane into the kitchen. An enormous black range filled the recess beneath the chimney. Matching blue china rimmed with gold lined the shelves of the dresser, with glasses and pewter tankards.

Keeping her hands out of sight was not possible. Jane flushed as their fingers touched round the cup.

'Don't you go to church then?' the girl asked. She was speaking English. Not since Mam died had anyone spoken to Jane in English.

'Chapel,' she said.

'Chapel.' She echoed the sing-song of Jane's voice and giggled. 'My name's Margaret. My mistress is poorly. The country's very dull. I prefer Chester.'

Jane stood picking at the rough edge of her thumbnail till a dog nudged her with its wet nose. A girl from Chester so nice and speaking to her! She might be her friend, for she could know nothing about Jane.

'How old is your brother? The one with the fair hair. The better-looking one?'

'Griffith?' Was he better looking than Richard? 'Twenty-five, I think.' Why bring him into it now and spoil everything?

'Would he be interested in meeting me, do you think?'

Jane shook her head. 'You'd not like him.'

'Why not?'

There was nothing easy to say.

'Tell him I'll be at the church gate tomorrow night at nine o'clock. My mistress will be in bed and I'll be free.'

Two nights later Jane woke with weight over her like a monster from a dark wilderness. She was dragged from the bed, leaving William whimpering in half sleep. Her face was slapped before she knew who the hand belonged to.

'Stop!' Jane choked. 'Get off me. What have I done?'

Griffith stood legs apart, face like a gargoyle with fury.

'What have I done?'

'What haven't you done? Did you have a message that you never gave?'

Jane's heart beat guiltily. Margaret. 'I didn't understand what she said.'

He took her arm and shook her.

'I didn't think she meant it! It was just in passing.'

'In passing? What right have you to decide what's in passing, Jane Evans?'

His arm was iron as though he longed to hurt her. He might. He had before. Instead he flung her from him and sat heavily on the bed.

'When do I ever have the chance to meet a sweet girl? And you ruin it for me.' Griffith tugged at his hair. 'She's back to Chester this afternoon. I met her in the village. She wondered why I never showed up.'

'I never meant to spoil it for you, Griffith,' Jane cried. She hadn't. Not really. But the truth made her feel bad.

William was sitting up in the bed wailing, stretching his arms up for Jane.

'This is the last night William is sleeping here with you. He's with us from now on.'

Griffith slammed the door behind him and Jane held William to her. What a mean thing for Griffith to do, and William barely six! So he would hurt her this way, would he? Such a wicked brother she had, and nothing she could do. She pressed William close and rocked her own misery away.

And now, with dawn light already turning the dark ceiling grey, in this strange bed in Painscastle, William was wrenched away from her anew.

An agony it was to think of him. He had saved her.

Please God let Griffith never suspect William. Make the boys treat him well.

She had made everything worse for them. That was the cold hard truth, though to be fair, as Mr Morgan said, her absence might be a spur to Griffith. Mr Morgan dribbled and was a loathsome old man, but on occasion he might talk some sense. If Griffith were to go now and find himself a girl, that would make everything better. Jane would have nothing bad to feel then, and he would neither.

CHAPTER 10

Like a Friend

THE DROVE FLOWED on, towards a horizon that was never reached.

The empty blue autumn sky was a child's picture of Heaven. A simple, homely place. Clean, not grand, just a few nice chairs and a table for God to sit with Jesus at His right hand. Angels flew around them, until the preacher poured scorn on them and that was a terrible loss. Angels were spotless women with gentle smiles and wings, who played harps and wore halos to dazzle you if you were bold enough to look into their faces.

Isaac jumped down from Banon and ducked down beneath her to examine the girth straps. He pulled hard. The saddle slipped. One strap dangled from his hand. He pulled the other tight.

'That'll need repair.' He frowned, examining the jagged edge before quickly stuffing it into his coat pocket. 'I should have noted that. That accounts for why I was unseated in the river.' The words were out. He clamped his lips and glanced sideways at Jane. He'd change the subject now.

'There's a sheep I found last evening with fly round its tail. We gave it the treatment but I want to check,' he said. 'If one sheep was to go down with the contagion we could lose the whole drove.'

'You believe in Heaven, don't you?' Jane said.

'I do. I wondered what you were thinking, Jane. You're very quiet this morning.'

'Where is it, then?'

'Are you thinking of David, Jane?'

'Do you think he might not have a place in Heaven, after he came to steal from you?'

'It's a small thing in a blameless life, Jane.'

Isaac did not know David as she did.

They walked a few strides in silence.

'Do you think it might count in your favour, Isaac, if you've been killed?'

He did not answer at once. He had a way of staring into the far distance when he was ordering his thoughts.

'It was a terrible accident, Jane. Uriah must have slipped.'

'He did not slip, Isaac.' Jane stopped. 'It was Rhys.'

Isaac's mouth worked from side to side with the rage boiling in him.

'Jane, we will mention this no more. You have to trust my judgement. I know what I am saying.'

His foot was in the stirrup and Banon broke from stillness to a gallop before Jane could open her mouth.

What about *him* trusting *her*? Her throat closed as though angry hands were squeezing – an old feeling, familiar, that hadn't been with her since she left home.

The river had to be crossed again, this time by a toll bridge, and then they were in England in a field that was like the fields in Wales in every way. As the fire died, Jane slipped away to find her resting place. Away from Isaac. Anywhere that was not near him.

Dark makes every sound sharp. The drove ponies were in the field next to her. That pawing of the ground, that huffing of breath did not come from them, but from the opposite direction, from the far side of the hedge. A thick hedge it was, and nothing could she see through it. Trees rose up behind it. The branches were shaking though there was no wind. A man was climbing up one of the trees, clear for a second before disappearing into the branches and leaves. Had someone come from home to find her? They missed her and wanted her back home. As quick as it was thought, it died away. She was not missed and no-one would come for her now. What then could this man be up to? Should she tell Isaac? She'd only to open her mouth for irritation to deaden his eyes. So stubborn and wilful men can be when they think they are right, and of course they always do. Let the cattle be rustled, let the drove be ruined!

Propped on her elbow, she watched Isaac moving like a black shadow amongst the eerie white sheep. The truth was, she was feeling the worse for not telling him. But at the sight of Rhys on the far side of the field, she lay back. David's hat was her pillow. She flicked her hair away from her ears. She'd not like anyone to creep up on her unheard.

Hereford was their first stopping place, to sell the geese. The drove was to graze in the common fields outside the town.

'Let me take the saddle in for you, Isaac,' Rhys offered.

'I'll do that myself, thanks, Rhys. Jane and Dai can manage the geese.'

Such a look Rhys flashed, but Isaac had his back turned. Isaac might think he noticed everything, but he did not. Being in a person's company over time reveals their faults.

Across the road from the field, where Rhys sat with a dark scowl on his face, Isaac paid the toll. Their job was to drive the geese down a street lined with houses and shops. Low cottages of brick with stone roofs sat between taller buildings with three layers to them, black and white: heavy oak beams making white plaster shapes. The further down the street they walked, the more people there were and the louder the noise.

The street opened out into a teeming market. Isaac led the way into a ramshackle covered building, like a roof on stilts where the walls had been forgotten. So many people: women in long dresses and bonnets with baskets hooked over their arms; men in tight jackets and hats. A girl carrying a tray of buttons round her neck smirked as she caught Jane's eye.

'Buttons, sir?' she said, brushing against Jane, who backed away, startled. Weasel Dai slapped his thighs, laughing.

'You're taken for a man, Jane!'

Never! How could that be, with her feeling herself to be Jane Evans, a young woman, and the same as ever?

'A smelly drover like the rest of us!' Weasel Dai laughed.

Isaac and the poultry merchant greeted each other and got down to business. Weasel Dai held the protesting geese up so the man could pinch their breasts. The pressure of glances and blatant stares had never been so great. Jane was more used to being invisible. Isaac was observant on this occasion, she had to grant him that, noticing her discomfort.

'You know this town, Dai, don't you?' Isaac said. 'Take Jane and show her the cathedral. I'll see the saddle mended first, then go on to The Grapes in about a half hour. Don't go mad now.'

No liking at all Jane had for Hereford. As she trudged down the street following Dai, looking at her feet, her mam came into her mind. To think that Mam had worked here, in such a place! She must have felt the same as Jane, no better than the cabbage leaves and filth on the streets, to run away with Tad to a place where she knew no one. They were the same, Jane and her mam, both fleeing from something unthinkable – a thought that made Jane heavy and light at the same time.

The cathedral was the most enormous building, rising up out of a perfect green, empty meadow. The cows would have been in Heaven there. Walking inside was like walking into another world of gloom, with cold space all around. To look up at the high ceilings was unbearable, bringing a sickness to the stomach. The floor was a marvel though. Yellow and red patterns with dragons and trailing leaves.

'Follow me.' Dai's low voice echoed in the emptiness.

Jane followed the lines of the floor, walking on tiptoe so her heels would not make a noise. This place brought on a shrinking feeling worse than the desolation of the Epynt. Concentrating on the patterns, she almost bumped into the first tomb, where a stone man lay at waist height with one foot missing. The other foot, in a thin pointed shoe, rested on a stone dragon. Or a dog, maybe. A beast like nothing Jane knew. He'd a hat on his head, a sword by his side. It must have been an age he'd been lying there.

Dead people lay all around, tucked into alcoves the length of the great wall. Full-grown men with their heads gone, all flat and grey and thin. Stone is such a horrible cold thing. Though dead flesh is colder and deader than stone. Poor David. This might be a reason to be grateful to be born a poor man. You would not have to lie for all eternity in this place. You would have the earth under you and the sky above.

Candles flickered from iron spikes, casting soft light on Mary's blue robe. Jane went alone into a side chapel where the figures were coloured, not so melancholy as the stone men on the shelves. A woman lay there, eyes closed, with a broken nose. She'd a beautiful dress, deep red like blackberry juice. Fancy making hard stone look like soft cloth! A foot poked out from underneath the skirt. Jane touched it and jerked back with horror. Mam, on the kitchen table: so cold when she touched her. She had not known she would be that way, because the fire was lit and the room warm for Aunt Anni to wash her.

A sudden heat swept over Jane. She couldn't breathe. Right across the cathedral she ran, towards the door, not caring at all about the noise of her boots on the floor.

Panting, she threw herself onto the soft grass. Dai came running after her.

'Jane, what's the matter?'

Jane lay trembling, from top to toe.

'I don't care for cathedrals at all!' she said.

Not a thing there was amusing and yet suddenly she was shaking with laughter – they both were, rolling round and aching. Dai straightened first, picked up his hat, and pulled her to her feet.

The Grapes was down a cobbled alley which led away from the cathedral. Dai peered through the window, shielding his face from the glare.

'He's there.' He tapped the glass. 'Reading the newspaper.'

Isaac came to the door adjusting his hat.

'Saddle's mended good as new. Money in my pocket from the geese.' He patted his coat. 'What do you make of Hereford, Jane?'

She glanced at Weasel Dai. 'It's too big. And I don't like the people here.'

'Do you not?'

He had a manner, Isaac, now she noticed, of seeming pleasant, but all the time his words made you feel you knew nothing at all. She was *not* the child she used to be.

Back in the field, while the men were inspecting the cattle cues, Jane sat picking the bark from her stick. That cold foot. She could not be rid of it, though it was long ago.

That morning Mam had taken to her bed with cramps, having eaten nothing. William, a scrap of a babe, was asleep in the rocking cot Tad had made for Griffith. It had rocked all the Evans babies to sleep. Mam's eyes were dark and glittery and her cheeks white as wool. But it had happened before. Aunt Anni was called for. She sent Jane for her tad and her brothers.

After it was over, Tad carried Mam from the bed to the kitchen table. Jane stood in a dark corner of the room, watching him smooth down her nightclothes and her hair too, with the air unbearably still all round him. He bent low over Mam's chest. Soft sounds came from him – like nothing Jane had ever heard before, deep and high at the same time and growing louder until she could not bear it, in this room so crowded and empty, with all the boys standing round. She must be somewhere else. Outside. At the door she stopped, biting her lip. She turned and walked the two paces to the table. She reached out to touch the nearest part of Mam, her foot, lying there so small and white. It was colder than ice, a dead cold.

Later, Aunt Anni came to the stable for her. Horses breathing in and out was the only comfort to be had.

'You said you were a healer.'

'There's things that can be healed and things that cannot, Jane. Baby William is calling for you.'

'He's calling for Mam.'

'No, for you, Jane.'

Aunt Anni found a wet nurse for William. Most days, Jane visited him after she had baked the bread on the flat stone the way Mam had taught her. Griffith helped knead the bread when her hands grew tired. Richard filled the kettle from the well. When something needed lifting from the fire the boys came forward. Splitting logs was a job for the older boys, but collecting kindling Jane was expected to do. David, when he appeared, always had a rabbit or mushrooms or berries and once a pheasant with its head blasted off and the meat full of shot – a danger to the teeth.

Mr Morgan brought their first sack of coal when he brought liquor for Tad.

'Coal lasts longer. Less work.'

'But it's not free.' Griffith sounded like Tad now.

Tad sat long hours at the table staring ahead saying nothing, drinking the beer the boys brought him or the liquor from Mr Morgan's still behind his Long House. Everything was made worse by liquor, but who dared say so?

A frequent visitor was Mr Morgan, the owner of the bull and the boar which serviced all the farms for miles around. When he was newly bereaved, Mam had taken pity on him and given eggs, which Jane had taken to him.

The first time she was willing enough.

The second time she frowned and twisted her face. Mam was sitting on the stone seat by the cowshed, wrapped in a woollen blanket although it was a warm June day.

'That is not charitable, Jane.'

'But Mr Morgan is old and he farts worse than the horses and I hate the way his lip hangs so.'

'Jane! I never took you for an unkind girl. Now go.'

Mam did not know the way Mr Morgan's breath had stunk of sweet liquor last time, nor how his eyes were bleary, and his tongue furred all his words. She didn't know, because Jane had not told her. Neither did Mam know that Mr Morgan had asked Jane to place the eggs in a bowl outside his back door, and when she was bending down, thrust his hand up her skirt and twiddled his fingers. It wasn't the sort of thing she could tell Mam, even if she were not ill.

After Mam died, Tad and Mr Morgan sat either side of the kitchen table with the bottle between them.

'We need a woman, John. Men do. We're less than half without them.'

Tad said nothing. Mr Morgan didn't need someone to talk with, just someone to talk to.

'Us older men can't be fussy. If she's getting on a bit herself, that would be acceptable. I'd like one with a bit of flesh on her... in the right places. We don't need them for breeding at our age. For comfort and cooking and keeping the house tidy.'

Jane had run away to be free of Mr Morgan, and here he was filling her mind as the drove prepared to leave. The stone woman replaced by Mr Morgan! Never had she been so glad to hear Isaac's whistle. Persuading reluctant pigs to be up and off pushed all other thoughts away.

Beyond Hereford the green fields of England on either side of the drove roads were hedged and cut into squares with no place for the common herd. The dotted farm houses and hamlets were pretty enough.

They passed queer-shaped brick houses pointing to the clouds.

'Oast houses,' Weasel Dai said. 'For the hops. Can you not smell the beer, Jane?'

He was nice, Weasel Dai. Like a friend. He *was* a friend. He'd this way to him, smiling sideways and talking out of the corner of his mouth. His eyes darted about like birds in the hedges. You didn't notice what he looked like once you knew him. He whistled too, tuneful, bright.

'Have you not tried the cider?'

She had not.

The land might be tame here, but the people were hostile, superior, turning away as they passed. Dai ran off ahead to catch a sheep which had led a group through an open gate.

Isaac took his place at her side.

'So, Jane, you do not like the English, do you?'

The amused tone in his voice must be ignored. 'I don't. Not at all.'

'Your mother was English, Jane.'

'I know it. She was different.'

'Do you like the Welsh, then, Jane?'

'Of course.'

'Do you like every single one of them? How about Mr Morgan, for instance?'

'You know I do not like him.'

'Just pointing something out to you, Jane.'

It was maddening that small way he made her feel, and worse – he was right. Forever looking at her he was, judging her, not allowing her to be other than the ignorant girl he knew back home.

'They're shaping up for war now, Jane. I read it in the newspaper in Hereford. The Russian Tsar is getting far too greedy. Trying to make friends with the British, thinking they will side with him against the French, but I think he's a shock coming.'

'Who?'

'The Russian Tsar. It's like a King, Jane. A Russian King.'

And now she was ignorant all over again. 'All these places and names. The world is a big place, and I've only got as far as England.'

Oatmeal was the meal for the evening: acceptable at the beginning of the day, but a disappointment at night when your mouth craves something tasty to reward hard work. Such a joy it was when Dai and Rhys slapped two rabbits down near the fire.

'How's that, then?'

'Grand, boys.' Isaac turned the rabbits over. 'A couple of fat does.'

While they were cooking over the fire on long-dampened spits of wood, their outsides burning black as coal, Jane moved into the gloom away from the fire. Pissing was easy enough, crouching with her skirt round her like a tent. It's not a thing you wish others to see.

She was adjusting her coat when she saw two men on horseback on the far side of the road, lurking in the thicket. Her heart jumped. How is that that only when your attention is taken for a moment, you are caught out? They *were* being followed. This time, she must tell Isaac. He could make her feel like a silly child and a burden, but that was better than being murdered and left in an English field to rot.

She hurried back to the fire. 'Isaac!'

'What now, Jane?' His voice was weary.

'Two men are following us.'

Isaac sighed and cleared his throat.

'Oh, don't listen to me at all,' Jane said. 'What do I know? Of course, I must be mistaken. I just thought it my duty to tell you, that's all.'

She stomped away, tossing her hair, to find a sleeping place. Let them steal up and butcher everyone, then he'd be sorry. She kicked twigs to the side with her boot. Isaac wouldn't be quite dead, just horribly injured, and neither would she, then she might live to hear him turn and say, 'I should have listened to you, Jane. I was guilty of the sin of pride. Please forgive me.'

Jane threw down her hat where her head would rest and settled herself on the ground. And she would forgive him and they would both live, with terrible scars, to tell the story to everyone at Tŷ Mawr.

Anger and fear kept rest away. She was forever sitting up to listen. Every flutter in the trees, every creak from the hedge was a man creeping up with his pistol cocked and ready. At least the dogs weren't barking. There they were now asleep by the fire.

Weasel Dai was drinking with the boys. Not as tall as the others, his shoulders slighter and his hat set in a jaunty way. Recounting a tale he was, and they were laughing with him. Not at how Jane had run howling across Hereford Cathedral, she hoped.

It was dark. A long way she had walked. She lay back and closed her eyes – waking frozen with fear, wide awake in an instant. Someone was near.

'Shall I sleep here, Jane? You're not asleep, are you? I've brought you a drop of the apple juice to taste.'

'Dai, you nearly stopped my heart!'

She snatched the leather bottle. Why did words always come out wrong so he'd not hear what she intended? She gulped and choked. Not sweet as she had been expecting, but foul and salty with a kick to it that was in no sense like apples.

Weasel Dai laughed. 'That's cider, Jane. Do you like it?'

'Not at all.'

'Shall I settle here, Jane?'

'If you like.' She shrugged. It *would* be good to have someone near, to treat her better than a silly girl and a nuisance.

'I'll be back.'

The stream of piss on the ground was heavy and long. Dai walked over to the fire, adjusting himself. The pigs snuffled and snored around her. He returned, protecting something precious with his hand.

He dented the earth with the heel of his boot. He held a fine white candle, tapering, smooth, pearly.

'Dai! Where did you get that?'

'It's nothing, Jane. Who could miss one little candle?'

'That's stealing.'

'Not stealing when it's something that doesn't matter to anyone. Not in my way of looking at it. Who's bothered? The Church has money enough. They'll not miss it.'

'*Thou shalt not steal*. That's a commandment!'

'What about all the stealing the Church has done, eh?'

She couldn't argue because she didn't know enough about that. She'd heard the men talking in the chapel doorway though, after the sermon. Thieving was a common subject. When it was a local event, like the theft of Mr Howell's undergarments from Mrs Howell's washing line, Jane would listen, but when it came to the Church or the English, her mind would drift.

It was hard to stay shocked when the candle looked so small and so pretty in the ground between them, transforming Dai's face, making their little space bright and the rest of the world darker.

CHAPTER 11

Remember the Sabbath

MORNING LIGHT BANISHED night shadows. Nothing lurking. Nothing to fear. Weasel Dai was gone and the day had a different feel to it. Jane stumbled to her feet. The earth was pale with the shape of her.

'What's happening?'

'What's not happening, do you mean?' Isaac was scattering the cut grass he had bought the day before in Hereford in front of the ponies. 'It's the Sabbath, Jane. *Remember the Sabbath day, to keep it holy*. If drovers work on the Sabbath and they are found out, there will be a hefty fine to pay. It's the law of the land and a good law.'

'I've lost count of the days myself.'

'That's my job, Jane.'

'We'll be here tonight then?'

'And making an early start, Jane. There's some who move as soon as midnight is struck. It's not against the law. But I'm a softer man than that.'

Here, as a gift, was a day for wandering. She took herself down the field to the copse to see if there was a stream where she might wash. The trees were not thick, just a few messy goat willows and a small stone bridge topped with grass.

Hardly above her ankles the water came, even midstream, and cold so it numbed her toes. Such a shock to look up and see a woman looking down on her. The sun behind made the figure light as a ghost.

Jane splashed to the bank, where her boots stood.

'Are you from the drove?'

Not a ghost, nor a woman's voice: a man's. Jane nodded. 'Not moving today, I trust?' His voice was all in his nose. A preacher man on his way to his church. His robe was black and his hat a strange low thing like a bowl with a brim.

'It's the Lord's day.'

'I know it,' she said.

He nodded and moved on.

And now, with nothing particular to do, Jane sat on the bank, picking the petals from daisies.

In the kitchen at Tŷ Mawr she was, when she saw Mam's ghost stretching up to the tin mirror on the mantelpiece. Holding her shawl close to her face, she stroked her cheek. Her head tilted to one side.

'Mam?'

'Jane!'

Mam vanished as Tad swung round: Tad dressed in Mam's skirt and blouse, which Jane herself had folded into the cedar box the day she died.

'What are you doing, Tad?' she whispered.

'*Cyfrinach.*' And that word was a terrible word. Spit and hurt and pain. 'A secret.'

He picked up the iron poker from the hearth, cutting the air with it as though it were a sword.

She couldn't move, couldn't speak until Mr Morgan's dog rushed into the house, squeezing past Jane's legs, sniffing for food. Tad kicked out at it, catching his leg in his skirt. He took Jane by the arm and pushed her into the pantry just as Mr Morgan arrived wheezing at the door.

The pantry door had a split in it where the wood had cracked; her view was clear. Ridiculous they were, the pair of them, in their dead wives' clothes with big boots sticking out under their skirts, bodies too big and moving all wrong. Mr Morgan had a thresher in his hand and an axe, and a coil of thick rope, which he threw to Tad.

'Ready, John?'

'Ready.'

Just before he left, Tad turned and looked straight at the crack in the pantry door. *'Cyfrinach.'* Such a mad, glittery look he sent, straight into her eyes.

Daylight faded rapidly those November evenings.

The boys returned from their work growling and hungry. They slurped their food in silence.

'Where's Tad?' Griffith was the first to notice Tad's absence.

Jane's cheeks burned as she fed scraps of food to William on her lap.

'Jane?'

'He's out with Mr Morgan.'

He gave her a long hard stare, then wiped his plate clean with bread. 'I'm off out.' At the click of his fingers the dogs ran to his heel.

Next morning the kitchen was empty and cold. Tad was not in his usual place at the table, sleeping with his head on his folded arms. Aunt Anni always said she could feel things in her bones: Jane's legs were heavy as lead.

No time to think with the baby to feed. She took William with her to the milking shed and sat him in the straw out of reach of the cow's kick. Pressing her head into the cow's side was usually calming with her silk soft udders and the squirt of the milk into the bucket, but all Jane felt was her bones.

Mr Morgan looming over the barn door made her jump and the three-legged stool tip beneath her. William started to cry.

'How's your tad?'

Against the light it was impossible to read his face.

'He's not back.' Jane picked up William and held him to her chest.

'Not back? Where is he, then?'

'I thought you'd know.'

Lifting the half-filled bucket, she pushed past him. The cow turned her head and lowed quietly.

'I know. I've not finished.' Jane led Mr Morgan across the yard. 'I've not told the boys about... you know...'

'About what?'

'The skirts.'

'Why not?'

It was hateful to be made to feel a fool when you thought you were doing the right thing.

Griffith was sipping tea in the kitchen.

'We were at the toll last night,' Mr Morgan explained. 'Doing a bit of damage, a group of us, telling them what we thought of their thieving toll... greedy bastards. We were the Rebeccas, your tad and I, dressed in our wives' clothes. I thought it would do your tad good – a bit of action, knowing his thinking on tolls.'

Jane's heaviness grew weightier. She knew the text. The preacher had delivered his sermon on Rebecca just a few weeks back: Genesis 24 verse 60.

> *And they blessed Rebekah, and said unto her, 'Let thy seed possess the gate of those which hate them.'*

A puzzler it was, as so many of the texts, for Jane took it as a story of sacrifice, nothing to do with vengeance at all. But that's how it was understood in these parts: the men dressing as Rebeccas to take revenge on the men who taxed them. There was a quiet nodding and an exchange of glances as the men left that chapel that day.

Aunt Anni, tapping her pipe out on the sole of her boot, told her it was all the rich wanting more and the poor getting angry.

'You can't keep the lid on a pot that's boiling,' she added, which was true, but didn't explain the men dressing in women's clothes.

'We'll go and search.' Griffith's voice was calm and quiet. He whistled the dogs. 'Richard, David, come with me. Jane, stay here with William. Don't leave this house.' His look was so sharp it pinned her to the chair.

Mr Morgan lingered after the boys left. His eyes flickered over Jane as she spooned gruel into William's mouth.

'You'd have been proud of your tad, Jane. Lashing out like a madman he was. Broke a few skulls. A hero, Jane. A hero.'

He pulled his stool up close till his breath was hot on her cheeks. He sat with his legs apart, his britches creased into the tops of his legs and his belly spilling over them.

Jane jumped up, swivelling William onto her hip.

'William needs air. And I've the pigs to feed and the eggs to collect.'

Her duties completed, Jane took the route across the top field and down to the river where they used to play. The field was not their own and it was not the usual way she walked. Something was leading her.

Tad was swinging gently from the branch of the oak overhanging the river.

The heaviness inside changed instantly to a floating, distant feeling, terrible because it was like feeling nothing at all. He was still dressed in Mam's skirt, all torn and heavy with mud. His head was tilted at the same angle as it had been when she saw him last – in the kitchen, stroking his cheek with Mam's shawl. She would not look at his face. As the boys arrived with the dogs and gathered round the tree, she walked back up the field, following her own muddy footprints, William wailing in her arms. Every step was heavier. Everything would be – from now and forever – changed.

Jane threw a plucked daisy away from her and breathed heavily. The animals were enjoying the Sabbath with an orgy of feeding. The dogs were sleeping the day away with barely a twitch to show they were still alive. Everyone, with no exceptions, Isaac had insisted, must attend his service. Over the far side, the boys were gathering. Jane stood to join them.

Isaac's body was the pulpit, his arms the lectern to hold *y Beibl*. In a field, his voice carried away on a restless breeze, it was hard to concentrate. Uriah led the singing. He closed his eyes and clutched his hat to his chest. Weasel Dai sat with Bryn, who turned his hat round and round in his hands, obviously itching to get it back on his head. Pedr slouched with his head between his knees; the younger boys were there; but where was Rhys? To be quite fair and certain, Jane looked right round the field. He was keeping out of her way – she knew why – and no surprise that he was not keen to be reminded of God and sin. But Isaac had given no choice. Everyone must attend.

Had Isaac not noticed?

She shifted her weight to catch Dai's attention. She coughed. He looked over, grinning. Behind her hand she mouthed 'Rhys?' making her eyes into a question. He looked around and shrugged.

Dogs were always the first to pick up danger. One of the corgis jumped up, barking, and in a second they were all up and off, charging over the field and scattering the sheep. Something was happening over the rise, where the field dipped down to the stream. The boys scrambled up and ran after the dogs. Jane followed, leaving Isaac holding the Bible in his hands.

'Give it up, you bastard!' a man screamed from the far bank. He had Rhys by the throat. A second man stood behind, holding the ponies' reins in one hand, the other arm hanging useless at his side.

'Leave him. Leave him.'

'You are dead meat!' the first man spat, hurling Rhys down. And the pair of them were up and away, galloping over the horizon.

There was no way they were to be caught. The drove ponies were up in the field, not even saddled. Even the dogs, which had followed into the far field, now hung back as though they too had concluded it would be a waste of breath.

Isaac came running. Without his hat, there was a wild look to him.

'What is it? Rhys? What's going on?' He jumped the stream to help him to his feet. Rhys wiped blood from his nose and spat into the grass.

'Nothing, it's nothing,' he mumbled, giving Isaac the longest, hardest stare, ignoring the hand he was offering and stumbling to his feet. To Rhys, the river stones must have been a bitter discovery too. These occurrences had to be part of the same story.

Try as she did to keep the words inside, they burst out.

'I told you, Isaac. They've been following us since Wales.'

Rhys was on his knees, dipping his head in the stream. 'They were after sheep, Isaac,' he said. 'They got nothing.'

Weasel Dai patted him on his shoulder. 'That's good going, Rhys, man. You gave them a hammering.'

Uncertainty was not often in Isaac's face. Jane tried to keep expression out of her own, though perhaps her eyebrows lifted a fraction.

'Jane, would you look at Rhys' face now? You could stop the bleeding.'

'Leave me. It's nothing – just leave me.' Rhys' voice was thick through the blood. He lurched off, hawking and spitting.

Jane's eyebrows rose higher.

'Alright, Jane. Now, everyone, let's get back to keeping the Sabbath holy.'

Jane hurried to fall into step with Isaac, who was marching fast away.

'May I say something, Isaac?'

'Is it an apology you want, Jane?'

'Not at all. I was only going to say that I noticed Rhys was not at the service. I suppose, in the circumstances, it was a good thing he was not, if he saved the sheep from the rustlers.'

Isaac said nothing, but quickened his step.

'And it's strange, is it not,' Jane was running now, 'that the sheep were all in the top field near us?'

A person must know when it is best to leave someone alone. Isaac was not in a receptive mood at all. She had placed a few thoughts inside his head; she must be content with that. He would think about what she had said now.

He paced over to the Bible, which he had laid on a box, protected by his hat, picked it up and muttered to Uriah.

'I will never knowingly bring a woman on a drove again.'

She was meant to hear him, otherwise he would have

turned away and mumbled quietly. A man who is cornered is always like that.

That evening, after the fire was lit, Uriah led them singing hymns which they all knew. She sat with Dai while Rhys scowled at the ground and did not join in once. Isaac stood behind the singers, scratching his cheek. He waited until the end of the final chorus, then beckoned Jane away.

'What?' Making things easy was not her way.

'I want to apologise to you, Jane. In my own defence, I was busy and preoccupied with the drove. You spotted the men following us. I was so full of the sin of pride, as you pointed out to me, that I took no notice. For this, I apologise.'

It's easier to stand your ground with your legs apart like a man. 'Your apology is only for this?'

'Everything else is dealt with, I believe, Jane.'

'*You* may believe it, Isaac, but I do not.'

CHAPTER 12

The Right Price

'STOW ON THE Wold where the wind blows cold,' Weasel Dai panted as they laboured up the long hill through thick woods. This was the place to sell the pigs and the sheep if the price was right. Not so easy to see if they were still being followed, though Jane was not concerned about that. If it was Rhys they were after, she'd have helped them, any way she could. He was walking by himself, head down, pinching his nose between his fingers, spitting, sending trails of phlegm into the grass.

No surprise that Rhys was to be left with Bryn-the-hat and the younger boys outside the town with the cows. No surprise that Rhys wanted to be in town with them. Bryn-the-hat would be no protection! There was a knowingness to Isaac's arrangements.

'Send for ale when you feel thirsty, boys.' Isaac's tone was kindly when he spoke to Bryn-the-hat.

Rhys had changed completely. Before the Sabbath, nice as pie he'd been; now he stomped away with his face ugly, to slump down under a lone elm in the middle of the field, leaning back and folding his arms across his chest.

Isaac shook his head.

'Jane, will you come with me? You are the pig expert.'

Sweet as sweet now, with the compliments and the smiles. It must be awfully hard to say 'I was wrong'.

The pigs inspected and nothing untoward detected, Jane picked up her hazel stick and swished it at the grass. The ditch in front of her was almost dry. Insects hovered above cracked earth. At the very bottom the mud was still dark. Now that would be something she could do, collect handfuls and slap it over the pigs. They'd be burned otherwise, with this sun beating down. There's nothing like spreading mud thick on a pig's back like she used to do back at Tŷ Mawr on the hottest days. Like when Morwenna's piglets were overdue. The size of her! When she spread her hands over her swollen sides, Jane felt the little ones pulsing.

Pigs never give birth in the broad daylight but always at night. Even after the hot day, there was a half moon and a film of frost in the puddles. Twice Jane had checked and twice nothing, but that third time when she hooked her lamp to the beam, the light caught a tiny clean piglet struggling free of its milky white sac. She picked it up and hooked her finger in its mouth, kissed it and placed it on Morwenna's teat. Such heat in Morwenna, always. Ten born in that litter, all in a whoosh, sucking and struggling. One she found clamped on Morwenna's back. And the last so weak and worrisome, she coaxed the end teat into its slack mouth and there was no response. A bigger bullying brother kicked out sideways right on the runt's head.

'Brute.' Jane pulled the bully from the teat and it screamed as though being murdered. 'You must watch out for your brothers. Show some guts,' she told the littlest one, fixing it onto the vacant teat. 'They'll trample all over you, else.'

She piled straw over the blood and mess. How clean the piglets were, how soft, how perfect: tiny trotters, petal ears, angel hair. The veins in their ears were like lace.

Who would slap mud on their backs and ears in this hot sun? Who would help deliver their babies at Tŷ Mawr now?

Dai sauntered over.

'Are you ready to part with the pigs, Jane?'

'I am. It's easier when you do not give them names and grow fond of them.'

'That's it, Jane. Fondness is a bind. You're better off without it.'

That was not entirely her meaning.

The pigs were flopped on their sides in the shade of the hedge near them. Dai twitched at them incessantly with his stick, making them flick their ears or tail. Why would he not leave them be?

'I was wondering, Dai, why does Rhys hate Isaac so? Have you not noticed it?'

'Rhys was bad in town last drove.' Dai clasped the stick across his knees and glanced up at her, but when she said nothing, continued. 'Drank a bit, chased out of town by locals, a girl – bit of stealing, most like. Bit of shooting. Isaac took his gun. Said Rhys would never be on his drove again. Rhys pleaded and begged. Isaac always gives another chance. Made Rhys promise – on the Bible, mind – he would never carry a gun on a drove. That was his condition.'

His eyebrows were raised watching for her reaction.

'Do you think that's it? I think it's something else entirely.'

Dai shrugged. Men had no curiosity, content with whatever was under their noses. No sense of the whys which made life interesting.

Isaac was ready. He waved his arm. Jane and Dai jumped up. This time Dai could use his stick as he wanted, whacking the pigs awake and onto their feet. The sheep were to enter from the south with Uriah. Jane, Isaac and Burr were to take the pigs in from the opposite side.

A fine town was Stow, with its wide streets of honey-stone houses. The market place opened up round an old stone cross. Hurdle fences divided most of the space right down to the bottom near the church. Every second building the length of the main street was an inn. Each had an arch wide enough to take a coach through to the stables at the back.

Pigs know when something bad is about to happen. The moment they were turned into the inn they were suspicious, trying to dodge back. Soft words were never going to move them, only a hard whack from Jane's stick. Once in the pens at the back, they quietened: no more point in struggling. Betraying a living creature turns a person hollow inside.

A deal had to be struck. Much stroking of chins was necessary, walking away, striding back again, not saying what you meant in an angry voice. Jane did not want to part from the pigs and yet it was bad seeing Isaac and the buyer standing back to back, as they were now, and the poor pigs sagging with the heat. Then, suddenly, a deal was done and the two men were like brothers, slapping money down and embracing each other.

Jane turned on her heel and marched firmly back out into the street.

'Are you up to a job now, Jane?' Isaac had the spirits of a man with a wad of money in his pocket. 'While Uriah drives the sheep up the chure, can you count them?'

'If I knew what a chure was, I could.'

'A passageway, Jane, built narrow to fit only one sheep at a time. I'll leave Burr with you now to hold the sheep. I'll be with Uriah feeding them through. Don't let our sheep mingle with other flocks, Jane.'

Trusted to be left alone and in charge – that was something to feel lighter about. A farmer was driving a huddle of sheep into one pen. Was it cream they fed to their sheep, these English farmers? It was not going to be easy, stopping their Llanwenogs from getting mixed in, though they'd be easy to pick out. Sheep were everywhere and the air full of their bleating and edginess.

Burr trembled with expectation. He sat close to Jane's heel, his tongue hanging out, panting; licking his lips when a sheep passed him. The day was as hot as any she could remember, with a light so dazzling on the windows of the houses it made her eyes ache. Imagine Rhys, under that elm. Like the one in the churchyard there, casting the gravestones into thick shade. Such a waste too, shade for the dead.

Was it not possible to have a thought about anything without the dead creeping in? David. Like he was all his life: sneaky, cunning, appearing when you least expected him.

Three English youths, leaning on the wall of the inn nearby, were staring in Jane's direction. Hereford had taught her what they would see: a shortish stout man in a hat and a long coat even in this boiling weather. A stranger, and a dirty one, loitering with no clear reason.

A distant rumbling pushed thought away in an instant as the first two sheep came charging up the chure. She hauled them forwards, digging her hands into their fleeces, hurrying them into the pens where Burr could keep them together. The third sheep arrived, with a wild look in its eye. A troublemaker. No time to stop. Another was on its heels and another behind that.

Wouldn't you know it – that wretch made a dash for it. For a fraction of a second, while Burr darted to the left, the sheep saw the opening to the right and shot away. Where one sheep goes, others follow.

'Burr! Come bye! Come bye!' He was off, as were the rest of the sheep, with more tumbling from the chure all the time. Which way to turn? The hurdle crashed to the ground and men appeared, shouting, behind her. By spreading her legs wide, she blocked the exit from the chure. Pandemonium.

Sheep everywhere. Farmers and buyers shouting, flailing arms and legs, kicking out the Welsh runts and swearing. Burr did his best, racing up the centre of the market to bring back the original mischief-maker.

Jane worked till the sweat blurred her sight and stung her eyes. This was terrible. The dam was about to break.

Never had she been so glad to see Isaac, with Uriah running up behind him.

'I'm sorry...'

'Don't stop counting, Jane. Let them out.'

Jane sprang back; the sheep poured out.

'...thirty-one, thirty-two, thirty-three...'

Uriah picked the sheep clear of the ground by the fleece and threw them to Isaac who had the hurdle back up and the pen secure. Only with the last stragglers in sight, the lame ones, was Jane able to stand and straighten her back and watch Burr bringing in the last of the escapees.

'That's seventy-five, I make it.'

'And that's a miracle, for it's seventy-five we sent up from the bottom.' Isaac was beaming, not angry with her at all.

She leaned back against the end wall of the chure in the thin shade of a house, wiping her brow on her sleeve.

'Here.' Uriah passed his flask. No matter what it was, it was wet, wasn't it? And she was dying of thirst. Water. Uriah stood next to her, his face curled up with remorse. This was her chance to make it comfortable between them. Whatever Uriah believed, he was not the murderer.

'Fine animals,' she said. The local sheep stood quiet in the next pen: wider, woollier. You had to say they were a superior-looking breed. 'And not one of them with the strength to run all the way from Wales!'

Uriah nodded and moved away to help Isaac, who was hefting a sheep up for a buyer to inspect its feet.

After all that hauling, Jane's back and legs ached terribly. There was only one place to sit and that was the step on the bottom of the market cross. The moment she took her weight off her feet, she knew what the problem was: that dull ache deep in her back like a bruise spreading from the inside.

How was she to manage this? So unfair, the things a girl has to think about. Men never had to consider the insides of themselves at all. Now she would have to be aware, day and night, slipping away with her rags to wash and dry them somehow. At least she had had the foresight to bring rags, wound now round her waist and wringing wet with sweat.

Once more she had the prickling feeling of eyes upon her. The three English lads were lurching towards her. If they'd seen a girl, they'd be sitting themselves next to her, nudging her, getting a blush out of her, touching if they could; hungry eyes would strip the clothes off her. But these eyes were hard and hostile. From the sway of their bodies, the low drooping way of their eyelids, they'd drink inside them.

Best move away; give them no grief.

She tried to stand but they loomed over her. It was impossible not to touch one of them, just a scrape, trying to dodge away.

'Hey! You! Who are you to push me?'

Say nothing.

'Eh? You Welsh bastard!'

She must keep walking with her head down, but two men jumped in front of her with arms folded across their chests.

'Don't you understand English? You ignorant Welsh pig!'

If she made her voice low it might be the better. Anything not to anger them further. 'I do. My mother was English.'

The drink meant it took time for the message to reach their brains.

'English mother, eh?' one sneered.

The other had eyes so close together there was barely space for a nose.

'Well, understand this. you half-Welsh bastard, you pushed my friend out of the way!'

'I'm sorry.'

'Sorrrry, so sorrry!' All three mocked her. One staggered towards her, pushing her hard on her shoulder. 'Eh? Eh?' He was asking nothing, but each time shoving her backwards. The second lad was dancing behind, shadowing, hands up like a fighter. The third copied him, mouth open and lips curled in a snarl. With a last mighty shove, Jane fell back over the step. He threw himself on top of her, knocking the air out of her, pulling back his fist.

'Leave her!' Isaac's voice was more powerful that any cudgel. He had the lad's fist in one hand, pulling him off by the collar with the other, holding him up like a puppy.

'*Her... her...?*' he stuttered.

'Cowards and heathen English with no respect.' Isaac spoke low and quiet and dropped him to the ground. The other two stood dumb, staring. They could make no sense of this through the drink.

'Come, Jane.'

Isaac's strides were long and fast. Jane followed, sniffing back the mucus pouring from her nose, wiping hot tears on her hand.

'I'm sorry, Isaac.'

He whipped round. 'Don't keep saying that, Jane. Just don't give yourself a reason for using the word.'

'It wasn't my fault, Isaac.' Indignation stopped her crying. 'I did nothing. They came at me, spoiling for a brawl. Just like all stupid men, thinking fighting such sport.'

Isaac nodded and put his arm round her shoulders.

'Not all men, Jane.'

CHAPTER 13

In the Darkest Hour

THERE'S NOTHING LIKE concern with yourself to take your mind off the absence of pigs. In the deep of the night in a field outside Stow, Jane woke; heavy, with a warm weight between her legs which could not be ignored. She sat up, wriggled out of her britches. They'd only be a nuisance. In front of her she could just make out the dark mounds of cattle and hear their breath and their jaws chewing.

She slipped quietly to the gate. The road was pale in the dark. The pieces of cloth were ready in her pocket.

Thank you, God, for putting rags into my thoughts when I escaped from Tŷ Mawr, when I might have forgotten them. And thank you for protecting me from those English beasts.

Across the road she had seen a stream. Noted it on the way into the field. Handy. Now all she had to do was place her feet either side. The low trickle assured her the water was there, though she could hardly see it at all. Her coat was a nuisance to be hitched up and held under her arms while she untied the heavy rag. Holding tight to one end, she let the other flop into the water dipping it in and out, still with her legs planted either side of the stream.

From nowhere, a hand clamped over her mouth, strangling the screech in her throat. She fell backwards, dropping the rag. Shocked, she twisted her head. Hands clamped under her arms, across her chest. She was being pulled. Her feet were dragging, heels catching. She was splitting in two. Twigs snagged on her clothes. She struggled, arching, flipping her body this way and that. A grip on her arm pinched through to the bone. Hot, thick panting filled her ears. The hand over her mouth was squashing her nose. She couldn't breathe. She shook her head from side to side till the hold slipped. She gulped air. She was flung to the ground. She kicked with all her strength but her arms were pulled apart. A sharp smack of a belt on her legs sent her rigid.

'Bitch! Bitch! Welsh bitch!' The words more vicious for being whispered.

Before she could scream, a different hand slapped over her mouth – a rough, stinking hand.

'Me first!'

'Sshhh!'

'Get on with it. I'm bursting!'

'Ram it in her mouth. That'd shut her up!'

The weight crushed the breath out of her. Her breast was grasped, squeezed, mauled. Her nipple pinched and twisted. Crushed, smothered, with the thick roll of a man's part pressed into her stomach. She knew what was to come. Think nothing. Think nothing. Be somewhere else.

Her skirt was riding up her legs. Sharp nails clawed at her thighs, forcing her legs apart. She couldn't breathe, she couldn't scream, but sounds there were that would not be kept down: stifled, choked eruptions. Suffocated shrieks.

They tensed suddenly. 'Damn it!'

The dogs! Oh, bless the dogs!

A sharp boot pushed her down the bank into the mud. Footsteps crashed away through the bushes.

All the dogs were creating now.

'Jane!' Isaac was calling. She groaned.

'Jane!' Rhys' voice, nearer. 'Where are you?'

'Here.'

They came crashing through the undergrowth, surrounding her, lifting her, helping her back to the road. Bryn-the-hat held a lamp.

'The bastards! Which way did they go?' Dai said.

She had no idea where they came from nor where they went. Nor did it matter in the least that she knew exactly who they were.

'Did they...?' Dai's voice was trembling.

'I'm alright. They did nothing.'

'Bastards!' Rhys spat. 'I'll kill them.'

'My Lord, Jane! Bring the lamp, Bryn,' Isaac said. 'You're bleeding.'

That was it. She remembered.

'I am, Isaac, and that's what I was attending to. Would you give me the lamp, Bryn? And Dai, would you stand by the gate so I know you are near? It would make me the easier to know you were all watching out for me.'

The dogs were asleep in an instant. The boys took a little longer. Eventually Isaac slept, though Jane knew he was waiting till he thought her asleep. She closed her eyes and breathed deeply. Safe under her blanket, her mind still whirled. The past was brought to life again, when she had thought it buried deep inside. That was the worst of it. If only she could fix on how good the boys had been, like brothers, and how they had saved her before the men had done the worst – she should be thinking of that. Not Tad.

Tad did things because he loved her and she must do what Tad said. It might have happened when she was little. She did not know. He would have been so heavy, and she so small, she would have been flat when he rose away from her.

That last time, after Mam died, when Tad came at her in the pigsty, up against the rough wall with the pigs sniffling round them, madness was in his eyes and his ears were blocked with his own pain.

'*Cyfrinach*,' he muttered. It was their secret.

It wasn't right. Nobody *said* it wasn't, but some things you know. When Tad burst out of the sty, she had followed, and there was Griffith standing in the yard by the well. In the top field, she had hitched her skirt up and squatted over the spring. She had thought Griffith gone, but then he spoke.

'If he hurt you, Jane...' She had spun round and Griffith's face was an agony. He cared, or he'd never have looked at her so. And that look had been there in his eyes that day on the cliff edge when he came for her. He cared. And she had shown no care for him.

CHAPTER 14

Truth Will Out

WAITING FOR SKINNY cows to fatten, time hangs heavy. They must stay in the grazing fields at Padbury until the cattle were plump for market. As the cows' ribs rounded, Jane's became more visible. Provisions were running low. When a person has little to do but watch others eat, they are full with thoughts of food: warm bread and scrap, fat *brithyll* from the stream, meat and potatoes and that fullness and weight in the stomach. Who would be there to feed them at Tŷ Mawr? Back home at the end of a day to a cold house and nothing to eat. Richard? Impossible. William, maybe. When little, he'd been at her feet while she kneaded the bread or cooked the *sucan*. The potatoes he'd rolled across the floor, crawling after them before she took them to cook, leaving him wailing. 'Oh,' she moaned aloud. Isaac looked up, sharp.

'What is it Jane?'

'Just a cramp. Nothing.'

Oh, William. I owe you everything and I did not think how it would be for you. And I miss you.

Why was it they were all so real to her now? Such an age she'd been running from them, and they were left miles and miles away, but here they were, still with her, her thoughts and feelings in a tangle. All this sitting around, that was the trouble.

'Hurry up and get fat, can't you?' She threw a stick at a grazing cow, which did no more than shake its ears.

Isaac laughed. 'Impatient to be away from us, are you?'

Isaac had no skill at all in knowing her thoughts.

Oh, William.

Sitting on her bed. Door bolted by Griffith. Moon outside, not caring at all. *Fel 'na mae* – nothing to be done. She must be wed to Mr Morgan within the week. A soft scratching outside. A barn owl's hiss. More like a kettle. She was at the window and there was William looking up from a pool of spread hay. Clogs and bundle went first, then she squeezed through the window feet first.

Letting go was easy. Falling was hard. No time for pain. Not a wisp of hay could they leave. They threw it over the barn door. A dog barked. A pig banged against the gate to the pen.

Over the fields they ran, all quiet emptiness. The meadows silver-blue sheets, the hedges thick, the trees tall. Down the empty village street they raced, past the inn and the silent cottages and St Cynwyl's, with its puffed-up cockerel weathervane silhouetted against the moon.

'Hide in the mine,' William whispered. 'I'll bring food. The drove's passing in a day or two. Go with them!'

'Don't tell Isaac, William. Smuggle me in, can you?'

'I can.' He was a man even though he was a child, his voice high and strong.

He left her at the empty Dolaucothi gold mines where the *coblynnau* lived and ghosts moaned and wailed in the deep dark. The gold was long gone.

She woke in the morning to the dark and the drip of water. The air was old and cold to breathe. So tired she was, with the push-pull of the night. Hunger gnawed at her. Was this a folly? Was this the chance to say: enough, go home, be safe and dry and fed?

'*Heiptro Ho! Heiptro Ho!*'

Her heart leapt at the sound of the teller's cry. The drove was coming. This night had been her test with its temptations. Hold fast, Jane, think of the cruelty and all the bad things they did to you and they would do forever.

Late that evening, Jane and Isaac sat either side of the fire. He was reading *y Beibl*. Preparing for the following day, no doubt. Three Sabbaths had come and gone while they were journeying. The letters were large to read in this light, but the book was a mighty size to bring all this way.

'Could you not have a smaller Bible, Isaac?'

'I could. But this one is precious to me, Jane!'

Jane watched the wood burn. Every now and again the fire would shift, setting sparks flying.

'Come here.' Isaac closed his Bible and patted the ground next to him. He was lying, stretched out and looking very tall, the ends of his great boots in the shadow the other side of the fire.

'Have you thought about what happens now, Jane?'

Jane jabbed at a burning log. 'God will make his plan clear!' Quick as silverfish the words came.

'I am thinking that you will not be persuaded to return home with me.'

'Never! For what would be the point of all this?' She spread her arms wide.

'As I thought. This could be the Lord putting ideas in my head, Jane, or just me speaking. You must judge.'

He was looking straight at her, but she could not look at him. There was a place in the heart of the fire that had need of poking.

'As you know, I have further business in London. I have packages from Mr Johns to be delivered to his cousin, Lady Alicia Blackwood. I am trusted. This is something I have done many times. Her husband, the Reverend, runs a mission. Johns sends money in remembrance of his son. Do you know of his son, Jane?'

She did, for hadn't she seen that plaque on the wall in the church with the boy's name in gold, underneath the names of Mr Johns' brothers killed at Waterloo. Such marvellous sharp-looking crossed swords were at the top of the stone, which was rolled up at the bottom to look like paper. All Hallows' Eve it was, when Gwendolyn from the inn had pushed Jane into St Cynwyl's Church, telling her she would see the man she was to marry. That was the superstition. The only man she saw was Jesus, hanging on the cross with blood dripping from his beautiful feet and hands, his face so sad it had made her cry and run for the door. It was locked. All night she had to stay, sleeping on a narrow wooden pew until she was discovered by the Reverend Howell in the morning. Arriving back at Tŷ Mawr, all she got was a beating.

Isaac was scratching his cheek. Hair on the face must be an irritation.

'As I said, Jane, I am trusted by Lady Alicia. I do believe that she might find employment for you. I know she has many charitable endeavours. You are a good and useful girl, Jane, honest and strong willed...' he glanced up at her. 'I will be anxious for you, Jane. The world is vast, but you will find your place in it, of that I am sure.'

Jane jumped to her feet. 'I know, Isaac. God will protect me, so no need for you to be worrying about me any more. I'm ready for sleep now. Good night.'

Whenever she said she was ready for sleep, she never was. A lady? Well, Jane must be like Sarah at the Johns' house.

Someone might teach her to coil her hair round her ears, though there was nothing she knew about being in a lady's house. No animals to look after, she supposed. But there were other things she could do to be useful. Exactly what, you cannot say in advance. When the dog bit Rhys, she knew what to do; she knew the herbs for Pedr's sickness and Dai's ankle; and when the pig was lame she was the one who saw it. You find things about yourself as you go along. She would be fine, she would. And she would not think about leaving Isaac behind, she would not. It would be a good thing not to have anyone who knew her, who could be scornful of her and treat her as a child...

Jane was asleep by the fire, her head on David's coat, when she stirred to the sound of fighting. Men! She would have rolled over and back into sleep, but for the sudden awareness that Isaac was no longer the other side of the fire. She sat up. The dogs were barking. The fire almost dead. Dark figures moved like shadows in the gloom.

'Jane!' She sprang to her feet. 'Jane!' Uriah's voice was shrill, distraught, coming from a dark place the other side of the ponies. They shuffled nervously as she pushed through them. She would have tripped over Uriah had he not spoken.

'Jane.' He was on the ground, his feet and hands tied.

'Are you hurt? What's happening?' She crouched down beside him. Without a knife, she could only pull at the knots and struggle to get him free.

'They have him, Jane. He was tricked into thinking there were rustlers picking off the cows, but it was Isaac they were waiting for.'

A thicket bordered the field. Sounds of a brawl were coming from it.

'Go back. Get a light from the fire, girl. Hurry!'

Winding dry grasses round a stick and lighting it takes an age when your heart is galloping. The light was almost spent before she reached the trees again, but there was still enough to make out Uriah bending over a second figure.

'Dai?'

His response was a gurgle and a spit.

Rhys' shrill voice rang out from the dense thicket. 'You bastard! Bastard! Give it up, will you?' Sounds of a struggle came from the trees. A smack had Jane tense. A sharp snap of something breaking followed. A piteous groan was drowned by a crash like a tree falling.

Uriah dived into the undergrowth, pulling his pistol from his belt. So badly Jane wanted to hang back, but the cries spurred her forwards.

A deafening shot sent a pheasant squawking into the air. Jane ducked, slamming her free hand over her ear. She saw nothing, and – after the shot – could now only hear as though through water.

Ahead in the clearing, lighter than the trees surrounding it, Isaac was being helped to his feet by Uriah. His hat was missing, his coat hanging strangely from his shoulders.

Three riders on horseback thundered away over the field, their shapes clear as the clouds moved away from a full moon – white flecks on the horses' necks, flashes of stirrups – until they disappeared over the rise. Three, not two. The dogs gave chase, squealing and yelping with fury.

'Whistle them, Uriah.' Isaac spoke in a winded way, leaning heavily on Uriah's shoulder as Uriah tucked his gun back into his belt. Two of the younger boys ran up to them, startled from their watch by the shot.

'Where were you?' Jane rounded on them. 'Were you not watching?'

Were they in on it too? The befuddled way they looked at her drove the thought from her mind.

'Feed the fire, Jane,' Uriah was breathless with anger, 'so we can see... what the bastards have done... Up boys... the animals... corral them... calm them down.'

Dai was struggling to his feet.

'Are you hurt, Dai?' Jane called. Lighting another grass torch she held it over her head to throw light on him. This fire needed fresh wood and coaxing. She should be on her hands and knees breathing into it.

'After them, Dai!' Uriah said. 'Go with the boys.'

Uriah was dancing between running forwards and keeping back with Isaac.

Dai took two stumbling steps and fell again.

'Dai!' Jane cried, running to him, sparks flying from her wispy light.

'I'm alright!'

'Leave him. Leave them all. They got nothing.' Isaac's voice behind her was stronger.

'He took a ride!' Uriah's voice was shaking. 'One of the ponies!'

'But nothing more.' Isaac's coughing had Jane running back to the fire. He was bent over, with one arm held over his chest.

The fire illuminated the dark wet of Isaac's shirt.

'Isaac! That's blood,' Jane said.

Uriah struggled to pull up Isaac's shirt.

'Don't fuss, man!' Isaac pushed him gently away.

'Did they cut you? Is that what they did?' Uriah's voice was breaking.

'No.'

'It's his nose,' Jane said. She turned to pour water from the leather bucket into a cup. 'Look,' she said, handing the water to Isaac, 'all bent to the side. Noses bleed worse than any part of you. I'll wash it and do my best, Isaac.'

'I'll be fine, Jane. No more damage than bare fists can do.' Isaac gulped at the water, swilling it round and round and spitting onto the ground.

Burr arrived ahead of the other dogs and sat trembling at Isaac's side, whimpering.

'Don't fret, Burr. They got nothing.'

Jane made a poultice, mashing her remaining comfrey leaves with water and the sparring of oats from the pan. She was a nurse to them all.

'Hold this to your nose, Isaac. It'll staunch the blood.'

Isaac flinched. 'Don't fuss, Jane.'

'Don't be a baby now.' She tilted his head back and stood over him.

'They got nothing, Jane,' he said, clasping his shirt.

'Rhys, was it, who did this to you, and made off with a pony with his friends?' She did not intend to speak but the words could not be stopped. 'All planned. I knew it!'

'It was Rhys.' The way Isaac hung his poor head, you could feel sad for the pain this must cause – never mind his nose. 'If he'd had a gun, Jane, I'd be done for now, don't you think?'

'I wouldn't speak for a while, Isaac,' Jane said.

CHAPTER 15

At Barnet Market

EXCITEMENT WAS GROWING. The pace lifted and the boys whistled and laughed. Barnet Market was in sight, at the bottom of a natural bowl ringed with elms, chestnuts, oaks and sycamores. Sand-coloured roads criss-crossed the sloping green fields, leading down to scattered houses, wooden shelters and the animal pens. Other droves there were, streaming down the slopes. For all of them, Barnet Market was the end.

But for Jane? David's boots grew heavier, his coat weightier on her shoulders. Soon she would be alone and that was a dismal thought. All her own doing, that was the worst of it. A melancholy place this market was for sure, with hundreds of cattle all unhappy with no fodder, waiting; milling around in a frenzy, with someone whacking them behind and pulling them forward with ropes.

Isaac, whose nose was still swollen as a beetroot, and Uriah were to stay with Pedr and two boys and the dogs to sell the cattle. He waved Dai and Bryn-the-hat away.

'You've done your job, boys, and I thank you for it. Look after Jane.'

A strange draining sensation came over her watching Isaac and Uriah steer their cattle into one of the far pens, as though a part of her was with them still – a ghostly, shadowy Jane. She'd not have been able to move had Dai not tugged at her sleeve, pulling her off balance. Food was on his mind – food and beer.

'Smell that, Jane?'

His head was up, his eyes closed, sniffing like a dog on a scent. He knew exactly where he was heading, and Bryn-the hat would follow like a puppy would his master.

They ate bloaters served by a woman in a green and yellow dress behind her stall.

'Bloaters and bread for thruppence.' Dai's eyes were alight. 'Have you ever eaten a bloater, Jane?'

She had not, and did not know the name.

'It's an ocean fish.'

Good and salty it was, and the bread soft and doughy. As soon as they had licked their fingers, they were off up the hill to the woman who sold bite-size bread and bacon, washed down with beer for fourpence.

Dai pushed a mug of frothing beer into her hand. 'You can't make your mind up about a thing before you try it.'

'All right, I will.' She threw back the cup and gulped it down without stopping, coming up desperate for breath.

Beer wasn't so bad. A bit mouldy tasting, but it was wet – and it was true, she felt no different. Full of wind, but nothing else.

At the top of the hill was a small beer tent, which had drawn a crowd.

'Are you coming in, Jane? Have you a taste for it now?'

A certain lightness had come to her, a feeling of separation between her feet and her head.

'I'll wait here.'

'Don't you wander off, now,' Dai warned her. 'You're still in our charge.'

'I'll walk as far as the horses there.'

Dai nodded.

All manner of horses there were at Barnet Market, although today was not a day for the races. Lined up they were, with their chests resting on long ropes. Buyers walked up and down the line inspecting them. Most of the horses had their eyes half closed and their heads sagging. Some had a harness on them and some just a rope halter.

Jane stopped by a fine draught horse. It towered above her, feathered foot resting on the tip and weight tilted. Its bottom lip trembled. So like Jessie after a hard day at the plough. She stroked its nose. The softest place in the world, that little piece of skin on a horse's nose, between his nostrils.

'You buying?' An old man with a quiet voice and a creased, gentle face came up to her. He'd bandy legs and leaned on a stick. 'Breaks my heart to let her go. My son used to help me with the cart, see. He's gone.'

'Dead?' The word was out like a squeak before she remembered. She would be seen here as a man. She lowered to a deeper note. 'I'm so sorry.'

'I hope not. Might be.' The man shook his head gloomily. 'Gone to the war.'

'God will look after him,' Jane blurted out.

'I doubt it,' he said, balancing bread on his hand. Watching the soft lips nuzzling his old wrinkled palm made Jane's throat tight. She moved on. A grey horse with a tangled forelock at the end of the line caught her eye. Quite the prettiest she had ever seen: mottled, shaded dapples on him like stones through water.

'Want your fortune told, sir?'

A ginger-haired, freckle-faced boy was at her elbow, staring at her with startling green eyes. He wore a dirty cap on one side; knee-length corduroy trousers and big, black boots on his feet. He held out a deck of cards, flicking the pack between his palms as though playing a concertina.

'Pick one. Go on.' He spread out a fan of cards.

There was no sidestepping him.

'For nothing. Honest.'

Jane picked a card and held it to her chest.

'This ain't no trick! I'm telling your fortune. I gotta see the cards, haven't I? Well, ain't that something! You'll have to pick another, so I can tell if I'm right.'

He fanned the cards again. Jane slipped one out and passed it to him. He whistled through his teeth.

'Well, I'll be...'

'What?'

'You're going on an adventure, right enough. Good things and bad things will happen... but you'll come home with a beautiful girl. You'll have to pick another for me to tell you what's going to happen between you and this girl.'

He thrust the cards under her nose.

'No, thank you. What's going to happen is going to happen. I'd rather not know.' She tried to move away but he dodged round and barred her path.

'That's three pennies you owe me, sir.'

'You said it was free.'

'The first one. Not after that.' His green eyes were sharp.

'I've no money at all.'

His eyes narrowed, vicious as a cat's. 'I'll set the peelers on you!' He grabbed her arm.

'I haven't, honest.'

'Leave her!' Dai picked the boy up with one hand and punched him to the ground.

'He owes me...' the boy snivelled.

'Can't leave you on your own for a minute, can I, Jane?' Dai grinned at her in a stupid way. He had no need to be so brutish to the poor boy.

'You've hurt him.'

'He'll live. You are an innocent, Jane, among villains.' He slung his arm round her shoulders. 'You come with me. I'll look after you.'

'Where's Bryn?' She did not like this weight on her.

'He's coming. I told him we'd meet behind the tent there.' He was steering her fast towards it.

'Don't you think...?' She must keep talking but his arm grew tighter, almost round her throat.

'Wait!' She trod deliberately on the outside of her boot and stumbled. Dai had his hand up to save her, but on her breast. An accident, surely – then he squeezed.

'Dai! Get off me! Let go!' She tried to wriggle free, but the more she squirmed the tighter his grip became, until he was dragging her past the end of the tent where the guy-ropes were pegged.

'Oi!' Bryn came running down the hill. Anger swept over Dai's face, changing to a sneer as he released her with a final squeeze. 'Dai, man. There you are. I thought you said the other side.'

Dai gave a careless laugh. 'No, I said down here.'

Dai was her friend. How could he? Jane walked away so they would not see her tears.

> Na chredwch i gyfaill, nac ymddiriedwch i dywysog.
> Trust ye not in a friend, put ye not confidence in a guide.

Jeremiah's words, and so true.

Isaac strode across from the pens, Burr at his heels. His bags were over one shoulder and that Bible held on his hip. He didn't appear to notice her distress.

'Jane! Where are the boys?'

She thought they were behind her.

'Ah, there they are. Everything is sold, and we are free men,' he called to them, pulling coins from his pocket. 'Here you are boys. That's an advance now. You don't want to fritter it all away in one go. Now, Jane, you're to come with me if you can bear to peel yourself away. The others may have finished their journey, but we've got a way to go still.'

That was it then. The drove was over. Dai was already walking towards two young women standing outside one of the marquees.

'Goodbye then, Dai, Bryn,' she called after them.

Bryn took his hat off and waved it in the air. Dai stopped and turned. 'I'll look out for you back home, Jane. Good luck.' He gave a funny nod and was gone. And that was it.

Not a moment was Jane given to think before Isaac steered her away with his free arm up the hill.

'Boys are boys, Jane. Do not be disappointed in them. Remember, eyes in the front of the head, Jane. I have made arrangements. First, we must make ourselves presentable. Mrs Bowman at the Queen's Arms is an acquaintance of mine. You can get yourself cleaned up there, Jane. She'll see you right. In the morning we'll travel on to London.'

A sudden panicky shaking had overcome Jane, like a pig knowing that something bad was about to happen. She bit the inside of her cheek, nodding.

'I've done fine with the animals, Jane. Just these two packets to deliver. And you. You can be off now, Burr. You start back with the other dogs. I'll catch up with you later.'

Burr looked up, panting. Isaac clicked his fingers. Burr's ears pricked. 'Home!' Isaac pointed over Jane's shoulder to the horizon. Immediately, Burr was off, skirting round the cattle pens and up the far hill without a backward look.

They had reached the end of the line of horses. The ginger-haired youth sat on a crate near the grey horse, still wiping blood from his lip with his sleeve.

'Have you three pennies, Isaac?'

She had never asked for anything. He gave them to her without saying a word.

She walked over and gave them to the boy. 'I'm sorry about your lip. Is it bleeding still?'

He shook his head, scowling, and pocketed the money.

'What's this? A charity case?' Isaac asked.

'He told my fortune. I owed it to him.'

'You fell for that? Dear me! The fortune was good, I trust.'

'He said I'll have ups and downs and meet a lovely girl.'

CHAPTER 16

Stepping into a Woman's Clothes

'WHAT A SIGHT in those terrible britches!'
Mrs Bowman opened the kitchen door in the yard behind the Queen's Arms and frowned at Jane. A stout woman in a grey dress and white apron she was, with a round face and purplish cheeks. Flesh rolled over the neck of her gown.

'And here was me thinking this was money earned easy! Come on then, let's be having you. You're right, Isaac. I doubted the size in a girl of her age. Now I've seen her… Bless you! I'll find clothes for her.'

'I'm off to the baths,' Isaac said. 'Will you feed her and give her board for the night, Ma'am? I'll be back in the morning to take her to London.'

First Burr gone, and then Isaac without a turn of his head, and Jane delivered like a package into a stranger's hands.

Jane followed Mrs Bowman across the yard. What a building this was, vast and built of the reddest bricks with fancy work round the windows – you'd not have taken it for an inn. A special room there was for the bath, with taps that poured water straight into it. A marvel. But this was Barnet.

'Step out of your clothes, dearie. I'll take 'em and burn 'em,' she said, as Jane started undressing.

'Not the boots!' Jane cried.

'There's no life left in these,' Mrs Bowman said, tossing them out of the door.

Though Jane braced herself for pain when Mrs Bowman lifted the scrubbing brush, she was not as rough as Mam, preparing her for chapel. The soap was greasy and gritty. But it was the smell of the paraffin for the vermin that took Jane's will; the dizziness in her head made her unable to stop Mrs Bowman cutting her hair. A terrible thing that made her cry out loud to see her own hair lying separate and abandoned in the dirt at the bottom of the bath and now she'd no chance of coiling her hair round her ears like Sarah.

'And I took you for a sensible girl. You'll thank me for this. None of that fiddle-faddle of rolling your hair up. You'll not know yourself, you'll see.'

That was the danger. She'd not know herself.

'Right, you can clean this bath out for me and then,' Mrs Bowman held out a cotton chemise, 'put this on yourself. You can eat in the kitchen and sleep in the box room if you've no objection to a straw mattress.'

Jane nodded. 'There's one other thing I need. Have you some rags? Just a few. Without them, I don't feel I can make the next step.'

To her surprise, Mrs Bowman hugged her briefly.

'Bless you, Jane. Don't you fret on that score.'

For so many nights on the hard ground, Jane's eyes had dropped almost as soon as the sun set. With her belly full of roast meat and cabbage, lying between cotton sheets on a straw mattress in a small room, falling asleep was impossible. Leaving home had been easy; leaving the animals – a wrench; but the drove, the company, the clear destination, the purpose – that was difficult. Without Isaac... she'd be adrift and alone.

A girl from a Welsh farm. What did she know? Only animals, and a few remedies. Now she would be in a place where such knowledge was not needed at all.

God, please don't leave me. I know You won't, but if You did, I don't know what I'd do. By tomorrow night, God, You will be the only friend I have.

Mrs Bowman came to Jane's room the next morning at dawn. Clothes hung over her arm.

'Quick, Jane. Isaac is waiting by the fishcoster's cart.'

Clothes Mrs Bowman had bought from the ragman. Such undergarments, with legs and a gusset between them, and a floor-length grey dress.

'Plenty of wear in this,' Mrs Bowman declared, holding it up. You could see the light through it, the material was that thin, the collar missing and there were patches in the sleeves and mends all over.

'These shoes should do. Bit on the large side. You can stuff the toes with paper.'

Flimsy and thin they felt after the boots, light so you missed the weight of yourself on the ground.

Mrs Bowman had a mirror in her hall where Jane could fit the whole of herself apart from the shoes. The woman who stood before her Jane would hardly have recognised: full bosom, thick arms, but a waist that curved in before the roundness of her hips. The hair was much shorter, darkish, neat and tidy, nothing wind-lifted or tangled at all. The face was familiar, though not looking as it felt from the inside: ruddy, full lips. Tad's eyes, dark and suspicious. Nothing of her Mam – a sadness. A small woman Mam was, with bones like a bird.

'Here's an old shawl. Isaac won't recognise you.'

He was waiting by the cart on the road outside. He'd his

Beibl under his arm and a bag across his chest. A hot rush came into her cheeks as Isaac looked at her and smiled.

'Don't say anything!'

Flustered, she took his hand to help her up into the cart, her skirts light and billowing round her bare ankles.

At the first hill the mule slowed, then stopped, flattening his ears no matter how the fishcoster whipped him.

'We'll walk!' Jane said.

How quickly a girl forgets the comfort of britches. Her skirts caught round her legs so she could barely keep up with Isaac. All shaven, hair cut and slicked back from his face and his boots glossed, he was barely recognisable himself.

Back on the cart either side of the fishcoster, they fair bowled along the flatter roads. A cap was pulled low over the man's eyes and he never stopped talking, but not in a conversational way with space for someone else to join in. As he talked, he flicked his whip from side to side to tease the poor mule's haunches. So annoying that must be, hauling heavy bodies around with that constant tickle on your rear when you are doing your best.

Such a rush everywhere, such speed. Carts and carriages travelling in each direction, some even overtaking in a way that stopped the heart, other coaches bearing down on them so fast. The sides of the road seethed with people. So much food right under your nose, all the time! Every few paces they passed a barrow piled with fruits and vegetables or men crouched over fiery braziers – leaving such smells in the air, your mouth was forever watering.

Shops too with meat or bread in the windows; boots lined up for you to wonder at; shops with bales of bright cloth; flower sellers. All manner of signs too: striped poles, brass globes, gold letters, green, cream. Painted pictures swung outside every inn and tavern, and they were not in short supply. Things, so many things, and not a sign of a place where anything might grow or be made. Such overwhelming life there was, all unknown – Jane shrank into herself. As small as she had felt in Hereford, the feeling was multiplied beyond belief in London.

As the buildings grew bigger and grander, the shops disappeared and the shrinking feeling grew worse. Trees shaded the pavements. The crowds vanished; the carriages became glossier and the horses slicker, holding their heads up in a superior way.

The cart turned into a quiet street with immense houses, all painted the colour of thick cream.

'This is it.' The fishcoster touched his cap.

'I'm much obliged.'

Never had Jane heard that word in Isaac's mouth before.

He jumped down and held his hand out to help Jane, though it was no further to jump than from Banon's back. He led the way up the prettiest path ever, black and white diamond shapes leading to three steps up to the grandest, blackest front door imaginable, with a shiny brass knocker the shape of a little hand. Isaac wiped his hand on his coat before lifting it. He glanced at Jane, hesitated for a moment and replaced it softly.

'Just one thing, Jane. I think it would be wise for you to say you are eighteen, should anyone ask. I want you to be given the respect and the responsibilities of a young woman, for that is what you are.'

He smiled and rapped smartly three times. Jane felt the knocks on her heart; she clutched her own hand with the other, her only comfort.

The girl who opened the door was no older than Jane, but her black dress and white apron had Jane shrinking further.

'We have come to see Lady Blackwood.' Isaac's smile was his most pleasant.

The girl's eyes wandered. You thought she was looking to the side and then you realised she was talking to you.

'Out.'

'The Reverend?'

'Out.' She held on to the edge of the door, suspicious.

'Could we wait? I am expected.'

The girl's eyebrows arched in a way Jane knew well from the likes of Gwendolyn in the village. The thing to do was walk a little taller.

'Wait here,' the girl said, pointing at two hard chairs in the hall either side of a table so shiny you could see yourself in the gloss. A glass dome of birds stood in the exact middle. Dead birds. But set as though they were living with tails all perked up and the wings half open. Their eyes were beads: the brightest, deadest thing about them.

A clock in a tall wooden box on the opposite wall ticked long minutes. If you watched the swing of the pendulum your eyes went heavy and you were in danger of slipping from the chair. Jane blinked and looked away. The red, green and blue patterned carpet was gorgeous, leading up a wide staircase with bannisters glossy as treacle, the brass stair rods gleaming. On the first landing was a window of coloured light. More beautiful by far this house was than any Jane had ever been in, and so very, very quiet.

Isaac cleared his throat and settled back with his eyes shut, *y Beibl* in front of him on his lap.

The faintest noises came from up the stairs, a long way away. A few words, all broken. The opening and shutting of a door.

The clock ticked on. A terrible whirring had Jane up and out of her seat before it struck the hour. Midday.

Somewhere far away above them, a door opened again.

'Go away! I hate you! I hate you! I hate you!' A child's voice, for sure. A scream followed; a thud; something breaking; a door slamming. Jane looked at Isaac but his face said: nothing to do with us, Jane. She sat back, folding her hands in her lap. If she'd been in her britches, she'd have spread her fingers.

Another woman, also in a black dress and white apron, ran down the stairs. Her hair was plaited and coiled round her head like Sarah's. Her face was bright red.

'Oh.'

Isaac half rose.

'We're waiting for the Blackwoods.'

The remaining stairs she took at a slower pace, patting her cheeks.

'He'll be back for lunch. I expect you heard, did you?' She jerked her head towards the stairs. 'One of her charity cases. I'd have put the little so-and-so on the streets, I would.'

The front door opened and immediately she was busy rearranging the dome of birds on the table, which needed no attention at all.

'You've visitors, sir,' she said, taking the Reverend's coat.

'Thank you, Clara! Ah, Isaac! I trust you've not been waiting long?'

The Reverend was small with white whiskers, red cheeks and gold wire-rimmed spectacles at the end of his nose.

'No, indeed,' Isaac answered for both. Just as well, as Jane's voice was gone.

'I've two packages this time,' Isaac said, reaching into his bag. 'And a note from Mr Johns.'

The Reverend read over the top of his glasses.

'I see, yes... yes, one for the war effort. Dear, oh dear... terrible thing, terrible... and one for the mission. Good man,

Isaac.' He weighed the packages, one in each hand. 'No problems, I trust.'

Isaac glanced at Jane. He raised his eyebrows, eyes wide, inviting her to speak. She could not; not to a reverend man staring at her over his spectacles, she could not.

'You could tell Mr Blackwood, Jane.'

'We were robbed at Erwood.' Out burst the words like a bullrush breaking.

'Nothing of value taken,' Isaac reassured the Reverend. 'Only a bag of river stones!'

'Good man!' Mr Blackwood laid his hand on Isaac's shoulder. His hands were very clean and smooth and he'd a gold ring on his little finger as big as a sparrow's egg.

And David. The words were loud in her own head. Isaac knew her mind. His breath was drawn to speak. It was her turn to stop him with a sharp look. Better to leave behind what was behind. Nothing could be made better by making the unspeakable into a story for a stranger.

'I'm sorry, I haven't introduced you. My cousin, Jane Evans. Jane – Reverend Theodore Blackwood.'

'You've not come all the way from Wales have you?' he said with a laugh, his face sobering as Jane nodded.

A distant thud and Clara was running back up the stairs, ignored by the Reverend – unless he was hard of hearing.

'My, my! Quite a walk. I believed it a man's province, bringing the animals?'

'Jane Evans here is the first woman I know of to come all the way,' Isaac said.

It's both a nice thing and a terrible screwing kind of agony to hear words like that.

'Gracious! Your feet must have been quite sore!'

What the purpose of his spectacles was, she couldn't imagine from the way he looked at her over them. He paused, waiting for her to say something. But she had not known it for a question.

'Jane was such a help to me, sir. She has a great knowledge of pigs.'

'Pigs! Well, I never!' He threw back his head and laughed, though Jane saw nothing amusing in this.

'I have care of them back home,' she said.

'Care of them! Well, well. You must talk to my wife. Caring is very much in her line.'

A scream, a bang and a thunder of steps broke their conversation. Clara appeared, calling from the landing by the coloured window.

'Come quick! He's stuck in the window. He's hurt bad!'

If someone calls in that urgent way, you just run, not stopping to wonder if you should. Up five flights of stairs Jane followed Clara, right to the top of the house, with her skirts hobbling her at every step. The last stairs were bare with no carpet or rods at all.

Clara flung the door wide. No time to hesitate, for there was a boy on the window ledge opposite, his body falling backwards, his legs mercifully pinned safely by the window. How he bellowed! His face was purple with it.

'Take him, Jane.' Isaac, who had run up behind her, heaved up the heavy window to release his legs while Jane grasped him under the arms. There was no weight to him at all.

'The sash has broken,' Isaac pulled at a frayed end of rope.

His skinny little legs were crushed and flat looking. Jane laid him on the cot bed, where his gasps gave way to great gulps. His eyes bulged. His lips were blue. He was stricken utterly.

'Breathe!' Jane said, hitting him across the face with the back of her hand.

He was shocked into a fit of hysterical sobbing.

'Now now, don't fuss so. It'll be alright.' She laid him on the truckle bed and pulled up his nightshirt to his knees. As she ran her hands over his legs, the boy's sobs redoubled.

'You're bruised, but no more than that. Wriggle your toes. Go on. I say you cannot.'

The boy's sobs quietened as he concentrated.

'You're like me. You can do two things at once. There you are! Wriggling around like baby mice. That's a good sign, see. You'll just have legs changing colour – yellow and blue and red. Won't that be something? And aching a bit, but that's all. If I had my arnica I could help you. What's this?' She sniffed a tin of jelly by his bed.

'Just grease for his chest,' Clara said.

'I could soothe your legs with this. Would you like that? I'll be gentle as anything.'

He'd a suspicious look to him, but who could blame him for that? His face was thin and colourless but for the grey under his eyes. He propped himself on his elbows to watch.

'Were you climbing out of the window?' Jane asked.

He nodded.

'What were you thinking of with such a long drop to the hard ground below? You are a lucky boy that the window caught you and saved you. That was God's doing. He saw the danger and brought it down – crash!'

'I was going to see my Mama,' he said, tears in his eyes.

'I don't think you'll find her outside the window, will you?'

'She's in Heaven with the angels.'

'My Mam's with the angels too,' Jane said, after a minute. 'Perhaps they know each other. What's your name?'

'Kenneth Lovelock.'

'Kenneth Lovelock. I'm Jane Evans. Do you know who you remind me of? I've a brother back home named William, always in scrapes and hurting himself. Once he fell on a bill hook and it went in one side of his leg and came out the other. I had to pull it out and patch him up. You should have heard the fuss he made. Much more than you.'

'Why do you talk funny – all up and down?'

'Up and down is it? That's like where I come from, up in the hills and down in the valleys. Shall I tell you about the farm where I live?'

Kenneth laid his head back on the pillow. His eyes, wide at first, gradually dropped as Jane told him of Morwenna, Fly and Glass and the white sheep on the hills.

Only when his face was to the wall and his breathing even did Jane pull the cover over him and sit back. More than a moment it took to pull herself free of the hills of Tŷ Mawr, back to where she was, in this attic room. Good it had been to be back home again, bringing each part to life as she spoke. Kenneth Lovelock, was it? His face was pale except for the pink mark where she had slapped him. She soothed it with her thumb.

She looked round. All alone? Now where was Isaac, and Clara? She had not heard them leave. The window was shut tight. Kenneth should not be left in a room without air, but the broken window was too heavy to lift. Should she go down now? Or stay?

She tiptoed to the door, which was not latched. Clara sat at the top of the wooden stairs with her head slumped on her folded arms.

'Got him off to sleep, have you? Spoilt little so-and-so. Thank the Lord that window came down, or we'd have a corpse on the road and I'd have my marching orders.'

'Thank the Lord indeed! Has his mother died, then?' Jane asked her.

'That's why Lady Alicia brought him here, till he's better or worse. Either way. She was watching you.'

'Who?'

'Her Ladyship! At the door.' Clara stood up. 'I'm to take you down.'

No time to do more than swallow and follow Clara, smoothing her hair and her skirt as she went.

'Jane.' Lady Blackwood rose from her upright chair at the dining room table. The exact same figure as Mr Johns – tall and thin with an elegant nose and eyes that looked deep into you. Her dark hair was parted in the middle with a white line that disappeared under her cap. White lace cuffs matched the edges of the cap. Her black dress had colours in it, like starlings' wings.

How rich the room was, with the table dark and polished and the chairs with seats of liver-red leather. The carpet was softer than grass. On the table, a bowl of apples bigger than any she had ever seen sat on a white lace runner, fancy as cow parsley. With too much to see, Jane had a longing for blinkers, like Jessie at the plough.

Isaac stood by the mantelpiece.

'Are you alright, Jane?'

Jane nodded. Lady Blackwood's eyes on her sent her squirming inside, her body still as a stone.

'You are to stay with me. Mr Davis and I have talked. It is all arranged.' Her voice was business-like, precise.

Isaac was looking with a strange softness in his eyes, like pride; a fondness that brought heat into her cheeks.

'I witnessed how you were with little Kenneth, Jane. I have plans for you, but we will discuss them another time. Mr Davis tells me you have been sent by God. Are you happy to stay with me, Jane, and help continue God's work?'

'I believe this must be the plan, Jane,' Isaac said, quickly. 'You told me He would provide the answer.'

Jane's words were taken from her. There was nothing to do but nod.

Lady Blackwood took a small handbell from the table and rang it at the door. Clara must have been right outside, for the door opened that instant.

'Show Jane to your room, Clara. She will share with you. Please make her comfortable and show her the house. I have business to attend to. Excuse me.'

As she left the room, Clara bobbed her head and bent one knee. Was that something expected of Jane?

'Come,' Clara moved out into the hall.

'Jane!' Isaac's voice was agitated. 'Don't go without saying goodbye to me.'

A terrible moment it was, to be standing with Clara in front of her and Isaac behind. His eyes so full of feeling, she had to look down.

'Jane. Look at me.' There was a crack in his voice. 'I am glad to leave you in safe hands. But I will miss your company. I wish to give you something. Something precious to me.'

Y Beibl. His *Beibl*. So big and awful heavy it was.

'This will be your comfort and guide you through,' he swallowed, making Jane swallow too, 'whatever lies ahead.'

For one fleeting moment, their eyes locked.

Clasping the big book to her chest, she looked away just as he pulled her towards him, his chin catching on her forehead and the hard covers of *y Beibl* cutting into her chest.

They sprang apart, both with a half-laugh.

But he still had her hand. He squeezed her fingers tight before letting them go.

CHAPTER 17

To War with *Y Beibl*

NEVER DO YOU know what God has planned for you. If you did, you'd burst for excitement and fear all mixed in. Looking down from the stern of a ship into the deep blue water, all stirring and rising and falling like your own feelings, was a thrill – though you could not see what was underneath, the depth of it, nor imagine what might be lurking there. More settling it was to press against the wooden rail at the stern, *y Beibl* at your feet, and count foamy white stepping stones stretching back to Marseilles. Before that, the watery trail, now dissolved, reached back to Southampton. And before that... *everything* led to this moment, on board with all these women – nurses going to the Crimea, a place Jane had never heard of until a few short weeks before.

Had she not been at the Blackwoods', she'd probably never have heard of the Crimea. For most of the year she'd been there, there was talk in the Blackwoods' kitchen of the war, but she did not know where exactly it was. Upstairs, sudden refreshments were required, meals prepared and then not eaten. Clara, when asked, knew nothing.

Out in the carriage with Lady Blackwood one day, taking mending from the orphanage to the Destitute Women, they were slowed by marching soldiers: so smart in their red coats and dark trousers, buttons gleaming – a person must be stone not to be moved by such a sight. Their eyes were fixed forwards, not a glance to either side, in spite of the people cheering and wishing them good luck and God speed. All their arms and legs moved at the same time, as though they were one being.

Lady Blackwood clutched the cross she wore at her throat.

'Off to the Crimea. Such brave boys!'

Jane had not liked to ask where the Crimea was. And never did she imagine for a moment that just weeks later she'd be following the soldiers herself.

Clara was the person usually summoned to Lady Blackwood's room. When Jane was sent for to help with packing, she was as bewildered as Clara was indignant. Every item on Lady Blackwood's bed must be folded in tissue and lavender. Why Jane had been chosen, she still could not understand, until Lady Blackwood said:

'God has spoken to us, Jane. We are to go out to the Crimea to help in any way we are able.'

Such a glitter she had in her eyes, standing so tall and fine, just her fingertips steadying herself on her writing desk. Without a moment's hesitation, Jane turned to her.

'God wants me to go with you, so I may be useful to you!'

Lady Blackwood smiled and nodded as though she was not surprised in the least.

'You are a girl of strength and spirit, Jane. There will be ways that we all may be of use. Of that I have no doubt.'

When Jane took the Reverend his sweet cocoa the next morning, he was bending over a large leather-bound book, open on the table in front of him.

'Ah Jane! I hear you are to accompany us. Would you like to see where we are going?' He left her no time to reply and she did not know if she would or not.

'England is here; and here's Wales, where you're from.'

Jane swallowed. Such a small green shape when it was so big, and on the same page as London, so very far away.

He turned the page, 'First to France, here. Then...' he turned another page, 'we sail all the way to Constantinople. Here is Varna, where our boys were waiting until they were summoned to sail to Calamity Bay,' he chortled, 'as it is known... to fight the war here...' His finger pointed to a small triangle edged in green. 'This is our destination.'

He tapped the book, but Jane could not see what he was indicating.

'Are you ready for it, Jane?' He closed the book, straightened and blinked at her over his glasses. Jane nodded.

There were three pages of blue between here and there.

Sea water bleaches everything white. Even the Reverend's coat sleeves, where he leaned on the rail of the *Sybil*, had ghostly lines on them. Ink still stained Jane's fingers. Surely, if she dipped her hands in the puddles of sea water on the deck daily and rubbed her fingers, she'd arrive with spotless hands. It was a good thing she had done for certain, penning that letter to Griffith before they sailed. Why she had not thought of it before, she did not know, for when Lady Blackwood mentioned it to her, finding her in the hall of the house given to them in Southampton with her bag packed and ready, she knew instantly it was the right thing to do. Such paper they had, and a special desk to sit at with all manner of inks and pens. Not an easy task at all to decide what to say, with the men loading the trunks into the cart and Jane's heart fluttering with the idea of the sea journey ahead. Her thoughts were more than she wrote. If Griffith could only know the effort it took.

He must have seen things her way by now. Isaac would have told him Jane was safe, told him how useful she had been on the drove. They would all have been proud of her. Griffith would know that Jane was left with Mr Johns' cousin, but he would not know where she was now, which was wrong. They would be worrying and she could stop that.

griffith.
I am saf. I am doing gods wil. I am gon with lady blakwod to the war. You may rite to me at the barraks. Tel Isaac I hav y Beibl with me. I forgiv you all.
Your sister jane.

When a child, Mam *made* her forgive when one of the boys said sorry for something horrible they had done to her. This was *true* forgiving, cleaning her inside out.

At sea, the weather changed quickly. The morning warmth became an afternoon of pitching and tossing, the wind screeching around the *Sybil*'s slippery decks in a fury. Jane would have clung on to the mast to stay out in the air, but a sailor with his hair tied back in a stiff pigtail ordered her below with a sharp point of his finger.

Emma and Ebba, the young Swedish girls the Reverend had brought to help with his mission, were sick before they left Marseilles. Jane's first job was to look after them; up and down the ladder with bowls and lemon water – hardly able to turn around, the cabin was so small. Such beautiful hair they had at the start of the journey: thick and coiled round their heads like golden ropes. To see it so messed up and trailing in the sick bowls was a pitiful sight. Jane slept on the floor between them to be on hand when they needed her.

Up on deck with the wind whipping her skirt, she must walk legs wide, like Richard returning from the inn. Lemons, the girls were moaning for lemons, and she must venture to the kitchens near the back of the ship to find one. Returning, the lemon in her hand, the *Sybil* lurched suddenly and violently just as a man covered in a cape was passing the other way: the Reverend, out for his daily walk.

'Miss Evans!' He was a genial man. They might have been in a London street on a summer's day. 'How are my girls?' He did not pause for an answer. 'You're a farm girl, aren't you? Get down to the horses, Jane. There's one in distress.'

Before they left Marseilles harbour she had seen a horse dangling from a sling above the ship. Until that moment the idea that horses might be necessary to a war had never occurred to her. Terrified they'd be, not knowing what was happening to them or why, hating all this pitching and rolling.

Back she stumbled beyond the kitchens, where a ladder took her to the hold. The smell was terrible: dung and strong urine overlaid with fear – the worst smell of all. It was dark and the horses were packed tight; the slings keeping them upright were barely visible. Two lanterns swung from the beam lighting up a terrified eye, a patch of chestnut, a sore chafed by the sling.

Near the end of the row, a man stood holding his lamp high. His nose was huge, his eyes dark and disappearing.

Jane squeezed through the hot bodies to join him. 'I'm Jane Evans. I've been sent.'

A horse lay on the ground with a broken sling swaying above. The snapped leg bone stuck right through the skin.

'What a thing to happen.' Jane stroked the horse's face. He was panting. There was no hope for him.

'Miracle worker, are you?' the man said, rubbing his nose and picking up his gun.

No wish at all she had to wait for the inevitable. Even muffled by the sacking wound round the horse's head, the single shot shocked the other horses to a violent jerking of their heads, a mad stamping of hooves. Above her, the hatch opened. Sailors ran down the stairs, pushing past Jane as she ran up onto the deck. Six men it took, straining on the rope to pull the horse up, dumping it at her feet while they wiped their foreheads and puffed their cheeks.

A fine chestnut he was, every part of him noble and strong, apart from the cruel split leg. What a waste to dispatch an animal like that without giving him a chance. No-one would kill a human being with nothing worse than a broken bone.

'Poor thing,' she whispered.

'Or lucky. Depends how you look at it.' The sailor spat into his hands. 'Right lads.'

The wind whipped the horse's tail into the air. The ship lurched; the men ran forward to the side. Not far to fall. The ship rolled back. If Jane clung to the mast she would stay upright. No splash, for the sea came up to take the body down.

For three full days and nights the gale blew, until it was impossible to think it would ever be over. A second and third horse died and were dumped at sea. A terrible place to end your life, in the middle of a journey to somewhere else. Even here, on the rough sea with the wood creaking, the girls moaning and the wind howling, David would come into Jane's thoughts in that space when she shut her eyes before sleep came. Hard it was to think he might have done a bad thing, for he'd had all the same lessons in the chapel as she had. *Ye shall not steal, neither deal falsely, neither lie one to another.* It would have broken Mam's heart for sure.

A particularly violent gust in the middle of the night woke Jane with an almighty crash. If the boat was to go down, she would rather be sleeping, with her eyes closed.

Please don't be angry with us, God. We are going to help!

Next morning The Reverend stood beside Jane on deck, watching the sailors wrestling to secure the remaining crates. Even in this weather he took his 'daily constitutional', holding his hat in his hand as the wind tore at his scarf. They were of one mind when it came to fresh air.

'One mast down. Two still standing. Straight through the captain's cabin roof! Several crates lost overboard, Jane. Someone will feel the loss of those!' he shouted. 'It is a cruel fate to lose them so close to our destination.'

'We are?' Jane's heart leapt.

'A day or two at most.'

'And the worst will be behind us?'

He smiled.

The wood creaked low as the boat rocked. The Swedish girls breathed deeply. Jane sat straight up, awake in an instant. Everything was still and calm.

'Thank you, God!' she said, squirming into her skirt and shirt and quickly climbing the ladder.

The sea was quiet and flat; the sails flapped weakly. Glorious it was: the morning sun in a golden sky, distant misty mountains rising out of the sea. The ship was close to land. A man fishing from a rock lifted his head, wrapped in a white cloth, to watch Jane watching him. Behind him a flock of long-legged bony sheep grazed in a golden field. This would be a scene to tell them of back home: all yellows and purples with not a speck of green anywhere at all.

Cheers drifted over the water. On the other side of the *Sybil*, a ship was passing in the opposite direction. Lady Blackwood, not seen for days, was now walking along the deck, her arm slipped through her husband's. She'd a black scarf over her hat, making her face look pale and thin, but there was a firmness in her look.

'Jane, I hear you have the makings of a good sailor.'

'I wouldn't trust the sea at all, Ma'am, for the next second it will be up and fighting.'

'Let's hope not, Jane.'

The Reverend had his telescope to his eye. 'Do you see, Jane? Constantinople.'

He pointed ahead of the ship to the land side. Truly, it was a magical sight: fine towers reaching into a golden Heaven, and rounded domes in between like the sun itself, half-risen above the horizon. Tall dark trees dotted around the buildings. The roll of the hills behind exactly echoed the shape of the domes. If Heaven were a city – which it wasn't – it would look like this.

'Mosques, Jane. Muslim churches. And minarets reaching up to their God,' he commented.

'Their God? Not ours?'

'Nice point, Jane. Nice point!'

The sea was now full of boats. Small rowing craft zipped to and fro across the paths of the bigger ships, like water boatmen. Up ahead the sea forked right and left and the mountains rose on either side. The *Sybil* was steering away from the magical city. Disappointing – like having the sweetest fruit dangled in front of you and snatched away just as juices filled your mouth.

They were heading for the far shore, where an enormous building filled the skyline. It had four turrets, thicker than the now misty and distant spires of Constantinople opposite. The size of it, the ugly block of it, set Jane's heart thumping.

All the nurses, with their bags and bundles, were gathering on deck. The Reverend was organising sailors to carry Lady Blackwood's hatboxes and trunks.

'Put them there. There!' He pointed with his stick.

Clutching her bag, *y Beibl* under her arm, Jane stood next to the Swedish girls. As the land ahead grew nearer, every good thing drained down her body, into her feet and down through the wooden floorboards.

The building grew massive, blocking out the sky.

'Scutari. The Turkish Barracks, I understand. Or was.' The Reverend waved his stick in the air again. 'Quite a sight.'

It was a sight indeed. You must move your head from side to side to see from one turret to the other; hundreds of windows staring out like empty eyes. The corner towers were five windows high. Only the tops kept a little magic, with their domes and decorations.

Along the shoreline and the rickety jetty, men watched, wearing the strangest clothes: baggy trousers, and their heads in cloths. The women were like jars, not going in at the waist at all, and their gowns were long and brown. Their heads were covered: cloth too, but more like shawls. A little boy ran along the shore followed by a dog with legs shorter than a corgi, though its body and head belonged to something more like a collie. Not so pretty. A terrible smell there was, stronger every second, like that rotting body of a badger she had found once in a thicket back home, seething with maggots that writhed on in her mind for days. She had only the sleeve of her shirt in which to bury her nose.

The anchor dropped with a rumble and a splash, and the sailors took the railing away. The nurses were lowered one by one into the rowing boat. To hold your skirts down, your hat on, your bag and Bible safe was not easy and required all your attention. Being passed down into the arms of a sailor with his shirt open and his chest so hairy was an undignified procedure. Lady Blackwood, however, was ladylike throughout, though she had four men and her husband to help her. She was a woman to admire for her composure.

The little boat rose up almost to the deck, only to plunge back down again. Lady Blackwood grasped the Reverend's hand. Were they now in peril of drowning in sight of their destination? The Swedish girls gripped the sides with white knuckles. The nurses were silenced.

The sun was fierce in these parts. Jane's cheeks would be on fire that night for certain. The water glittered. Up and down, up and down. Only when they were dangerously laden with boxes and crates, the sides almost level with the water, did the rowers fix their blades into the leather grooves to row them briskly across the final stretch of water.

Jane gripped the sailor's hand to step onto the wooden jetty. Two soldiers leaned against an ox cart by the landing pier. Not like soldiers at all – more like statues of clay for the thick mud that covered them. They were looking at nothing; not in a blind, milky way, but as though they did not want to see. What had they witnessed to make them like this?

A long, steep path wound up the hill to the building.

'Last leg!' said the Reverend, striding out to follow a Turk who was bent double under the Blackwoods' portmanteaux. the Reverend's words might be bracing as usual but even *his* heart must be falling with every step he climbed up that treacherous steep hill, thick with sucking mud. The smell, bad on the quay, grew worse: a sweet, rotting stench, unsettling the stomach worse than the heaving sea had. Breathing through the mouth was the only way.

Even when the ground levelled out alongside the building, the mud was so weighty and the sun so strong, it felt like wading through a river; the water dragging her skirt and pulling her down.

CHAPTER 18

Beyond Imagining

NOTHING, NOTHING ON this earth could be as desperate as this place: it was full of sights no one should ever witness. Terrible. Terrible. *Now* the meaning in the soldier's eyes on the jetty was clear: they did *not* want to see. How dreadfully, painfully Jane wanted to run back down to the boat before it sailed away. Take me home, she'd beg the sailors. I want to go home.

Her mind screamed: run! But her legs were rooted as tree trunks. Everyone huddled together like geese in the lobby, the only comfort being together. No-one said a word. Silenced by the haunting cries and moans rising from the floor to the high ceilings and wrapping all around them. Men, too many to count, stretched away to a point in the far distance along the longest corridor you might imagine, so close together there was no room to step between them. Soldiers with scraps of their uniforms still clinging to them: fragments of red or blue and frayed tartans, cloth smeared with the mud and blood of war. Bones with the skin tight over them. Unspeakable. Ripped open. Like meat. And the smell so powerful it was not a smell at all. Even the straw on the floor, where it could be seen, was dark as evil itself. She'd not leave her pigs in filth like this.

The new nurses had their hands to their faces, and even Lady Blackwood held her cuff to her nose. The Reverend ran his finger over his nostrils as though squashing them might help. Jane held *y Beibl* tight.

Please God, make me strong enough! Please, God, please.

She forced her eyes wide for fear of closing them and never opening them again. She must not even blink. She must talk to herself and do as she said: look at one man. Just the one. Start at the head and work down to the toes, stay with each part. The third mattress on the right-hand side would be fine: a man, more a boy, with hair like wet sand; head back, white throat with the veins thin and blue; eyes too big for a face no more than a skull; shirt of rust – earth or blood. Shivering, every part of him.

She had no more words for herself. God was the only hope. Please God, do not let me down and I won't let You down.

'Nurse!' A faint touch on her ankle made her clutch the arm of the nurse next to her to stop her scream.

'Sorry,' she whispered. The nurse patted her arm.

At her feet a poor soldier on the floor had stretched out to touch her, that was all. His eyes were haunting, full of fear, pleading. To look away was the worst thing in the world to do, but she could not stop herself. A nurse in a Scutari sash came hurrying down the ward – but Jane had failed! The first test! And now she would never like herself again, ever.

'Forgive me!' she whispered.

Just in time, the nurse slid a pot under the poor man. The sounds were beyond words and the stench unbearable. What to do? Where to look? Lady Blackwood closed her eyes as her husband squeezed her arm.

The group waiting all turned together in relief at the soft swish of a skirt and the pad of feet on the wooden steps behind them.

'Alicia, dear friend.' The two women hugged each other. 'James.' The Reverend removed his hat and bowed. The other nurses were smiling again. Jane's face too, she realised, was stretched into a grin. And now her throat was knotted with a strange desire to laugh. Everything was tall and straight about this woman: her nose, her neck, her back, the parting in her dark hair. Her lace collar and simple cap were clean and white. Such a fine nose and grey eyes and a calmness to her she had: she was in charge and that was all she needed to know. It was hardly believable that she had the power to overcome such desperate sights and smells. Miss Nightingale. The nurses had talked of her often. It could be no other. The mercy was that she had not witnessed Jane's shame.

She turned and smiled faintly, one smile for all three of them: Emma and Ebba and Jane.

A short pause followed, where normally there would be a discussion of the weather or the journey.

'Where shall we begin, Florence?' Lady Blackwood asked.

Miss Nightingale held Lady Blackwood at arm's length to look straight into her face.

'Tomorrow. You must be tired.'

Lady Blackwood said quickly, 'This is why we have come.'

That touch on the arm, the way the two women gazed into each other's eyes, twisted Jane's throat. Breathless she was with the up and down of her feelings, worse than the boat.

Miss Nightingale nodded. 'Follow me. Mind the third step!' she warned. 'It's broken.'

Down they went into a courtyard as big as a field. Round every corner, behind every door was something to punch the breath from you. A barracks with a hospital inside. A hospital with a village inside! An actual village with stalls and shelters, men and women everywhere, dressed like the people on the jetty in those strange clothes. You could not believe it if it were not there in front of you and you walking through it. A man sat poking a fire while a second man ladled

155

liquid from a pot into a mug held out by a soldier leaning on a crutch. Behind them a broken fountain dribbled into puddles. A huddle of men smoked under a cart tipped to the side, with only one giant wheel holding it up. A dog lay near two skinny horses; washboard ribs and heads hanging low. The dog was very still. One horse shifted its weight and a cloud of black insects rose from the dog's muzzle.

Jane fixed her eyes quickly on Miss Nightingale. Such a fine profile she had, with her neck curving over her high collar. The folds of her grey skirt were so neat and her waist so small.

Where shall we begin? Now that was the kind of person to be, brave and composed. If all this was a shock to Jane, used as she was to the farmyard and a rough life, what must it be like to Lady Blackwood?

Miss Nightingale gestured towards an opening under the stairs, before nodding and turning back. As she went up, a young man in a turban and a tight soldier's jacket came down the steps, saluting Miss Nightingale as he jumped the third step. His lower body was covered with no more than a piece of cloth that hung loosely down and round and up again. His legs were brown as branches and his feet wide and pale with dry mud.

He approached with a smile of broken, blackened teeth, and English words strung together in a line. You knew the meaning of each one singly; together the sense was lost.

Husband and wife consulted.

'Jane,' Lady Blackwood said. 'You will stay with me. Your Bible will be taken ahead and kept safe. You might have need of both your hands.'

Hard this was to part with something so precious, even for a short while. What now would steady her and give her strength? What would she do if she never saw it again? The thought kept her hands on her Bible a fraction longer than she should as she handed it to the man, who smiled warmly. There was no knowing how else to read a person in this place. In everything, she must do as Lady Blackwood wished.

'Ali! Me! I bring back! I bring back!' he grinned at Lady Blackwood as he led the Reverend and the Swedish girls up the steps and away. 'Come!'

'He is to arrange accommodation, Jane.'

If only she had realised in time how suited she could have been to helping the Reverend spread the word. The Bible she *did* know about, and she could sing hymns.

'Are you ready for this, Jane?' Lady Blackwood asked.

A question Jane could not answer as she wished to. She *had* to be. No turning away now, however she felt inside. Never again would she turn way from a plea for help. Never. Though God would understand. He always did. There was nothing in the world He had created that was beyond Him.

Jane nodded and they turned and walked through the open cellar door. Usually a deep breath is necessary to meet difficult situations. But this breath turned her stomach. Thank God for the cover of the dark so no-one could see her gagging. Gradually, light from the doorway lit up scenes in the darkness. Scenes from a nightmare, mad and ghoulish.

Strong enough is all I ask, God. Please.

Close to her feet two women sprawled out on the dirt floor – *women!* – a child – a *child!* – motionless nearby. Slumped against a brick pillar another woman sat, her bare legs stuck straight out like a doll's. From a pile of rags on the ground next to her rose a bald head. So wrong it was to see a bald woman. Leaning on one of the brick supports stood a naked girl, a man sucking on her breast. So dreadful, so sad, the way the girl's head hung as though she was not there at all and this was not happening. Unbearable. Jane looked away, down to her feet, where a small boy crouched alone on the floor, eyes too big for his tiny face of bone. Behind him, a scraggy dog licked at the foulness.

'Away!' Jane rushed at it, waving her arms. The dog yelped and slunk behind the legs of a mule standing there in the semi-darkness.

Shocking! Shocking! On and on, endless horror, stretching back into the dark. Everything so foul-smelling and disgusting. Who were these women? Children? Babies? Where did they come from? Soldiers she expected, even those broken, bleeding men in the ward upstairs, though not such numbers. But women!

Her skirt was pulled. 'For the love of God, help me.'

There, on the floor, a woman crouched on all fours, looking up with desperate eyes.

'It's coming! It's coming!'

'What? Oh, my God!' This must happen outside. Not here! Seizing the woman under the armpits, Jane started to pull.

A second woman tapped her on the arm. 'Too late! Grab the poor mite!'

It was all so quick. The mother groaned, the baby slithered out and Jane caught it, hot and wet and long. It would have fallen on the floor had she not.

'You poor little creature!' Jane held it to her chest and wiped it with her skirt as best she could. 'To be born into this!' A thick pink rope linked it still to its mother. Aunt Anni had always attended to that part. There was nothing here to cut it with.

'Look away!' the second woman, not a hair on her head, touched her side teeth and lifted the cord. 'Give her to me.'

The sound! Blood was in Jane's own mouth as the baby cried, a thin grating wail.

'Here!' The baby was passed back to her, all slippery and

hot. She wrapped it in her shawl. 'A girl! Take her!' she said to the mother.

She must be like the Reverend, and try to be bright even when she felt desolate.

The mother turned away. 'You take her. Throw her to the dogs. Spare her.'

Jane clutched the baby tight.

'That's a terrible thing to say!' she whispered. 'The most terrible thing I've heard in my whole life.'

'Jane!' Lady Blackwood was calling. 'Where are you? Oh, my good Lord.' She touched the baby on the cheek, then said briskly to the second woman. 'Take her. Persuade the mother to put her to her breast. Jane and I have work to do!'

Lady Blackwood's crisp order was a relief. Jane must do as she was told, and yet, to leave them like this... She passed the tiny body to the bald friend.

'Here, lady.' The woman held Jane's shawl out to her.

Jane shook her head.

'Keep it, please; and I'm no lady.'

CHAPTER 19

Fighting Spirit Is What We Need

A SHELF MIGHT be a good place for a Bible, but a hard place to sleep. Ali's mother's mother's house in Üsküdar, where they were to lodge, was a brisk walk along the cliffs, out of the reach of the sounds from Scutari. The air was cleansed by the sea breeze. Jane was to sleep on the shelf next to the Swedish girls. *Y Beibl* would be her pillow so that all the good could rise from it in the night and give her its strength. How else could she meet the morrow?

Bleak and heavy as she had ever been, Jane lay on her back, staring into the dark. Are you punishing me, God? Her eyes would not close for fear of what they would see. How could You allow this to happen, God? If You are so powerful... Why did You let me come? There's nothing I can do here. I am not able, I cannot; I am a disappointment to You and to myself.

In the morning, she would plead with the Reverend that she was more suited to help him. Chapel she was, not C of E, but at least she was not Roman. Emma and Ebba might then help Lady Blackwood. Underneath the words, she knew it would not happen. Such a heavy feeling weighed her down.

The partition was thin. The Blackwoods had a loud, clear way of speaking, as if they had never tried to speak quietly.

'Women, you say? Good gracious!' the Reverend said. 'Shall I extinguish the light?'

'Why they are here, Heaven alone knows.'

'I'm sure you are right there. And He has called the right person to attend to them, if I may say so, Alicia.'

But *I* am not the right person – Jane screwed up her face in an agony to stop the leaking from her eyes, which would do nothing but mark the cover of *y Beibl*.

The sight of Emma and Ebba, with their soft faces, plaiting their hair the next morning pushed all thoughts of speaking to the Reverend away. Last night's thinking was a weakness she must put behind her. Black tea and dry bread is not much, but coarseness and hunger Jane was used to. Dawn was breaking as they set off along the high cliff path. Nurses from other lodgings filed along the road to the Barracks. Silent, heads down. No choice either. Not their place to question or even to think. Just follow orders.

The Reverend and the Swedish girls turned at the junction in the road while Jane followed Lady Blackwood to the Barracks with a fleeting pang of words unspoken. The crying of gulls and the wash of the sea filled one ear; the other echoed with the vast emptiness of land. A strange buttery sky tinged with pink had Jane yearning suddenly for the colours and shapes of home, the bowl of the hills, the green moss and the purple oaks.

'Beautiful day!' Lady Blackwood commented. She'd a wonderful straight back and her head was always up. She held her skirts as though she was about to dance and spoke to Jane over her shoulder. 'A stick would make this walk easier, Jane, don't you think? Though where we would find such a luxury, I do not know.'

What a fine thing, to rustle when you walked. Imagine

your skirt stiff with the petticoats, and running your hands over the smoothness of the silk. Your hands would not snag, for they'd be white and smooth; and those shoes, the softness of them, it would be like walking on air. Though here the thickness of a boot might be better suited, and there would be no matter if your hem trailed in the mud if your clothes were all the colour of mud to start with.

A strange quiet hung over the courtyard and of the women there was no trace, though they'd left them clustered at the cellar entrance. Perhaps they had moved back for warmth, though no-one in their right mind would retreat where the air was worse. Poor things, of course they were not in their right minds, not any minds at all. Where was that baby? It was too dark to see with no lamp. How far the cellar stretched back she had no idea, apart from imagining the endless corridors above. In the dark, no dawn had broken.

'Come, Jane. Before we can make any plans, we must see what's what and leave ourselves no surprises,' Lady Blackwood said. 'Ah, Ali, with a lamp! Just when we need you!'

Ali walked ahead, holding the lamp high. You'd have thought his arms would scorch, but he never flinched. Lady Blackwood followed, nodding to all the women she passed. A few nodded back, though most turned away. Of the baby there was no sign.

'Move away from there!' Lady Blackwood's voice ahead was half shout, half whisper. Jane could only see the faintest outline where Ali held his lamp. 'You're lying in filth. Have some sense.'

Jane stood where she was, waiting. Lady Blackwood returned, holding her handkerchief over her face.

'Outside, Jane! We need to formulate a plan of action.'

So sweet was the idea of being outside, away from this

place, Jane almost broke into a run. A shape suddenly loomed up in front of her. A ghost! A ghoul! A man stood swaying for a second, before his knees twisted sideways as his body crumpled to the ground.

'Ali!' Lady Blackwood shouted. 'Quickly!'

Ali put the lamp down to take the man under his arms and drag him out to the courtyard. A thin grey face he had, with his eyes wide and staring; but he was not dead. A pulse throbbed in his neck. Jane could have stepped forward, helped, told them of the pulse. Taken charge. She could. Was not her place to do more than look?

'Ali, water!' Lady Blackwood turned back to the man. 'What is your name?' Her voice was very loud. The man stared through her.

'Perhaps he's not British,' Jane said.

'He's British alright. That's a soldier's belt.'

A young woman, skin like marble, arms across her chest thin as bones, stood in the cellar doorway, watching.

'Begging pardon, Ma'am. He don't know who he is nor where he is neither – lucky man.'

'What do you mean?' Lady Blackwood's voice was so haughty sometimes. Jane pinched her lips together.

'He came the other day. I thought he'd gone.'

'A soldier should be upstairs.'

Ali arrived back with a cup of water, which Lady Blackwood sniffed suspiciously. 'Where did you get this?'

Ali shrugged and pointed into the darkness.

'I have no wish to kill him!' She emptied the water on the ground, where it lay before gradually seeping into the saturated earth. 'Get it from the fountain.'

Ali shrugged and gave Jane a sideways smile. It was hard to know whose side to be on.

When Ali returned, Lady Blackwood rubbed the rim of the cup in her skirt before pouring the first drops. The soldier's lips parted. His adam's apple rose and fell.

'Ali, take him upstairs. Up!' she said, pointing at the sky.

Ali shook his head. 'Not dead.'

'No, the hospital, I mean.'

'Ah.' Ali grinned at Jane. 'He die there soon. Very soon.'

This was not a matter for a smile, but Ali was so friendly. Jane had no wish to be seen as disagreeable in any way. She had no wish either to sit with Lady Blackwood, especially while being watched by the woman with the marble skin. But when Lady Blackwood sat and patted the bottom step, she could not refuse.

'At the moment, I don't think we can afford to have feelings, Jane. They will only hinder us.'

Calmness, action: this must be the way of a lady.

'We should make a list of all the things we should do and all the things we need.' Lady Blackwood unclipped a small notebook and pencil from another chain on her belt.

A woman Jane had not seen before, with cheeks sunken and the mouth of one who has no teeth, came out of the cellar to watch Ali struggle up the steps with the man. Just a thin cotton skirt she had, with a piece of cloth tied round her neck to cover her front.

'You!' Lady Blackwood said. Jane bit her lip. She did not mean anything by it, but Lady Blackwood spoke in a way that would have made her brothers angry. 'What is your name?'

'Mrs Naylor, Ma'am. Resident of hell.'

'That is talk I do not appreciate, Mrs Naylor. Fighting spirit is what we need. Come and help us. I have so many questions. Tell me about food.'

Mrs Naylor took a step forward, but kept her distance. 'What food?'

'You must have food to live.'

'We eat when we can, whatever we can. Sometimes the men bring us things. Some of the Turks are kind.'

Lady Blackwood pursed her lips. 'How do you cook?'

'Same as them upstairs – pots in the kitchen.'

'Fuel?'

'All the trees are gone for miles around. There's always people selling things but we've no money. We earns it when we're desperate, some other way.'

Lady Blackwood cleared her throat. 'And the third – bodily function. Where do you... relieve yourselves?'

'Where we can. We tried outside at first, but most move back... Can't see nothing there.'

The silence hung heavily. For a long moment the muscles in Lady Blackwood's face twitched. Her eyes flicked from side to side. She's like me, Jane thought, wanting to get up and turn away. But she can't and neither can I.

Mrs Naylor stayed standing in front of them. So thin she was, with her bones all sharp and her eyes with all life washed from them. Her feet were swollen, ugly, not like human feet at all, with bloodied sores and cracks that made you wince for knowing how painful they would be.

'We'd not have got this far if we'd not the fighting spirit, Ma'am,' she said quietly.

Lady Blackwood was not used to being spoken to unless in answer to her question.

'We all come down from Varna. Marched all the way with the children and babes. Weeks it took. Some didn't make it this far. We had nowhere to go, see, when the men went for the fighting – the ones who hadn't died of the fever waiting. No-one thought of us – the wives, cooks and washerwomen. When we drew stones back in England, us wives, to see who would go, we thought we were the lucky ones.'

Lady Blackwood cleared her throat. She turned to Jane.

'Varna, Jane, is a long way from Constantinople.'

Mrs Naylor stared into the distance. This was a story that was two things at once: shocking and stunning. Walking all that way with no proper shoes on your feet! That was as brave a thing to do as any Jane had heard. Wales to Barnet was an achievement to be proud of – well, Reverend Blackwood said it was and so had Isaac. But that was truly nothing.

I have been guilty of pride and I'm sorry for it, God. And now I will make up for it. I will.

And after everything they had endured, to be pushed into the Barracks cellar and forgotten. Hard to know which was worse: to be a man, fighting for nothing you understood, being injured so your life would never be the same; or a woman, forgotten and invisible.

'I think we should pray,' Lady Blackwood said. 'I am feeling the need for help to begin this task, Jane. *Dear Lord, do not forsake us. We are mortals and we need Your help. Help us, we pray.* Jane? Have you anything to add?'

'*Amen.*'

That afternoon men arrived, ordered from Ali by Lady Blackwood, to make improvements. They'd faces like chestnuts with bright eyes, baggy trousers and cloths round their heads and over their shoulders. The cloth was wool, sheep's wool. Like theirs back home, only a different brown. They must have carded it, spun it and woven it just like they did in Tŷ Mawr.

A faint haunting sound drifted over the Barracks. Immediately the men fell onto their knees, holding their hands in front of them and bowing down until their foreheads touched the earth.

'Gracious! They are praying, Jane,' Lady Blackwood explained. 'I thank the Lord I am Church of England.'

A walk is stretched and lonesome when you are wretched in your own thoughts. She should not be here. She should be walking up the lane to Tŷ Mawr with the hedges on either side, the oak at the fork, the fields all fitting together, tucked into the valleys and folded into the hills. That's where she belonged. A wave of longing swept over her. A yearning. Deep inside. *Hiraeth.*

Here, she was of no use to herself nor anyone. A person has to be strong and powerful with no shame or fear to be of use in a situation like this. Lady Blackwood was born to it. She was not. The problem was too big and she was too small; she should have stayed at home. She thought she could face anything because she knew nothing. She had no good feeling about herself at all.

CHAPTER 20

A Helper, Not a Nurse

WORDS MUST HAVE lifted from Jane's Bible pillow in the night, for they were there in her mind as she woke.

Wait on the Lord: be of good courage, and He shall strengthen thine heart. Wait, I say, on the Lord.

Too dark it had been to read *y Beibl* when Jane climbed up onto her shelf in the mother's mother's house the previous night, and lay with her head on its hard cover. Waiting is what she would do then, though it might mean the attending kind of wait as well as the patient kind. Both would be fine.

What a country. No understanding this weather. This day's bitter wind made the walk along the cliff hard. Clouds spread over the entire sky like a lid. Dismal and cold as it was, her heart was the stronger.

A woman with a large bundle stood waiting under the arch of the Barracks. Like a beetle, she scuttled towards them, bent right over with a black shawl covering her head, blocking their way. She opened her bundle there in the mud. Bread. She nodded and thrust half a warm loaf into Jane's hands. She brought her hands to her mouth. Her gesture changed, flicking her thumb over her fingers repeatedly.

'Money,' Lady Blackwood said. 'At least there is bread to be bought. Come.'

Money certainly was the way to solve a few problems. Once at Tŷ Mawr they had had no oatmeal and no money either. Sour bread made from acorn flour was all they had until a pig was sold. How wretched and hungry they'd been. And this was so much worse. Without money, the women in the cellar were powerless.

As they arrived at the cellar, the first snowflakes fell. Soon it was swirling round like feathers, flakes spiralling up as others tumbled down, white on the foulness of the courtyard. Mrs Naylor stood in the cellar doorway rubbing her arms.

'We're minus two, Ma'am. Mrs Hicks and Mrs Bailey died in the night.'

'Fever?' Lady Blackwood pursed her lips.

'Fever, Ma'am.'

'I do not like this, Jane.'

Death. Now that was something you could never get used to, a test to all faith. The preacher might say what he liked, but it was never enough. Here it was easier not to know a person's name, a help to think of them as minus two – though in this place, death might not be such a terrible thing.

'Miss Nightingale has asked for a report on the courtyard, Jane. A little weather must not daunt us!'

Lady Blackwood had her umbrella; Jane the shawl Lady Blackwood presented her after Jane had given her own away, saying, 'Acting on impulse is not always sensible, Jane.' The shawl was by far the finest Jane had ever had, but not the warmest. If only she had David's coat. Mrs Bowman should never have taken it. Rather, she should not have allowed Mrs Bowman to take it. The snow fell fat and white, dissolving into the muddy ground, though sprinkling the soaked grass roofs in white.

'Mrs Naylor is to move the mothers and babies near the cellar entrance in our absence. Two hundred and thirty women and children were counted yesterday. Did you know that, Jane? Let's see what they can manage for themselves. You may hold the umbrella.'

Not an easy task, though it took her mind from feeling awkward. Lady Blackwood was tall and would change directions unexpectedly, skipping over puddles to walk on drier ground, darting sideways to peer behind a stall or under a crate. Imagine, the men there, or the women, seeing her dancing after Lady Blackwood. What would they think? A lady's maid with no more use to her than that. If only she were given a chance to do more. 'Keep up, Jane!' was all Lady Blackwood said, as though she was dawdling on purpose.

Lady Blackwood was forever 'tsk-tsking' and shaking her head but the truth was, nothing here was as terrible as the cellar. A broken cart provided shelter for the top half of a soldier in a filthy coat. His legs were dusted with snow.

'Remind me to check on the way back, Jane, to see if he has moved.'

Soldiers huddled round a heap of rubbish, smoking, drinking – keeping a Turkish pedlar busy, poised ready to pour, holding out his hand to grab the coins. Not a drop would he give until the money was in his purse.

'The Devil's at work in this place, Jane!' Lady Blackmore muttered, as she passed swiftly on. Such a certainty she had about everything.

No-one in their right mind thinks drunkenness a good thing, but you could understand anyone here drinking themselves into numbness. If you want evidence of the Devil's work, look in the cellar, or the hospital wards – though Jane did not believe in the Devil. If monsters didn't really exist, nor those giants and ogres of the stories – why should the Devil? He was something made up to keep children scared and good. Evil was the work of bad men.

The fourth side of the courtyard was burned out completely. The fire that had raged must have been monstrous. Hard to imagine on a day like this, but flames must have leapt to the skies. And the heat! No-one would have been able to get near it. Quite ruined it was now, the damage unrepaired with no roof tiles on the blackened rafters. The steps still looked sturdy. Jane must test their strength. Lady Blackwood followed her.

Brown eyes peered out from every corner, until you thought you would go mad with everyone looking at you. Every broken tile, half-burned piece of timber and broken glass had been used to make shelters. It took the breath away, the inventiveness of it all.

The whinny of a horse was a joy in this mad world, not striking Jane as odd, for nothing was odd any more.

'Gracious! Stables. Well, I never!'

More horses than stables. A group of them stood gloomily with their eyes shut and coats darkening. Animals are all the same – what they don't see isn't happening.

Two boys stood flat to the wall under the roof – a Turkish boy and an English boy with a bandaged arm in a dirty sling. He saluted them with his good arm.

'Ma'am! Cavalry, Ma'am. What's left of them.'

The horse nearest Jane shuddered violently and coughed in painful spasms. A man lurched out of the stables. His face was red and fleshy; he stood unsteadily, staring at them. He'd not listen to her. Better to alert the boys.

'That horse is not well at all!' Jane said.

'He's not!' the man agreed, slurring his words. 'Nor's any of 'em. Still, better to peg it here than shot by Rooshains. That's what I say.'

'I think we have seen enough,' Lady Blackwood said briskly. Horses, now, *that* Jane could have helped with. She knew about them. She understood. But women – she was not suited to women at all.

Back in the cellar, Jane wrapped her soaking shawl round her waist like an overskirt. If she put it down, she'd not see it again. Mothers and babies pressed together in the cellar entrance and the light like sheep on a cold night. There she was! The baby she, Jane, had helped into the world. The mother, her friend and the baby in her arms, right at her feet. Now that was something to lift the spirits!

'I've been searching and searching,' Jane said, crouching, not wanting to be above them.

The friend shrugged. 'I've a bad feeling about them both.'

Her face was sour, now seen in the light.

'Don't say that!' Jane said quickly. 'Keep the baby warm as you can,' she said, fastening the shawl over her head. 'You've got to look out for them both now, do you hear?'

Not as hard as she would have imagined, giving orders to these women, older than her though they were. She had no requisition slip. Lady Blackwood was busy, but this was an emergency.

The kitchen was a damp basement room the far side of the rickety steps, the tiny windows running with water inside. Two of the older nurses, sleeves rolled above their elbows, stirred vast coppers. Orderlies queued for their rations of raw meat. Standing waiting with so much at stake was not easy. At last the nurse in charge turned to her.

'List?'

'I need milk. There's a baby dying.'

'There's many dying. Where's your slip?'

'Just a little, please.'

The old nurse looked at her, sucking air through her cheeks. 'You'll get me in trouble. Here, this is all I can spare.'

There was barely enough to cover the bottom of the cup.

'It'll be worse tomorrow. More on their way. I've not enough to feed a hundred and we've near two thousand.'

The friend was standing where Jane had left her, with the baby in her arms.

'Do you want to feed her?' Jane said, offering her the cup.

The woman shook her head and handed the baby to Jane. So small and light she was. Jane touched her lips with the cup. Nothing. No response.

The world stopped turning.

'Give her to me,' the woman said.

This could not be. The desolation could barely be kept inside. How could Jane be so undone? One tiny baby. Lost was all sense of what was big and what small.

'Jane! What's the matter with you?' Lady Blackwood had caught her again. 'Pull yourself together. Run upstairs and find where to go for supplies. We need cups and blankets immediately.'

Thank God, or God through Lady Blackwood, for giving her an order – simple. She must do something that took her away, fast; that made her legs and body work, not her feelings. Up the rickety stairs and into the lobby she ran. Breathless, she stopped at the top of the steps. Two orderlies with the ropey arms of older men were struggling down the lobby steps opposite her towards the outer arch of the Barracks where a bullock cart stood waiting, snow on his horns. A soldier hung between them, wearing nothing but a thin shirt. They shouldn't be taking him out in the snow. What were they thinking of?

One grabbed the man's feet, the other his arms and with a sudden heave they threw him up into the cart. The shock of it! She had not thought him dead. But of course he was.

She *should* have known. Punches came from everywhere. Constantly reeling Jane was, like that poor man fighting Mr Jerrard in the back of the Drover's Inn, cowering and bloodied, hands over his face, doing nothing to protect himself.

A nurse came down the stairs into the lobby in her long grey tweed dress, the Scutari sash across her chest. 'You'll get used to it.'

'I don't want to get used to it.' Truly she did not.

'Believe me, you do! What do you want up here?' the nurse asked. 'I'm Nurse O'Connor. You're Jane, aren't you? I heard about you.'

It's unnerving to find you are known to a person you did not know existed. 'I was sent to ask where to get blankets.'

'Blankets!' Nurse O'Connor laughed. 'Chance would be a fine thing. There's nothing to be had here without a requisition slip. And no provision for women at all! Rules and regulations! The Purveyor is king – he's sitting on a treasure trove of the things we need and will he let anything out of his sight? No, he won't! Not without the right docket!'

Jane sat on the top step. She should not be here. If only Aunt Anni were by her side, she'd talk sense. 'Self-pity's a wasted feeling,' she'd say and she'd be right. How could Jane feel so bad for herself, with those women suffering so, and those poor boys, no older than David, dying with no-one to care or even know. Boys who *had* to come.

The young lad with his arm in a sling was walking through the courtyard. About William's age but with straight brown hair falling over his eyes. He stopped, scraped up a handful of snow, shaped it into a ball and tossed it in the air. He saw Jane and smiled. A powerful thing, a smile, in such a place. William would have thrown it hard at her face for certain, but this boy threw it on the ground.

'Saw you just now. I'm Bobby Robinson, Miss Nightingale's messenger.'

'What happened to your arm?'

'Shot at Alma. Ain't too bad. Led them into battle with my drumming. I'll not drum again. Still, a messenger's better than a drummer, I reckon.' He was a boy, but spoke like the soldier he was pretending to be. 'What's your name?'

'Jane. Jane Evans.'

'Pleased to meet you, Jane.' He ran up the steps and saluted her with a click of his heels. His smile dropped. He was looking past her into the lobby. 'Are you alright, sir?'

A soldier in a ripped red coat stood swaying, about to fall. There was no saving him. He was past that point. His weight took him tumbling back down the steps. He must have come through the Barrack arch by himself. He was a grown man and Bobby only a boy with one good arm. The steps were slippery with snow.

'I can manage!' Bobby said.

'I know you can, but he could just hook the other arm round my neck.'

'I'm sorry,' the soldier moaned.

'No need,' Jane said. 'Are you hurt bad?'

He winced as she stretched his arm along her shoulder. 'Am I making it worse?'

'No.' He wiped his face with his free hand. His fingers were long and lean, but cut and bleeding. Together they lugged him up to the lobby, Bobby keeping one step ahead. Lovely hair the soldier had on him, black and curling. And crawling! His arms too and his neck, thick with vermin and now she would be too. Dreadful, this fine man in such a terrible state. An orderly came running down the stairs. He'd white side-whiskers like sheep's tails down either side of his face.

'Alright, sir. Let's get you up to the officer's ward. I'll take over, Missy.'

Such a look he gave Jane, as though she was meddling where she shouldn't. An officer! But what difference did it make? He was a wounded soldier.

'Thanks, Jane,' Bobby said quickly. He must have seen the hurt on her face. 'He didn't know you for a nurse. Without the uniform.'

'Thanks, Jane,' the officer echoed.

'I was wondering, Lady Blackwood, Ma'am,' Jane said, after delivering the news about the blankets. 'If I should wear a uniform?'

'Uniform?' Lady Blackwood stared at Jane as though she were a cockroach. Had she returned with better news, perhaps Lady Blackwood would have been more amenable. 'What uniform?'

'Like the nurses.'

'But you are not a nurse, Jane, are you? More a helper.'

A helper. Like a child when she was not a child at all. The child left far behind in Wales. And in her own clothes Jane would have to stay, and no-one would know who she was nor why she was there, just as she herself did not.

CHAPTER 21

Comfort

IT WAS HARD to say day by day that things were improving until you stopped and saw everything was less bad, though still worse than you had ever experienced in your life before arriving here. There were ways to act without Lady Blackwood's orders: feeding a child when the soup was running through her fingers and she had no spoon; drawing the tooth of a woman whose face was stretched like a pig's bladder. Small deeds – great satisfaction!

A marvellous organiser was Lady Blackwood. She must be admired for that: unruffled and calm, crisp in her silk clothes with her back still straight and her cuffs clean. With the women's cellar more ordered, Jane was lent upstairs when asked for. In the hospital wards things were as bad as they had ever been. Desperate men arrived continually, the need for bandages constant. A storeroom had been cleared in the cellar on the far side of the courtyard, with access from a staircase in the far lobby. There Jane helped rip linen into bandages or stuff sacking with straw for mattresses. Such a relief it was to listen to the nurses' chatter after the silence of the cellar. There, no-one had the spirit to talk and nothing to talk about either.

'Did you hear?' Nurse O'Connor said, always full of news. Great meaty forearms she had, and a great ripping style. 'Queen Victoria herself has sent a Christmas letter to us all.'

'Christmas!'

'Did it steal up and take you by surprise, Jane? The festive season's done nothing to anyone here. Tempers and arguments such as you can't believe! A button in the meat... men not paying for their drinks... a bonnet not suiting... jealousy worse than the cholera! You'd think with all these men to choose from...'

The air was thick with tiny fragments of torn fibre.

'How people can argue here, of all places, is beyond belief!' Jane said.

Nurse O'Connor laughed. 'How old did you say you were, Jane? Arguing is what makes people human. If the small things are large, you don't have to worry about the really big things. That's what makes the world go round.'

Was she always to be treated as ignorant and laughed at? There was plenty Jane knew that Nurse O'Connor did not.

An older sister came bustling into the store room to pick up supplies. She'd a black gown and a white cap that should have been starched, but was sagging like a bird with broken wings. A tiny Christ hung on a cross round her neck. Wasn't there enough dying here? If you had a cross at all, it should be empty after Christ had risen and left His body behind.

'You'll have to work faster than this!' she said.

'A Roman,' Nurse O'Connor said, wrinkling her nose. 'Jane – did you hear about Nurse Hopkins?' There was a gleam in her eyes. 'Sent home in disgrace.' When Jane asked no questions, she added, 'Found with a soldier. What's the harm, I say. Those French have got the right idea if you ask me. Bring their own comfort. Who thinks about our boys' needs? It's a service, that's my way of looking at it.'

One of the younger orderlies stuck his head round the door and whistled loudly.

'You're wanted!' he said to Nurse O'Connor.

'No rest for the wicked,' she said, passing her half-rolled bandage to Jane.

When two start a job together and one leaves, it's lonesome. Jane's hands were sore. There was no lanolin here to rub into them. Right, wrong? *In disgrace with a soldier.* Not the first and not the last. Everything is challenged here. Lady Blackwood would be scandalised. Fixed were all her thoughts about life, fed to her whole on a silver spoon when she sat on her velvet cushion in her high chair. Most certainly the soldiers' needs were not considered. Though never had Jane thought of it as a need. Food, yes. Comfort, now that was the word. Had they not comfort women in Wales? The young boys talked of them, the older ones disappeared up into the hills above Pumsaint and returned without comment.

Perhaps if you had been married and lost your husband, it wasn't so wrong. And what about Christ and Mary Magdalene with her evil spirits and sin? Christ forgave her and she was his friend. David told her when she was young that Mary Magdalene was a comfort woman, but Jane hadn't known what he meant. David told her to ask the preacher, who hit her on the head with his Bible when she did. David nearly split himself in two laughing.

The window from the cellar store room was high up. It looked out onto the courtyard. Only feet and legs to the knees could be seen, often bare and plastered in mud, with an occasional pair of wooden shoes or scuffed boots.

As Jane looked up, there, framed in the high window, was a pair of black polished riding boots. They moved away, one foot dragging slightly after the other.

She could not say if the weakness started in her legs and rose up, or in her head and flooded down through her body. A weakness, like a faint, squeezed her stomach and set her heart fluttering like a moth behind glass, leaving her damp and breathless. How glad she was that Nurse O'Connor had been called away so she could not see the colour rising in her neck. God works in mysterious ways indeed.

If she stood on tiptoes and craned her neck, she could see him. That same officer. Someone had cleaned his coat and his boots. He steadied himself on the shafts of the broken cart. He had a look of Isaac about him, standing with his weight on one foot, his shoulders broad and strong.

Christmas Day itself was a day like any other apart from the Reverend arriving to conduct a short service in one of the wards, which was serving as a chapel. Mrs Haskins, a woman in a poorly way, asked Jane to take her baby.

'Do, Jane,' begged Mrs Naylor. Faint wisps of hair covered her head now, but she'd sores and cracks on her head that should have been hidden by hair. 'You can't start a child soon enough with religion. Give us some peace at the same time, Jane. It's not much to ask, is it?'

Certainly it wasn't, though Jane was not the type to take a baby for the love of jiggling it about as some women were.

Listening to the Christmas story with a baby in your arms made the words different. Mary must have looked down on that tiny peaceful face asleep on the hay. Jesus would not have had this white pinched look to him. He'd have been more like a Turkish baby, with big eyes and brown skin.

The baby began to wriggle. Jane shifted it to the other arm. The Reverend was saying a prayer.

'Lord, be with us. Teach us humility to submit to Your will in all things, knowing that You, Lord, in Your infinite wisdom, have a plan for us, even though we may not comprehend what that plan may be.'

Devise a plan, write it down and you were halfway to solving the problem. That was Lady Blackwood's way. But

God, the bigger plan... that was harder. More like a plan gone wrong. Submitting was not easy. Not necessarily right. Not in every situation. Not if you knew what you were being asked to submit to was wrong.

Singing came from a place untroubled with thinking. Carols were rousing, the tunes familiar. Every face was hopeful. Everyone a servant in the eyes of the Lord, even Lady Blackwood with her nose pinched and her cheeks flushed, Emma and Ebba with their eyes closed and plaits quivering; nurses, orderlies, some of the women and children from the cellar, wounded men – the ones who could totter from their beds – all were present.

And there he was again. The officer. In the very front row. His coat like the holly, as red as any blood, his dark hair curling over his collar. He moved his head from side to side, singing up to the roof, out of the window. Before she could look away, he had caught her eye with his. Stronger was the feeling that flooded through her than the shaft of Christmas light which broke at that very moment through the open window, illuminating a patch of flaking plaster right above the Reverend's head.

The courtyard was more crowded than ever. Christmas was good for business, especially in this winter sun. Mrs Naylor queued by a drink seller with her arm round Mrs Haskins' waist. How peeving. It was not for this kind of peace she had taken the baby. Taking advantage, in Jane's book.

'Mrs Haskins!' The baby stretched out his arms and started wailing, desperate to be away.

Mrs Naylor rounded on her, clearly not grateful or contrite in the least.

'It's Christmas Day, Jane. Who are you to judge us?'

She had said nothing! All she was doing was returning

the baby. Judge them? Was that how she was seen? Too long with Lady Blackwood, was that it? Did the women not see her as having a mind of her own?

Jane sat on the bottom step and lifted the baby to her shoulder. If his empty stomach was pressed, perhaps he would stop grumbling.

Bobby Robinson pushed through the crowd.

'Hello, Jane! Look what he gave me.' He held up a shiny gun cartridge.

'Who?'

'Him.'

Bobby flicked the bullet casing in front of the baby to catch the sun. The baby wailed, quite beyond distraction.

The officer, leaning on a barrel, lifted his mug and smiled at them.

'On the mend, is he? That's good.' Speaking fast hid her fluster. Quite sick she felt, suddenly, and ridiculous, knowing that now she would be seeing him raising that mug over and over that day, and at night she would lie awake for hours with her hands clasped between her legs to contain herself, with *y Beibl* hard under her head.

CHAPTER 22

Shock and Exhaustion

WHEN EVERYTHING IS unexpected, nothing surprises any more.

'Come and look, Jane!' Bobby was waiting for her on her way down to the cellar one morning. He'd a cream envelope in his hand. he led her to the lobby, where a black woman in a large yellow hat and a blue and white striped skirt was walking down the far stairs to the arch.

'Did you see her face?' Bobby said.

'I did.'

'Black.'

Her clothes were more astonishing. Such a hat, and the stripes on her dress so joyful.

Bobby turned the envelope over in his hand.

'For Miss Nightingale!' he said. 'Have you smelt the bread cooking, Jane? A man came all the way from London to make it for us, 'cos he says fresh bread will turn the fortunes of the war.'

'I hope he's right, though it seems like madness to me,' Jane shrugged.

'It's all mad,' Bobby said cheerfully. 'Sanitary inspectors are arriving from England today and I'm to show them round.' He looked at the envelope in his hand, from a boat docked that morning from England. 'Says "Urgent".'

'Have we our orders?' Jane asked Lady Blackwood, as she hung her shawl on one of the hooks Ali's father had put up on the wooden beam. He would not touch the brick pillars. Such a weight above depended on them. Happier than Jane had seen her, Lady Blackwood sat behind the table Ali's father had made for her. Now she could sort her papers and place them in neat piles: jobs already completed on one side; jobs to be completed on another. She was reading the letter Bobby had just delivered.

A sacking screen had been fixed across the cellar to the right of the table for the birthing. Screams cannot be kept out by a piece of sacking, but this was the nearest to privacy that could be achieved. The room doubled as a place where the dead could wait until they were collected by the ox cart. Silence, like noise, had a way of seeping through sackcloth.

'Requests, Jane. They are requests.'

Orders – when spoken to Jane, whatever Lady Blackwood might like to call them.

'Oh dear.' Lady Blackwood's sigh was long. 'This cholera's getting the upper hand, I fear. One might have hoped for good news from the front by now. Oh, Jane. A letter has come for you.'

'For me?'

'It's been on quite a journey, Jane, but it has found you – a miracle of a kind.' Lady Blackwood smiled as she passed the letter to her.

Isaac's hand. Jane's heart was beating fit to burst. She stuffed it quickly down her shirt. She must wait. She could not open it here. But she could not wait. At every step it crinkled. She must find a quiet spot, with light. Behind the screen was ideal.

With shaking fingers, she peeled it open.

The words of Griffith Evans to his sister Jane, 4th day of March.

Written by Isaac Davis, cousin.

Jane

You should not have done what you did. It was wrong and unchristian thinking only of yourself. The Bible tells us to think of others. It tells us to honour our father and mother. They are gone so you should honour me, Jane. I was not thinking of myself. I have not done so in all my life. I cannot. I am the eldest. I have to think of Tŷ Mawr, for no-one else will. All the lives — people, animals — the house and all the moneys, every day as it arrives, with no end. And the future too. It is not for me to wonder what I want.

Mr Morgan has been a good friend to Tŷ Mawr all his life. It was a small thing, Jane. You would not have moved far. You could have had care of your pigs. Think of all the pigs that will not now be born because of you.

He is a fair man and not a beater like some. You know him for what he is. A stranger might be more to your liking at first but later his darkness would let you down. There would be no letting down with Mr Morgan.

And what of us, with everyone laughing and judging? And Mr Morgan. What of him? It is hard to say this to your sister but I hope I will see you no more. I do not want to know what has happened to you. You might as well be dead. No,

185

that would be better, for then I would think kindly of you and visit your grave. I have no kind thought of you, Jane, nor any thought at all.

Griffith

Terrible, terrible words. How could he be so cruel, so unfeeling? Jane crushed the letter in her hand, then remembered it was written by Isaac so smoothed it across her body. All in Isaac's hand and no message from him at all. Now would Isaac see everything as Griffith saw it and agree with him? Why could Isaac not have explained to Griffith that being sold to a horrible old man was certainly not a little thing... Indeed it was not. Isaac should have told Griffith that everything was God's will. How could she have done other than obey Him? *That* would have been wrong! What a terrible brother he was, to be sure. *He* was the one thinking only of himself, and yet he had no understanding of it.

March! Eleven months it had taken to reach her. For certain, he had not received her letter written in Southampton when he wrote it. By now he must feel differently, yet the power of this letter shattered her.

Could Isaac not have refused to write such words? At least, he did not need to send them.

Never would she go home, whatever happened. And now the thought of that was like falling into the deepest bottomless pit of nothingness. She would not think of Griffith or Tŷ Mawr more, just as he would not think of her.

The vicious summer heat burning and drying the world helped make it impossible to think of cool green fields and icy rivers. Insects desperate for blood plagued the sickest women most, finding sore places to settle and poison. Terrible that children grew so used to flies crusting their eyes and dry lips, they barely brushed them away. The stench intensified. The lice swarmed. Rats plagued them all.

Exasperated, Lady Blackwood ordered every item of clothing burned and the whole cellar scrubbed with paraffin. Everyone was to be issued with new clothes donated in the 'Free Gifts' from England. The children and sickest women were to sit in the courtyard until the fumes did not sting their eyes. But the courtyard scorched so in the sun, they had to move round with the meagre shade like a sundial.

Lady Blackwood was suffering from exhaustion. Jane must manage on her own for a few days while she rested. Kept busy, Jane now had no time for worry, no chance to sink into the misery inside herself since Griffith's cruel letter. No thoughts of the past or the future pulled her away from the day she was in. All was smooth as smooth.

At the end of the day Lady Blackwood returned, Jane was sitting with the women to eat on a spotless floor near the entrance to catch any movement in the air. Lamps hung from Ali's hooks created pools of light, though attracting insects in their thousands, casting strange moving shadows on the floor and making the recesses darker.

Eating was a silent time. The stew was watery with no sustenance in it at all. Jane's gums were tender. Gnawing dry bread was a tussle between pain and hunger. No herb robert or greater plantains grew in these parts. A worrisome thought that your teeth might be working themselves loose. There's no second chance with teeth. No, she must not allow her thoughts to burrow inside. Stop them with a text!

My God, my strength, in whom I will trust.

She had thought Lady Blackwood had gone, when her voice, always till now calm and controlled, came raging from the recesses of the cellar.

'Out soldier! Out! I will not tolerate this lewd behaviour. We have children here!'

Lady Blackwood had flushed a woman from the dark, naked apart from a shawl which barely covered her shoulders. Her breasts were so small. A large, brutish soldier stumbled after her, fumbling with himself. However quickly a person turns away, it is never before you have seen that hideous part – gross, swollen. One woman giggled, but most acted as though nothing had happened. Lady Blackwood confronting this beast was a stirring sight. Her arm was straight, pointing all the way to the tip of her finger.

'Don't you curse at me, soldier!'

His face was hard, rough. His fists curled at his sides.

Jane knew the signs. Hadn't she seen them often enough? She knew what to do. On her feet she was, as he drew breath to hurl who knew what filth at Lady Blackwood, stepping between them and speaking straight into his face: not harsh but gentle, soothing. His face changed from angry to leering. He lunged for her. Seeing him off balance, Jane dodged to one side and pushed him out.

From the dark behind her, a woman cheered. Someone banged a plate with a spoon.

Lady Blackwood said curtly, 'Thank you, Jane,' before turning on the woman. 'And as for you, Mrs Hunt...'

Mrs Hunt was fastening her blouse. 'What do you know about anything, you with your airs and graces?' she shouted. 'It's all very well for you. Back to your husband each night. Brought him with you, didn't you? And what about us, eh? Husbands dead and buried and us with no money... anything to escape all this, this...' her arms flailed about '...hell!'

With a toss of her head, she flounced out. The spoon was banged again, twice, halting as silence fell. It was a hard situation with right on both sides.

Lady Blackwood picked up her notes.

'Things seem to have been allowed to deteriorate in my week of absence. A pity,' she said as she left. So grossly unfair, and Jane must say nothing. She crashed the plates together and threw them into the tin tub. Mrs Hunt was right! What did Lady Blackwood know?

Jane's name was on the rota and Mrs Naylor's not at all, but she stayed to help stack the plates.

'Don't think bad of Mrs Hunt, Jane. Her friend died last night. Helped each other all the way from Varna.'

The plates were greasy, the water cold. And now Jane's feelings were all up and down again. Imagine, seeing your friend die, washing her naked body, sewing her into a sheet, staying with her behind the screen until the orderly took her away. No surprise that Mrs Hunt sought comfort. Jane carried the dirty water across the courtyard to throw it down the pit dug at the side of the courtyard near where the rubbish was burned. Being so close to death, it was no wonder a person would try to feel alive in whatever way was in their power.

One lamp was to be left burning, with Mrs Naylor charged with extinguishing it. Low on oil. That must be added to the list for the Purveyor.

'Goodnight!' Jane said.

'Goodnight, Jane!' The voices came from many places. She left with a lighter heart.

A small fire was burning in the courtyard next to one of the drinking stalls. Mrs Hunt sat on the end of the cart swinging her legs. Poor Mrs Hunt. Jane had been too quick to judge.

A man in the shadows stood holding the wheel, running his hand up and down her leg. She stopped, numb. So much she did not want it to be – she looked down, but had to check... of course it was: *her* officer! All charitable feelings vanished as a fury swept through her. Had there been any child near, she would have grabbed it, slapped it and shouted, shaking it by the shoulders until it cried.

Sitting in the courtyard beside the abandoned cart in the heat of the next morning, washing screaming children from a bucket between her legs, did nothing to change Jane's mood. Perhaps she was a little on the rough side and held their arms more firmly than sometimes.

A madness it was, she could see that now, to allow her feelings to turn her stupid. Why would a man, any man, look at her when they had the likes of Mrs Hunt available to them, swinging her legs like that with hardly a stitch to cover her? Who could blame him? It was a lesson. She must remember who she was, what was expected of her, and be as useful as she could be. That was why she had begun the day taking the bandages she had rolled herself, unbidden, up to the ward. All would have been fine had Nurse O'Connor, taking the bandages, not mentioned the numbers of men she had dying of the cholera, as though Jane had life easy in the cellar.

'We've cholera there too. Deaths every night,' Jane had said, with some heat.

She could not help noticing Nurse O'Connor's sash, when Jane had none.

As she began the long walk back down the ward, an elderly nurse came from a side ward, following a man in a blood-stained white coat who picked his way as if avoiding cow muck in a farmyard. He'd socks pulled up over his trousers. Two orderlies came towards him, meeting at a mattress halfway down the ward. The soldier on the mattress squealed and scuttled back against the wall, shaking.

'No, no... it's better! I can feel it.'

Such a look in his eyes, like a rabbit under the cosh. Jane, not the old nurse with a sour face and eyes, unaware of what was going on, took the soldier's hands, soothing the fingers, all thoughts of Mrs Hunt vanished. This she could do without a thought. Men or animals are alike: a calm voice will talk them docile. Quietened, the poor boy allowed the orderlies to pick him up and carry him down the ward. Jane followed, babbling on about the streams and the pastures and the birds in the hedges, though the smell of his leg, hanging down putrid and black, made her sick to her stomach.

At the end of the ward, the man with the bloody coat picked up a terrible-looking saw he'd left against the wall.

'Thank you, nurse,' he muttered.

Nurse! Jane looked round but the sour-faced nurse was nowhere. He knew her for a nurse! But when she arrived back in the cellar and happened to mention it to Lady Blackwood, her answer was: 'Not now, Jane. You've the children to prepare.'

A new arrangement this was: mothers and children badgering the Purveyor for rations themselves, and a fine job they did of it, screaming and crying and banging their tins till the poor man could stand it no longer.

'When you have finished, Jane, I would like a word with you,' Lady Blackwood called from the cellar entrance.

What had she done now – or not done? Here she was again, vexed and worried. Why does someone sitting behind a desk always make you feel like a child at school, like when she had stood in front of Mr Norris' desk after she bit Thelma Jones on the arm. How could she have explained to him what it felt like to have the other children snorting at her, holding their noses as she passed, curling away if she came too near them?

She stood waiting until Lady Blackwood looked up. 'Ah, Jane. Miss Nightingale wishes to see you.'

'Me?'

Lady Blackwood smiled. 'Is that so strange?'

'I've done nothing, Ma'am. You know that. Not the milk, surely – it was only a drop and it was a matter of life or death.'

'Jane. Why must you think badly of yourself when others think highly of you?'

Highly? Of her? Now that was a new thought, for no-one – certainly not Lady Blackwood – had ever given her a hint of such a feeling.

A staircase of iron spiralled round the tower at the end of the first corridor. Miss Nightingale's quarters were at the top. Dizzy Jane was when she arrived at the door. Dry as dirt her mouth, not a drop of moisture. If she was asked to speak, she'd have no voice.

What must she look like? Her hair wild with no cap and her skirt not yet replaced. If only she'd had a uniform! That child had sicked on her dress that very morning and she had not bothered to clean herself properly.

She could not stay here forever. She knocked.

'Come!'

Like Lady Blackwood, Miss Nightingale sat at a desk covered with paper in neat piles, the edges all together. Her ink pot was open; she wrote busily, her pen flowing over the pages. She did not look up.

A light airy room it was. A breeze fluttered the pages. Outside the high window birds, screamed to and fro. Martins, with nests right under her roof.

'I have a fine view of Constantinople, Miss Evans. Take a look from the window!'

Miss Nightingale was smiling at her, no anger or disaproval in her grey eyes.

'I have had a good report of you, Miss Evans. I have consulted with Lady Alicia. I witnessed you myself just now in the ward downstairs.'

All of a fluster Jane was to have been watched and not to have known it.

Miss Nightingale held the cream envelope in the air. 'Authority at last. I am to visit the hospitals in the Crimea. Would you come with me to Balaclava? The need for nurses is great there too.'

Too full for speech, Jane nodded.

'Within a few days, Jane. Time to make a few arrangements. Having waited so long, I wish to be away at once. Bobby will be part of the team, and Mrs Brown my new companion.'

CHAPTER 23

Forsaken

'THE BLACK SEA'S a ridiculous name,' Jane said to Bobby, who was hanging over the side of the *Empress of India* to catch the spray on his face.

Three days they had been sailing from Scutari, through calm blue waters.

'It can turn black in a second, Jane, no warning. Lots of ships wrecked and all the men drowned.'

'Not most of them,' Jane said. How else to account for the sick and wounded that poured constantly into the wards?

'But that's why it's called "black", Jane. See that?'

She should not have mentioned it. As though reminded of its reputation, a wind blew in from nowhere, pushing the *Empress* towards a line of dark cliffs at speed. They'd smash for sure, to end up as driftwood and fish food. The closer they sailed, the higher and more monstrous the cliffs became, towering over them and blotting out the sky. Giant waves hurled against the solid line of rock in white rage. Of the harbour there was no sign at all.

Bobby stood facing forwards while Jane sat clinging to her Bible. The wind pulled Bobby's hair back, making a skull of his face. Not in the least perturbed he was, pointing to an ancient tower on the skyline. 'Balaclava!' he shouted.

He must have been mistaken. She struggled to her feet. No opening in the cliffs of any kind.

I do not want to end my life in the water, God. Please. Remember, I cannot swim. Her prayer was interrupted, so swift was the response, as the *Empress* veered round, sending her sprawling as it rolled. A quick dodge to left and to right and they were into the numbing silence of sheltered water.

She was pulling herself up again as they hit the stench, invisible but as solid as any cliff. That loathsome, rotting, fetid smell of early Scutari days hung over this place, with a power to turn your body inside out and sink your spirits into your boots.

Jane's mouth filled. She ran to the side to spit. Below, the water was red and scummed. The *Empress* bumped against something. A body, bloated and gross, rolled over gently, the jacket buttons strained to bursting point.

Jane looked up quickly. The *Empress* was nudging its way into a narrow inlet full of masted ships. Up on the right, behind the tower, a wall with crumbling turrets followed the line of the rock face down to the water: an ancient fort, but still standing. A deep ravine cut away up behind the line of the wall at right angles to the harbour, as though some monstrous hand had brought an axe down on the rocks.

Side by side they stood as the ship nudged into dock, Bobby as silent as she was. Four horses waited on the quay, their riders dressed in red coats, the only colour in the entire scene. Miss Nightingale's reception committee, no doubt. A long, straight waterfront stretched into the distance. Grey with mud it was; the men working the ships were knee deep in it. Even the sky was in keeping with the mood: overcast and ominous.

Never should Jane have thought it a good move coming here, when all she had had to complain about was Lady Blackwood telling her what to do, and an irritation with the routine and the children. When would she ever find contentment with where she was?

Bobby's arm was round her waist.

'Cheer up, Jane! Things will get better, you'll see.'

'Don't say that, Bobby. You cannot know.'

Mrs Brown appeared as the sailors were tying the boat to the wooden posts.

'Go to the General Hospital along the quay, Jane. This sailor will take you. Tell Miss Davis to prepare for a visit from Miss Nightingale tomorrow. Miss Nightingale will be resting. Her headquarters will be on board for the time being. Bobby, you must stay here to take messages as and when she... come on, what are you waiting for?'

The sailor walked fast, legs apart, like a man steadier on the rolling sea. Hurrying to keep up with him, concentrating on *y Beibl* and her bag kept Jane's mind from working.

A miserable sight to see a fine building fallen into such a sorry state. Once the hospital must have been so elegant, built for the likes of the Blackwoods – the nobility of Balaclava. Fled, no doubt, to safer places. Right at the end of the quay it was, a narrow road leading on and up the valley.

Inside was a thousand times worse than the sad outside – a large room packed with bodies, most lying up on those strange shelves a foot from the floor, with no space at all between them. Everyone was occupied. Broken men reduced to pain and misery, their body casings split and the contents spilling out, gory and morbid. The air was thicker than ever. Shrunken, weak, inadequate Jane was, worse than before. So many eyes there were all focused on her that she was desperate to run back, but she must step forward.

One nurse, with her back to Jane, was bending over the first mattress.

'I'll be with you when I've finished.' A voice – a Welsh

voice, up and down like her own – nearly had Jane weeping with relief. 'There now.'

The nurse's face was drawn and tired, but she'd the eyes of a robin, which lit up as she smiled, tilting her head to one side. Wisps of grey-brown hair escaped from her cap and stuck to her forehead.

'What's your name?'

'Jane Evans.'

'A fellow Welshwoman! Doubly blessed. I'm Betsy Davis. Call me Betsy, everyone does. Where are you from?'

'Caio.'

'And I'm from Lanycil. Bala. Way north of you. A farm, was it, you grew up on?'

'It was.'

'Me too. Now, won't we have a lot to talk about? We'll share *hiraeth* and bring ourselves to tears, but we'll understand and won't that be a comfort! We'll celebrate your arrival, won't we boys?' She beamed around her. 'Bless them. I try to bring a little brightness to their days. Who would want them to suffer worse when any of it can be avoided, I don't know. Follow me.'

Betsy's kitchen was built into the rock; a smell of bare earth mingled with old meat.

'Lift the curtain, Jane. Put your bag there. You can sleep with me. Privy's round the side. Watch the bucket. Set to catch water from the roof.'

Just the one pallet on the floor in the alcove and no window at all. *Y Beibl* Jane laid on the bed, with her possessions on top of it.

In the kitchen, Betsy took a bottle from a crate on the floor. She pulled the cork, sniffed. 'Brandy. The best. The smell is enough for me, but a drop does the men a world of good.'

She offered Jane the bottle. 'Look at your face!' She burst

out laughing. 'Not a sin, you know, whatever they told you back home.'

'No, no! I'm just used to things done by the book.'

'By the book, eh?' Betsy's eyes were flinty. A laugh softened them. 'Don't take any notice. Just teasing. You're here, aren't you, and that makes you a fellow survivor of Scutari and rare, and a Welsh girl and the answer to my prayers.'

A homely, warm woman was this Betsy. The kind of woman to like at once.

'I was sent on ahead to tell you to expect a visit from Miss Nightingale tomorrow.'

Betsy rammed the cork back into the bottle. 'What an honour indeed. Not to help me then?'

'No – well, yes. I am to help you.' The news should have been broken more gently. 'I *am* a nurse.'

Betsy sniffed. 'And what does Madam expect? A red carpet?'

The door in the ward banged open. 'Bring the drinks, Jane. Take them round. Introduce yourself.'

Two dark-skinned men with beards and woollen pill-box hats stood in the doorway with a soldier slumped between them. His head lolled. Blood soaked the front of his shirt and dripped onto the floor. The mud of the battlefield was still on him.

'The Tatars bring the injured men down to me,' Betsy said to Jane. 'Budge up now,' she said to the man on the end mattress. 'You'll have to share. Put him here. My poor boy,' she said helping him down. 'You lie there now. You're safe with Betsy. I won't be a moment.'

She scurried back down the ward to where Jane still stood with the tray.

'I've never known a nurse stand and stare so! Take one to him. Go on now. Give the tray to me. Help him to drink it.'

Jane slipped her hand under the boy's shoulders and lifted his head. His breathing was shallow, his face so white. She tipped the glass. The brandy smelt strong, trickling from the corners of his mouth.

The silence of the room magnified the drip-drip-drip on the floor: blood leaking from his body, pooling under the platform. She gave his hand a gentle squeeze. His fingers loosened. He held something there. A morsel of paper.

'Do you want me to take it?' She read it aloud. 'Gwyneth. Llanwrda. That's three of us Welsh here! Isn't that something? Llanwrda. I know that place. Just over the hills from where I live. Gwyneth's your girl, is she?'

Sound bubbled in his throat. There was nothing to be done and yet she must do something. With your eyes closed, seeing is clearer and your voice is the stronger.

'My, it's a beautiful day in Llanwrda! The wind is chasing the clouds over the sky and the mountains are purple and the noise from the sheep is ridiculous. They make the worst mothers, don't they? Always losing their babies and causing such a din. I've the sweetest little lamb brought into the kitchen today, half dead... It'll be fine now in the warm. I'll get milk and feed it up till it thinks I'm its own mother and soon it'll be bouncing around, making a nuisance of itself, messing up my kitchen and annoying the dogs. The moment this little fellow is weaned he'll be back with the others, jumping and butting, kicking and racing for no reason but the joy of being alive.'

Her own face was stretched into a smile. She glanced down. Nothing was different, yet everything was different. She eased the hand away and pushed the smeared paper into the front of her dress. His blood was still dripping.

Betsy stood at the end of the mattress.

'I should have told the Tatars to wait. I knew it wouldn't be long. Help yourself in the kitchen, Jane, if you'd like a bit of comfort... What the eyes don't see... that's my motto.'

Jane sat at the kitchen table, the bottle untouched in front of her. The paper fragment was brown with dry blood. Gwyneth, Llanwrda. One day, she would find Gwyneth and tell her she had sat with her man's hand in hers and told him stories of sheep on the hills, and when she had finished he was gone. She did not even know his name.

Terrible, she felt now. A hollow of misery. It could not be this one man dying that was making her feel so bad, not at all. Her own words had taken her back home, so she thought she was there. He was dead but home was vanished, leaving her further away than ever and empty with longing in this silent dark place. She would keep the note safe in *y Beibl*. The text was already in her ears.

Later, in Betsy's alcove, she turned to Matthew 27. When the words were spoken out loud they had a Welsh sound to them.

Eli, Eli, lama sabachthani...
My God, My God why hast Thou forsaken me?

CHAPTER 24

Patience, Experience, Hope

WITHOUT HER BOOTS, Betsy walked so silently that she was peering over Jane's shoulder the next morning before Jane knew she was there.

'Tsk! Jane! Matthew 27. That's a miserable page to be reading from and should only be read on Good Friday. Forsaken we are not and I won't have such thoughts here. If you want a text, then Romans 5 is the one I tell my boys: *We glory in tribulations also: knowing that tribulation worketh patience; And patience, experience; and experience, hope.'*

She tucked her hair into her cap and tied it tight under her chin as she spoke. 'Enough of all this forsaken nonsense, Jane. I'd not taken you for a wallower.'

That was not fair. A wallower she was not and she would show it. She had made a shameful impression on a Welshwoman of certainty and strength and good cheer. No-one likes a misery, least of all the person who *is* that misery. Sometimes a lesson must be learned over and over. Strands of Betsy's long grey hair lay on her pillow. They would be a good marker for the text.

Sounds of crashing and banging came from the ward. Dark-skinned women with dark dresses were cleaning the floor with such vigour that not a word was spoken and all to be heard was the swish of their brushes. They might be Turks too or the people who lived here – Crimeans, were they? – she did not even know that. The few able-bodied soldiers had shunted up one end, the bed-ridden left marooned. Betsy stood, red faced, in the middle, issuing sharp commands.

'Change Thomas Fisher's dressing, if you're up to it,' Betsy told her. 'I've no time to attend to the men. Everything's for Madam now.'

Jane must be up to it. She *was* up to it, though she did not know where the bandages were, nor the cloths nor the water nor anything. Betsy she would not ask. Whatever the state of Thomas Fisher, he would show her.

He wore a woollen hat over his ears and his eyes were closed. With his beard and side-whiskers he had the look of the *bwca* who lived in the barn rafters, according to David, waiting to frighten her.

'Could you shuffle forwards so I can reach you, Thomas Fisher? I'm to change your dressing. You'll have to show me where exactly.'

His eyes snapped open. He snatched off his hat and scooted to the end of the mattress. One leg, complete with boot, hung down. The other ended in a thick stump above where the knee should be.

'Not a pretty sight.' Thomas apologised. 'Don't mind about me. Do what you have to.'

She fetched water and cleanish bandages, though Miss Nightingale would not call them so. Thomas' stinking bandage was stuck.

'We could soak it.'

'Give it a good tug.' Thomas braced himself on his arms.

'I find singing helpful for pain.'

'I'm not a musical man, Miss.'

'Jane. Plain Jane.'

It was not pleasant the way the stump moved up and down like a giant blind worm.

Only the strength of the wail from behind her would have taken her concentration from Thomas' leg.

'Jane!' Bobby stood at the door, his face crumpled in misery.

'Hold this wet cloth on it, Thomas. I'll be right back.'

'She's taken ill – Miss Nightingale,' Bobby cried. 'She should never have come. It's the air. Nothing a lady should breathe.'

Someone had placed a three-legged stool outside the door. The wooden seat was already warm from the sun. Jane led him there and pressed his shoulders to make him sit.

'I'm sure she'll be alright.' A silly thing to say – she regretted it as soon as the words were out.

'You don't know that, Jane. You've seen the men drop. And she's a woman!'

'Women are stronger than men.'

'Don't say that, Jane. It's not true. You know it and I know it. If women are strong, why do men do the fighting?'

This conversation was not helping. 'Let's pray God won't take her.'

Bobby's face was agonised. 'Come with me, Jane, please!'

The men had caught the gist of the news. Of course they had. Betsy's face was full of hope as she waved Jane away.

A solemn procession they made along the quay, following Miss Nightingale's stretcher away from the boat towards the sea and then up the ravine. Only the brightness of the weather was at variance with the mood. A smooth rock path led them up the valley along the side of a trickling stream. Sheltered it was, but the sun was soon beating fiercely on them, bouncing off the pink rocks to either side. Mrs Brown opened an umbrella to shield Miss Nightingale's face. So pale it was and fine, like a statue in Hereford Cathedral.

'I should have carried that!' Bobby cried.

'Where are they taking her?' Jane asked a sailor toiling up before them, his cap in his hand as though this were a funeral procession.

'Castle Hospital. Air's better there.'

Miss Nightingale would not have liked the General.

A nurse and doctor were waiting on the wooden verandah to escort her and Mrs Brown inside. No more than a large wooden hut was this hospital. The door closed. The stretcher bearers came out. The procession trooped off down the valley leaving Jane and Bobby sitting side by side on the verandah step in the full glare of the sun. Only the birds were unconcerned, chattering from thorny bushes or calling far overhead. Bobby threw stones at a broken tree stump.

In an empty mind, thoughts enter with feelings all in one: Thomas Fisher. Guilt. Jane sprang to her feet.

'I have to go, Bobby. There's nothing we can do here. Come back with me.'

He shook his head. He'd never leave until Miss Nightingale could leave too.

In the hospital, gloom had descended like a fog.

'What will we do without her?' one man cried.

'Continue as we have always done.' Betsy was brusque. 'I have finished poor Thomas' dressing, in case you were wondering, Jane.'

Thomas was lying back on his mattress with his hat on. The sun is cruel to a man who is unable to wriggle away into the shade.

'I'm sorry I deserted you,' Jane said.

'Think nothing of it,' Thomas said.

'There'll be another to fill her shoes, there always is,' Betsy continued, an opinion she should have kept to herself.

Betsy might have thought the same on reflection, for by the afternoon she called Jane to the kitchen.

'Here,' she passed a bowl to Jane. 'A milk pudding. Take it up to her with my best wishes. Tell her all the men are praying for her.'

The power of prayer is impossible to judge. It might have been the strength of Miss Nightingale's own constitution – who knew? News came after an agony of days that she was recovering. Just time enough for Jane to know Betsy as the warmest, kindest woman she had ever met, with a core of strength. To be like Betsy was all she wanted now: selfless, cheerful, confident and doing what she could to make each man comfortable in spirits, if not in body.

The broken men were upsetting as ever. Talking, as she cleaned wounds and bandaged, kept pain as far away as it can be kept. Not one man was here because he had chosen to be. War was a job where none else was to be had. Behind every single man was a family at home without food on the table: mothers, sisters, wives, children. Jane would sit with her mind fixed on the neatness of the bandage, not allowing a wrinkle, covering the parts most stained where she could, to keep the stabbing thoughts away: *she* was here *because* of a choice she had made.

Fortunately there was not much time to think, with only local girls to help and the occasional doctor riding down from the field hospitals to spend as little time as possible in the ward, though the brandy was lower when they left. At the end of the day, sleep overcame Jane before she felt the solid Bible under her head, and she was on her feet and working before she had time to think. The days were so sunny and warm it was hard to imagine the booms heard faintly at night were men being blown to bits only a few miles away.

As the men slept in the noonday heat, Jane slipped away to join Bobby in his vigil at the Castle Hospital. The ravine was a different world. Where the narrow valley opened into the harbour, she passed a small shack set back in a green sweep of meadow. Once, a goat was up on his hind legs nibbling blossom from fruit trees. Once, she nodded at two children washing in the stream beyond a second, uninhabited wooden shack. A white dog stood near them but turned to accompany Jane up the ravine. Great when an animal chooses you. What must those children make of this strangeness come into their lives? A dog would not wonder at all.

Miss Nightingale was back on her feet! The news travelled as fast as fire down from the ravine, through Balaclava to the Hospital one morning. The men were ecstatic; Betsy less so, stomping off to the quayside to take delivery of fresh rations. She arrived back breathless with excitement: the doctors had advised Miss Nightingale to return to England at once.

'England. Are you sure? Am I to go too?' The ground was shaking under her feet and Jane with it. No sooner settled than she was to be uprooted, once more on the receiving end of someone else's orders. England! She could not. But then, maybe she could. England. Then home! But no. That could never be. *You might as well be dead. I have no kind thought of you, Jane, nor any thought at all.* Oh, Griffith, why could he not forgive if she had forgiven him? His sin was the greater.

'Stay here with me!' Betsy beamed.

No time to think one thing or another before Bobby arrived, bursting through the door with news.

'It was a plot, Jane. The doctors. Sending her to England when she did not know! Trying to be rid of her. She will not have it. She's back to Scutari, Jane, and you and I with her.'

'Are you certain, Bobby? She said I was to go?'

'Tomorrow morning. On the tide.'

Pulled this way and that, how could a person not feel adrift and uncertain? Not back to Scutari! No. She liked it better here with the men and Betsy – the ease of her: a Welshwoman, with no airs of a grand lady. She would stay if she could – but could she? Could she even trust her own decisions? If ever she needed someone to tell her what to do, it was now, and she had no sense of God's will, nor her own.

Betsy was not as distressed by the thought of Jane leaving as might have been hoped. She stood in the middle of the ward cutting bread against her chest for the men. Her eyes flicked from side to side, calculating.

'Before you go, Jane, one more thing you can do for us.'

She disappeared into the kitchen, shedding bread crumbs as she went. Rats would be the next problem, for sure.

'Look at your long face,' Betsy said, returning with a large parcel. 'Here was me thinking you'd be glad to be back where things are done by the book.'

'I like your way, Betsy. If I had a choice, I'd stay here.'

'Would you now? Then stay.'

Jane's heart leapt, but fell again. 'I have to go.'

Betsy's eyebrows lifted.

'Kadikoi is not far from here. There's a woman I know with chickens. Her son who brought them down before is dead. Take her this in exchange.' A heavy sacking parcel it was. 'There's only the one road. You'll know the place. It stands back from the track on the right, half an hour's walk from Kadikoi along the Woronzoff Road – a little farm shack with goats and hens around it. And you hurry back now! It's a quiet morning but things can change fast.'

Twenty-eight days was all it was since first Jane had walked along the quay from the *Empress of India* to the General

Hospital. In four days she'd be back in Scutari and under Lady Blackwood's disapproving eyes.

The stench was still foul here, the harbour so crammed that the water between the boats could hardly be seen. Another fine day with blue sky and a cooling breeze, though the road leading up the gentle slope to the plains was a channel of churned mud. Her skirt she held up to save it from the worst. New clothes – now that would be something. Perhaps at last she would have earned that Scutari sash.

The land levelled out to a plain of gentle bumps and undulations. Far above, huge birds wheeled in easy circles, like they did in the wildest places in Wales, looking for carrion no doubt. Not a thought to dwell on. A group of soldiers in ragged caps ran past, muskets at the ready. They did not see her. At the top of a slight rise they ducked down and disappeared. In the distance, mountains rose to snowy peaks. Dark clouds swelled over them as black as the mountains themselves. Were they coming this way? She'd better hurry.

The farm was all on its own, in a field of low, knotted vines: yellow-green leaves sheltering bunches of green grapes. Chickens scratched outside. An old woman crouched behind a goat, milking. Jane coughed. The woman turned quickly. Her face was sunken and suspicious. She waved a bony arm over her head, telling her to go.

Jane showed her the sacking parcel.

'Chickens? Chook-chook.'

The woman nodded at the parcel and stretched out her hand for it.

Jane held on: 'Chickens.' She held up two fingers.

The woman spat out a torrent of words. Sounds would not move Jane. The woman disappeared – cursing, no doubt – and returned with two birds dangling, squawking, from her hand, flapping wildly. Fair exchange. The parcel was ripped open, a soldier's greatcoat held up and shaken. Was it not wrong to give a coat away? Think of the winters! Though without food, the men would have no need for a coat.

A cloud covered the sun, taking the colour from the scene. A mournful, whistling noise whipped towards them over the emptiness. The chickens' talons curled in her hands.

The second whistle must have been a squall of wind. The ground burst open. Drops like solid rain spattered her face.

'Get down!' a voice yelled.

No time to understand before she was thrown into the air. The earth smacked into her. Her hands were empty. The air was white feathers of snow.

CHAPTER 25

The British Hotel

L YING IN SUCH deep blue peace, everything must be all right. Just fine. Dreamy, floaty, part of the blue, not separate at all.

A shadow fell over her. She might be dead. So hard it was to force her eyes open. A girl was leaning over her. A girl with a black face. Wide brown eyes.

She held a cloth to Jane's head. 'I'll take you to the hotel. Mama will be back soon. She will know what to do.'

She *was* dead. A hotel?

'Can you stand?'

How could she, with no legs? But yes, her legs were there – yet far away and not under her control.

'Put your arm round my shoulders. Quick, before they start shellin' again. Trust me. Not far.'

No sensations. Nothing. So tired. Eyes so heavy.

Someone was bathing her face, gently, carefully. A long way away. In the clouds, maybe. Slowly, her eyes opened. Near her, not far away at all, the black-faced girl sucked her bottom lip. The skin on her hands was smooth, her palms so pink.

Jane's eyes closed all on their own.

Hands cupped her ears. Her hair was lifted, strand by strand, and dipped in water. The sound of the cloth squeezed and the dripping water was beautiful. Someone was looking after *her*.

A lark was singing high up, not far away. But she was inside. On a bed. Her hands hurt. Scratches. Chickens' feet! Where were they? She sat up. That girl. This place? A room with whitewashed walls, a window with lace curtains. The sun pouring in. Flowers in a vase by her bed. A tin mirror on the back of the door. Like a dream, this was. She breathed deeply then sniffed. Onions. Onions cooking. There are no smells in dreams.

The door opened. 'Hello. I'm Sally. What's your name?'

'I'm Jane. Where am I? What happened?'

'This is the British Hotel. You were wounded. Do you remember?'

'I was going to get chickens.'

'And I was going to take honey.' The girl beamed. 'All wasted! Your clothes were so sticky. We took them to wash.'

Yes, Jane was wearing a cotton nightdress now. Not her own at all. And now her head felt odd – tight. A bandage? How did she get this?

'Mama cleaned you up good. She gave you something so you'd sleep a long time. You'll be right as rain soon. She told me to feed you when you woke. She'll be back soon.'

Had Sally spread wings and told Jane this was Heaven when she brought her eggs and onions on a china plate, Jane would have believed her and not been surprised in the least. Happy she would be to tell the preacher in Caio he was wrong. There *were* angels and they had black faces and skin like polished wood.

She could eat and drink the cold water, though her head was throbbing now and everything was still distant, as though on the other side of the lace curtains.

'Is this the war?'

Sally giggled.

'Not this part. War don't take up all the time. What do men do when they're not fighting? Ever thought of that? Rest now. I've customers to attend to.'

Blissful, but on a breath everything became real. This was ridiculous, behaving as though she had been injured in the war! What about the men in the General? And Betsy! What would she be thinking? The chickens! And the boat! Bobby. They would not leave her behind, surely?

She must go. Now! But her legs were weak under her. Sally. She must find her to explain. If she could reach the door, she could hold onto the frame. She opened it. A corridor. On the opposite side a door stood open to a world that could *not* be real! Shelves lined the walls from floor to ceiling, filled with bottles of all shapes and sizes: jars of pickles and preserves, nuts and fruits; fish that peered through the glass; things the like of which she had never seen before. Wooden barrels stood on the floor next to sturdy wooden tables with chairs and stools.

Two officers in fancy red jackets, gold twists down the front and on the shoulders, sat at the table, with a bottle between them and two glasses.

'Ah!' One turned towards her. He'd a wonderful thick moustache. 'Come and join us.'

She only had a nightdress on. She answered from the door. 'I've a boat to take this day.' The words were awkward lumps in her mouth.

'Leaving us so soon? We've only just met. You cannot imagine how it delights the heart to have the company of a woman. Stay, do! Where were you thinking of going?'

Never had she been spoken to like this; so polite they were. And they were officers! She twisted inside.

'Scutari.'

'Out of the question!' He gave an exaggerated shudder. The face the other made was comical. 'Stay, and increase your chances of a happy old age.'

Sally, in a white starched pinafore, arrived through a doorway behind the counter, with plates, knives and forks.

'Sally, tell her not to go.'

'Jane! What you doing? Back to bed! You not going nowhere without my Mama say so.'

'There, you see. We are all in agreement.'

Why shouldn't she stay? For a while. Didn't she deserve it? God's reward, maybe. And the officers had begged her to stay! No man had ever begged her to stay anywhere, certainly not one in a uniform with such a moustache.

That afternoon, Sally draped Jane's shoulders in a fine green shawl with a scarlet fringe and led her out to the steps at the front of the hotel. Shirts flapped their arms from the washing line. Meadows swept down to the tidy lines of vines stretching away to the mountains. The road down to Balaclava was way before the mountains. Balaclava. Not far away. This could not be right. She should not be here at all. The officers were only teasing her, surely. She should be with the wounded soldiers.

A woman appeared round the bend in the road riding a wide grey horse. Her dress was as yellow as gorse; on her head she wore a wide hat the same bright blue as her cape. A leather bag was strapped across her chest. The horse was an easy-looking creature, dull compared to its rider, whose face was black as Sally's.

She called out as soon as she saw Jane. 'Feeling better? That's what I like to see!'

Such a smile she had on her.

A stooped man with a grumpy, hanging face came from the back of the house to help her dismount.

'I have to go to Balaclava,' Jane said, the panicky fluttering inside making her words fast and breathy. 'There's a boat leaving in the morning.'

'There's always boats leaving. I'm Mrs Seacole. I brought my supplies from Jamaica but there's plenty of goodness growing here if you know what you're looking for. And I do. This, see?' She opened her bag and took out a bunch of yellow-headed flowers with long silver saw-toothed leaves. 'Silverweed. Growing by the path. Wonderful for the bleeding and the cramps. Take one. Smell it!'

So peppery and powerful it was. 'Let me have a look at that head. Come, follow me.'

She led the way through the room where the men were drinking, shedding her hat and her cape as she went.

'Good afternoon to you all. Unless it's evening already. No sense of time out here. I'll be joining you directly. Sally, fill their glasses.'

In a wooden room at the back, the ceiling hung with drying herbs, Mrs Seacole placed the flowers on the table top and sat Jane on a chair. With care, she pulled at the skin near the wound until fresh blood started to trickle down.

'Good, good.' Mrs Seacole tilted Jane's head. With her face so close, her breath was warm. Such a sweet-sweaty motherly smell she had. 'I seen you before, I think. Scutari. Came all the way from Jamaica to be a nurse. But she did not want me. Well, look what I got instead!'

Mrs Seacole was winding a bandage firmly round Jane's head. 'Treat yourself good and the more good you'll have to give. Think of it from where I stand – a girl to look after with a wound that will heal; what a change from my poor boys. Every day I ride out with my medicines to look for the soldiers left on the ground. Pitiful and wretched. I hold them and talk, often times nothing more. But if that's all I can do, it's a blessing.'

'I've an aunt like you.' Aunt Anni appeared so suddenly and so real in Jane's mind – the smell of tobacco and wild herbs caught the back of her throat.

'Looks like me, does she?' Mrs Seacole laughed. 'Look at your skin, now!' She handed Jane a small pot. 'Rub this into your poor, starving skin... and you get Sally to do your hair for you. We owe it to the men, Jane, to look our best. They're doing the killing and we'll do the caring. Think of a man's spirits. They're helpless without us, Jane. And think of my dear Sally. A girlfriend at last in a country of men.'

As she lay that night, clean again in Sally's bed, Jane listened to the sound of men laughing, with Mrs Seacole's voice rising above them. Is this Your will, God, that I should stay here a while? Did You save me for this? If the answer was yes, that would smooth the worries away. Life doesn't have to be a struggle to be worthwhile. You can learn from good people in good easy places.

The smell of the crushed silverweed was strong on her hands. She'd keep it and use it as another keepsake in *y Beibl* and remember Mrs Seacole forever. The exact right text was in her mind, 1 Corinthians 12:

> *For to one is given by the Spirit... the gifts of healing...*
> *To another the working of miracles.*

What a hat she wore, and the colour of those clothes, the yellow shining like the sun. If a man was lying out there dying, imagine him looking up and seeing her riding towards him. Who better to take your hand and lead you through?

CHAPTER 26

A Thing of Beauty

A PIG WAS screaming for its breakfast. Had she slept late? The boys would be screaming too for their food and Griffith beating her soon after. She sat up. Her head throbbed. In an instant, she remembered. A great thing it is to be alive and not dead in a muddy hole along with scraggy chickens. This was the nicest place she had ever woken in, with the nicest people near, who wanted her here and cared for her. And a pig screaming is the best sound in the world!

Her legs were weakish but held her as far as Sally's cot, where she knelt to look out of the window. Pens small as the ones at the market in Llandovery stretched back to a row of beehives. The fences round them were woven from sticks and odd pieces of wood. Long-eared white goats nibbled the yellow grass. Mrs Seacole's sturdy grey horse grazed in one pen with its back to its next-door neighbour, a sleeker bay with a black tail flicking sideways in the breeze. It stood with its chest right up to the fence, ears pricked and longing on its face. A fine milking cow with sagging udders grazed next to the horses and, in the far pen, a few bony long-legged sheep shared accommodation with half a dozen brown chickens.

Jane tiptoed to the door and opened it a fraction. No-one in sight. Voices came from the kitchen opposite. She grabbed the blanket and darted across. Such a smell of baking there was, her mouth was full of water.

Sally looked up from the pot she was scouring. 'Quick! There are men about.' She pulled her inside. 'Wait here while I fetch your clothes.'

Mrs Seacole, head tied in a scarlet scarf, came into the kitchen carrying a china bowl.

'Like figs? Try one.'

Purple on the outside and soft and green inside they were, the seeds in jelly like tadpoles, but with a smell of sun and wonderful sweetness.

'How's your head?' She fastened an apron over her dress.

'Much better. It's nothing.'

Mrs Seacole took a ball of pastry from a bowl, slapped it down, shook flour onto the board, and rolled up and down so quickly it was smooth and flat and round in a second.

'Senna tarts, Jane. When the inside of a man is functioning well, then the outside can. I've blancmanges to make and my rice pudding is the best in the Crimea. You know what tomorrow is, don't you?'

Jane didn't.

'The Queen's birthday. We'll celebrate in style!'

Jane's clothes were dry. Paler and stiffer than before but warm from the sun, they were better than when she had first put them on in Scutari, folded and crushed from the long journey from England. By the time she was dressed, the tarts were baking and the kitchen full of smells that made breathing bliss. Mrs Seacole appeared in another enormous hat, with her bag strapped across her chest.

'Take the tarts out, Sally. Don't let them burn. Jane, I've arranged for a cart on its way to Balaclava to stop and take you down.'

Her face must have shown the sinking in Jane's heart. Why had she said the wound was nothing? She had made too light of it.

'It's what you want, isn't it?'

'Yes. Yes.'

Yesterday it was. Now, all she wanted was to stay. But Mrs Seacole was gone, sweeping out of the front door. Her grey horse stood saddled and waiting.

'Pray that the ice is delivered in time,' Mrs Seacole said, mounting, tilting her hat. A large black feather curled down to her shoulder. 'Champagne must be served chilled. It's been grand making your acquaintance, Jane. You take care now.'

Jane shielded her eyes to watch her go. At the road, the horse broke into an easy, lolloping canter. If only she'd begged her to let her stay. She would have said yes. Furious Jane was with herself for ruining everything yet again.

A girl can change her mind. It wasn't that she didn't dare go back. She did not want to. Simple. And who in their right mind would? She was being played with. Again. To be shown the sweet things of life and then sent back to hell was worse than if she had never seen them at all.

She sat heavily on the step to wait. Red poppies had opened up overnight in the grass. Such a strong, brilliant colour to them, and the petals so delicate and thin. A poppy picked was a poppy dead in Wales. The petals would fall like drops of blood, leaving a sad green stem.

Three men arrived mid-morning, their arms full of brightly coloured flags and bunting to decorate the hotel. Union flags, the red, the white and the blue – the poppies, the clouds and the sky – soon covered the front of the hotel completely. Usually there's nothing like flags flapping to bring cheer into the heart, but here they were mocking her, like the children at school in Caio.

The cart arrived when the men were standing back to admire their work. The mule was the thinnest creature ever, with not an ounce of flesh on his bones and his long ears without the strength in them to stand straight. The sides of the cart were raised.

Sally ran to Jane's side and squeezed her hand as Jane clambered up next to the driver. Too full Jane was of remorse to say much to Sally, whose deep brown eyes were watery. 'I wish you did not have to go.'

The cart lurched away over the rough ground. There was distance enough. Sally must not see how much Jane did not want to go. She should wave. She turned in her seat. There, in the back of the cart, was a tangle of broken men – and Jane unprepared once more. A slap and a punch all at once. She could not wave, but covered her face with her hands, a bitter swill flooding her mouth.

It's a hateful thing to realise, once more, that you are drowning in self-pity and not thinking of the poor men at all. She faced forward but could not free her mind from what was so close behind her. Please God, make them dead, for else they would be suffering so, jolting along this potholed road. But why would they bother to take dead men to Balaclava? She turned back to look again at what she did not want to see. A desperate look in a man's eye locked with her own. Not all dead. A confused pile of arms and legs and muddied boots, top to tail and half on top of each other. Blood seeped everywhere, filling the air with its iron stench, mixing with the mud. Still in view were the flags decorating the hotel.

A knot of uselessness gnawed at her as she fixed her eyes on the mule's backside, where the leather harness divided round its tail. The wind had dropped. Clouds were piling up ahead, going nowhere. At the side of the road, two great birds lifted away from a dead horse. Its neck was stretched out, its teeth bared in a horrible grin. Further away more birds were feeding, heads down, shoulders hunched like ugly old men. They were squabbling, rushing at each other with wings out and naked necks stretched. Grisly red threads trailed from their beaks. No need to see what they were feasting on. Man was meat. She must not get used to it, she must not! The day the bile did not rush into her mouth was the day when she was lost.

The nearer they drew to the turning down to Balaclava, the slower their progress until, with a violent lurch, the cart tipped into a deep rut and stuck fast. The groans from the back were piteous. The mule had not the strength to make any further effort, however much the driver lashed at his haunches. He stood beyond feeling.

Although the road was mud, to the left a grassy field, flecked with flowers, stretched into the distance. Soldiers were moving, too far away to know if they were friend or enemy. If asked, they might help, or they might shoot.

The driver had given up and was now sitting on a small hillock of grass, picking mud from his clothes. The road stretched empty in both directions. The distant soldiers appeared not to have noticed them. They were constructing something, piling sacks one on top of the other. She would have to approach them. There was no other option.

Jane was searching for the driest route when the ground started shaking. Three riderless horses came galloping across the plain from east to west. They would pass right between her and the soldiers. Their heads reached out in front of them in a desperate way. One was still saddled. The stirrups were thrashing. The reins of another dangled alarmingly near his legs. From their frenzied eyes it was obvious they had no idea what they were fleeing from or fleeing to. Unspeakable, to bring horses into a war and frighten them witless. Such a dreadful, senseless, wicked thing, a war.

The soldiers had stopped their work to watch. Jane was close enough to see their British caps, though they were working in their shirtsleeves. One with a shocking scarred face and rough, tufted hair held the pole. A tarpaulin lay on the ground beside them. Was it some sort of a tent they were putting up?

Jane waved her arms.

The officer in charge straightened sharply.

'Well, well!' he called out. 'We meet again!'

Once more a slap and a punch, but this shock was of a wondrous kind, as though she had stepped from one terrible world to a marvellous one. Cleaned up, his face looked younger, browner. He'd that look of Isaac round his eyes, though his hair was finer, his body slimmer. Everything was changed into this instant, this chance. Never ever should you despair, for you have never reached the end.

'What happened to your head?'

Forgotten completely, she hardly knew what he was talking about until she touched the bandage.

'Oh, nothing.'

'What circumstances bring you here, I cannot imagine.'

The mission would cover her flustering. 'Our cart is stuck completely in the mud. I've come begging for help. We've wounded soldiers in a terrible state.'

He would admire her for that surely. He was not to know she was only travelling with them by chance.

'Of course. Hubbard, take the men to free her cart.'

Hubbard, the soldier with the scarred face, dropped the pole to the ground and nodded to the other men. Could the officer not be the one to help her?

'Good luck!' he said, brushing hair from his eyes.

'Thank you.' A mercy indeed that he could not read her disappointment. At least as she walked back he would see her hair light and clean, hanging down beneath the bandage, and her clothes fresh.

'Jane, isn't it? Precious few things of beauty in these parts!' He held out a flower, a white daisy. 'Brave little thing!' he said, handing it to her.

No knowing which he meant, and no matter. She would keep that flower forever. She would.

God moves in mysterious ways indeed. To think that evening Jane was sitting in the very shack she had passed daily on her way up the ravine to the Castle Hospital. Now, here she was, on her own. Betsy herself suggested it to her. So hard she had hugged Jane, as she had thought her lost and taken the blame for it for sending her for the chickens.

'You sleep up there, Jane. It's empty, and the truth is: I put up with you in my bed for a short time, but with you gone, I've remembered the pleasure of being on my own.'

The candle stub sent flickering light over *y Beibl*, open in Jane's lap. Now she could sit and read and read until the light gave out or her eyes became too heavy. How proud Mam would be of her now, for hadn't she taught her from her own Bible all those years ago? How Jane had wriggled and sighed, with the words all jumbled and dancing about in front of her eyes, making her want to dance too. Her own living quarters! Was this – being saved from death, having the comforts of life dangled in front of you, returning and being rewarded like this – was this God's plan? For her. When you thought to see the plan, there were always awkward questions lingering, unanswered. The men in the cart, for instance? What was God's plan for them?

The boat had sailed with Miss Nightingale and Bobby on board. They had gone; she was left. But Jane had survived the pain and the shock of war itself, making her the better equipped for her job here at the General, for sure. Now she had met two more women she wanted to be like: Betsy, who trusted herself and took orders from no-one, and Mrs Seacole, turned away from Scutari when she'd come all that way to be a nurse, and who now was a true nurse. No purveyor. No dockets and regulations.

Jane took the silverweed from her pocket. Such a strong peppery smell it had, even wilted like this. She turned the pages of the Bible until she reached 1 Corinthians 12: *For to one is given by the Spirit... the gifts of healing.* That was Mrs Seacole. The yellow flower heads would stain the page, but there was no help for that. Paper was precious and she could not bother Betsy after she had given Jane all this.

Certainly, the British Hotel was for the officers, and not for the likes of Thomas Fisher and the soldiers in the General. But officers have to be cared for, for they have to lead, don't they? *And* put themselves in danger and be wounded. Her mind was back to the lobby in Scutari, with the officer swaying like a falling tree. Now what were the chances of that? Meeting up on the vast plains above Balaclava. And he remembered her name!

'A thing of beauty.' He must have meant the flower. 'Brave little thing!' She twirled it now in her fingers. Wilted, for he'd taken it from the earth which fed it. Song of Solomon. That would be the place.

> *I am the rose of Sharon, and the lily of the valleys. As a lily among thorns, so is my love among the daughters.*

Not daughters exactly – soldiers. And this flower was no lily, but it was white and the sentiment was the same, whatever its name was. There were times when you had to press your own meaning into the words. The Song of Solomon. Such a book. No wonder it was not mentioned in chapel. Full of love and passion. If such feeling was in the Bible, how could it be wrong? If the world was ruled by such emotions, not fighting and war, it would be such a place.

No-one could see. She touched her lips with the petals and spread them carefully on the page. She shut the Bible gently and squeezed it to her chest. *Y Beibl* made a good pillow, tipping her head so she could see down the valley. Wetting her fingers, she pinched the candle flame and clasped her hands between her legs.

The wooden beams were close to her head. If she sat up in the night, she would be in danger of injury. Logs should be drying here for winter, or animals resting: goats or low creatures that would not mind the slant of the roof. The air smelt of wood, earth, grass and burnt tallow.

Stars were bright in the black sky above the hills on the far side of the water. The officer might be looking up at the same stars at this same moment.

That night she dreamed she was held tight on Mam's lap while the last log split and settled under the black kettle. She'd a book in front of her, held by Mam's hands. A beautiful English Bible with a brown cover and pages so wide she'd to move her head to see it all. The words danced and came alive in Mam's mouth – which was behind her, and strange, for the words were in front. Mam would point at the words and say them until Jane said them too. And some of the squiggles became pictures, like the swine, which was a pig like the one in the sty outside, and the silly man fed it jewels. They laughed together but it brought a fit of the coughing on Mam, who pushed Jane from her lap and lay straight on her alcove bed, gasping for the root tea Aunt Anni had left – but Jane did not know where it was. The coughing drowned Tad's boots on the mat and the door slamming and him running to the bed: 'My pride, my own, my Mary,' not seeing Jane at all, and not helping find the tea.

Now the Bible was face down on the floor and the dogs were walking on it with wet feet, and Tad's boots were trampling mud into the hook rug which Mam had made. And now Mam would never shake the mud off for herself and she would die for the want of the tea. And Jane must shake and shake and shake that rug forever, with the pain inside growing, and she was as much in need of the root tea and no-one in all the world knew.

CHAPTER 27

Fever

BEING WOKEN BY a pain gnawing your insides is not the best start to the day, even in your own hut in a beautiful valley away from all the horror below. Ignoring it was not possible. Jane kneaded deep into her stomach, then smoothed her hands round her hips to her back. She rubbed to either side of her spine. The tenderness was not there; definitely it was not the kind of ache that sends a woman to her rags – something, thankfully, that had not happened for many months. Mrs Naylor had told her it was common, what with the heat and the poor diet and the illness, and to be thankful for it.

'You're not worrying on another score, are you Jane?' Her smirk had been most irritating. 'Or are you such an innocent you don't know what I mean?'

'Mrs Naylor, I am a farm girl!' Jane had said.

By the time Jane reached the General Hospital, she was clammy and cold. Distant cheering and the sound of shrill bugles drifted down over the harbour from another world altogether. The birthday celebrations must have begun. Betsy was handing round the first toast of the day in her assortment of cups, mugs, bowls and even the odd glass. Brandy might help settle pain.

'The Queen!' All the men who were able stood to attention. Hair had been slicked down, boots buffed. Joe Stallard had his coat buttoned to his neck, his cheeks made red with the tightness. Thomas Fisher had removed his hat. Arnold Castle, always the one the other men asked to write letters home for them, took his brandy but sloped away outside to the stool in the sun.

The heat and toasts made Jane dizzy. Fresh air might help.

'Are you not wishing the Queen a happy birthday?'

Arnold's eyes never left his page. His handwriting was very neat and even.

'I'm not in the celebrating mood, Jane.'

That was understandable.

'I'd drink her health if she called us all home. Now that would be worth drinking to. She don't care about my health. And I don't care much about hers.'

Flies buzzed in front of them. A dog stopped, balancing on three legs while he scratched his fleas. She *did* care though, Queen Victoria. Hadn't she sent a letter to Scutari last Christmas that cheered their spirits so? As soon as the Queen heard how cold they were, she and the Princesses started knitting hats for the soldiers as fast as they could. And now Scutari was in Jane's mind and a twist inside of something she should have done. It made a difference thinking someone dead when they were alive, or alive when they were dead.

'Could you write a letter for me, Arnold? I could do it myself but I'm not in the writing mood.'

'I could, willingly, Jane.' He smoothed paper over his knee.

'*Lady Blackwood. I am not dead. I was shot but mended now. There is much to do here.*'

She paused, breathing rapidly as a pain gripped her. Arnold had dipped his pen, ready for the next sentence. She patted her cheeks.

'*I would like to stay. Greet Bobby for me.* How do you end a letter to a lady, Arnold?'

227

'Same as to anyone else, if it were me.'

'Write *Jane*.'

He folded the paper and offered it to her, just as another pain was rising like a distant wave.

'Could you post it for me? *Lady Blackwood. Scutari.*'

She gripped the doorframe as the wave threatened.

'Are you alright, Jane?'

Pain took her voice and squeezed her eyes. Sweat broke out on her forehead.

The rush down the ward was a desperate one. The privy was a place to avoid if you could; alive with flies, dark and evil-smelling.

After several minutes, she staggered out, sucking the fresher air, only to be sent back instantly with a feeling that her whole insides were turning to liquid. Her waste was splattery and foul.

'Go!' Betsy said. 'Come back in your own time.'

Jane hurried along the quay. At the entrance to the ravine she stopped, bending over and groaning quietly. With her hut in sight she stopped again, leaning against the rock, panting. Voices echoed down the ravine. Thank the Lord she had not been caught squatting. At the top of the ravine, soldiers with a stretcher were moving around the hut where Miss Nightingale had been. Someone must be hurt, but there was nothing she could do about that. Not in this state.

In her hut, she sank to the ground; cold earth beneath her was nothing new. She curled up, drawing her knees to her chin, holding her feet in her hands to warm them. Her hands were cold too. Sleep was impossible with feet like ice.

She woke shivering. It was black. How she wished for a blanket or Betsy to snuggle up to. So utterly terrible she felt, crying like a child, teeth chattering out of all control.

Lying back, she was suddenly hot as fire, flinging out her arms and legs to feel the night air.

A sudden thought stabbed like a dagger of ice. Is this where I am to die? Who will find me? Please don't let me die! I'll be left on the hill with my bones all mixed up and no-one to visit me ever. I want to be home!

Judging by the light when she woke, it was late, but she was quiet: her head was warm, not hot. Many soldiers and women she'd seen feverish and raving, eyes brittle as glass, mouths parched. She was not like that. She checked her neck, her chest and pressed her hand into her stomach. A soreness, no more. A protest, that was what it had been, a warning from her body. As Mrs Seacole had said, there's nothing you can do of any use to yourself or anyone if you become ill.

Her legs unreliable, she stood leaning against the wooden frame before squatting in the grass behind the hut. There was nothing but sound wanting to come out of her. A good sign. She would begin by walking up to the fort to test her legs, and then, in her own time, return to the hospital.

Her weak body protested the long climb. Definitely worth it, though; such a grand view there was from the fort: on top of the world. From here anyone could see why Balaclava had been chosen for the fleet. A great hiding place for the ships. The Black Sea, stretching left and right in a wide sweep, had a morning glitter to it.

Deep breaths of salty air would clean her insides. There must be more for her to do or she'd be in her hut, shivering, with burning fever. The purpose of illness, if you recovered, was to see everything fresh and wondrous and your own place in life miraculous.

What a place to build a fort! Kings or generals always made wise choices, without a thought for the poor labourers toiling up the hill in the heat carrying the vast blocks of yellow stone. Now that too was something to be thankful for – to be born now and not back then. What a desperate hard time they must have had of it in those far-off days.

She walked on to the place where the path split, one way continuing along the cliff, the other down behind the Castle Hospital at the head of the ravine. Someone was sitting on the verandah.

'Jane. We meet again.'

The fever had burned all thought from Jane's head. She froze, unable to speak until she saw his torn shirt and his arm held awkwardly to his chest.

'Are you wounded?'

'I fell in the races. What does it matter?' He was distracted, peevish. 'My men brought me here. There's no doctor! Unbelievable!'

'Shall I look at it?' Blood rushing into her cheeks was maddening. 'I'm a nurse.' Well, she was.

'Should I take my shirt off?' He began to ruck his shirt with his good hand.

She shook her head quickly. 'No need.'

She held his arm, feeling the length of it up to his shoulder. It was wrong: the joint was lumpy and misaligned.

'This will hurt,' Jane warned.

'Do you know what you're doing?'

'You see that bush on the path behind me? What can you see behind it?'

'Behind? How can I see behind – arghhhh!'

Immediately the arm softened, Jane jerked it up and round, pulling with one hand, pushing with the other. The ball clicked back into the socket.

'You deliberately tricked me!' Furious, his eyes.

'But it feels better now, doesn't it?'

He circled his arm round and round.

'It does. It truly does!'

'My aunt taught me.'

'What more can you do?' he said. His eyes were bright now. 'My ribs are sore. I couldn't lift my arm before and now...'

There in front of her, he took off his shirt. He'd a smooth and young-looking chest with the skin brown at his neck where his shirt had been open. His collar-bones were sharp and the place where they met a deep triangle.

A healer does not think of who she is touching. But when Jane drew back, her face flushed.

'You're a miracle worker, Jane. No pain! Nothing to stop me rejoining my men. How can I thank you?' he said, windmilling his arm. He'd a sweaty, unwashed smell to him. His hair was black and greasy.

'You should not hurry back, in my opinion,' Jane said.

'This is war, my dear.' His eyes were soft, crinkling at the edges. 'My man will be back soon with my horse.'

She had to speak or it would all be over. 'I love horses. We've one at home.'

'You ride, do you?' His head tipped, his eyebrows rose up under his hair line. Jessie pulling the plough was in her mind as Jane nodded.

'We might ride one day.' His eyes were the deepest she had ever seen. Such a way he had of holding her in them.

But he would not know how to reach her. 'I sleep in a shack just down from here, and I work at the General Hospital on the quayside...'

'Ah! One day I might surprise you.'

He turned back to the hospital hut. It was her signal. He meant for her to go, but she could not move until he had shut the door.

CHAPTER 28

A Fallen Woman

THE REAL WAR might be being fought up on the plains, but the battles continued in the hospital. Life against death, day after day.

Nothing is how you wish it to be. Expectations that the officer would be true to his word faded to hope and then to resignation. The only thing to do was not to wish for anything at all.

One evening Jane trudged up the ravine. The sinking sun burned the pale rocks a deeper pink. The heat was still intense. Her hands were blood-stained from the day. Nothing but stones to mark the dry bed of the stream and no chance of dew on the grass to clean them either. Not possible these days to read her Bible without leaving the pages smeared with brown.

Blood – so startling the colour of it, the amount of it, the smell so strong – had lost its power; as had those terrible, bleeding, ripping wounds. Shock is a state that cannot remain for long.

'You'll get used to it,' that nurse had said. A terrible thought back then but the truth was, she had.

You clean. You bandage. You wash, praying the water clean. You bind. You tend until the blood scabs to a shell, the skin mends. That's the best you can hope for: that the black doesn't triumph over the red.

Jane passed her shack, where the air would be trapped and baked all day, and pulled herself up the slope to the clifftop, though her legs complained and her heart beat fit to burst.

The Black Sea glittered. The whole sky scorched red. Nothing moved. Sometimes a desperate melancholy takes you so suddenly there is nothing you can do to prepare yourself for it; a person comes into your mind, startling as if they had jumped out from behind a rock.

Isaac.

It was hard not to sob or call out his name. No-one would hear if she did, but she could not have that name turned to sound. Where was he now? Sitting outside his cottage knitting socks for the pigs, maybe; whittling drumsticks for George; or chopping wood for Aunt Anni, with the sweat darkening his shirt. A powerful surge of feelings and thoughts this was to be sure, tightening every muscle in her body with a longing and a yearning to hold him and be held.

'Well, well!'

The shock would have sent her over the cliff had her body not had the sense to jump backwards. There, riding up from the fort, was the officer on his silver roan horse, followed by the man with the scarred face on a skinny bay.

'I like to take a ride in the evening. Empties the mind. Doesn't it, Hubbard?'

The man's face bunched into an ugly grin.

The officer's red coat was slung over his saddle. His white shirt was open to the waist.

'What brings you here? Jean, isn't it?'

'Jane.' She could hardly say her own name.

'Going my way?'

Now she certainly was.

'Give Jane your horse, Hubbard. She likes to ride, I recall. The camp's not far. Bess and I will bring her back later.'

Such a look Hubbard gave her as he dismounted, turning quickly to follow the goat path down to the Castle Hospital. Not an idea of helping her into the saddle! Was he jealous? Angry that she, Jane Evans, a nurse, had been chosen over him and he dismissed.

Forgotten but recalled in an instant: the joy of sitting above the earth like this, the hardness of the leather saddle over the heat of the horse's body. The power of it and her own surrender. Her reins were slack because there was no need for her to guide it. Her horse followed his at a leisurely pace, its cheek nuzzling the roan's flank, eyes almost closed. Jane's mind was emptied now; she had nothing to say and neither did he. Not awkward at all, but easy, companionable.

They passed an old monastery, the gold of its onion domes dull and flaky.

'Used as a hospital now, I believe.' The first words he had spoken, and directed more to the air than to her. 'The old couple in charge drink morning, noon, and night – making so much noise, the sick can get no sleep.'

Beyond it was an old orchard. Apples were ripening beneath the leaves, flecks of red and pink. The trees themselves were twisted and old, mottled with lichens.

The officer dismounted, Jane followed. He sat twisting a grass stem in his fingers, looking straight ahead over the wide shimmering sea. Jane sat a little distance away from him, her back turned. A wonderful sound, horses ripping at grass, snorting gently, bits clanking. Breathing had never been so hard. In and out, you would not believe a person could hardly remember! She would not turn for fear he might not be there.

From the far corner of the orchard, a cow started bellowing over and over without stopping – a sound of terrible distress. Jane jumped up. Beyond the last apple trees, a small section of cliff had slipped down, leaving a grassy ledge with a vertical drop beneath to the sea. The anguished cow bellowed from the higher part of the grass, while her calf stood on the overhang with its legs splayed out and head bobbing in bewilderment.

He strode past.

'No!' She covered her eyes. He'd fall straight down into the sea, leaving her bellowing with the cow. Her breath stopped and her heart too, as did the cow's cries. Silence. She peeked between the fingers of one hand. The cow's head was down, ready to charge, not understanding at all. Visible to the waist, with the sky on fire behind him, the officer was heaving the calf up in front of him over the cliff edge. It fell on its side, stood and skittered forward as though nothing had happened. The mother licked its rump as it nudged her udder. A sweet little thing, with one brown patch on its back, like a slipped saddle. As the officer pulled himself up by his arms, the cow turned, ears forward, threatening.

'Women are so ungrateful!' he said, brushing the soil off his hands.

'We are not to be judged by cows, surely!' Jane said.

He laughed, striding fast to where his horse was grazing under the tree, Jane following.

He turned slowly to face her, smiling. He stretched out a hand. He meant for her to take it. He did. He pulled her to him, stroking her hair flat to either side of her face until his hands were on her cheeks. Jane closed her eyes. She must not tremble so. He sat and pulled her arm for her to sit too. His arm was round her. He turned her head and kissed her on the mouth. Never, never had anyone done that. It was sweet and soft. She must keep her mouth tight, though she wanted to gasp for breath and he was nudging, pushing until he forced it open. That tongue was a shock, a slippery, darting thing. Why would he want to do that? She pulled back, half laughing, half choking. He'd such a strange hard look in his eyes as he pushed her back onto the grass. He was too strong. And now there were twigs sticking in her back which she could not move because he was rolling on top of her, squashing the breath from her. This was not right. This was not what she wanted at all.

'No!' she whispered. 'No!' Immediately a hand was over her mouth, pressing so hard her teeth would cut the flesh. She pushed his chest with all her strength. He grabbed both wrists in one hand and wrenched them back over her head.

Her mouth was free. 'Get off! Get off!'

She could not think because her skirt was pulled up. His hand was on her leg. The inside. No! He could not. He must not. She looked up into his face. His mouth was open, brutish, baring his teeth like a mating dog. His eyes were turned away, not seeing her. It was not him at all. She fought and kicked and squirmed and flailed but she could not stop him. He pushed into her. It was terrible. It hurt. Oh, it hurt. She could not breathe in, only out and out and out again with every jab and grunt.

Suddenly it was over. One moment of stillness before he pulled away and rolled off her. She was alone on the grass. Quite still.

Gradually the sounds of the insects came through the pounding of her blood, then the pulling of the grass and the swishing of the horses' tails. Gulls cried over the sea.

She opened her eyes. She could not keep them shut forever. Branches fanned out over her, dark leaves with fiery sky behind them.

He was standing a way off, hooking his braces over his shoulders. He did not even glance at her as he mounted his horse and sat waiting, looking out over the sea.

She pulled down her skirt and stood up. One boot was lying a way off in the grass. She fetched it and slipped her bare foot into it. Taking her time, she pulled herself up into the saddle.

Walking hurt. The trot was worse. The gallop overwhelming. She lay her head on the bay neck. The strong smell of horse sweat was a comfort. If she and the horse were one thing, she could not be hurting.

Back past the monastery they rode, and along the cliff path. The sky was a purple bruise now. At the top of the ravine, he was out of sight. Her horse slowed, its shoes slipping on the rock. Jane leaned back. Outside the hut, he sat waiting. He would not look at her. She dismounted. He took the reins without a word.

'How could you?' she whispered. She was looking up; he looked down, expressionless. No pity. No regret.

He did not say goodbye, but turned the horses away up the ravine.

Inside, Jane sat on her straw pallet for a long time, doing nothing, thinking nothing. Her thighs ached with bruising. Her skirt was ripped. No remembering how. Her skin was split and bleeding, her shirt torn. She ripped the cotton away and dabbed her blood with it. Not all keepsakes were good ones. All must be important. She lit her candle stub to see the words.

> *Now unto Him that is able to keep you from falling, and to present you faultless before the presence of His glory with exceeding joy...*

She reread the words out loud, closed the big book and lay back with her head on its cover, her chest tight with self-pity.

She didn't realise... she never imagined... She did not even know his name. She clenched her fists and beat them onto the hard-baked floor. Why had God not saved her? She had fallen. A fallen woman. And how is it the fault of the person who falls? If you fall over an object, or slip on ice or lose your balance, you cannot be blamed. There was nothing she could have done. He was too strong.

Over the hills, sharp points of starlight were appearing as the sky darkened. Was it that he was an officer and she a lowly nurse that he treated her so? Should she have had that thought in her head and protected herself? How is it wrong to think the best of a person?

It had happened and the world would never be the same and she would never be the same, because this was after and that was before.

She must not be judged. I will not judge myself. Judging is God's job.

CHAPTER 29

Letters

CONSOLATION MUST BE found in appearing no different. Sailors nodded or called as Jane walked to the hospital the next morning. As familiar a sight she must be as the stringy ill-tempered camel, pulling crates with that superior look on its face. No-one could know how her head teemed. How could she – how dare she – feel so destroyed with these poor soldiers, their lives shattered all for nothing? She should not feel as bad as she did, but she could not help it. A man, one brutish man, that's all it was... Without a doubt, he would never think of her again... while she could think of nothing else, and that was so unfair. The worst thing was that she had been so deceived... by him or herself? Her boots weighed heavier than they had in the winter with the mud clinging to them.

'Letters, Jane! Just come from the boat.' Arnold sat on his stool at the door.

Two. Which to open first? One, the hand unknown; the other, Lady Blackwood's.

Scutari, July 15th

My dear Jane,

You might as well stay where you are. I share your conviction that God has a purpose for you.

Everything here continues smoothly. We have a

> *reading room for the men in the courtyard and a*
> *coffee house past the laundry. Almost civilised!*
>   *Bobby sends his best wishes, as does the Reverend.*
> *May God continue His watch over us all.*
> *Your handwriting is much improved.*
> *In haste,*
> *Alicia Blackwood*

Yesterday, the meaning would have been entirely different. God's purpose, was it? The words added to the pain.

Arnold was watching her face.

'Not good news? Are we to lose you?'

Jane shook her head. 'No, I'm to stay. Good news.' She smiled quickly and turned the second letter over.

The letters were large and uneven, not the easiest. She unfolded it. Not too long. Her eyes skipped to the last line.

Your loving brother Griffith.

Written by himself then. Not Isaac. Perhaps he was on another drove. Griffith's thoughts would be private this time, at least.

Loving brother. This must be bad news. She read quickly so the shocks would not hurt.

> *Sister,*
> *Isaac gives me a good report and says you are*
> *away at the war as a nurse. Time has passed and*
> *time is a healer. We miss your help here. The*
> *animals are well. Mr Morgan died. I have the*
> *bull and the boar. You would be free if you had*
> *stayed. May God take care of you better than I*
> *did.*
> *Your loving brother Griffith*

All thoughts and muscles and all the parts inside knotted and squeezed, like cloths being wrung out. The scene was sharp in front of her on the baked quay: Isaac in his drover's hat; Griffith, Richard and William, with Glass and Fly panting at their feet; Jessie in the barn, the cattle and sheep on the hills. Mr Morgan was dead, was he? Her sole comfort must be that the bull and the boar were at Tŷ Mawr. She had not ruined Griffith's life after all.

You would be free if you had stayed... And she would not be here now, standing but fallen, in this bleak, baked, forgotten wasteland.

'News from home?' Arnold reached out and touched her arm. 'We're the lucky ones, Jane. Imagine life here without you in it.'

Cruel words are easier to hear than kind ones. Arnold and Griffith. She would have been undone had Betsy not screamed from the doorway.

'Jane Evans. Could you possibly spare the sick and the dying and a desperate woman some of your precious time? Or are you going to stand chatting all day long?'

CHAPTER 30

Tourists of War

E VERYTHING MUST END some time, even this war. Talk of the siege of Sebastopol was everywhere. This *would* be the end. In the gathering excitement, no-one paid Jane much attention. Nothing, she believed, could ever distract her thoughts from herself for more than a minute or two, not even the soldier who staggered inside, blood spilling over his boot like a spring – and when she took his boot off, his foot came with it. Three men it took to tie him to the bed and help with the strapping of his leg in three places. He died. And all Jane could feel was numb until she thought of herself. Four weeks and two days, and her misery was not lifted in the least.

She stood on the edge of the baked quay. The harbour had lost that scummy boiling of red froth since the clean-up. The water lapping the ships was clear. Tiny fishes darted to and fro. A cormorant dived and reappeared far away from where she had expected it to surface.

Words travel far over calm water, particularly voices used to being loud and clear.

'Is this it? Is Sebastopol far?'

A woman in a pale yellow gown, the frill of a petticoat peeking out over her white boots, made her way down the gangplank of a ship which had recently docked. She wore white gloves and held a fancy parasol over a straw bonnet.

A man in a light suit with a monocle followed her. Sailors trailed after them with suitcases and hatboxes. Three more men, raucous and jovial, were joined by three women twittering like birds.

They stood in a group on the quayside. The man with the monocle looked about him. His eye passed quickly over the group of Tatars usually employed to unload the boats.

'Is there no transport?'

The women looked round.

A portly man with a shiny red face and spats suggested they walk.

'Walk!' The women laughed, with the sound of tinkling crystal. 'What fun!'

An odd sight they made, processing out of Balaclava following a line of Tatars bent double under hampers, hatboxes, trunks and leather bags.

Arnold stood up, muttering, and disappeared into the hospital. Thomas Fisher leaned on his crutch on the hospital doorstep, smoking. He no longer wore his hat, and his hair had become quite untamed.

'Come to see, haven't they? The "fun". The siege. The last great push. Should be quite a spectacle. From the right vantage point.'

Enraged, Jane pushed past Thomas Fisher and ran the length of the ward to the kitchen.

Betsy's arms were a-quiver with white feathers as she plucked a bird for the pot.

'It's wrong! Turning killing into sport! I can't bear it!'

Betsy put her feathery arm round Jane's shoulders. 'It's so wrong, I'd pray a shell would come their way – if that were the kind of thing to pray for.' She gave Jane a squeeze. 'Are you alright, Jane? You've been quiet these last days. And now you're raging worse than I've ever seen you.'

'I am. It's just – everything!' It was hard to keep the tremble from her voice.

'I know. The straw and the camel's back, that's what it is.'

The winds coming down from the plain carried gunfire from the siege like distant thunder. On the first day, casualties were so numerous that there was no chance for Jane to return to the ravine. English, French, Turks – it no longer mattered. Hardly a place to walkt without stepping on someone, and clothes ripped from men as they died, for bandages.

A strange silence settled in the heat of the second day. Outside was the only escape from the thick stench and the pitiful moaning of the men. Arnold stood to let Jane doze on his stool, leaning back against the wall. Sleep she needed badly, but every time she closed her eyes, she saw inside herself: broken things all confused and turning, waking her with the keenness of a knife in her belly.

A curious commotion came from the Sebastopol road. Two Tatars came into sight, carrying the woman in lemon towards them. Her straw bonnet was askew, her pale skirt spattered with mud. The man in the linen suit ran after her, hatbox in one hand, suitcase in the other. His face was wet with sweat and his monocle swung on the end of a chain, flashing in the sun.

The Tatars dumped the woman on the hospital doorstep and stood with their hands out. The woman whimpered and fell into Jane's arms. It was tempting to drop her.

'Arnold...' Jane nodded to the stool. Such a dark look he had on his face as he pushed it under the lemon skirts. The man fumbled in his pocket.

'How much should one give?' he asked Jane. 'She's hurt her ankle. Absolutely no-one up there to help us. Nightmare,' the man said, as the Tatars walked away smiling.

The woman's stays were too tightly laced. They'd have to be eased.

'Water,' she gasped.

'Rum?' Jane said. Water was precious. If she'd offered poison, the woman could have been no more horrified.

'Dear God, the things I have seen.' Some women, when they start to talk, cannot stop. 'A grand vantage point and I cannot fault the hampers. The field glasses were our undoing. Things far away and out of sight should be left that way. The French were to make the first assault, the English the second. A colonel instructed us on the uniforms of each rank and nationality. Such a perfect day! The countryside reminded me of the South Downs. All promised so well.'

She paused only to draw breath and start again. 'I lifted my glasses in expectation of a glorious sight.' She patted her cheeks with her handkerchief. 'Men were falling in every direction: into the air, to the side, backwards, into pieces. Consumed in smoke and fire. Hideous beyond words!'

Her breathing was rapid and shallow, her face very white.

'We sprang to our feet and fled for our lives, leaving the hampers, the rugs, everything. Somehow, in the confusion, I tripped. Victory, we were promised. Not carnage. What are you doing, girl?'

'Your corset's too tight.'

'Get your filthy hands off me!' Even looking up, the woman had the look of one looking down.

'How could you turn war into an amusement?' Fury made Jane fearless. 'You disgust me!'

She turned and swept back into the hospital, the watching men at the door parting to let her pass.

'Well said.' Thomas Fisher patted her on the shoulder.

'How dare you!' the woman cried. 'Come back! What about my ankle?'

A faint cheer like a ripple of wind the following day hushed everything it touched. No-one dared even wonder. Jane froze near the door, a bandage half-wound round her fingers, until a Turkish soldier burst into the room, waving his gun.

He screamed a word, took Jane's free hand and kissed her on the lips. Immediately he ran to the door and stood shooting into the sky.

'Get away with you! Away!' Betsy ran after him, clapping her hands, but with a smile on her face Jane had never seen. All around them men, clambered out of their beds, even the bed-bound, embracing each other, weeping. One man fell down on his mattress face-first and did not move.

'I'll not bloody well believe it. I'll not believe it!' Joe Stallard stood shaking in the middle of the ward.

The increasing noise from the harbour was confirmation. The air crackled and boomed, gunfire drowning whoops of joy and cheering.

'I'm bloody well believing it!' Joe grabbed Betsy round the waist and they whirled and danced the length of the ward, leaping over the men who lay in their path. Betsy's cap was askew, her face glistening as she hugged Jane, kissing her again and again on her cheeks. Strong, gummy kisses.

'We did it, Jane, we did it! Sebastopol is ours! Read your Isaiah tonight, Jane. *He will swallow up death in victory; and the Lord God will wipe away tears from off all faces*. If this doesn't call for a celebration, I don't know what does. Worth all the sacrifices!'

Worth it? Was Betsy mad? She'd seen them, all the broken men. And each one part of a family back home: wives, sweethearts, mothers, fathers, brothers, sisters, children, chapels, villages, inns, shops. Robbed. Empty shapes there would be, everywhere. Emptiness stretching to eternity with lives never lived. How could that be worth it?

Loneliness is to be in a celebration and not be in the celebrating mood at all. The only thing to do was drink herself numb, shrink the distance she felt from everyone else.

By the evening, when Betsy lifted the last bottle to the evening light in a kitchen chaotic with dirty cups and plates, the distance had disappeared, and all problems with it. The world had an unsteady feel to it, the floor a slope not noticeable before, like a ship in a storm.

Jane steadied herself on the edge of the table and lifted her mug. 'I've a toast: to no more blood, no more deaths, no more maggots and rotten bandages and sights no person should ever see. To all of that!'

'Lord, love you, Jane, for the innocent you are!' Betsy squeezed her shoulders. 'It's only Sebastopol has fallen. This may be the beginning of the end, but the end is not even in sight. The last man will be killed after the ink is dry on the peace treaty, because the man with the gun didn't know it was peace. Plenty more work for us yet.'

Jane was instantly punched sober and steady. Better never to have let the dark feelings free, for it was worse to be shocked by them all over again.

'I'm back to the ravine tonight.'

Betsy nodded. 'As you wish, Jane. As you wish.'

All Jane wanted now was to run, run away until the breath hurt in her chest. She did not stop when she reached the hut but clambered on up to the fort, stumbling over rocks she could not see in the twilight, tripping on nothing at all. In this unsteady state, sitting on the wall was risky, with the rocks falling away below her to the sea. I don't care. I just don't care!

Sitting dangerously on the edge, her boots dangled into nothingness. The sea shimmered silver far below. But she *did* care. She leaned back, holding on to the stone wall, and stared up to the Milky Way, trailing over the sky. God's fishing net: trying to keep everyone safe, but with a terrible tear in it and everything spilling out.

She lay down behind the wall. This would be a good place to close her eyes. The earth smelled of the goats that must have chosen this exact place to shelter. He might be dead, her officer. Shot from his horse and bleeding into the thirsty soil. The thought did not make her feel better. He might be living still. That thought made no difference, for she would never know. She was so alone. Suddenly, a weighty arm was round her shoulders. She leaned her head against his old coat. The smell of him was strong: animal smells and the sweat of hard work. He was with her, and she, Jane, so much herself with him.

Isaac? Why was she thinking of him? Not dead, surely? He'd not appeared in her head to tell her that? Most certainly she would not want to be on the face of the earth, not even tucked behind a wall like a goat, if he were not on it somewhere. Please God, may he be sitting on the bench outside his house in Caio, looking up at the same sky, thinking of me.

A thought is the strongest thing. It can travel faster than a comet and shrink the universe to nothing.

CHAPTER 31

Into The Breach

BETSY WAS NEVER wrong. The fighting continued. A terrible cough spread round the hospital, then a chronic suffering of the bowels, which was worse – much worse. Arnold Castle's chest went weak again and he took to his bed, staring into nothing all day long, his fingers clean of ink. A distressing thing to see, men growing sicker when they were near recovery. Awful to be needed for your good cheer when you have next to none to give and are near empty yourself.

A storm had been brewing for days. Ships had not been able to sail and none had arrived. Betsy was down to the last case of brandy and fretting, when a sailor came bursting into the hospital.

'A ship is outside the harbour, stuck and can't come in on no account. But there's a special passenger on board so a skiff's been sent to bring her in.'

His excitement ignited hope in the men, shared in the looks they exchanged. The special passenger could be one person only, though no-one dared to say her name.

Betsy was in the kitchen attacking a sheep's head with a cleaver when Jane went to collect her shawl.

'I'll not tell you who I'm thinking of!'

Right in the centre Betsy struck, and the two halves fell to either side on the table, one eye in each. Her anger brought on her cough, until she was doubled over and heaving.

Bobby himself sauntered in to make the announcement that Miss Nightingale would stay at the Castle Hospital, now her headquarters. She would make her postponed visit the next day. He acknowledged Jane with an inclination of the head and a salute. Such a man he was now, with his trousers halfway up to his knees and his rough, growling voice.

'You wouldn't know Scutari, Jane!' His chest swelled with pride. 'It's clean and nice and we've classes in the day and singing and all sorts. Men are going home now. No babies for months. Only one nurse sent home for moral laxity!' He said the words with a swagger, though his eyes suggested he did not know exactly the meaning. 'Abandonment, Miss Nightingale calls it. And it's a terrible thing. She has an owl now, and we've a tortoise called Jimmy and a cat. Miss Nightingale's come herself to make things nice here too.'

'Things are quite good here,' Jane said, picking at her tattered clothes. No crates from England had been brought ashore for weeks.

Pandemonium broke out the moment Bobby left: fetching and carrying the entire day, mending, scrubbing the floors with ammonia until the men who could help had watering eyes. Everything was carried out to the sound of Betsy screeching, throwing pots and pans and coughing. Worse, her temper, than the storm outside.

Jane's back was desperate sore at the end of the day, her whole self exhausted, but worse than that was the sense of thoughts held back, building a force inside her head that would burst. She must find a place where they could break. 'I have to go. I'll sleep the night in my hut,' she said to Betsy.

'We're not finished. I need you here. I won't allow it!' Betsy shouted after her. 'You selfish, good-for-nothing...'

'Can I come with you too?' Thomas Fisher whispered as Jane sped past him.

She should stay. But she did not want to. The wave of feelings pushed her forwards along the quay past Miss Nightingale's skiff. The wave must not break. Not yet. Her fast walk turned to a run up the ravine, her breath rasping. She threw herself into her hut, prostrate onto her blanket, her face flattened by the Bible.

Abandonment. No more babies.

Her breasts were sore under her.

She could not close her eyes, but stared along the uneven compacted ground to the wooden planks of the wall, growing darker as the light faded. A baby. No! Not possible!

She was abandoned.

She sat up suddenly, hugging her knees.

How could You, God? I did not deserve this. No, no, I'm sorry, I know I'm to blame. Not You. But please, God, do not let this happen or else I will never be able to go home.

Home was where she should be. Not here at all. She should be safe in her bed under the thatch of Tŷ Mawr, in the village of Caio by the Afon Annell, ringed by green fields below the purple mountains. How could she ever have complained at looking after three healthy men? Aunt Anni – she moaned her name. I need you now so very much. All the women went to her, girls too. Some had the babies and some did not. Aunt Anni would help them just the same.

To think of the impossible made it all worse. Jane was here. Things were as they were. She must speak to Betsy, even if she slapped her and shouted and called her a harlot. But then she would shrug and bring out the brandy and say, 'What will be, will be.' Betsy would know what to do.

Jane walked quickly along the quay. Not having managed to sleep until dawn was breaking, the day had a late feel to it. The wind had blown out its fury and once again the water lapped, the boats creaked. Miss Nightingale's three-masted boat was nudging its way through the smaller boats to the quayside. Sailors with coiled ropes stood ready on the deck. Betsy would be busy preparing for the visit, but she would benefit for sure by having her mind diverted by Jane's situation. Caught in her own thoughts, it took a moment for Jane to feel the strange atmosphere in the General. Something had happened. The men's faces were sombre. No-one was speaking.

'Morning, Jane,' Thomas Fisher whispered quietly, jerking his head towards the kitchen.

In the doorway, a tall woman in a long black dress, a neat cap over her hair, stood with her back to Jane.

'Please reconsider, Mrs Davis.'

Betsy's voice came from inside. 'Once my mind is made up, it is made up.'

'Very well. If you will excuse me. I have a position to be filled.' She turned. Jane bowed her head. She never could get the way of a curtsey.

'Ah, Miss Evans. I had forgotten about you. Glad to see you looking well,' Miss Nightingale said.

'As you too,' Jane mumbled. 'You were poorly last time.'

'I was. Please excuse me.'

Miss Nightingale's skirts rustled as she walked.

'Don't say nothing!' Betsy stood trembling, one hand clutching the kitchen table. Her face was a terrible white colour, her cheeks livid. Her hat was on her head, an old coat over her arm, her bag in her hand.

'You're exhausted, Betsy. Things will get better. I'll do more if you let me.'

'Pour us a drink, Jane. A big one. I'm off, as you see.'

'You can't go, Betsy. What about us?' Thomas Fisher leaned on his crutch in the kitchen doorway.

'You'll manage. I've run this hospital my way for all these months. She needn't think she can come in here with a letter from the Prime Minister or the Queen herself. I've worn myself to the bone. No-one is going to tell me what to do!'

She threw back her head, drank, coughed, finished the drink and quietly replaced the mug on the table.

'Next time we meet, Jane, God willing, it will be in the sweetness of home.'

Hope was dashed away again and now everything was as terrible as it could be. Betsy was marching down the ward, shaking each man's hand in turn. As she leaned over the last mattress, the man held on to her cape.

'Don't go, Betsy. Don't leave us.'

'Control yourself, sir!' Betsy said. 'You'll have forgotten me as soon as I am out of the door.'

'No, Betsy. Never.' He was sobbing, the poor man.

'You've been a mother to us all, Betsy! No-one forgets his own mother,' Arnold Castle said quietly. Thomas Fisher put his arm round Joe Stallard's shoulders as all the men murmured agreement.

Betsy sniffed.

'God bless you all!'

Not a man could lift his head to watch her push open the door, head high, eyes looking straight ahead.

A terrible gloom settled on the men. If Jane were flattened too, what good would that be to anyone? She was needed. She could do this: step into the breach, fill their stomachs, give them drink to warm their spirits, nurse them and comfort them too. She could.

'Get on with it, Jane.' She spoke more sharply to herself than anyone else ever did, and she took more notice.

'Right, Mr Stallard, would you be up to counting the spoons if I was to put them on your bed? We'll need to make a record of everything we have in here for Miss Nightingale to inspect. Could you do the writing, Arnold? You have the pen and paper and your hand is the finest. I could be doing with some help in the kitchen if we're to have food ready for this evening. We'll all want feeding, no matter how sad we are. I'll do my best, I promise you that. And I know you'll help me. And before supper we'll all drink a toast to Betsy. What do you say?'

CHAPTER 32

A Root, Not a Branch

MRS HORTON WAS insufferable. Just because she had been appointed to take over the General Hospital, that gave her no excuse to act as though she had been anointed. Had she no idea how well Jane had managed before she arrived? Did she not consider that it had been three whole weeks since Betsy left? No. Clearly. She had no idea because she would never consider there might be life at all without Mrs Horton at the centre of it.

Back in Betsy's alcove, Jane placed the docket between the pages. Romans 11. Mrs Horton would be remembered by a requisition docket...

> *Boast not against the branches. But if thou boast, thou bearest not the root, but the root thee.*

Proud Jane was of all she had done. Self-appointed as she had been – there by circumstance or design – she had managed. The General Hospital Balaclava had run smoothly.

She, Jane, was a root, not a branch. A root lives on after all the branches have gone, taking nourishment where it can. Insignificant to look at but strong. It might not know where it is going but it will grow deeper and deeper in the faith that it is travelling in the right direction, surviving drought or plenty, cold or heat.

Mrs Horton was a branch. Branches wave about, drawing attention to themselves, but lose their leaves when the wind blows or the cold pinches or the drought shrivels them. Not for herself did Jane feel sorry, but for the men, though enduring Mrs Horton's strict regime might hasten recovery.

Betsy's room at the back of the kitchen had been a convenient place to sleep, necessary for the night calls and the occasional unannounced visits from a doctor. Jane had been wondering how to block the open wall of her shelter in the ravine with the winter coming on – and now she didn't have to. In the alcove there was enough room to stretch up when she took her shirt off, with no fear of knocking herself senseless on the slanting roof as there was in the hut. She had no free time at all without the walks to and from the ravine, but as the weather was worsening, the quayside reverting to mud and her boots worn thin, this was no sacrifice.

In charge! The words had a fine ring to them, which would have burst her shirt with pride had she not lost the weight on her with the scant food and the hard work. Not the least bit nervous she felt, not now, for hadn't her whole life led up to this moment? How proud Aunt Anni would be if she knew. She must think of her aunt and find an answer to every problem. Or of Lady Blackwood, a lady to be admired so for her calmness, particularly now Jane was not with her. Step by step, Lady Blackwood had brought about changes that anyone would have thought impossible. Such strength, such faith. Or of Mrs Seacole. Jane might not have the same colours in her clothes, but she must be as sunny and warm as she was. Or of Betsy, with her good heart, making her own rules – not for herself, but for her boys. A little bit of each of them was in Jane now. With God's help, she'd run this hospital just fine.

All she had to do – over and above what she had always done – was think ahead, and give jobs to the people who would do them best. Bobby would help her as Miss Nightingale had no immediate plans to return to Scutari, he informed her. At night, he would go to HQ in case he was needed and return to help Jane with the morning tea.

Barely a wink of sleep she had, thinking through the day ahead as she had never done before. She must be the one to rise at dawn and light the fire and fetch water. Unless she collected the bread from the Armenian woman up the hill, there would be no food. The Tatars must be organised to find fuel, or they would be without for the following day. She must go down to the quay to find what might suit her needs on board ships newly arrived. Flexibility not rigour. Plans must be adapted round what was available.

Cabbages and a few withered turnips Betsy had left her, together with lumps of meat with a greenish tinge to them. A lengthy boil would be needed. One man had sighted a rat in the ward. Vermin must be a priority. Where there was one rat, it was almost certain there were more. Put the meat on first, then see to every man's dressing personally, examining, deciding on doses of laudanum. Yes, medical supplies must be checked and calculations made. Oh, and the bandages. Someone else could roll them and make them ready. She must try to board up the broken window more effectively than Betsy had managed. Poor Arnold Castle's mattress was mouldy through soaking and he now preferred to sleep doubled over on the stool. The hospital Jane ran would be clean and cheerful. Only when she had visualised it could she sleep, and then fitfully, listening, watchful for first light.

Salt. That was vital. All bandages must be rinsed in it.

Rain gushed into the water bucket outside like a waterfall. A sudden memory stabbed her: on the drove, trudging along in the pouring rain. Next to her, Isaac's head was down so the water ran along the brim of his hat and dripped down over his nose. He'd looked across at her just as she looked at him. He put out his tongue as though to catch the water and smiled. So long ago. Not her, surely; another Jane altogether.

Bobby arrived the second morning, beaming. 'Something to keep in a safe place here, Jane,' he said, handing her a note. 'It's got Miss Nightingale's signature on the bottom and it's personal from her to you.'

The writing was even, sloping, with no crossing out at all.

> Jane,
>
> I am indebted to you for stepping into the breach. Lady Blackwood always spoke of you as a trustworthy girl, with a God-given vocation. Qualified reinforcements will be found in Scutari, but a ship may take four days or more, as you know. The doctor will visit daily, as he should have done all these months. Robert will bring your daily allocation of provisions. If you have sick men in need of special diets, the doctor will sign the necessary forms. Please send to me if you have need to.
>
> Yours gratefully,
>
> F Nightingale

Buffeted by feelings, she was: excited, but with a growing annoyance. *Qualified reinforcements*.

Jane tucked the note into her shirt. She would press it between appropriate pages of *y Beibl* when she had time. One day she might be proud of it, but not now. *Qualified reinforcements*. She jabbed the turnips in the stew, keeping them under the bubbling surface. Boiling meat has a nasty smell to it.

Bobby sat shredding cabbage, chewing on a stalk.

'Don't eat it. I could use that.'

He pulled it out of his mouth and handed it to her.

'No. Keep it. The thing is, Bobby, I can manage by myself and I don't need anyone else to order me around. It's not the way things are done here and I've grown used to it.'

'Miss Nightingale likes things done proper, Jane.'

'And what I do is not proper?'

'I didn't mean that. You are as proper a person as anyone I know.'

The compliment was hard to hear. 'It's so hot in here. Open the door, Bobby, before we boil.'

Another day was soon over. Nothing of any consequence went wrong. Dr Hall visited in the foulest mood, muttering under his breath words that Jane thought wiser not to hear.

Procurement of the next case of brandy was something she was not sure how to accomplish. The tipple she offered Dr Hall meant opening the last bottle. It brought him no noticeable cheer. He pronounced Joe Stallard a malingerer, declaring him fit to return to the front line, his thigh wound a 'mere scratch'. Even her loudest hums as Jane escorted the doctor from the ward did not drown Joe Stallard's curses. When she mentioned special diets and forms, the doctor's eyes looked as though they might reduce her to cinders.

'Get them from Miss Nightingale! She's the only one with authority around here, it seems.' Ramming his hat on his head, he stomped off through the sheeting rain.

Less than a week after Joe had left, he was back again, brought by cart from the fighting. He'd a shot wound to his shoulder. His shirt was ripped and black with mud and blood.

'Not as bad as it looks, Jane. Might have saved my life, that,' he said as she cleaned it and dressed it as best she could. "Cos here I am, back again.'

Sufficient experience Jane had had by now to know the odour that escaped from the wound on his thigh.

'He should never have sent you back!' she exploded, peeling off the fetid bandage. Joe took her hand and patted it between his own, hot and gritty with dirt.

One of the newer arrivals, a surly soldier, refused to empty the waste. He only had the one arm injured. No-one was suggesting that this was a pleasant task, but it was one that had to be carried out to avoid a more unpleasant situation. He must see that. Here at the General, everyone who could helped, for all their sakes.

The first time Jane asked, he simply ignored her. The second time, he said, 'I don't take orders from a woman.'

There was no third time. Thomas Fisher and Arnold Castle somehow picked him up and threatened to drop him in the waste barrel if he ever dared speak to Jane like that again.

Though pushed away, worry crept through Jane's defences. She was ragged and ill-tempered. Twice every night she was woken by the same soldier, a lad of sixteen with his front teeth knocked out and a cut on his cheek. He had wandered into the General dazed and confused, discovered by a sailor hidden among empty crates. Terrible nightmares he suffered, waking screaming, drenched in sweat.

'It came at me, Jane: a beast... like the Devil... I turned and ran and he got me... and his fingers was splitting my skin... he's going to bite my head off, Jane, I know it!'

'It was a dream!' Jane rubbed her thumb over the back of his hand. 'Go back to sleep.'

'It's waiting for me!'

'No, it's flown away.' Jane yawned. She could have closed her eyes and fallen asleep right by him, but by the time she

260

tottered back to bed, after a cold visit to the privy, she was wide awake. That's when the fears came out of the shadows, turning her rigid. It could not be. There simply was no time to think about herself. Nor was it possible to think that a life could be growing in a place where so much life was ending.

Until Mrs Horton arrived.

It wouldn't have been easy even if Mrs Horton had been the nicest, sweetest person in the world, to have someone tell you how to do the very things you've been doing for months without thinking. A sour look she had to her, this *qualified reinforcement*. Her mouth was a line with no lips at all.

'I will conduct the doctor's round with him. I will attend to any new patients and their medical requirements. I see you more as a helper with the care and the washing. I have brought the standard requisition dockets from Scutari. Please make sure they are filled in correctly should the need arise. Now, I wonder about my accommodation.'

Mrs Horton could have Betsy's room and welcome.

Rain or no rain, window or no window, Jane would be back in the ravine. As she walked along the quay, everything released: the thoughts that had been squashed away springing up and overwhelming her. The dull ache in her back since the morning now turned into cramps that stopped her, took her breath, folded her up until they passed. Inside, tiny hands were gripping tight. Don't make me go. Let me live. But by the time Jane stumbled into the hut, the grip had turned to pain. The hands had slipped, dissolved into blood and there was nothing to be done.

Inside the hut, everything was dank, neglected. Squeaks came from under the mattress. She pulled away the blanket. A nest of mice, pink and hairless, the size of her thumb, and the mother streaking away, just a scaly tail under the wall. Let them live. She threw the blanket down on the earth and curled onto it. This pain she knew, though not this bad. Blood, brown as the river, clotted like liver, she caught and folded into the blanket.

Was this not what she had prayed for? Hadn't God taken pity on her after all? The pains subsided. The sky was ink black. Her thinking went one way, her feelings the other. Rags she had in here. She felt for them in the dark: damp and unused for months, half nibbled away. She sat on her haunches and stared over the dark field. She was empty. No secret. No life. Nothing. No link to the best and the worst. No feelings left.

She took the blanket and with numb hands scrabbled into the wet earth a pace away from the hut. Sticky and cloying as the blanket itself was this Crimean soil. Lying on the bare earth inside the hut with no covering but her shawl, she was cold, so cold. Morning would come as it always did.

In the first light, she took *y Beibl* from under her head and searched through the psalms for Psalm 102:

> *For my days are consumed like smoke,*
> *and my bones are burned as an hearth.*
> *My heart is smitten, and withered like grass...*
> *By reason of the voice of my groaning*
> *my bones cleave to my skin.*

CHAPTER 33

Thoughts of an Ending

PARIS IS FAR from Balaclava. The peace agreed there made no difference. Better it was not to consider anything changing, knowing the madness would go on and on, day after day. That way you could not be further downhearted.

Mrs Horton, declaring Betsy's alcove damp, cold and unhealthy, and unsuitable in every way, made other arrangements. Jane was content in the alcove. Miss Nightingale left for Scutari, taking Bobby with her.

Another Christmas came and went, no baby to hold.

Almost without it being noticeable, men started to leave until, for the first time, there was space to move between the mattresses. Gradually, the balance shifted until more men had gone than remained. Better it was in every way to wash the men and prepare them for embarkation than to patch them up for war, and yet every time a soldier grinned at her and talked of home, Jane's stomach tightened.

'You'll be home, Jane, before long. Back with the animals. Why the long face?' Thomas Fisher caught her fretting at the doorway. Arnold's stool was empty. One day he had gone, without saying goodbye. Perhaps goodbye was not that important. You were there or you weren't.

'And you, Thomas, why have you not gone?'

'I have no-one particular to return to, Jane. Do you?' Thomas hesitated.

'I do not,' Jane said. Why was she lying to him? Now. When she never lied, because lying was useless. You cannot change the way things are with words. 'Well, in truth... I do, but this person is taken and I cannot think of him.'

Thomas took his pipe from his mouth.

'I believe you do think of him, Jane.'

You can't see the red in your own cheeks, but you feel it and know you are betrayed. She picked some flakes of porridge from her shawl. 'Sometimes.'

Joe Stallard died. He was discovered quiet and still when Jane took his soup to him, the day his name was on the list for embarkation.

'No!' she said, tipping the soup so it spilled on him. 'You're going home!'

It could not be borne. She put the soup down and cried and cried, great howls and sobs which she could not control coming from her.

'Stop it at once. What is the matter with you? You should never form such attachments. Unseemly!' Mrs Horton was tugging Joe's shirt over his head.

'I'll do it,' Jane said, wiping her face. The last she could do for him and for herself was prepare his body with care.

By the time the Tatars arrived to carry him away, her sadness was back inside. Everyone was silent for the time it took to carry him down the ward. Thomas Fisher took his pipe from his mouth and saluted from the doorstep, and Jane walked out to watch the cart labour up the hill.

'Don't say anything!' she warned Thomas.

'Recovered, I hope.' Mrs Horton said later that morning, turning Jane's sadness to rage. 'As there is not much more that needs doing this morning, I suggest you return to your quarters to prepare. You must be ready to leave at a moment's warning.'

And now the rage was turned to a feeling heavy as dread, but feathery as excitement at the same time. Impossible and yet possible. This day was one she had not dared to dream of. A long, long way there was to go to wind up the thread connecting Balaclava to Tŷ Mawr. That Jane knew. Many would never reach the place they wanted most to reach.

Everything here looked the same. The ships, the quayside, the puddles. The sky was low and heavy, the path in the ravine slippery. Rivulets cut jagged passages over the stones, the stream was full and brown. In the ravine all was so peaceful. So unaffected. As it had always been since the fort was built, since before that.

This would be the last time she climbed this rocky path. The small farm in the corner of the green field she had never visited. Out on the grass, a heifer was grazing. Never before had Jane seen anything but goats there, or the sandy dog. The brown patch on the heifer's back was like a slipped saddle. She stopped, holding out her hand to touch the rocky wall. No two calves have patterns the same. It was the calf the officer had rescued at the monastery. It was! She ran through the wet grass, slowing as the heifer backed nervously away. A stake held it on a short rope. Grass hung from its black lips.

The boy ducked out of the low farm shack pointing at the heifer and then at Jane.

She touched her chest. 'Mine? A man brought it for me?'

He nodded, smiling as she was smiling.

'He remembered.'

She gathered her possessions – few, apart from *y Beibl*.

'Thank you. Thank you,' she whispered, avoiding the puddles on the quay. 'Better than words. Much better. I knew he was sorry. I knew it.'

When she returned, Thomas Fisher was leaning on his crutch in his usual place by the door, sucking his pipe.

He smiled at Jane. 'Well?'

'Well, what?'

'Happy now, are you? Were you surprised?'

'Surprised?'

'A gift from all the men, with our gratitude and affection.'

'No!' Jane hid her face in her hands. How could she have believed for one moment in a happy ending? Surely, if she had learned one thing in all this desperate time in this desolate place, it was that things do not always get better, they get worse too. And now she must force a smile and she could not, knowing that the likes of Thomas Fisher and all the other men were worth a thousand of him, though she could not feel it.

'Don't take on so, Jane! We meant to please you. Her passage is arranged on the same boat as you and everything taken care of.'

She could not look up.

'You have done so much for us, Jane.'

Jane's chest was pressed hard into the railing of the *Empress of India*. The wood was dead, the sheen quite gone. Fine salt spray on her cheeks did nothing to soften the sting of the sun, which had burned all the clouds away: a round scorching force with no pity in it at all. The light on the water glinted sharp as metal. Her sight was fixed on the point where the prow cut through the sea like a plough, tossing water clumps over the white foam.

You'd have thought the *Empress of India* would be a boat of joy, of singing and cheerfulness, full as it was of the ones touched by Lady Luck – or an angel, maybe, or fortune, or fate, or chance, or God... who could say which? All alike:

returning against all odds. No explaining the heavy silence. No words in any tongue.

Survived Jane had, but a war was raging inside her: the thoughts on the top, in her head, clear and right; but underneath a bleakness which was not in words at all. She had been tested and found strong enough, but where was the limit of that strength?

On board a ship full of men is not a good place to be a woman. Blood leaked once more into her rags – thin and rusty as though her insides were still weeping. Every piece of clothing she was not wearing, she ripped into rags. There was only salt water to rinse them. If she were being punished, nothing could have done a better job than those chafing rags.

Standing was better, gripping the rail. Or moving. On a ship there is nowhere to go but round and round. From the stern, the cold-eyed birds followed without a flap of their wings, the water covering the very presence of their ship. Better it was to lean over the prow and face forwards.

The purse Mrs Horton had given her before she left Balaclava hung heavy at her waist. Miss Nightingale's doing: making sure wages were paid – thinking of a way for money to be sent safe to soldiers' wives left at home with nothing. Imagine seeing how things could be and then making them happen. Lady Blackwood too. The secret was not to have a moment of confusion, nor mind what people thought of you. Always grumbling about them the nurses were, but Miss Nightingale and Lady Blackwood were good women too, leaving their own easy lives in England for work so desperate.

The wives left behind could not know that the wives who had gone out with the men, to cook and wash and have babies, had had a worse time, though they might have envied them when they went. Abandoned and forgotten when the men got their marching orders for war. Like Mrs Naylor said, they'd been to hell – and survived. Or not. There were so many left in the earth far away with no stone to mark them.

It's a kind of loneliness for no-one to know the way your life has been. But there was Betsy. If you can journey overseas and live in strange lands for months, surely you can find a fellow Welshwoman a few hills away! At the least, Betsy would know what was in Jane's head and her bones, though they might never talk about the General Hospital at all.

More likely to see Betsy than anyone else, though she'd like to see Mrs Seacole and Sally, who had saved her life. The men said there was no time when the officers left the British Hotel to thank Mrs Seacole or say goodbye, or pay their bills. Terrible to think of her and Sally alone with no-one to make sure there was money in her purse, and no-one to bring cheer to but the old man with the long face.

How glad Jane was she had those strange silverweed leaves pressed between the pages of *y Beibl*, so peppery she could sense them right now. Aunt Anni might know them, though Jane had not. The thought that so soon the old lady might be burying her nose into them had Jane shivering.

Suddenly, she was sitting on the stone seat in the courtyard at Tŷ Mawr, Aunt Anni next to her: bonnet on her head, her great boots sticking out straight in front of her. Aunt Anni! Oh, Jane's heart fair leapt, catching the breath in her throat. The old lady placed a hand on Jane's knee. *Fel 'na mae...* Her knuckles were gnarled, the freckles on her skin like an egg. Try as she might, Jane could not feel the weight of her hand. Her breath was caught, but her heart was aflutter. As good and as bad a feeling as any she had had!

She must touch something alive, get away from this sharp light with power to make the unreal real and the feelings too large to hold inside. The heifer. Her heifer. She picked up her bag and *y Beibl* and ran, stepping over the legs of the men sprawled on the deck. The quickest route was down the narrow staircase to the engine room, where stokers worked bare-chested in the heat. Huge pistons, like the limbs of giant grasshoppers, clanked and roared, drowning all other sound.

The animal smell was not hard to follow. A heavy door opened to a vast empty space. One lantern hung above the same man with the large nose who had shot the horse with the broken leg on the journey out. He was sweeping the dung from the stalls built for an entire cavalry, though only four shadowy horses were returning.

'I'm Jane Evans. The cow's mine. I came out with you.'

'I'm Thomas.' If he remembered her, he did not show it.

Small the heifer looked, dwarfed by the horse in the neighbouring stall – a broad-backed chestnut with an ugly stump where its tail should be flowing. So pretty, this heifer, the brown hair of the slipped saddle patch curling where it met the white, her nose so broad, her eyes soft. Unconcerned she was by the dark and the space and the quiver of the engines through the boards. If a cow has food, there's nothing much can trouble it.

Jane moved through the light to the next horse, a sleek, placid bay with plaited mane.

'Woe is me if anything happens to her,' Thomas said. 'That's the Major's wife's horse. She and the Major sailed a day or two ago. Better class of ship. Suitable for officers but not their horses. Left these in my care.'

The furthest stall was in deep shadow. The horse snorted and skittered nervously on the boards.

'Woah there, Bess!' the man said, throwing down the broom to catch her halter and pull her head down into the light. 'Don't trust strangers, horses!' he muttered.

'Bess!'

Another punch in her belly. How could this be? *His* horse; the same silver roan she had watched pulling the grass in the apple orchard. Just as the wound was healing, the scab split open. Still, scabs do form, again and again; that's the miracle, and pain can be endured.

She turned back to pat the heifer's neck. Firm and warm it was, with the white fur curling soft through her fingers. Her heifer. Her own. A gift from the men. This was the grandest feeling: she had done what she could. Never had she thought to find inside herself what she had found. A proper nurse she had been to them all – they knew that and she knew that – even with no uniform to say she had. Proud she was to be taking this gift home. Aunt Anni would understand, though her brothers might scoff. Jane would march into Caio holding her head high and the rope in her hand and the heifer behind her. So pleased Aunt Anni would be to see her Jane again. She'd not show it – she was not the touching kind, but her old eyes would be washed with joy. She'd laugh and nod at the cow, which would not astonish her in the least.

'Acquainted with Bess, are you?' he said. 'Jane Evans? I remember now. Name stuck, 'cos I'm Thomas Evans.'

Jane turned back to face the horse, whose eyes were rolling in fear. Only a selfish, unfeeling man could bring an animal to a war.

'Easy now, Bess – calm!' She ran her hands over her neck and face, spoke softly into her ear, looked her straight in her huge dark eye. 'We're going home.'

The seas were calm and the wind favourable the entire journey from the Black Sea to the Mediterranean, a circumstance which might make one think that God had at last taken pity on this ship of survivors. In Marseilles a great fuss was made on the quayside, with cheering and all manner of food brought on board. New hay and straw was loaded for the animals, happy enough in their gloomy half world: comfortable and fed and watered daily.

The celebratory mood continued after the ship sailed from Marseilles, though the plenty and richness of the French food was not what Jane wanted. Plain, digestible bread and cold meat eaten in the quiet of the hold suited her better.

'Hard to know what's on a heifer's mind,' she commented to Thomas, as she chewed her crust carefully.

'If they have a mind,' Thomas said rubbing his nose.

'Oh they do, though there's not a lot of passion in a cow.'

'You don't want passion in an animal that gives you milk.' Thomas was a horse man. Jane held her hand to the heifer's nose. Broad and hot and wet, with the firmness of fish under her hand. 'I'm calling her Kadi. Kadi from Caio. Caio is my home. Do you like it?'

Thomas snorted.

'Horses have names! Why not a cow? From Kadikoi – that's where I was shot.'

She glanced at him, but Thomas was not the kind of man to need a story.

Sudden cheering came from above. Heard through the noise of the pistons, it was loud. On deck it must have been thunderous. It could mean only one thing.

'Go and see,' Thomas said.

The men were so crushed together at the front it was a wonder the whole ship didn't tip forwards and disappear under the waves. A dark line on the horizon separating the sea from the sky was all there was to see, but it grew and grew. As it became solid land, the wispy thoughts in Jane's mind became real: the house, the yard, the two dogs, Griffith, Richard, William, Aunt Anni. She'd be outside her cottage standing with her mouth agape, until she busied herself with her pipe or gave Jane the basket and nodded towards the chickens. And Jane would be quivering with the need for Aunt Anni to wrap her arms round her. But there would also be Isaac. Isaac. Suddenly, desperately, now it was possible, she wanted to see Isaac more than anything; to hug him – no, to let him hug her, press her close and never let her go away again.

CHAPTER 34

Another Country

JANE WAS AS fast down the gangplank in Southampton as a person carrying a Bible and a bag and leading a heifer can be. The air made her head light and the busy dock scene had her reeling: spring air, but folded into it tar and brine and the traces left clinging to the clothes of the survivors. No seas left to cross, but still in another country. The shorter the distance, the more unendurable it became.

From Southampton she would walk with Kadi to the Prince Regent Inn on the Winchester Road, not a great distance but one that took an age – a cow is a creature with a slow pace and a mind not to be hurried. All was arranged: she would meet up with Thomas, who would bring the horses. The Major himself would collect his wife's horse – the sleek bay with the plaited mane – in a special horse carriage with two compartments. He would take Kadi on to Thomas' brother in Salisbury and explain everything to him. Jane could ride on with Thomas, making all speed on the other two horses, following the old Roman way to his brother's house. His brother Albert was a railwayman. He would arrange for Jane's onward journey to Hereford.

'I do not want to arrive in a train!' Jane said. 'And there's no train that would take me near where I am going.'

'There are trains all over England now,' Thomas said. 'I thought you wanted speed!'

'No further than Hereford,' Jane said.

The last stage of her journey must be the walk on the drove route over the Epynt with Kadi. With the words spoken, the plan was firm in her mind. It would be better that way. It would take an age, but each step she took would stitch her back into the land, like binding the hem of a skirt to prevent fraying and make it strong.

As far as Hereford, a force like a storm inside her pushed her forwards. A long day and a longer night and yet another day it took, up over the downs, down to the chalk streams, where Thomas insisted they dangle their feet and watch the trout hiding in the shadows. Finally, they made speed following the straight route west until the spire of Salisbury Cathedral rose sharp on the horizon.

Being reunited with Kadi in the small, muddy paddock behind Albert's house, Jane was filled with a happiness she had almost forgotten. A feeling short-lived when she found she must stay two more nights until a train could take her via Bristol to Hereford.

'I could walk the distance in less!' Jane said.

Albert's smile faltered.

'Hardly, Jane,' Thomas said. His nose purpled with irritation. 'And what about Kadi? No iron cues on her yet and Albert's arranging that too. Be patient.'

They were doing everything they could, which made it worse. No interest in the cathedral spire she had, nor any other fine sight. The knowledge that she should be better behaved was painful. She could not look at Thomas, not wanting to see his disappointment in her.

'I'll be the guard on the train, Miss Evans. You can ride in the end carriage with me. The cow will travel in the cattle truck. No expense to you, Miss Evans. The honour of having a woman who has nursed with Miss Nightingale will be the railway's. And...' Albert's face was shining with the pleasure of yet more good news. 'I have sent a message by telegraph to your family, Miss Evans, so they may expect you.'

There was no keeping the shock from her face.

'You told me it was Caio they lived,' Thomas said.

Could he not have asked? By telegraph! From the Crimea to England maybe; but from England to Wales? Anger, tight and hot, flooded mind and body.

> *Be not hasty in thy spirit to be angry:*
> *for anger resteth in the bosom of fools.*

So tiresome, those texts that came into her mind unbidden. A sudden urgency for the privy was the only way to stop herself shouting words she would regret later.

On this occasion – she agreed with her own reasoning as she sat there on the wooden seat – she was being foolish; foolish but reasonable too. Odd that anger felt unfamiliar. Now, how could she be angry about such a small irritation when she had not felt anger over all the dreadful things she had witnessed?

Anger resteth in the bosom of fools. Mam had said those very words many times when Jane was raging at David for all the sins he committed against her – pushing her in the river, taking her clogs and filling them with mud, locking her in the barn with the *bwca* – and she was all for killing him.

Anger resteth in the bosom of fools.

That's not the whole truth, surely? Would it not be right to be angry at all the terrible things she had witnessed? The big and the small. What had Nurse O'Connor said? If you make the small things large, you don't have to worry about the really big things.

275

So small this was, the scene she had in her mind: walking in unannounced, quietly tying Kadi to the porch post, tiptoeing over the flagstones, kicking the boots out off the way, tapping gently on the door. She would put down *y Beibl* on the ledge, for now it would be safe. Surely that way the boys would not have time to be anything but glad to see her.

You can't make things happen as you want. The soil box was full, with a handy shovel so no need to dirty her hands. Was that what life was, forever trying to distinguish the things that mattered from the things that did not?

Albert left for the station before dawn on the Monday morning. Jane had bathed, and accepted the clothes Albert's wife had found for her, including a blue straw hat she insisted Jane must keep. Never had she worn such a hat before. Quite a sight she would make, pushing open the door at Tŷ Mawr and standing there in a long dark dress with a fine hat on her head.

Thomas offered the silver roan but Jane preferred the chestnut for the ride to Salisbury station. He rode behind her, leading Kadi on a rope halter. The weather had turned chill. Kadi's breath rose into the air like will-o'-the-wisps.

Thomas was not a man for lingering or for saying what could not be said. Outside the station Jane jumped down, patted the chestnut's neck, gave Thomas the reins and took Kadi's rope. She was just transferring *y Beibl* to the other arm when she realised Thomas had turned away.

'Thank you, Thomas,' she called after him – such an inadequate word. He raised a hand but did not turn. Goodbyes are wrenching, tearing things, as painful now as ever, which was ridiculous. You'd have thought she'd be used to them by now.

Bess. Not since that first shock in the hold had Jane

thought of her by name. That way, she was Thomas' ride. Now, fleetingly, she was Bess, her silver roan flank fading into the distance. Where Thomas was taking her, she did not know. She did not want to know.

Noise is a good mask to feelings, and when a train is being loaded with animals, a station has to be the noisiest place on God's earth. Sparrows were unaccountably fond of this place, cheery and chirping and unconcerned by the terrible din. Pigeons cooed contentedly from the iron cross-beams.

A bird fluttered down, setting Jane's heart racing. Could she not now hear flapping wings without dread of being shot? The memories were so near in her body and so very far away in her head. She was bringing back fears and feelings she had not considered. What lay ahead? After she had opened that door to Tŷ Mawr, it might not be easy. It never was.

A man was striding towards her in greatcoat and boots, with a cap on his head. 'What do you think of our station, Miss Evans? Grand, isn't it?'

'Albert!'

'Only just stopped the rule that top hats must be worn on the platform. Us railwaymen are smart as the army.'

'Smarter.'

'And you should know.' He clicked his heels and touched his cap. 'Come with me.'

Behind the train, a huddle of penned cows waited knee deep in mire with no grass or hay in sight. Two men in waistcoats and cloth caps were coaxing them one at a time to a gangplank and into a tall truck at the end of the train. A similar wagon was coupled to it, its door fastened with a wooden beam. In the gap beneath, a line of cows' nostrils stretched up into the air.

Kadi would not like it.

'Allow me?' Albert took the rope from Jane's hands and

277

passed it to a man, who led Kadi away. Tears, absurd tears, filled Jane's eyes. Ridiculous to feel so for a cow when she had shed hardly a tear for any of the dying men. Because she could not. Too big. Too many tears. Such a comfort it was, to feel deeply for small things.

It took time to settle into the lumpy movement of the train, but like a horse, the faster it went, the easier it became. Soon the town was behind. They were hurtling through countryside: fields and hedges and farmhouses, though there was no sense of them when all you could smell was coal, and all you could hear were the pistons and the rattle and shake of metal. Animals they passed – sheep and cows grazing in fields, unaffected by this demon hurtling past. The animals Jane knew in Caio would have been scattered to the four winds for fear. Could it be that these were used to it already? Was it such an age she had been away?

They chugged over a viaduct, the river beneath them black as lead. A barge was passing underneath at that very moment. Though the face of the man with his hand on the tiller could not be seen, his head shone as though greased. A stumpy dog ran up and down the barge roof, barking, though not a sound reached Jane's ears. A horse with feathered feet laboured along the towpath, led by a woman with bare feet. The railway line ran so near the roofs of houses, she glimpsed the reflection in a mirror of a girl coiling her hair. Passing through other people's lives: a faint touch here, a barely visible mark there.

Jane turned her hand and relaxed her fingers to better see the lines on her palm. That ginger-headed boy at the fair in Barnet: what had he said, now? Jane would go on a journey and have lots of adventures and come home with a lovely girl. And so she had. The line down the centre bisected her

278

palm. That meant a long life. Isn't that what Aunt Anni said? Always she turned Jane's hand over to examine it, as though it was telling her things Jane's words could not. Aunt Anni! Her toes curled at the thought of her. Not long. Not long.

'You should have seen the engine done up for the celebrations.' Albert didn't like to be silent. 'We all helped with the decorations. Flags all over. French and the one with the crescent moon and a star on it... and in pride of place our Union flag. All of us railwaymen in our finest. We did you proud. Wish you could have seen it.'

'I wish I could.'

'The Lamb and Flag down the road is the Alma Tavern now, and all the street names and engines too... Lord Raglan, and I don't know who else. You've changed the face of England!'

The train slowed. The engine hissed. The pistons ground.

'Bristol!' Albert said. 'Change trains. They've narrow gauge up to Hereford. Wish I could take you further. But I'll pass you into the care of a friend of mine. Stanley will see you safe. Still time for you to change your mind and transfer to the South Wales line?'

Jane shook her head. More and more certain she was that the quiet way would be the better way. From Hereford she could retrace the route up and over the Epynt. A new person fitting into an old life cannot be rushed. Completion must be an unhurried affair.

Beyond Bristol, the countryside took on a more familiar feel: orchards filled with pale frothy blossoms on dark winter branches and ringed with stone walls; elms and chestnuts guarding circles of dark earth in green fields; the distant purple hills, solid and misty at the same time.

Stanley, who had said nothing after Albert had delivered her into his care, took his watch from his waistcoat. 'Hereford.

Right on time!' He rolled his shirtsleeves and began to turn his wheel, easily at first but with increasing strain until the veins stood out on his forearms. With a terrible shudder and a hiss of water on pistons, the train finally stopped.

Quite a leap it was from the van to the ground. Jane threw out her bag to soften her fall. She jumped with *y Beibl* under her arm, landing winded with her hat over her eyes.

She laid down *y Beibl* on her bag to adjust her hat.

She felt the touch on her arm and heard the voice at the same time.

'Jane.'

CHAPTER 35

Isaac

IN THE SAME instant you can know and not know. A slow age it took to look from the boots, up the legs, the greatcoat, to Isaac's face, dark under his hat.

'Am I to help you to your feet, Jane? Is that what you are waiting for?'

Jane hugged *y Beibl* tight. He must speak. She could not.

'You have the Bible still.'

'It has been with me all the time.'

They stood, awkward, for the silence was so stretched.

'It feels…,' he said finally, '…with you standing in front of me, you've been gone only a short while.'

'To me, it's a lifetime.'

'Jane! The same as you ever were!'

'No, Isaac. I am quite changed.'

'I am come to take you home, Jane.'

If Stanley had not come up, there might never have been a way to move.

'Alright, Miss Evans?' He gave Isaac a suspicious look.

'Isaac, my cousin, has come to meet me.'

Stanley nodded but his eyes were still narrow. 'The cow is unloading now.'

'I've a cow, Isaac. Kadi. I know you'll like her.'

Isaac nodded. 'This is my Jane. I've brought ponies. But I've a feeling this cow will choose the pace.'

All was the same and all different. They took a road that avoided the centre of Hereford, linking up with the toll gate where Jane and Dai had taken the geese. She did not want the three Englishmen to come to her mind, but they did, though they did not pass the place where it had happened. She was struggling with them once more: black night, nothing to be seen, a hand over her mouth, under her arms, across her chest as she was dragged, twigs snagging her clothes, nails clawing her thighs... and now it was not dark at all, but the officer's face above her and the sky blue and the horses ripping at the grass. He stood there, his back to her, slipping his braces over his shoulder, and now she had lost her shoe.

The mind is a wonderful and a terrible thing. All those memories, more and more each day, some to transport you to places of joy, but some also to places of anguish. Was it not in a person's ability to take that power away? Make things pale, shadowy, distant as they should be so that then she could say the words and mean them:

I will not fear what flesh can do unto me.

All those unspeakable things that had happened had been in the autumn with winter ahead – and this was spring with winter behind. Look at the hedges now, with the hawthorn bursting out in its new green life!

Isaac was some paces in front of her. Leading Kadi, she was always slowing the pace. Every now and again she had to jerk the rope and kick the pony forward.

'Is Rhys still at Caio?' she asked as she drew level.

'Ah.' In that simple sound she wished Rhys had not been the first person she asked about, but it took her away from where she had been.

'I wondered when I saw the tree where we rested.'

Isaac looked away, his jaw working. 'It seems a lifetime ago.'

'You said it was as though I'd only been gone a short while?'

Isaac turned back. His teeth were still so even, a whole row and not one missing. 'It's both, Jane.'

'And I was going to say it's as though we were only just here. I see time now as some kind of trickster.'

'I know what you mean, Jane.'

They rode in silence, but an easy, comfortable silence, with the ponies' hooves clipping the road surface, Kadi's a soft under-note. The breeze chased dry leaves along in front of them. The hedges either side of the road shivered. The blackthorn was alive with little brown birds.

'I have food and drink, Jane.' Isaac touched his saddlebag. 'I thought we'd make Willersley tonight. Remember, Jane? We'll cross the Wye tomorrow to Wales.'

'At Erwood.'

'We could cross at another point.'

'No. Erwood.'

With Isaac there was no need to say more.

As they ambled along, thoughts came and went from Jane like the clouds scudding overhead. What a mercy that Kadi's udder was still too small to bang against her legs and add to her discomfort. Her head was low and the rope taut, as if the ponies were always going just that little bit too fast for her.

'I should like to know about Rhys, Isaac.'

A man who will not look you in the eyes is a man who feels uncomfortable with himself.

'I should have taken more notice of my mother's opinion of you and trusted you. There are things I should have taken greater notice of while I could. Rhys is no longer in the village, Jane.'

Isaac had that sideways manner in answering a question that Jane remembered now, with a prickle of irritation.

'What do you mean?'

'He did some bad things, Jane. He killed a man in

Llandovery. A drunken fight... a fellow who only had one good arm – a disadvantage in a brawl.'

Jane pulled the pony to a halt.

'Did he hang?'

'He would hang if he were caught and brought to trial, but no-one knows where he is.'

Jane's mind tumbled. Justice for David she wanted – Rhys dead. But the idea of Rhys hanging like Tad was terrible. Seeing both sides of a situation is not as satisfactory as seeing only one. A person is left bewildered.

Isaac too was stationary by her side and all three animals were eating the grass in a frenzy.

'I have thought about David, Jane, and your conviction about that and about Rhys being involved in trying to rob me at Erwood. Over time, adding all things together, I came to the conclusion that you were probably right.'

'*Certainly* is the word you need.'

'It's hard to believe what you don't wish to believe, Jane.'

His look was pleading.

'I know it,' Jane said, kicking the pony and giving a sharp tug on Kadi's rope. Isaac followed. His pony drew level.

'Rhys' brother was in the war, Jane. Killed. Word came just after Rhys fled. Awful distressed they were, the family.'

'There were so many, Isaac.' A low voice is easier to control when you fear feelings will overpower you.

Isaac reached across and held her arm. 'You are a brave, strong woman, Jane, and I am so proud of you.'

Jane looked down with a snort. 'Oh, Isaac, I'm not used to that kind of talk. And I wasn't brave at all. I was just there.'

'God sent you, remember. And kept you safe. *Then shalt thou walk in thy way safely, and thy foot shall not stumble.*'

'Indeed.' Jane pulled over to the far hedge. 'Look, two blackbirds together! Good fortune will follow.'

CHAPTER 36

Changes

THE SMELL OF a thing is a memory in itself. The first sign was the cool on her cheeks. Jane breathed deeply the heavy, strangely earthy air. It could have overwhelmed her. That she was prepared for. But the thought that came with the sight of the river, swollen and deep with winter colour, was that all the time she had been elsewhere it had been here, rushing on without ceasing.

Isaac jumped down to pay the Willersley Bridge toll.

'I can pay my way,' Jane said, taking coins from her purse. A good feeling, having your own money. Was it in Miss Nightingale's thoughts that you could return without the need to beg from those you returned to, making them the better pleased to see you? Not Isaac. He was pleased, she knew. But her brothers.

Isaac stood back. 'You've returned a wealthy woman, have you, Jane?'

'I have.'

The five then marched across, the boards echoing in a dull rumble as the water rushed beneath.

'Shall we take a bite here, Jane – let the animals feed?'

Sitting side by side with Isaac, watching the river flow, dividing round the arches of the bridge, she was almost home. A kingfisher darted upstream, a flash of blue so fast you doubted you'd seen it. A dipper hopped from stone to stone in the shallows. A coot threaded in and out of the reeds by the bank. Weed spread under the water like wet hair. A shady bank of violets right beside her put Aunt Anni in her thoughts again.

'Keep your eyes always alert, for God will provide,' she would say. You could tell, by the sweet and strange smell of them, and the colour so strong for such a small thing, that violets would soothe a cough and strengthen the lungs.

'They were growing right by where we sat,' she'd tell her aunt, and all else could follow, tumbling out in whatever way it came. Oh, the longing for that meeting was a seizing thought which hunched her shoulders to her ears.

'You alright, Jane?' Isaac asked, as Jane slipped the flowers into her pocket. They'd be wilting for sure when she arrived, but that would not matter for they'd be boiled for the cure, and Aunt Anni would know she had been thinking of her and had learned her lessons well.

The first drops of rain pocked the surface of the water. Isaac stood and pulled a coat from his saddlebags.

'Put this on, Jane. I'd a feeling you'd not be prepared for our weather.'

Not Elisabeth's, she hoped as she fastened it, glad Isaac could not know her mind.

A sharp wind was finding ways to chase up her sleeve or burrow down her neck. Jane turned up her collar and tucked her chin close to her chest. The hat was a problem, threatening to fly away.

'Could you put this in your saddlebag without ruining it?'

'Jane, with pleasure. Such a fine hat does not suit you and I didn't like to say.'

'It does indeed suit me. It was only for fear of losing it.'

'It's a grown woman's hat.'

'And I am a grown woman.'

He had not meant to offend her, that she knew as she rode on. But she was no longer his little Jane who knew nothing. She was not.

They passed the chapel at Llandeilo Graban and Cousin Frederick's farm. There was no need to go in. All the way down to Erwood, Jane watched herself, waiting to feel a panic inside, the rising of a grief not at rest. Nothing came. The crossing was strangely calm. Though she stood on the spot where David had lain, all she saw were stones, grey and smooth. Perhaps she had seen too much of death.

April is a mischievous month, like a child: sweet as sweet one minute, vicious and angry the next. Snowflakes started to fall halfway up the Epynt, grey swirling against a leaden sky. Snow stuck to the long grasses as the ground levelled, mounding round the base of the clumps. It clung to the ponies' eyelashes and forelocks, falling dark as Jane looked up but landing white at her feet, turning the world around them to soft silence.

Isaac's head was down, deep in thought. He'd a strange way with him of knocking his knuckles against his teeth. No guessing what was on his mind, and anyway with this blank landscape came the wish to be white and blank. For so long she had carried too much inside.

On the drove, all those months ago, the innkeeper had told her he had had to dig himself out, with drifts right over the door. Inside the inn, she could believe it from the way the snow covered the windows, turning the light inside yellow and strange.

Sitting by the fire, she was thawing in a deep place. They had eaten, and drunk warm beer. Isaac sat one side of the hearth, Jane on the rocker on the other. Steam rose from her socks and the heat was burning her toes.

287

'Do you know who I'm thinking of, Isaac? The person I long most to see?'

Isaac leaned forward. Without his hat, his hair hung dark to his shoulders.

'Jane, give me your hand. I have been trying to find the right time to tell you.' His thumb soothed her palm over and over. 'My mother is dead.'

The fire flickered and cracked.

'Your Aunt Anni is dead.'

Jane slid her hand away, but couldn't move. In the silence you could think you might not have heard anything. This couldn't be. It couldn't be. Aunt Anni *must* be there. She *was*.

'It happened in October. I was back from the autumn drove.' Isaac's eyes were fixed on her face but Jane could look nowhere but down. 'She brought eggs over in the morning, enquired after Elisabeth – had her remedy been of any help? I had to say it had not. She shook her head and said *fel 'na mae*... and she gave a look which puzzled me. Not at the time, but later, when I thought about it. She patted George's head and left, saying there was no urgency for the bowl. I did not see her again that day. The next day I sent George over with the bowl and she was asleep. After I had attended to Elisabeth, I went over myself. A wonderful morning, Jane, a day to lift the heart – full of birdsong and the apples red on the trees. She was asleep, Jane. Her final sleep. In her rocking chair in front of the fire. But the fire was dead.'

Nothing could keep Jane inside, for she would burst with the smoke and the light from the flames as the wood turned to dust. She ran for the door. Outside, thick grey flakes were falling onto deep snow. Beautiful it would be, to be part of all this, cold and white and covered until she was nothing. She walked away towards the blankness. Not a sound there was, other than her breathing. She stopped to hear the emptiness, but though she held her breath, the drumbeat in her temples would not be silenced.

'Jane!' Isaac would follow, of course. 'Jane! What in God's name do you think you are doing? Jane. Look at me.'

He pulled her head round and pinched her cheeks.

'I am not having this, Jane. I'm not having it! What were you thinking of?'

'I'm not thinking at all.'

His voice was gentle as he put his arm round her to guide her back inside. 'Of course you're not.' Jane laid her head on his chest.

Sleep, oblivion. So deeply Jane craved it, but it would not come. Such a longing there was in the men in the Crimea for sleep, relief from unbearable waking hours and the pain of life. Aunt Anni was old, tired maybe. She was Tad's aunt, and he died a lifetime ago. Release for her, more than relief, perhaps. But why could she not have waited just that little bit longer?

Her homecoming was not meant to be like this. It should be full of joy, like the drovers' return when Jane was younger. Such occasions they had in the inn, with the music and the songs: Uriah, pewter mug in his hand and his eyes closed, singing, and Tad with him; Isaac beating his drum and the boys with their fiddles. All the village gathered, crammed together with no room to move. The Reverend Howell, cheeks bright red, was among them to say a prayer if he could be heard; Mighty Michael and Ma Penny; Mr Morgan probably, though mercifully out of sight as she recalled it; as were the boys, over the far side of the room no doubt; the dogs asleep on the floor, and the babies with them; even Aunt Anni sitting on the settle in the corner, pipe in her mouth, tapping her knee to Isaac's beat, and Jane squeezed beside her.

Jane preferred to walk on alone, leading her pony. A gusty wind made the going hard, carving a way through the white. Isaac, Kadi and his pony would be behind, but too distant for her to hear the squeak of the snow as they trod. The ground and the sky were one thing; no knowing the undulations under the white, nor any way to be sure of the direction. Without warning, Jane was floundering, drowning. Beating with her arms made her sink further.

'Help me!' she shouted, but her voice was muffled. The snow was freezing to her cheeks and in her mouth when she felt Isaac behind her, grasping her under the arms.

'Keep still – don't thrash so. Let me try the other way.'

He was in front of her, bending down, pulling with all his strength until suddenly she was free, falling forwards on top of him. They lay shaking with laughter.

'Jane!' It was a moment. It was. When the laughter died away and all was suspended.

Jane rolled away and sat pulling at clumps of snow stuck in her skirt and hair.

'Did she ask about me, Isaac? Did she mention me?'

'She did, Jane. As often as I saw her. And she talked to you and prayed for you every day. And when we worried about you, she reassured us that you were well. She knew it.'

'In her bones, most like.' Jane took a handful of snow and rubbed her face with it.

'In her bones,' Isaac agreed, standing and brushing the snow from his coat.

That evening they sat by the Spite Inn fire, their feet in a tub of hot water. The animals had been fed and bedded down. A shoulder of lamb turned on a spit over the fire, its skin crisping. The fire sizzled as fat dropped into the flames.

'I'll be seeing the boys so soon now,' Jane said. 'All this time I've had and I hardly know how to feel.'

Jane wriggled her toes. Their feet touched.

'That's enough for me,' Isaac said, pulling his feet out of the tub quickly.

Jane had a cloth which the landlord had given her.

'I'll rub your feet like Aunt Anni did to me when I was little girl, while you tell me the news from home.'

The way a foot is shaped, the spread of the toes, the soft arch of the instep and the turn of the ankle can be fine indeed. Sparse hairs grew along the ridge of Isaac's foot with a tuft on the first joint of each toe. The top was as smooth as water but the underside tough as leather. Jane traced each toe, her fingers circling over the joints, drawing blood to the tips.

Isaac spoke without opening his eyes. 'How a man is supposed to speak with someone meddling with his feet like this, I do not know.'

'Meddling, indeed. Have them back then.'

'I'll not offer to return the favour, Jane, for fear of your being disappointed in me,' he said, pulling on his stockings.

Jane opened her mouth to protest, but pressed her lips together again quickly.

'Everyone at Tŷ Mawr is well enough, though everyone has a story.' Isaac hesitated. 'Elisabeth is not well at all. Failing, I think you could say.'

'I'm sorry to hear that, Isaac.' Sometimes it is a blessing that the truth behind words cannot be known.

'I pray her suffering may end soon, Jane. I hope you do not think the worse of me for that.'

'I do not.'

Isaac looked down at his feet. 'George is grand. He plays the side drum at the inn now when I am away.'

'He must be so grown I'd hardly know him.'

'He misses his grandma.'

'Of course he does.'

'He does not like to have the cottage empty beside us.'

'Who looks after the hens now?'

'That's the thing, Jane. That's the thing.'

The kitchen door opened. The innkeeper's wife came forward to test the lamb. She pronounced it ready and took it away to carve. Great wooden platters they had, filled with fatty lamb and potatoes and greens. A good meal should not be spoiled with talking, but as soon as the plates were taken away, she must speak.

'Before I left, I had no thought of how bad things were for the boys.' She picked up the poker and disturbed a shower of sparks from the crumbling logs. 'I'm sure they did the best they could.'

Isaac nodded. 'Don't be nervous of meeting them, Jane.'

'I'm not. I must have been an awkward, stubborn creature. Concerned only with my own feelings.'

A warmth spread over her as she spoke, the fond look on Isaac's face a reward in itself.

'But it was the right thing I did. For I have found myself to be a person I would never have been if I had stayed here.' Jane spoke the words and it was so.

'You will be pleased to hear Griffith is married now, with a child,' Isaac told her. 'Richard is to be wed to Sarah from the Big House...'

'Sarah? David's Sarah?'

'Richard's Sarah now, and a girl who has had a hard time and deserves our pity, Jane.'

Jane burned with the reproach. 'Did I ever tell you, Isaac, that you remind me of Mr Norris sometimes?'

'Mr Norris the schoolteacher?'

'Indeed.'

'Ah, Mr Norris passed on last year. And Mr Morgan too. But I didn't think you'd mind about that.' He smiled at her.

'And William. Tell me about William?'

'He's a fine young man, Jane. Good on the farm, but he's that roving streak that reminds me of you. I've promised to take him on the next drove to see what he makes of the life.'

'I don't think William would be right for that life at all, Isaac,' Jane said quickly. 'He needs to be home with me.'

'We must trust in God, Jane, as you did, that He will guide William in his decisions and all will be for the best.'

Jane knew well that this was an argument that pushed a person into a place from which there is no obvious escape.

'There's not the same room at Tŷ Mawr now,' Isaac continued. 'And there's a different situation when a person finds herself in a sister-in-law's house. Things change, Jane.'

'Are you meaning me, Isaac?'

'My mother's cottage lacks an occupant, Jane.'

CHAPTER 37

A Story

THE CREST OF the hill was a good place to stop. The entire village was there in front of Jane, for the first time in four years: streets and houses, the stream, dark trees, and green fields – all held in the bowl of the hills. This was the feeling, the *hiraeth*, the longing settled. A slow filling moment she had before sliding down from the pony, handing the reins to Isaac.

'I'd like my hat.'

Isaac pulled it from his saddlebag, and held Kadi while she reshaped it and put it on her head. She would walk into the village down the Drovers' Road, sedate and calm, like the woman she was. Only her insides would be skipping and nervous, and no-one else would know.

It was a rare morning. The sky over Dolaucothi woods was solid blue. Ahead in the clearing stood the stubby standing stone and beyond it the path up to the chapel. No stopping now. There would be time to visit. Plenty of time. Her mind was on the living.

Over the bridge, St Cynwyl's Church was clear, the weathervane cockerel on the tower flashing in the morning sun. Outside the inn, Mrs Davis was sweeping her step. She looked up and dropped her broom.

'Jane Evans is home! Jane Evans is home!' she shouted.

In a village, words spread faster than fire. Doors opened

the length of the street. Women ran out, men followed: dogs barked, children cheered. The Reverend Howell hurried down the church path, clutching his cross to his chest.

'I'm taking Jane to Tŷ Mawr,' Isaac said, and the crowd parted to let her pass.

A young man with wide shoulders stood at the fork in the road. William! She said his name but he did not move.

'William!'

When he ran to hug her, he was a little boy, and then he was the young man again, holding Jane in the air as though she was the baby.

'Put me down! Mind my hat now.'

No-one else came running down the road.

'Where is everyone?' Jane said.

'Griffith's horse-hoeing the wheat. Richard's busy somewhere. Let's go up to the farm. What's that you've brought us, Jane?'

'Isaac?'

'No, that.'

'"That" is Kadi. She has come all the way with me from the Crimea, and she's mine.'

'Don't know what the cows will make of her,' William said. 'She's a bit...'

'What?'

'Different from the cows round here.'

'Well?'

'That's all I'm saying, Jane.'

'Let's go on up,' Isaac said.

Richard was walking across the yard with a bale of straw. Such a big man he was, with his hair blacker and wilder than she remembered. 'Ah, you're back,' he said. 'Could do with a bit of help round here.' He threw the bale down. 'And what's that with you?'

'This is Kadi. She's travelled all the way from the Crimea with me.'

'I doubt she'll last long. Miserable creature. Or have you brought your own supper?'

He was not going to make her feel stupid. She would not allow it. 'She's as special as any cow I have ever seen.'

Richard shook his head. 'Not changed a bit, have you?'

And now she looked again at Kadi, she saw a thin, small cow with markings dull as shoe leather, ribs like a washboard and sharp jutting hips. 'She'll fatten soon on Welsh grass. It will be like Heaven here, Richard, compared to where she's come from.'

'Is that so?' he snorted. 'Are you staying for a cup of tea before you go marching off again?'

Richard was the one who had not changed! Isaac was at her elbow, steering her away towards the farmhouse.

Saved by the dogs, Jane's heart leapt again as they came streaking into the yard. What a commotion they made, leaping and dancing round Jane's feet. Jessie turned into the yard, harness clanking and then, for a second, she saw Tad – but it was Griffith, with mud on his boots and his hair on end from the ride.

'So, Jane. Back in one piece.' Griffith's hair was fairer and thinner, with a little more of his forehead showing. His arms were thick with muscles. 'Lie down!' he growled as Jane stroked and kissed the dogs. So uncomplicated, dogs. No hanging on to anything bad at all – love and joy unfailing.

'I am.'

It was awkward standing opposite like this, with neither moving to touch the other.

'I'm so glad to be home,' Jane said. 'With everything so... just as it was when I...'

'We've had it hard, Jane. Very hard.'

'As have I, Griffith.'

'And no-one to blame but yourself, Jane.'

She pressed her lips together and glanced at Isaac.

'That is true – one way of looking at it,' she said.

Everything was the same: the house with its green thatch; the porch with the boot scraper. The door opened. Sarah stepped shyly into the porch. What had happened to her in four years? Hair streaked with grey; a thin, lined face. 'Sarah! You look... different,' Jane said.

'Welcome home, Jane.'

She would have melted at those first kind words had another woman not appeared in the doorway with a baby in her arms. Griffith walked forward to take the infant.

'Meet your Aunt Jane. Jane, this is David – we named him for his uncle.'

He'd the face of an old man in a bonnet, and was wrapped tight as a parcel in a shawl of fleece.

'Don't drop him, Jane,' the voice was unmistakable.

'Margaret!'

'It's never too late to pass on a message, Jane.' She sidled up to Griffith, smiling her tombstone grin, and slipped her arm round his waist.

'As you see Jane, some amends have been made,' Griffith said. He smiled. He actually smiled.

'He's so small,' Jane said, returning the baby and stooping to kiss Fly and Glass, who were panting with jealousy.

'Who do you think he looks like?' Margaret asked.

'Neither of you. Someone quite different.'

Everyone laughed and something awkward was broken, though she had not thought the comment amusing.

Later that day, Jane delivered Kadi to fresh pasture and walked down to the stream. The hedges were full of blossom and new scrunched-up buds of a green so vivid it almost hurt to look at them. She stopped to break off a short twig, though taking a live branch was not easy, bending it this way and that. The stream meandered and gurgled. An old tune drifted on the wind. Griffith was back hoeing in the Dipped Field, singing to his horse. White gulls followed the plough just as they had the ship. Rooks were cawing over the Dinas, and high above the distant hills a pair of buzzards circled, mewing soulfully.

She sat on the bank, watching the water flow past. There was the oak tree where Tad's body had hung. Odd to imagine him in Mam's clothes climbing up that stout straight trunk, for there was no other way to reach the branch which leaned out over the water; strange too that she had not pondered it before. She might make a story from the fragments that came into her mind: Griffith, rope in his hand, staring at her as she washed herself in the spring in the upper meadow. If a person does something wrong for a reason they believe is right, is it less wrong? A person who did such a thing must have cared for Jane so very much. But a story is not the truth and how could anyone know? It was past. Over.

A short rope still dangled there, but that's where they had swung and dropped into the water on hot summer days as children: Griffith and Richard, David, Jane too, and William. If she listened, she could hear their screams.

CHAPTER 38

Aunt Anni's Boots

BEHIND THE CHAPEL, things had changed. David was there, by Mam and Tad in the one plot. Aunt Anni lay, a more obvious mound, a short distance away. Room had been left for Isaac beside her. And space for Jane next to David. Then she and Isaac would be side by side. Elisabeth would be buried at Cilycwm with her family, wouldn't she? Here, now, in this place, it was not wrong at all to be thinking about Elisabeth this way. Reasonable. She was not expected to last the winter. Margaret had told her so that very morning, sitting nursing the baby long after he had fallen asleep, while Jane kneaded the bread. Such a look Margaret gave Jane, such a smirk on her face.

'That Isaac is a handsome man, is he not, Jane?'

Jane said nothing, but punched the dough hard.

Aunt Anni would like the signs of spring. Jane laid the twigs of bud and blossom where she judged her hands to be, folded on her chest, and patted the grass. Maybe if she waited, a thought would come into her head. But none came. Or a feeling of Aunt Anni, somewhere near. None came.

'I'm back,' she said, loud enough for anyone to hear.

How to be different here, where nothing much had changed, that was the difficulty. Walking a clear path sorts muddled thoughts, especially as the way up the hill was as familiar as the line on her own hand. She had returned, and that in itself was a miracle which she must be forever thankful for – and she was. What you prepare for, guard against, never happens. Griffith could have been unforgiving, as might they all, and no-one might have talked to her at all. It is the things you have not thought of that overwhelm you. Aunt Anni not being here – never had she thought of that, but the most unexpected was to realise that no-one could ever know what she had seen, what she had done. That was a loneliness in itself, and she had not thought to be alone.

A blackbird was singing from the hedge below Ma Penny's broken cottage. Jane hopped over the stile but the bird wasn't disturbed. His beak was the brightest yellow and his eyes like cut coal.

A grizzled corgi charged out of Isaac's cottage towards her, hackles bristling.

'Burr!' Jane patted her skirts, and he flattened his ears at his foolish mistake. 'Forgotten me, have you?'

He rolled over, pawing the air, begging forgiveness. His muzzle was quite grey.

'He hasn't forgotten.' A boy the size William had been when he pushed Jane into the drove came out of the house. He'd the sharpness of Elisabeth in his cheekbones, but his father's eyes and hair.

'And neither have you, I hope, George.' He would not wish to hug her. 'What a man you are now, just like your tad.'

He pulled his drum strap over his shoulder to beat a demonstration of his skill.

'Quite the drummer boy now, I hear, playing reserve at the inn. What next!'

Isaac stood in the doorway behind him. 'Quiet now, George. Think of your mother.'

'Is Jane to live in Grandma's cottage now?' he asked.

'Ask Jane,' Isaac said.

'I cannot live at Tŷ Mawr. They wish to treat me as though these past years have not existed. I am ready to leave. I'm quite content in my own company.'

'I'll show you inside.' George was already taking off his drum, but Isaac held him back.

'I think Jane would like some time alone, wouldn't you?'

Jane sat in the rocker by the empty grate. Aunt Anni's pipe was on the mantelpiece by the tins. No thought at all Jane had of taking up the pipe. Bundles of herbs dangled from the ceiling. Aunt Anni must have gathered them herself. They must not be left to waste into dust.

Upstairs in the tiny room which smelt of old apples and mice, Jane knelt on the floor on the rag mat Aunt Anni had hooked. She cupped her hands under her chin as she leaned on the windowsill. Plenty wide enough for *y Beibl*. From here she looked over the valley to Tŷ Mawr. The henhouse was right beneath her, and behind it Aunt Anni's field with its two old apple trees. Kadi would be happy there.

Better is the end of a thing than the beginning...

Was this God's plan? Had He led her here? There were never going to be answers unless she gave them herself, though who planted the knowing that came before the words, she could not say. Was this story already written or was she writing it herself? The question would be the last thing, not the answer.

Neither the chapel nor St Cynwyl's could she see from this window. Only the purple hills. She must speak.

'I have run the race that You set me, God. I have been pure in my heart. I have kept faith. I have done all that has been asked of me and I have not wavered. I may not have been always meek, God, for meekness is not in my nature. You made me to be strong.'

Tomorrow she would take the soldier's note from *y Beibl* and walk to Llanwrda to find Gwyneth.

'There's a fire downstairs needs lighting.' She had not heard Isaac's boots on the stairs. In this room he could not stand upright, the ceiling was so low. 'And a space here that needs filling.'

'I don't think it would be right to crowd in on Margaret, do you?' Jane asked.

Isaac covered a smile with his hand, but Jane read it in his eyes.

'Did you keep Aunt Anni's boots? Mine are finished,' she said, stepping out of them.

'They're downstairs in the porch with her coat and her hat and her stick.'

'Have we the same size feet, would you think?' Jane stood on the oak floor, wriggling her toes for Isaac to judge.

'I wouldn't know that, Jane. Why don't you try them on?'

Glossary

Welsh terms

brithyll	trout
bwca	goblin, sprite
coblynnau	goblins, imps, sprites
cyfrinach	secret
Fel 'na mae	That's how it is
Heiptro Ho!	(traditional drover's cry)
hiraeth	nostalgia, homesickness, longing
mam	mum / mother
rhyfel	war
sucan blawd	oatmeal porridge
tad	dad / father
y Beibl	the Bible

English terms

feller	person whose job it is to tip animals over so that a blacksmith can shoe them
teller	person who warns farmers with his cry of *Heiptro Ho!* that the drove is about to pass through, so they may corral their animals

Acknowledgements

Thanks to everyone who has been part of this drove.

To all my writing buddies at Bath Spa: Samantha, Helen, Beth, Sarah and Andrew; to Colin; to Val. To Amanda and Becky, Jane, Mina, Di, Mary and Ali who keep me going now and everyone else who has borne with me on the ups and downs of this saga;

Special thanks to Pip Morgan for the final edit, making Jane's story publishable at last; to Carolyn Hodges at Y Lolfa who guided Jane to her final destination; and to the Welsh Books Council for making this possible;

To Tricia Wasvedt, for her wise help, but mostly for her conviction that Jane would go to the ball – words that have kept me persevering more than she can know;

To Chris who has suffered and rejoiced with me along the way;

And lastly, to the real Jane Evans, and the inspiration of all the unsung women of that time, whose lives were truly heroic.

Christine Purkis
January 2019

PUFFIN B

Boy

Roald Dahl was born in 1916 in Wales of Norwegian parents. He was educated in England before starting work for the Shell Oil Company in Africa. He began writing after a 'monumental bash on the head' sustained as an RAF fighter pilot during the Second World War. Roald Dahl is one of the most successful and well known of all children's writers. His books, which are read by children the world over, include *James and the Giant Peach*, *Charlie and the Chocolate Factory*, *The Magic Finger*, *Charlie and the Great Glass Elevator*, *Fantastic Mr Fox*, *Matilda*, *The Twits*, *The BFG* and *The Witches*, winner of the 1983 Whitbread Award. Roald Dahl died in 1990 at the age of seventy-four.

Books by Roald Dahl

THE BFG
BOY: TALES OF CHILDHOOD
BOY *and* GOING SOLO
CHARLIE AND THE CHOCOLATE FACTORY
CHARLIE AND THE GREAT GLASS ELEVATOR
THE COMPLETE ADVENTURES OF CHARLIE AND MR WILLY WONKA
DANNY THE CHAMPION OF THE WORLD
GEORGE'S MARVELLOUS MEDICINE
GOING SOLO
JAMES AND THE GIANT PEACH
MATILDA
THE WITCHES

For younger readers

THE ENORMOUS CROCODILE
ESIO TROT
FANTASTIC MR FOX
THE GIRAFFE AND THE PELLY AND ME
THE MAGIC FINGER
THE TWITS

Picture books

DIRTY BEASTS *(with Quentin Blake)*
THE ENORMOUS CROCODILE *(with Quentin Blake)*
THE GIRAFFE AND THE PELLY AND ME *(with Quentin Blake)*
THE MINPINS *(with Patrick Benson)*
REVOLTING RHYMES *(with Quentin Blake)*

Plays

THE BFG: PLAYS FOR CHILDREN *(Adapted by David Wood)*
CHARLIE AND THE CHOCOLATE FACTORY: A PLAY *(Adapted by Richard George)*
FANTASTIC MR FOX: A PLAY *(Adapted by Sally Reid)*
JAMES AND THE GIANT PEACH: A PLAY *(Adapted by Richard George)*
THE TWITS: PLAYS FOR CHILDREN *(Adapted by David Wood)*
THE WITCHES: PLAYS FOR CHILDREN *(Adapted by David Wood)*

Teenage fiction

THE GREAT AUTOMATIC GRAMMATIZATOR AND OTHER STORIES
RHYME STEW
SKIN AND OTHER STORIES
THE VICAR OF NIBBLESWICKE
THE WONDERFUL STORY OF HENRY SUGAR AND SIX MORE

Roald Dahl

Boy Tales of Childhood

PUFFIN

Find out more about Roald Dahl
by visiting the website at
roalddahl.com

PUFFIN BOOKS

Published by the Penguin Group
Penguin Books Ltd, 80 Strand, London WC2R ORL, England
Penguin Group (USA) Inc., 375 Hudson Street, New York, New York 10014, USA
Penguin Group (Canada), 90 Eglinton Avenue East, Suite 700, Toronto, Ontario, Canada M4P 2Y3
(a division of Pearson Penguin Canada Inc.)
Penguin Ireland, 25 St Stephen's Green, Dublin 2, Ireland (a division of Penguin Books Ltd)
Penguin Group (Australia), 250 Camberwell Road, Camberwell, Victoria 3124, Australia
(a division of Pearson Australia Group Pty Ltd)
Penguin Books India Pvt Ltd, 11 Community Centre, Panchsheel Park, New Delhi – 110 017, India
Penguin Group (NZ), 67 Apollo Drive, Rosedale, North Shore 0632, New Zealand
(a division of Pearson New Zealand Ltd)
Penguin Books (South Africa) (Pty) Ltd, 24 Sturdee Avenue, Rosebank,
Johannesburg 2196, South Africa

Penguin Books Ltd, Registered Offices: 80 Strand, London WC2R ORL, England

puffinbooks.com

First published in Great Britain by Jonathan Cape Ltd 1984
Published in the USA by Farrar, Straus & Giroux 1984
Published in Puffin Books 1986
This edition published 2008

7

Text copyright © Roald Dahl Nominee Ltd, 1984
All rights reserved

The moral right of the author has been asserted

Made and printed in England by Clays Ltd, St Ives plc

British Library Cataloguing in Publication Data
A CIP catalogue record for this book is available from the British Library

ISBN: 978-0-141-32276-6

www.greenpenguin.co.uk

Penguin Books is committed to a sustainable future
for our business, our readers and our planet.
The book in your hands is made from paper
certified by the Forest Stewardship Council.

Contents

Repton and Shell, 1929–36 (age 13–20)

For
Alfhild, Else, Asta,
Ellen and Louis

An autobiography is a book a person writes about his own life and it is usually full of all sorts of boring details.

This is not an autobiography. I would never write a history of myself. On the other hand, throughout my young days at school and just afterwards a number of things happened to me that I have never forgotten.

None of these things is important, but each of them made such a tremendous impression on me that I have never been able to get them out of my mind. Each of them, even after a lapse of fifty and sometimes sixty years, has remained seared on my memory.

I didn't have to search for any of them. All I had to do was skim them off the top of my consciousness and write them down.

Some are funny. Some are painful. Some are unpleasant. I suppose that is why I have always remembered them so vividly. All are true.

R.D.

Starting-point

Wendy House

Alfhild Ellen and Else me and Astri
Radyr

Papa and Mama

My father, Harald Dahl, was a Norwegian who came from a small town near Oslo, called Sarpsborg. His own father, my grandfather, was a fairly prosperous merchant who owned a store in Sarpsborg and traded in just about everything from cheese to chicken-wire.

I am writing these words in 1984, but this grandfather of mine was born, believe it or not, in 1820, shortly after Wellington had defeated Napoleon at Waterloo. If my grandfather had been alive today he would have been one hundred and sixty-four years old. My father would have been one hundred and twenty-one. Both my father and my grandfather were late starters so far as children were concerned.

When my father was fourteen, which is still more than one hundred years ago, he was up on the roof of the family house replacing some loose tiles when he slipped and fell. He broke his left arm below the elbow. Somebody ran to fetch the doctor, and half an hour later this gentleman made a majestic and drunken arrival in his horse-drawn buggy. He was so drunk that he mistook the fractured elbow for a dislocated shoulder.

'We'll soon put this back into place!' he cried out, and two men were called off the street to help with the pulling. They were instructed to hold my father by the waist while the doctor grabbed him by the wrist of the broken arm and shouted, 'Pull men, pull! Pull as hard as you can!'

The pain must have been excruciating. The victim screamed, and his mother, who was watching the performance in horror, shouted 'Stop!' But by then the pullers had done so much damage that a splinter of bone was sticking out through the skin of the forearm.

This was in 1877 and orthopaedic surgery was not what it is today. So they simply amputated the arm at the elbow, and for the rest of his life my father had to manage with one arm. Fortunately, it was the left arm that he lost and gradually, over the years, he taught himself to do more or less anything he wanted with just the four fingers and thumb of his right hand. He could tie a shoelace as quickly as you or me, and for cutting up the food on his plate, he sharpened the bottom edge of a fork so that it served as both knife and fork all in one. He kept his ingenious instrument in a slim leather case and carried it in his pocket wherever he went. The loss of an arm, he used to say, caused him only one serious inconvenience. He found it impossible to cut the top off a boiled egg.

My father was a year or so older than his brother Oscar, but they were exceptionally close, and soon after they left school, they went for a long walk together to plan their future. They decided that a small town like Sarpsborg in a small country like Norway was no place in which to make a fortune. So what they must do, they agreed, was go away to one of the big countries, either to England or France, where opportunities to make good would be boundless.

Their own father, an amiable giant nearly seven foot tall, lacked the drive and ambition of his sons, and he refused to support this tomfool idea. When he forbade them to go, they ran away from home, and somehow or other the two of them managed to work their way to France on a cargo ship.

From Calais they went to Paris, and in Paris they agreed to separate because each of them wished to be independent of the other. Uncle Oscar, for some reason, headed west for La Rochelle on the Atlantic coast, while my father remained in Paris for the time being.

The story of how these two brothers each started a totally separate business in different countries and how each of them made a fortune is interesting, but there is no time to tell it here except in the briefest manner.

Take my Uncle Oscar first. La Rochelle was then, and still is, a fishing port. By the time he was forty he had become the wealthiest man in town. He owned a fleet of trawlers called 'Pêcheurs d'Atlantique' and a large canning factory to can the sardines his trawlers brought in. He acquired a wife from a good family and a magnificent town house as well as a large château in the country. He became a collector of Louis XV furniture, good pictures and rare books, and all these beautiful things together with the two properties are still in the family. I have not seen the château in the country, but I was in the La Rochelle house a couple of years ago and it really is something. The furniture alone should be in a museum.

While Uncle Oscar was bustling around in La Rochelle, his one-armed brother Harald (my own father) was not sitting on his rump doing nothing. He had met in Paris another young Norwegian called Aadnesen and the two of them now decided to form a partnership and become shipbrokers. A shipbroker is a person who supplies a ship with everything it needs when it comes into port – fuel and food, ropes and paint, soap and towels, hammers and nails, and thousands of other tiddly little items. A shipbroker is a kind of enormous shopkeeper for ships, and by far the most important item he supplies to them is the

fuel on which the ship's engines run. In those days fuel meant only one thing. It meant coal. There were no oil-burning motorships on the high seas at that time. All ships were steamships and these old steamers would take on hundreds and often thousands of tons of coal in one go. To the shipbrokers, coal was black gold.

My father and his new-found friend, Mr Aadnesen, understood all this very well. It made sense they told each other, to set up their shipbroking business in one of the great coaling ports of Europe. Which was it to be? The answer was simple. The greatest coaling port in the world at that time was Cardiff, in South Wales. So off to Cardiff they went, these two ambitious young men, carrying with them little or no luggage. But my father had something more delightful than luggage. He had a wife, a young French girl called Marie whom he had recently married in Paris.

In Cardiff, the shipbroking firm of 'Aadnesen & Dahl' was set up and a single room in Bute Street was rented as an office. From then on, we have what sounds like one of those exaggerated fairy-stories of success, but in reality it was the result of tremendous hard and brainy work by those two friends. Very soon 'Aadnesen & Dahl' had more business than the partners could handle alone. Larger office space was acquired and more staff were engaged. The real money then began rolling in. Within a few years, my father was able to buy a fine house in the village of Llandaff, just outside Cardiff, and there his wife Marie bore him two children, a girl and a boy. But tragically, she died after giving birth to the second child.

When the shock and sorrow of her death had begun to subside a little, my father suddenly realized that his two small children ought at the very least to have a stepmother to care for them. What is more, he felt terribly lonely. It was quite obvious that he must try to find himself another wife. But this was easier said than done for a Norwegian living in South Wales who didn't know very many people. So he decided to take a holiday and travel back to his own country, Norway, and who knows, he might if he was lucky find himself a lovely new bride in his own country.

Over in Norway, during the summer of 1911, while taking a trip in a small coastal steamer in the Oslofjord, he met a young lady called Sofie Magdalene Hesselberg. Being a fellow who knew a good thing when he saw one, he proposed to her within a week and married her soon after that.

Mama Engaged

Harald Dahl took his Norwegian wife on a honeymoon in Paris, and after that back to the house in Llandaff. The two of them were deeply in love and blissfully happy, and during the next six years she bore him four children, a girl,

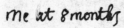

me at 8 months

another girl, a boy (me) and a third girl. There were now six children in the family, two by my father's first wife and four by his second. A larger and grander house was needed and the money was there to buy it.

So in 1918, when I was two, we all moved into an imposing country mansion beside the village of Radyr, about eight miles west of Cardiff. I remember it as a mighty house with turrets on its roof and with majestic lawns and terraces all around it. There were many acres of farm and woodland, and a number of cottages for the staff. Very soon, the meadows were full of milking cows and the sties were full of pigs and the chicken-run was full of chickens. There were several massive shire-horses for pulling the ploughs and the hay-wagons, and there was a ploughman and a cowman and a couple of gardeners and all manner of servants in the house itself. Like his brother Oscar in La Rochelle, Harald Dahl had made it in no uncertain manner.

the house at Radyr

But what interests me most of all about these two brothers, Harald and Oscar, is this. Although they came from a simple unsophisticated small-town family, both of them, quite independently of one another, developed a powerful interest in beautiful things. As soon as they could afford it, they began to fill their houses with lovely paintings and fine furniture. In addition to that, my father became an expert gardener and above all a collector of alpine plants. My mother used to tell me how the two of them would go on expeditions up into the mountains of Norway and how he would frighten her to death by climbing one-handed up steep cliff-faces to reach small alpine plants growing high up on some rocky ledge. He was also an accomplished wood-carver, and most of the mirror-frames in the house were his own work. So indeed was the entire mantelpiece around the fireplace in the living-room, a splendid design of fruit and foliage and intertwining branches carved in oak.

He was a tremendous diary-writer. I still have one of his many notebooks from the Great War of 1914–18. Every single day during those five war years he would write several pages of comment and observation about the events of the time. He wrote with a pen and although Norwegian was his mother-tongue, he always wrote his diaries in perfect English.

He harboured a curious theory about how to develop a sense of beauty in the minds of his children. Every time my mother became pregnant, he would wait until the last three months of her pregnancy and then he would announce to her that 'the glorious walks' must begin. These glorious walks consisted of him taking her to places of great beauty in the countryside and walking with her for about an hour each day so that she could absorb the splendour of the surroundings. His theory was that if the eye of a pregnant woman was constantly observing the beauty of nature, this beauty would somehow become transmitted to the mind of the unborn baby within her womb and that baby would grow up to be a lover of beautiful things. This was the treatment that all of his children received before they were born.

a letter from Papa

... The best tonic both for body & brain I should say is plenty of fresh air & exercise. Long deep drafts of sea air before breakfast, in fact before every meal & skipping should ... eat any chemical concoction.

Kindergarten, 1922–3
(age 6–7)

In 1920, when I was still only three, my mother's eldest child, my own sister Astri, died from appendicitis. She was seven years old when she died, which was also the age of my own eldest daughter, Olivia, when she died from measles forty-two years later.

Astri was far and away my father's favourite. He adored her beyond measure and her sudden death left him literally speechless for days afterwards. He was so overwhelmed with grief that when he himself went down with pneumonia a month or so afterwards, he did not much care whether he lived or died.

If they had had penicillin in those days, neither appendicitis nor pneumonia would have been so much of a threat, but with no penicillin or any other magical antibiotic cures, pneumonia in particular was a very dangerous illness indeed. The pneumonia patient, on about the fourth or fifth day, would invariably reach what was known as 'the crisis'. The temperature soared and the pulse became rapid. The patient had to fight to survive. My father refused to fight. He was thinking, I am quite sure, of his beloved daughter, and he was wanting to join her in heaven. So he died. He was fifty-seven years old.

My mother had now lost a daughter and a husband all in the space of a few weeks. Heaven knows what it must have felt like to be hit with a double catastrophe like this.

Here she was, a young Norwegian in a foreign land, suddenly having to face all alone the very gravest problems and responsibilities. She had five children to look after, three of her own and two by her husband's first wife, and to make matters worse, she herself was expecting another baby in two months' time. A less courageous woman would almost certainly have sold the house and packed her bags and headed straight back to Norway with the children. Over there in her own country she had her mother and father willing and waiting to help her, as well as her two unmarried sisters. But she refused to take the easy way out. Her husband had always stated most emphatically that he wished all his children to be educated in English schools. They were the best in the world, he used to say. Better by far than the Norwegian ones. Better even than the Welsh

Me and Mama
Radyr

ones, despite the fact that he lived in Wales and had his business there. He maintained that there was some kind of magic about English schooling and that the education it provided had caused the inhabitants of a small island to become a great nation and a great Empire and to produce the world's greatest literature. 'No child of mine', he kept saying, 'is going to school anywhere else but in England.' My mother was determined to carry out the wishes of her dead husband.

To accomplish this, she would have to move house from Wales to England, but she wasn't ready for that yet. She must stay here in Wales for a while longer, where she knew people who could help and advise her, especially her husband's great friend and partner, Mr Aadnesen. But even if she wasn't leaving Wales quite yet, it was essential that she move to a smaller and more manageable house. She had enough children to look after without having to bother about a farm as well. So as soon as her fifth child (another daughter) was born, she sold the big house and moved to a smaller one a few miles away in Llandaff. It was called Cumberland Lodge and it was nothing more than a pleasant medium-sized suburban villa. So it was in Llandaff two years later, when I was six years old, that I went to my first school.

Me, six

The school was a kindergarten run by two sisters, Mrs Corfield and Miss Tucker, and it was called Elmtree House. It is astonishing how little one remembers about one's life before the age of seven or eight. I can tell you all sorts of things that happened to me from eight onwards, but only very few before that. I went for a whole year to Elmtree House but I cannot even remember what my classroom looked like. Nor can I picture the faces of Mrs Corfield or Miss Tucker, although I am sure they were sweet and smiling. I do have a blurred memory of sitting on the stairs and trying over and over again to tie one of my shoelaces, but that is all that comes back to me at this distance of the school itself.

On the other hand, I can remember very clearly the journeys I made to and from the school because they were so tremendously exciting. Great excitement is probably the only thing that really interests a six-year-old boy and it sticks in his mind. In my case, the excitement centred around my new tricycle. I rode to school on it every day with my eldest sister riding on hers. No grown-ups came with us, and I can remember oh so vividly how the two of us used to go racing at enormous tricycle speeds down the middle of the road and then, most glorious of all, when we came to a corner, we would lean to one side and take it on two wheels. All this, you must realize, was in the good old days when the sight of a motor-car on the street was an event, and it was quite safe for tiny children to go tricycling and whooping their way to school in the centre of the highway.

So much, then, for my memories of kindergarten sixty-two years ago. It's not much, but it's all there is left.

Llandaff Cathedral School,

1923−5

(age 7−9)

Else, me, Alfhild

A picnic with Mama

The bicycle
and the sweet-shop

When I was seven, my mother decided I should leave kindergarten and go to a proper boy's school. By good fortune, there existed a well-known Preparatory School for boys about a mile from our house. It was called Llandaff Cathedral School, and it stood right under the shadow of Llandaff cathedral. Like the cathedral, the school is still there and still flourishing.

Llandaff Cathedral

But here again, I can remember very little about the two years I attended Llandaff Cathedral School, between the age of seven and nine. Only two moments remain clearly in my mind. The first lasted not more than five seconds but I will never forget it.

It was my first term and I was walking home alone across the village green after school when suddenly one of the senior twelve-year-old boys came riding full speed down the road on his bicycle about twenty yards away from me. The road was on a hill and the boy was going down the slope, and as he flashed by he started backpedalling very quickly so that the free-wheeling mechanism of his bike made a loud whirring sound. At the same time, he took his hands off the handlebars and folded them casually across his chest. I stopped dead and stared after him. How wonderful he was! How swift and brave and graceful in his long trousers with bicycle-clips around them and his scarlet school cap at a jaunty angle on his head! One day, I told myself, one glorious day I will have a bike like that and I will wear long trousers with bicycle-clips and my school cap will sit jaunty on my head and I will go whizzing down the hill pedalling backwards with no hands on the handlebars!

I promise you that if somebody had caught me by the shoulder at that moment and said to me, 'What is your greatest wish in life, little boy? What is your absolute ambition? To be a doctor? A fine musician? A painter? A writer? Or the Lord Chancellor?' I would have answered without hesitation that my only ambition, my hope, my longing was to have a bike like that and to go whizzing down the hill with no hands on the handlebars. It would be fabulous. It made me tremble just to think about it.

My second and only other memory of Llandaff Cathedral School is extremely bizarre. It happened a little over a year later, when I was just nine. By then I had made some

friends and when I walked to school in the mornings I
would start out alone but would pick up four other boys
of my own age along the way. After school was over, the
same four boys and I would set out together across the
village green and through the village itself, heading for
home. On the way to school and on the way back we
always passed the sweet-shop. No we didn't, we never
passed it. We always stopped. We lingered outside its
rather small window gazing in at the big glass jars full of
Bull's-eyes and Old Fashioned Humbugs and Strawberry
Bonbons and Glacier Mints and Acid Drops and Pear
Drops and Lemon Drops and all the rest of them. Each
of us received sixpence a week for pocket-money, and
whenever there was any money in our pockets, we would
all troop in together to buy a pennyworth of this or that.
My own favourites were Sherbet Suckers and Liquorice
Bootlaces.

One of the other boys, whose name was Thwaites, told
me I should never eat Liquorice Bootlaces. Thwaites's
father, who was a doctor, had said that they were made
from rats' blood. The father had given his young son a
lecture about Liquorice Bootlaces when he had caught him
eating one in bed. 'Every ratcatcher in the country', the
father had said, 'takes his rats to the Liquorice Bootlace
Factory, and the manager pays tuppence for each rat. Many
a ratcatcher has become a millionaire by selling his dead
rats to the Factory.'

'But how do they turn the rats into liquorice?' the young Thwaites had asked his father.

'They wait until they've got ten thousand rats,' the father had answered, 'then they dump them all into a huge shiny steel cauldron and boil them up for several hours. Two men stir the bubbling cauldron with long poles and in the end they have a thick steaming rat-stew. After that, a cruncher is lowered into the cauldron to crunch the bones, and what's left is a pulpy substance called rat-mash.'

'Yes, but how do they turn that into Liquorice Bootlaces, Daddy?' the young Thwaites had asked, and this question, according to Thwaites, had caused his father to pause and think for a few moments before he answered it. At last he had said, 'The two men who were doing the stirring with the long poles now put on their wellington boots and climb into the cauldron and shovel the hot rat-mash out on to a concrete floor. Then they run a steam-roller over it several times to flatten it out. What is left looks rather like a gigantic black pancake, and all they have to do after that is to wait for it to cool and to harden so they can cut it up into strips to make the Bootlaces. Don't ever eat them,' the father had said. 'If you do, you'll get ratitis.'

'What is ratitis, Daddy?' young Thwaites had asked.

'All the rats that the rat-catchers catch are poisoned with rat-poison,' the father had said. 'It's the rat-poison that gives you ratitis.'

'Yes, but what happens to you when you catch it?' young Thwaites had asked.

'Your teeth become very sharp and pointed,' the father had answered. 'And a short stumpy tail grows out of your back just above your bottom. There is no cure for ratitis. I ought to know. I'm a doctor.'

We all enjoyed Thwaites's story and we made him tell it to us many times on our walks to and from school. But it didn't stop any of us except Thwaites from buying Liquorice Bootlaces. At two for a penny they were the best value in the shop. A Bootlace, in case you haven't had the pleasure of handling one, is not round. It's like a flat black tape about half an inch wide. You buy it rolled up in a coil, and in those days it used to be so long that when you unrolled it and held one end at arm's length above your head, the other end touched the ground.

Sherbet Suckers were also two a penny. Each Sucker consisted of a yellow cardboard tube filled with sherbet powder, and there was a hollow liquorice straw sticking out of it. (Rat's blood again, young Thwaites would warn us, pointing at the liquorice straw.) You sucked the sherbet up through the straw and when it was finished you ate the liquorice. They were delicious, those Sherbet Suckers. The sherbet fizzed in your mouth, and if you knew how to do it, you could make white froth come out of your nostrils and pretend you were throwing a fit.

Gobstoppers, costing a penny each, were enormous hard round balls the size of small tomatoes. One Gobstopper would provide about an hour's worth of non-stop sucking and if you took it out of your mouth and inspected it every five minutes or so, you would find it had changed colour. There was something fascinating about the way it went from pink to blue to green to yellow. We used to wonder how in the world the Gobstopper Factory managed to achieve this magic. 'How *does* it happen?' we would ask each other. 'How *can* they make it keep changing colour?'

'It's your spit that does it,' young Thwaites proclaimed. As the son of a doctor, he considered himself to be an authority on all things that had to do with the body. He could tell us about scabs and when they were ready to be picked off. He knew why a black eye was blue and why blood was red. 'It's your spit that makes a Gobstopper change colour,' he kept insisting. When we asked him to elaborate on this theory, he answered, 'You wouldn't understand it if I did tell you.'

Pear Drops were exciting because they had a dangerous taste. They smelled of nail-varnish and they froze the back of your throat. All of us were warned against eating them, and the result was that we ate them more than ever.

Then there was a hard brown lozenge called the Tonsil Tickler. The Tonsil Tickler tasted and smelled very strongly of chloroform. We had not the slightest doubt that these things were saturated in the dreaded anaesthetic which, as Thwaites had many times pointed out to us, could put you to sleep for hours at a stretch. 'If my father has to saw off somebody's leg,' he said, 'he pours chloroform on to a pad and the person sniffs it and goes to sleep and my father saws his leg off without him even feeling it.'

'But why do they put it into sweets and sell them to us?' we asked him.

You might think a question like this would have baffled Thwaites. But Thwaites was never baffled. 'My father says Tonsil Ticklers were invented for dangerous prisoners in jail,' he said. 'They give them one with each meal and the chloroform makes them sleepy and stops them rioting.'

'Yes,' we said, 'but why sell them to children?'

'It's a plot,' Thwaites said. 'A grown-up plot to keep us quiet.'

The sweet-shop in Llandaff in the year 1923 was the very centre of our lives. To us, it was what a bar is to a drunk, or a church is to a Bishop. Without it, there would have been little to live for. But it had one terrible drawback, this sweet-shop. The woman who owned it was a horror. We hated her and we had good reason for doing so.

Her name was Mrs Pratchett. She was a small skinny old hag with a moustache on her upper lip and a mouth as sour as a green gooseberry. She never smiled. She never welcomed us when we went in, and the only times she spoke were when she said things like, 'I'm watchin' you so keep yer thievin' fingers off them chocolates!' Or 'I don't want you in 'ere just to look around! Either you *forks* out or you *gets* out!'

But by far the most loathsome thing about Mrs Pratchett was the filth that clung around her. Her apron was grey and greasy. Her blouse had bits of breakfast all over it, toast-crumbs and tea stains and splotches of dried egg-yolk. It was her hands, however, that disturbed us most. They were disgusting. They were black with dirt and grime. They looked as though they had been putting lumps of coal on the fire all day long. And do not forget please that it was these very hands and fingers that she plunged into the sweet-jars when we asked for a pennyworth of Treacle Toffee or Wine Gums or Nut Clusters or whatever. There were precious few health laws in those days, and nobody, least of all Mrs Pratchett, ever thought of using a little shovel for getting out the sweets as they do today. The mere sight of her grimy right hand with its black fingernails digging an ounce of Chocolate Fudge out of a jar would have caused a starving tramp to go running from the shop. But not us. Sweets were our life-blood. We would have put up with far worse than that to get them. So we simply stood and watched in sullen silence while this disgusting old woman stirred around inside the jars with her foul fingers.

The other thing we hated Mrs Pratchett for was her meanness. Unless you spent a whole sixpence all in one go, she wouldn't give you a bag. Instead you got your sweets twisted up in a small piece of newspaper which she tore off a pile of old *Daily Mirrors* lying on the counter.

So you can well understand that we had it in for Mrs Pratchett in a big way, but we didn't quite know what to do about it. Many schemes were put forward but none of them was any good. None of them, that is, until suddenly, one memorable afternoon, we found the dead mouse.

The Great Mouse Plot

My four friends and I had come across a loose floor-board at the back of the classroom, and when we prised it up with the blade of a pocket-knife, we discovered a big hollow space underneath. This, we decided, would be our secret hiding place for sweets and other small treasures such as conkers and monkey-nuts and birds' eggs. Every afternoon, when the last lesson was over, the five of us would wait until the classroom had emptied, then we would lift up the floor-board and examine our secret hoard, perhaps adding to it or taking something away.

One day, when we lifted it up, we found a dead mouse lying among our treasures. It was an exciting discovery. Thwaites took it out by its tail and waved it in front of our faces. 'What shall we do with it?' he cried.

'It stinks!' someone shouted. 'Throw it out of the window quick!'

'Hold on a tick,' I said. 'Don't throw it away.'

Thwaites hesitated. They all looked at me.

When writing about oneself, one must strive to be truthful. Truth is more important than modesty. I must tell you, therefore, that it was I and I alone who had the idea for the great and daring Mouse Plot. We all have our moments of brilliance and glory, and this was mine.

'Why don't we', I said, 'slip it into one of Mrs Pratchett's jars of sweets? Then when she puts her dirty hand in to grab a handful, she'll grab a stinky dead mouse instead.'

The other four stared at me in wonder. Then, as the sheer genius of the plot began to sink in, they all started grinning. They slapped me on the back. They cheered me and danced around the classroom. 'We'll do it today!' they cried. 'We'll do it on the way home! *You* had the idea,' they said to me, 'so *you* can be the one to put the mouse in the jar.'

Thwaites handed me the mouse. I put it into my trouser pocket. Then the five of us left the school, crossed the village green and headed for the sweet-shop. We were tremendously jazzed up. We felt like a gang of desperados setting out to rob a train or blow up the sheriff's office.

'Make sure you put it into a jar which is used often,' somebody said.

'I'm putting it in Gobstoppers,' I said. 'The Gobstopper jar is never behind the counter.'

'I've got a penny,' Thwaites said, 'so I'll ask for one Sherbet Sucker and one Bootlace. And while she turns away to get them, you slip the mouse in quickly with the Gobstoppers.'

Thus everything was arranged. We were strutting a little as we entered the shop. We were the victors now and Mrs Pratchett was the victim. She stood behind the counter, and her small malignant pig-eyes watched us suspiciously as we came forward.

'One Sherbet Sucker, please,' Thwaites said to her, holding out his penny.

I kept to the rear of the group, and when I saw Mrs Pratchett turn her head away for a couple of seconds to fish a Sherbet Sucker out of the box, I lifted the heavy glass lid of the Gobstopper jar and dropped the mouse in. Then I replaced the lid as silently as possible. My heart was thumping like mad and my hands had gone all sweaty.

'And one Bootlace, please,' I heard Thwaites saying. When I turned round, I saw Mrs Pratchett holding out the Bootlace in her filthy fingers.

'I don't want all the lot of you troopin' in 'ere if only one of you is buyin',' she screamed at us. 'Now beat it! Go on, get out!'

As soon as we were outside, we broke into a run. 'Did you do it?' they shouted at me.

'Of course I did!' I said.

'Well done you!' they cried. 'What a super show!'

I felt like a hero. I *was* a hero. It was marvellous to be so popular.

Mr Coombes

The flush of triumph over the dead mouse was carried forward to the next morning as we all met again to walk to school.

'Let's go in and see if it's still in the jar,' somebody said as we approached the sweet-shop.

'Don't,' Thwaites said firmly. 'It's too dangerous. Walk past as though nothing has happened.'

As we came level with the shop we saw a cardboard notice hanging on the door.

We stopped and stared. We had never known the sweet-shop to be closed at this time in the morning, even on Sundays.

'What's happened?' we asked each other. 'What's going on?'

We pressed our faces against the window and looked inside. Mrs Pratchett was nowhere to be seen.

'Look!' I cried. 'The Gobstopper jar's gone! It's not on the shelf! There's a gap where it used to be!'

'It's on the floor!' someone said. 'It's smashed to bits and there's Gobstoppers everywhere!'

'There's the mouse!' someone else shouted.

We could see it all, the huge glass jar smashed to smithereens with the dead mouse lying in the wreckage and hundreds of many-coloured Gobstoppers littering the floor.

'She got such a shock when she grabbed hold of the mouse that she dropped everything,' somebody was saying.

'But why didn't she sweep it all up and open the shop?' I asked.

Nobody answered me.

We turned away and walked towards the school. All of a sudden we had begun to feel slightly uncomfortable. There was something not quite right about the shop being closed. Even Thwaites was unable to offer a reasonable explanation. We became silent. There was a faint scent of danger in the air now. Each one of us had caught a whiff of it. Alarm bells were beginning to ring faintly in our ears.

After a while, Thwaites broke the silence. 'She must have got one heck of a shock,' he said. He paused. We all looked at him, wondering what wisdom the great medical authority was going to come out with next.

'After all,' he went on, 'to catch hold of a dead mouse when you're expecting to catch hold of a Gobstopper must be a pretty frightening experience. Don't you agree?'

Nobody answered him.

'Well now,' Thwaites went on, 'when an old person like Mrs Pratchett suddenly gets a very big shock, I suppose you know what happens next?'

'What?' we said. 'What happens?'

'You ask my father,' Thwaites said. 'He'll tell you.'

'You tell us,' we said.

'It gives her a heart attack,' Thwaites announced. 'Her heart stops beating and she's dead in five seconds.'

For a moment or two my own heart stopped beating. Thwaites pointed a finger at me and said darkly, 'I'm afraid you've killed her.'

'*Me?*' I cried. 'Why just *me?*'

'It was *your* idea,' he said. 'And what's more, *you* put the mouse in.'

All of a sudden, I was a murderer.

At exactly that point, we heard the school bell ringing in the distance and we had to gallop the rest of the way so as not to be late for prayers.

Prayers were held in the Assembly Hall. We all perched in rows on wooden benches while the teachers sat up on the platform in armchairs, facing us. The five of us scrambled into our places just as the Headmaster marched in, followed by the rest of the staff.

The Headmaster is the only teacher at Llandaff Cathedral

School that I can remember, and for a reason you will soon discover, I can remember him very clearly indeed. His name was Mr Coombes and I have a picture in my mind of a giant of a man with a face like a ham and a mass of rusty-coloured hair that sprouted in a tangle all over the top of his head. All grown-ups appear as giants to small children. But Headmasters (and policemen) are the biggest giants of all and acquire a marvellously exaggerated stature. It is possible that Mr Coombes was a perfectly normal being, but in my memory he was a giant, a tweed-suited giant who always wore a black gown over his tweeds and a waistcoat under his jacket.

Mr Coombes now proceeded to mumble through the same old prayers we had every day, but this morning, when the last amen had been spoken, he did not turn and lead his group rapidly out of the Hall as usual. He remained standing before us, and it was clear he had an announcement to make.

'The whole school is to go out and line up around the playground immediately,' he said. 'Leave your books behind. And no talking.'

Mr Coombes was looking grim. His hammy pink face had taken on that dangerous scowl which only appeared when he was extremely cross and somebody was for the high-jump. I sat there small and frightened among the rows and rows of other boys, and to me at that moment the Headmaster, with his black gown draped over his shoulders, was like a judge at a murder trial.

'He's after the killer,' Thwaites whispered to me.

I began to shiver.

'I'll bet the police are here already,' Thwaites went on. 'And the Black Maria's waiting outside.'

As we made our way out to the playground, my whole

stomach began to feel as though it was slowly filling up with swirling water. *I am only eight years old*, I told myself. *No little boy of eight has ever murdered anyone. It's not possible.*

Out in the playground on this warm cloudy September morning, the Deputy Headmaster was shouting, 'Line up in forms! Sixth Form over there! Fifth Form next to them! Spread out! Spread out! Get on with it! Stop talking all of you!'

Thwaites and I and my other three friends were in the Second Form, the lowest but one, and we lined up against the red-brick wall of the playground shoulder to shoulder. I can remember that when every boy in the school was in his place, the line stretched right round the four sides of the playground – about one hundred small boys altogether, aged between six and twelve, all of us wearing identical grey shorts and grey blazers and grey stockings and black shoes.

'Stop that *talking*!' shouted the Deputy Head. 'I want absolute silence!'

But why for heaven's sake were we in the playground at all? I wondered. And why were we lined up like this? It had never happened before.

I half-expected to see two policemen come bounding out of the school to grab me by the arms and put handcuffs on my wrists.

A single door led out from the school on to the playground. Suddenly it swung open and through it, like the angel of death, strode Mr Coombes, huge and bulky in his tweed suit and black gown, and beside him, believe it or not, right beside him trotted the tiny figure of Mrs Pratchett herself!

Mrs Pratchett was alive!

The relief was tremendous.

'She's alive!' I whispered to Thwaites standing next to me. 'I didn't kill her!' Thwaites ignored me.

'We'll start over here,' Mr Coombes was saying to Mrs Pratchett. He grasped her by one of her skinny arms and led her over to where the Sixth Form was standing. Then, still keeping hold of her arm, he proceeded to lead her at a brisk walk down the line of boys. It was like someone inspecting the troops.

'What on earth are they doing?' I whispered.

Thwaites didn't answer me. I glanced at him. He had gone rather pale.

'Too big,' I heard Mrs Pratchett saying. 'Much too big. It's none of this lot. Let's 'ave a look at some of them titchy ones.'

Mr Coombes increased his pace. 'We'd better go all the way round,' he said. He seemed in a hurry to get it over with now and I could see Mrs Pratchett's skinny goat's legs trotting to keep up with him. They had already inspected one side of the playground where the Sixth Form and half the Fifth Form were standing. We watched them moving down the second side . . . then the third side.

'Still too big,' I heard Mrs Pratchett croaking. 'Much too big! Smaller than these! Much smaller! Where's them nasty little ones?'

They were coming closer to us now . . . closer and closer.

They were starting on the fourth side . . .

Every boy in our form was watching Mr Coombes and Mrs Pratchett as they came walking down the line towards us.

'Nasty cheeky lot, these little 'uns!' I heard Mrs Pratchett muttering. 'They comes into my shop and they thinks they can do what they damn well likes!'

Mr Coombes made no reply to this.

'They nick things when I ain't looking',' she went on. 'They put their grubby 'ands all over everything and they've got no manners. I don't mind girls. I never 'ave no trouble with girls, but boys is 'ideous and 'orrible! I don't 'ave to tell *you* that, 'Eadmaster, do I?'

'These are the smaller ones,' Mr Coombes said.

I could see Mrs Pratchett's piggy little eyes staring hard at the face of each boy she passed.

Suddenly she let out a high-pitched yell and pointed a dirty finger straight at Thwaites. 'That's 'im!' she yelled. 'That's one of 'em! I'd know 'im a mile away, the scummy little bounder!'

The entire school turned to look at Thwaites. 'W-what have *I* done?' he stuttered, appealing to Mr Coombes.

'Shut up,' Mr Coombes said.

Mrs Pratchett's eyes flicked over and settled on my own face. I looked down and studied the black asphalt surface of the playground.

''Ere's another of 'em!' I heard her yelling. 'That one there!' She was pointing at me now.

'You're quite sure?' Mr Coombes said.

'Of course I'm sure!' she cried. 'I never forgets a face, least of all when it's as sly as that! 'Ee's one of 'em all right! There was five altogether! Now where's them other three?'

The other three, as I knew very well, were coming up next.

Mrs Pratchett's face was glimmering with venom as her eyes travelled beyond me down the line.

'There they are!' she cried out, stabbing the air with her finger. ''Im . . . and '*im* . . . and '*im*! That's the five of 'em all right! We don't need to look no farther than this, 'Eadmaster! They're all 'ere, the nasty dirty little pigs! You've got their names, 'ave you?'

'I've got their names, Mrs Pratchett,' Mr Coombes told her. 'I'm much obliged to you.'

'And I'm much obliged to *you*, 'Eadmaster,' she answered.

As Mr Coombes led her away across the playground, we heard her saying, 'Right in the jar of Gobstoppers it was! A stinkin' dead mouse which I will never forget as long as I live!'

'You have my deepest sympathy,' Mr Coombes was muttering.

'Talk about shocks!' she went on. 'When my fingers caught 'old of that nasty soggy stinkin' dead mouse . . .' Her voice trailed away as Mr Coombes led her quickly through the door into the school building.

Mrs Pratchett's revenge

Our form master came into the classroom with a piece of paper in his hand. 'The following are to report to the Headmaster's study at once,' he said. 'Thwaites . . . Dahl . . .' And then he read out the other three names which I have forgotten.

The five of us stood up and left the room. We didn't speak as we made our way down the long corridor into the Headmaster's private quarters where the dreaded study was situated. Thwaites knocked on the door.

'Enter!'

We sidled in. The room smelled of leather and tobacco. Mr Coombes was standing in the middle of it, dominating everything, a giant of a man if ever there was one, and in his hands he held a long yellow cane which curved round the top like a walking stick.

the cane

'I don't want any lies,' he said. 'I know very well you did it and you were all in it together. Line up over there against the bookcase.'

We lined up, Thwaites in front and I, for some reason, at the very back. I was last in the line.

'You,' Mr Coombes said, pointing the cane at Thwaites,

'Come over here.'

Thwaites went forward very slowly.

'Bend over,' Mr Coombes said.

Thwaites bent over. Our eyes were riveted on him. We were hypnotized by it all. We knew, of course, that boys got the cane now and again, but we had never heard of anyone being made to watch.

'Tighter, boy, tighter!' Mr Coombes snapped out. 'Touch the ground!'

Thwaites touched the carpet with the tips of his fingers.

Mr Coombes stood back and took up a firm stance with his legs well apart. I thought how small Thwaites's bottom looked and how very tight it was. Mr Coombes had his eyes focused squarely upon it. He raised the cane high above his shoulder, and as he brought it down, it made a loud swishing sound, and then there was a crack like a pistol shot as it struck Thwaites's bottom.

Little Thwaites seemed to lift about a foot into the air and he yelled 'Ow-w-w-w-w-w-w-w-w-w!' and straightened up like elastic.

''*Arder!*' shrieked a voice from over in the corner.

Now it was our turn to jump. We looked round and there, sitting in one of Mr Coombes's big leather armchairs, was the tiny loathsome figure of Mrs Pratchett! She was bounding up and down with excitement. 'Lay it into 'im!' she was shrieking. 'Let 'im 'ave it! Teach 'im a lesson!'

'Get down, boy!' Mr Coombes ordered. 'And stay down! You get an extra one every time you straighten up!'

'That's tellin' 'im!' shrieked Mrs Pratchett. 'That's tellin' the little blighter!'

I could hardly believe what I was seeing. It was like some awful pantomime. The violence was bad enough, and being made to watch it was even worse, but with Mrs

Pratchett in the audience the whole thing became a night-mare.

Swish-crack! went the cane.

'Ow-w-w-w-w!' yelled Thwaites.

''Arder!' shrieked Mrs Pratchett. 'Stitch 'im up! Make it sting! Tickle 'im up good and proper! Warm 'is backside for 'im! Go on, warm it up, 'Eadmaster!'

Thwaites received four strokes, and by gum, they were four real whoppers.

'Next!' snapped Mr Coombes.

Thwaites came hopping past us on his toes, clutching his bottom with both hands and yelling, 'Ow! Ouch! Ouch! Ouch! Owwwww!'

With tremendous reluctance, the next boy sidled forward to his fate. I stood there wishing I hadn't been last in the line. The watching and waiting were probably even greater torture than the event itself.

Mr Coombes's performance the second time was the same as the first. So was Mrs Pratchett's. She kept up her screeching all the way through, exhorting Mr Coombes to greater and still greater efforts, and the awful thing was that he seemed to be responding to her cries. He was like an athlete who is spurred on by the shouts of the crowd in the stands. Whether this was true or not, I was sure of one thing. He wasn't weakening.

My own turn came at last. My mind was swimming and my eyes had gone all blurry as I went forward to bend over. I can remember wishing my mother would suddenly come bursting into the room shouting, 'Stop! How dare you do that to my son!' But she didn't. All I heard was Mrs Pratchett's dreadful high-pitched voice behind me screeching, 'This one's the cheekiest of the bloomin' lot, 'Eadmaster! Make sure you let 'im 'ave it good and strong!'

Mr Coombes did just that. As the first stroke landed and the pistol-crack sounded, I was thrown forward so violently that if my fingers hadn't been touching the carpet, I think I would have fallen flat on my face. As it was, I was able to catch myself on the palms of my hands and keep my balance. At first I heard only the *crack* and felt absolutely nothing at all, but a fraction of a second later the burning sting that flooded across my buttocks was so terrific that all I could do was gasp. I gave a great gushing gasp that emptied my lungs of every breath of air that was in them.

It felt, I promise you, as though someone had laid a red-hot poker against my flesh and was pressing down on it hard.

The second stroke was worse than the first and this was probably because Mr Coombes was well practised and had a splendid aim. He was able, so it seemed, to land the second one almost exactly across the narrow line where the first one had struck. It is bad enough when the cane lands on fresh skin, but when it comes down on bruised and wounded flesh, the agony is unbelievable.

The third one seemed even worse than the second. Whether or not the wily Mr Coombes had chalked the cane beforehand and had thus made an aiming mark on my grey flannel shorts after the first stroke, I do not know. I am inclined to doubt it because he must have known that this was a practice much frowned upon by Headmasters in general in those days. It was not only regarded as unsporting, it was also an admission that you were not an expert at the job.

By the time the fourth stroke was delivered, my entire backside seemed to be going up in flames.

Far away in the distance, I heard Mr Coombes's voice saying, 'Now get out.'

As I limped across the study clutching my buttocks hard with both hands, a cackling sound came from the armchair over in the corner, and then I heard the vinegary voice of Mrs Pratchett saying, 'I am much obliged to you, 'Eadmaster, very much obliged. I don't think we is goin' to see any more stinkin' mice in my Gobstoppers from now on.'

When I returned to the classroom my eyes were wet with tears and everybody stared at me. My bottom hurt when I sat down at my desk.

That evening after supper my three sisters had their baths before me. Then it was my turn, but as I was about to step into the bathtub, I heard a horrified gasp from my mother behind me.

'What's this?' she gasped. 'What's happened to you?' She was staring at my bottom. I myself had not inspected it up to then, but when I twisted my head around and took a look at one of my buttocks, I saw the scarlet stripes and the deep blue bruising in between.

'Who did this?' my mother cried. 'Tell me at once!'

In the end I had to tell her the whole story, while my three sisters (aged nine, six and four) stood around in their nighties listening goggle-eyed. My mother heard me out in silence. She asked no questions. She just let me talk, and when I had finished, she said to our nurse, 'You get them into bed, Nanny. I'm going out.'

If I had had the slightest idea of what she was going to do next, I would have tried to stop her, but I hadn't. She went straight downstairs and put on her hat. Then she marched out of the house, down the drive and on to the road. I saw her through my bedroom window as she went out of the gates and turned left, and I remember calling out to her to come back, come back, come back. But she took no notice of me. She was walking very quickly, with her head held high and her body erect, and by the look of things I figured that Mr Coombes was in for a hard time.

About an hour later, my mother returned and came upstairs to kiss us all goodnight. 'I wish you hadn't done that,' I said to her. 'It makes me look silly.'

'They don't beat small children like that where I come from,' she said. 'I won't allow it.'

'What did Mr Coombes say to you, Mama?'

'He told me I was a foreigner and I didn't understand how British schools were run,' she said.

'Did he get ratty with you?'

'Very ratty,' she said. 'He told me that if I didn't like his methods I could take you away.'

'What did you say?'

'I said I would, as soon as the school year is finished. I shall find you an *English* school this time,' she said. 'Your father was right. English schools are the best in the world.'

'Does that mean it'll be a boarding school?' I asked.

'It'll have to be,' she said. 'I'm not quite ready to move the whole family to England yet.'

So I stayed on at Llandaff Cathedral School until the end of the summer term.

Going to Norway

The summer holidays! Those magic words! The mere mention of them used to send shivers of joy rippling over my skin.

All my summer holidays, from when I was four years old to when I was seventeen (1920 to 1932), were totally idyllic. This, I am certain, was because we always went to the same idyllic place and that place was Norway.

Except for my ancient half-sister and my not-quite-so-ancient half-brother, the rest of us were all pure Norwegian by blood. We all spoke Norwegian and all our relations

lived over there. So in a way, going to Norway every summer was like going home.

Even the journey was an event. Do not forget that there were no commercial aeroplanes in those times, so it took us four whole days to complete the trip out and another four days to get home again.

We were always an enormous party. There were my three sisters and my ancient half-sister (that's four), and my half-brother and me (that's six), and my mother (that's seven), and Nanny (that's eight), and in addition to these, there were never less than two others who were some sort of anonymous ancient friends of the ancient half-sister (that's ten altogether).

Looking back on it now, I don't know how my mother did it. There were all those train bookings and boat bookings and hotel bookings to be made in advance by letter. She had to make sure that we had enough shorts and shirts and sweaters and gymshoes and bathing costumes (you couldn't even buy a shoelace on the island we were going to), and the packing must have been a nightmare. Six huge trunks were carefully packed, as well as countless suitcases, and when the great departure day arrived, the ten of us, together with our mountains of luggage, would set out on the first and easiest step of the journey, the train to London.

When we arrived in London, we tumbled into three taxis and went clattering across the great city to King's Cross, where we got on to the train for Newcastle, two hundred miles to the north. The trip to Newcastle took about five hours, and when we arrived there, we needed three more taxis to take us from the station to the docks, where our boat would be waiting. The next stop after that would be Oslo, the capital of Norway.

When I was young, the capital of Norway was not called

Oslo. It was called Christiania. But somewhere along the line, the Norwegians decided to do away with that pretty name and call it Oslo instead. As children, we always knew it as Christiania, but if I call it that here we shall only get confused, so I had better stick to Oslo all the way through.

The sea journey from Newcastle to Oslo took two days and a night, and if it was rough, as it often was, all of us got seasick except our dauntless mother. We used to lie in deck-chairs on the promenade deck, within easy reach of the rails, embalmed in rugs, our faces slate-grey and our stomachs churning, refusing the hot soup and ship's biscuits the kindly steward kept offering us. And as for poor Nanny, she began to feel sick the moment she set foot on deck. 'I hate these things!' she used to say. 'I'm sure we'll never get there! Which lifeboat do we go to when it starts to sink?' Then she would retire to her cabin, where she stayed groaning and trembling until the ship was firmly tied up at the quayside in Oslo harbour the next day.

We always stopped off for one night in Oslo so that we could have a grand annual family reunion with Bestemama and Bestepapa, our mother's parents, and with her two maiden sisters (our aunts) who lived in the same house.

When we got off the boat, we all went in a cavalcade of taxis straight to the Grand Hotel, where we would sleep one night, to drop off our luggage. Then, keeping the same taxis, we drove on to the grandparents' house, where an emotional welcome awaited us. All of us were embraced and kissed many times and tears flowed down wrinkled old cheeks and suddenly that quiet gloomy house came alive with many children's voices.

Ever since I first saw her, Bestemama was terrifically ancient. She was a white-haired wrinkly-faced old bird who seemed always to be sitting in her rocking-chair, rocking away and smiling benignly at this vast influx of grandchildren who barged in from miles away to take over her house for a few hours every year.

Bestepapa was the quiet one. He was a small dignified scholar with a white goatee beard, and as far as I could gather, he was an astrologer, a meteorologist and a speaker of ancient Greek. Like Bestemama, he sat most of the time quietly in a chair, saying very little and totally over-whelmed, I imagine, by the raucous rabble who were destroying his neat and polished home. The two things I remember most about Bestepapa were that he wore black boots and that he smoked an extraordinary pipe. The bowl of his pipe was made of meerschaum clay, and it had a flexible stem about three feet long so that the bowl rested on his lap.

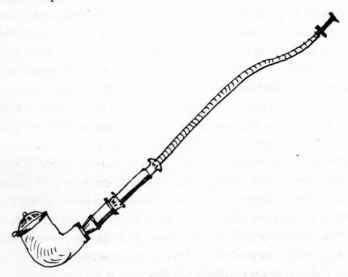

All the grown-ups including Nanny, and all the children, even when the youngest was only a year old, sat down around the big oval dining-room table on the afternoon of our arrival, for the great annual celebration feast with the grandparents, and the food we received never varied. This was a Norwegian household, and for the Norwegians the best food in the world is fish. And when they say fish, they don't mean the sort of thing you and I get from the fishmonger. They mean *fresh fish*, fish that has been caught no more than twenty-four hours before and has never been frozen or chilled on a block of ice. I agree with them that the proper way to prepare fish like this is to poach it, and that is what they do with the finest specimens. And Norwegians, by the way, always eat the skin of the boiled fish, which they say has the best taste of all.

So naturally this great celebration feast started with fish. A massive fish, a flounder as big as a tea-tray and as thick as your arm was brought to the table. It had nearly black skin on top which was covered with brilliant orange spots, and it had, of course, been perfectly poached. Large white hunks of this fish were carved out and put on to our plates, and with it we had hollandaise sauce and boiled new potatoes. Nothing else. And by gosh, it was delicious.

As soon as the remains of the fish had been cleared away, a tremendous craggy mountain of home-made ice-cream would be carried in. Apart from being the creamiest ice-cream in the world, the flavour was unforgettable. There were thousands of little chips of crisp burnt toffee mixed into it (the Norwegians call it *krokan*), and as a result it didn't simply melt in your mouth like ordinary ice-cream. You chewed it and it went *crunch* and the taste was something you dreamed about for days afterwards.

This great feast would be interrupted by a small speech of welcome from my grandfather, and the grown-ups would raise their long-stemmed wine glasses and say 'skaal' many times throughout the meal.

When the guzzling was over, those who were considered old enough were given small glasses of home-made liqueur, a colourless but fiery drink that smelled of mulberries. The glasses were raised again and again, and the 'skaaling' seemed to go on for ever. In Norway, you may select any individual around the table and skaal him or her in a small private ceremony. You first lift your glass high and call out the name. 'Bestemama!' you say. 'Skaal, Bestemama!'

Bestemama and Bestepapa (and Astri)

She will then lift her own glass and hold it up high. At the same time your own eyes meet hers, and you *must* keep looking deep into her eyes as you sip your drink. After you have both done this, you raise your glasses high up again in a sort of silent final salute, and only then does each person look away and set down his glass. It is a serious and solemn ceremony, and as a rule on formal occasions everyone skaals everyone else round the table once. If there are, for example, ten people present and you are one of them, you will skaal your nine companions once each individually, and you yourself will also receive nine separate skaals at different times during the meal – eighteen in all. That's how they work it in polite society over there, at least they used to in the old days, and quite a business it was. By the time I was ten, I would be permitted to take part in these ceremonies, and I always finished up as tipsy as a lord.

The magic island

The next morning, everyone got up early and eager to continue the journey. There was another full day's travelling to be done before we reached our final destination, most of it by boat. So after a rapid breakfast, our cavalcade left the Grand Hotel in three more taxis and headed for Oslo docks. There we went on board a small coastal steamer, and Nanny was heard to say, 'I'm sure it leaks! We shall all be food for the fishes before the day is out!' Then she would disappear below for the rest of the trip.

Fra Havna, Rössesund   Eneret A. Mathisen fotograf Tønsberg

We loved this part of the journey. The splendid little vessel with its single tall funnel would move out into the calm waters of the fjord and proceed at a leisurely pace along the coast, stopping every hour or so at a small wooden jetty where a group of villagers and summer people would be waiting to welcome friends or to collect parcels and mail. Unless you have sailed down the Oslofjord like this yourself on a tranquil summer's day, you cannot imagine what it is like. It is impossible to describe the sensation of absolute peace and beauty that surrounds you. The boat weaves in and out between countless tiny islands, some with small brightly painted wooden houses on them, but many with not a house or a tree on the bare rocks. These granite rocks are so smooth that you can lie and sun yourself on them in your bathing-costume without putting a towel underneath. We would see long-legged girls and tall boys basking on the rocks of the islands. There are no sandy beaches on the fjord. The rocks go straight down to the water's edge and the water is immediately deep. As a result, Norwegian children all learn to swim when they are very young because if you can't swim it is difficult to find a place to bathe.

Sometimes when our little vessel slipped between two small islands, the channel was so narrow we could almost touch the rocks on either side. We would pass row-boats and canoes with flaxen-haired children in them, their skins browned by the sun, and we would wave to them and watch their tiny boats rocking violently in the swell that our larger ship left behind.

Late in the afternoon, we would come finally to the end of the journey, the island of Tjöme. This was where our mother always took us. Heaven knows how she found it, but to us it was the greatest place on earth. About two hundred yards from the jetty, along a narrow, dusty road, stood a simple wooden hotel painted white. It was run by an elderly couple whose faces I still remember vividly, and every year they welcomed us like old friends. Everything about the hotel was extremely primitive, except the dining-room. The walls, the ceiling and the floor of our bedrooms were made of plain unvarnished pine planks. There was a washbasin and a jug of cold water in each of them. The lavatories were in a rickety wooden outhouse at the back of the hotel and each cubicle contained nothing more than a round hole cut in a piece of wood. You sat on the hole and what you did there dropped into a pit ten feet below. If you looked down the hole, you would often see rats scurrying about in the gloom. All this we took for granted.

Breakfast was the best meal of the day in our hotel, and it was all laid out on a huge table in the middle of the dining-room from which you helped yourself. There were maybe fifty different dishes to choose from on that table. There were large jugs of milk, which all Norwegian children drink at every meal. There were plates of cold beef, veal, ham and pork. There was cold boiled mackerel submerged in aspic. There were spiced and pickled herring fillets, sardines, smoked eels and cod's roe. There was a large bowl piled high with hot boiled eggs. There were cold omelettes with chopped ham in them, and cold chicken and hot coffee for the grown-ups, and hot crisp rolls baked in the hotel kitchen, which we ate with butter and cranberry jam. There were stewed apricots and five or six different cheeses including of course the ever-present gjetost, that tall brown rather sweet Norwegian goat's cheese which you find on just about every table in the land.

After breakfast, we collected our bathing things and the whole party, all ten of us, would pile into our boat.

Everyone has some sort of a boat in Norway. Nobody sits around in front of the hotel. Nor does anyone sit on the beach because there aren't any beaches to sit on. In the early days, we had only a row-boat, but a very fine one it was. It carried all of us easily, with places for two rowers. My mother took one pair of oars and my fairly ancient half-brother took the other, and off we would go.

My mother and the half-brother (he was somewhere around eighteen then) were expert rowers. They kept in perfect time and the oars went *click-click*, *click-click* in their wooden rowlocks, and the rowers never paused once during the long forty-minute journey. The rest of us sat in the boat trailing our fingers in the clear water and looking for jellyfish. We skimmed across the sound and went whizzing through narrow channels with rocky islands on either side, heading as always for a very secret tiny patch of sand on a distant island that only we knew about. In the early days we needed a place like this where we could paddle and play about because my youngest sister was only one, the next

63

sister was three and I was four. The rocks and the deep water were no good to us.

Every day, for several summers, that tiny secret sand-patch on that tiny secret island was our regular destination. We would stay there for three or four hours, messing about in the water and in the rockpools and getting extraordinarily sunburnt.

Me, Alfhild, Else Norway 1924

In later years, when we were all a little older and could swim, the daily routine became different. By then, my mother had acquired a motor-boat, a small and not very seaworthy white wooden vessel which sat far too low in the water and was powered by an unreliable one-cylinder engine. The fairly ancient half-brother was the only one who could make the engine go at all. It was extremely difficult to start, and he always had to unscrew the sparking-plug and pour petrol into the cylinder. Then he swung a flywheel round and round, and with a bit of luck, after a lot of coughing and spluttering, the thing would finally get going.

When we first acquired the motor-boat, my youngest sister was four and I was seven, and by then all of us had learnt to swim. The exciting new boat made it possible for us to go much farther afield, and every day we would travel far out into the fjord, hunting for a different island. There were hundreds of them to choose from. Some were very small, no more than thirty yards long. Others were quite large, maybe half a mile in length. It was wonderful to have such a choice of places, and it was terrific fun to explore each island before we went swimming off the rocks. There were the wooden skeletons of shipwrecked boats on those islands, and big white bones (were they human bones?), and wild raspberries, and mussels clinging to the rocks, and some of the islands had shaggy long-haired goats on them, and even sheep.

Now and again, when we were out in the open water beyond the chain of islands, the sea became very rough, and that was when my mother enjoyed herself most. Nobody, not even the tiny children, bothered with lifebelts in those days. We would cling to the sides of our funny little white motor-boat, driving through mountainous white-capped waves and getting drenched to the skin, while my mother calmly handled the tiller. There were times, I promise you, when the waves were so high that as we slid down into a trough the whole world disappeared from sight. Then up and up the little boat would climb, standing almost vertically on its tail, until we reached the crest of the next wave, and then it was like being on top of a foaming mountain. It requires great skill to handle a small boat in seas like these. The thing can easily capsize or be swamped if the bows do not meet the great combing breakers at just the right angle. But my mother knew exactly how to do it, and we were never afraid. We loved every minute of it, all of us except for our long-suffering Nanny, who would bury her face in her hands and call aloud upon the Lord to save her soul.

In the early evenings we nearly always went out fishing. We collected mussels from the rocks for bait, then we got into either the row-boat or the motor-boat and pushed off to drop anchor later in some likely spot. The water was very deep and often we had to let out two hundred feet of line before we touched bottom. We would sit silent and tense, waiting for a bite, and it always amazed me how even a little nibble at the end of that long line would be transmitted to one's fingers. 'A bite!' someone would shout, jerking the line. 'I've got him! It's a big one! It's a whopper!' And then came the thrill of hauling in the line hand over hand and peering over the side into the clear water to see how big the fish really was as he neared the surface. Cod, whiting, haddock and mackerel, we caught them all and bore them back triumphantly to the hotel kitchen where the cheery fat woman who did the cooking promised to get them ready for our supper.

I tell you, my friends, those were the days.

A visit
to the doctor

I have only one unpleasant memory of the summer holidays in Norway. We were in the grandparents' house in Oslo and my mother said to me, 'We are going to the doctor this afternoon. He wants to look at your nose and mouth.'

I think I was eight at the time. 'What's wrong with my nose and mouth?' I asked.

'Nothing much,' my mother said. 'But I think you've got adenoids.'

'What are *they*?' I asked her.

'Don't worry about it,' she said. 'It's nothing.'

I held my mother's hand as we walked to the doctor's house. It took us about half an hour. There was a kind of dentist's chair in the surgery and I was lifted into it. The doctor had a round mirror strapped to his forehead and he peered up my nose and into my mouth. He then took my mother aside and they held a whispered conversation. I saw my mother looking rather grim, but she nodded.

The doctor now put some water to boil in an aluminium mug over a gas flame, and into the boiling water he placed a long thin shiny steel instrument. I sat there watching the steam coming off the boiling water. I was not in the least apprehensive. I was too young to realize that something out of the ordinary was going to happen.

Then a nurse dressed in white came in. She was carrying a red rubber apron and a curved white enamel bowl. She put the apron over the front of my body and tied it around my neck. It was far too big. Then she held the enamel bowl under my chin. The curve of the bowl fitted perfectly against the curve of my chest.

The doctor was bending over me. In his hand he held that long shiny steel instrument. He held it right in front of my face, and to this day I can still describe it perfectly. It was about the thickness and length of a pencil, and like most pencils it had a lot of sides to it. Toward the end, the metal became much thinner, and at the very end of the thin bit of metal there was a tiny blade set at an angle. The blade wasn't more than a centimetre long, very small, very sharp and very shiny.

'Open your mouth,' the doctor said, speaking Norwegian.

I refused. I thought he was going to do something to my teeth, and everything anyone had ever done to my teeth had been painful.

'It won't take two seconds,' the doctor said. He spoke gently, and I was seduced by his voice. Like an ass, I opened my mouth.

The tiny blade flashed in the bright light and disappeared into my mouth. It went high up into the roof of my mouth, and the hand that held the blade gave four or five very quick little twists and the next moment, out of my mouth into the basin came tumbling a whole mass of flesh and blood.

I was too shocked and outraged to do anything but yelp. I was horrified by the huge red lumps that had fallen out of my mouth into the white basin and my first thought was that the doctor had cut out the whole of the middle of my head.

'Those were your adenoids,' I heard the doctor saying.

I sat there gasping. The roof of my mouth seemed to be on fire. I grabbed my mother's hand and held on to it tight. I couldn't believe that anyone would do this to me.

'Stay where you are,' the doctor said. 'You'll be all right in a minute.'

Blood was still coming out of my mouth and dripping into the basin the nurse was holding. 'Spit it all out,' she said, 'there's a good boy.'

'You'll be able to breathe much better through your nose after this,' the doctor said.

The nurse wiped my lips and washed my face with a wet flannel. Then they lifted me out of the chair and stood me on my feet. I felt a bit groggy.

'We'll get you home,' my mother said, taking my hand. Down the stairs we went and on to the street. We started walking. I said *walking*. No trolley-car or taxi. We walked the full half-hour journey back to my grandparents' house, and when we arrived at last, I can remember as clearly as anything my grandmother saying, 'Let him sit down in that chair and rest for a while. After all, he's had an operation.'

Someone placed a chair for me beside my grandmother's armchair, and I sat down. My grandmother reached over and covered one of my hands in both of hers. 'That won't be the last time you'll go to a doctor in your life,' she said. 'And with a bit of luck, they won't do you too much harm.'

That was in 1924, and taking out a child's adenoids, and often the tonsils as well, without any anaesthetic was common practice in those days. I wonder, though, what you would think if some doctor did that to you today.

St Peter's,

1925-9

(age 9-13)

St. Peters uniform

Jack Hobbs
Cumberland Lodge Lland...

Duckworth Butterflies my house
St. Peters
me in front row

Asta Else Alfhild me
Cardiff 1927

First day

In September 1925, when I was just nine, I set out on the first great adventure of my life – boarding-school. My mother had chosen for me a Prep School in a part of England which was as near as it could possibly be to our home in South Wales, and it was called St Peter's. The full postal address was St Peter's School, Weston-super-Mare, Somerset.

Weston-super-Mare is a slightly seedy seaside resort with a vast sandy beach, a tremendous long pier, an esplanade running along the sea-front, a clutter of hotels and boarding-houses, and about ten thousand little shops selling buckets and spades and sticks of rock and ice-creams. It lies almost directly across the Bristol Channel from Cardiff, and on a clear day you can stand on the esplanade at Weston and look across the fifteen or so miles of water and see the coast of Wales lying pale and milky on the horizon.

In those days the easiest way to travel from Cardiff to Weston-super-Mare was by boat. Those boats were beautiful. They were paddle-steamers, with gigantic swishing paddle-wheels on their flanks, and the wheels made the most terrific noise as they sloshed and churned through the water.

On the first day of my first term I set out by taxi in the afternoon with my mother to catch the paddle-steamer from Cardiff Docks to Weston-super-Mare. Every piece of clothing I wore was brand new and had my name on it. I wore black shoes, grey woollen stockings with blue turnovers, grey flannel shorts, a grey shirt, a red tie, a grey flannel blazer with the blue school crest on the breast pocket and a grey school cap with the same crest just above the peak. Into the taxi that was taking us to the docks went my brand new trunk and my brand new tuck-box, and both had R. DAHL painted on them in black.

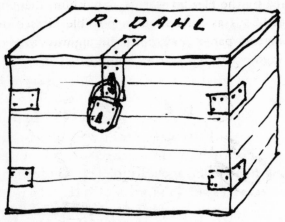

A tuck-box is a small pinewood trunk which is very strongly made, and no boy has ever gone as a boarder to an English Prep School without one. It is his own secret store-house, as secret as a lady's handbag, and there is an unwritten law that no other boy, no teacher, not even the Headmaster himself has the right to pry into the contents of your tuck-box. The owner has the key in his pocket and that is where it stays. At St Peter's, the tuck-boxes were ranged shoulder to shoulder all around the four walls of the changing-room and your own tuck-box stood directly below the peg on which you hung your games clothes. A tuck-box, as the name implies, is a box in which you store your tuck. At Prep School in those days, a parcel of tuck was sent once a week by anxious mothers to their ravenous little sons, and an average tuck-box would probably contain, at almost any time, half a home-made currant cake, a packet of squashed-fly biscuits, a couple of oranges, an apple, a banana, a pot of strawberry jam or Marmite, a bar of chocolate, a bag of Liquorice Allsorts and a tin of Bassett's lemonade powder. An English school in those days was purely a money-making business owned and operated by the Headmaster. It suited him, therefore, to give the boys as little food as possible himself and to encourage the parents in various cunning ways to feed their offspring by parcel-post from home.

'By all means, my dear Mrs Dahl, *do* send your boy some little treats now and again,' he would say. 'Perhaps a few oranges and apples once a week' – fruit was very expensive – 'and a nice currant cake, a *large* currant cake perhaps because small boys have large appetites do they not, ha-ha-ha . . . Yes, yes, as *often* as you like. *More* than once a week if you wish . . . *Of course* he'll be getting plenty of good food here, the best there is, but it never tastes *quite* the same as home cooking, does it? I'm sure you wouldn't want him to be the only one who doesn't get a lovely parcel from home every week.'

As well as tuck, a tuck-box would also contain all manner of treasures such as a magnet, a pocket-knife, a compass, a ball of string, a clockwork racing-car, half a dozen lead soldiers, a box of conjuring-tricks, some tiddly-winks, a Mexican jumping bean, a catapult, some foreign stamps, a couple of stink-bombs, and I remember one boy called Arkle who drilled an airhole in the lid of his tuck-box and kept a pet frog in there which he fed on slugs.

So off we set, my mother and I and my trunk and my tuck-box, and we boarded the paddle-steamer and went swooshing across the Bristol Channel in a shower of spray. I liked that part of it, but I began to grow apprehensive as I disembarked on to the pier at Weston-super-Mare and watched my trunk and tuck-box being loaded into an English taxi which would drive us to St Peter's. I had absolutely no idea what was in store for me. I had never spent a single night away from our large family before.

St Peter's was on a hill above the town. It was a long three-storeyed stone building that looked rather like a private lunatic asylum, and in front of it lay the playing-fields with their three football pitches. One-third of the building was reserved for the Headmaster and his family. The rest of it housed the boys, about one hundred and fifty of them altogether, if I remember rightly.

As we got out of the taxi, I saw the whole driveway abustle with small boys and their parents and their trunks and their tuck-boxes, and a man I took to be the Head-master was swimming around among them shaking every-body by the hand.

I have already told you that *all* Headmasters are giants, and this one was no exception. He advanced upon my mother and shook her by the hand, then he shook me by the hand and as he did so he gave me the kind of flashing

the Loony Bin !

grin a shark might give to a small fish just before he gobbles
it up. One of his front teeth, I noticed, was edged all the
way round with gold, and his hair was slicked down with
so much hair-cream that it glistened like butter.

'Right,' he said to me. 'Off you go and report to the
Matron.' And to my mother he said briskly, 'Goodbye,
Mrs Dahl. I shouldn't linger if I were you. We'll look after
him.'

My mother got the message. She kissed me on the cheek
and said goodbye and climbed right back into the taxi.

The Headmaster moved away to another group and I
was left standing there beside my brand new trunk and my
brand new tuck-box. I began to cry.

Writing home

At St Peter's, Sunday morning was letter-writing time. At nine o'clock the whole school had to go to their desks and spend one hour writing a letter home to their parents. At ten-fifteen we put on our caps and coats and formed up outside the school in a long crocodile and marched a couple of miles down into Weston-super-Mare for church, and we didn't get back until lunchtime. Church-going never became a habit with me. Letter-writing did.

Here is the very first letter I wrote home from St Peter's.

> Dear Mama   23th Sat
>
>   I am having a lovely time here. We play foot ball every day here. The beds have no springs. Will you send my stamp album, and quite a lot of swops. The masters are very nice. I've got all my clothes now, and a belt, and, ties, and a school Jersy.
>   love from
>   Boy

From that very first Sunday at St Peter's until the day my mother died thirty-two years later, I wrote to her once a week, sometimes more often, whenever I was away from home. I wrote to her every week from St Peter's (I had to), and every week from my next school, Repton, and every week from Dar es Salaam in East Africa, where I went on my first job after leaving school, and then every week during the war from Kenya and Iraq and Egypt when I was flying with the RAF.

... Major Cottam is going to recite something caled "as you like it" To night. please could you send me some conkers as quick as you can, but dont send to meny, just send them in a Tin and wrap it up in paper

My mother, for her part, kept every one of these letters, binding them carefully in neat bundles with green tape, but this was her own secret. She never told me she was doing it. In 1967, when she knew she was dying, I was in hospital in Oxford having a serious operation on my spine and I was unable to write to her. So she had a telephone specially installed beside her bed in order that she might have one last conversation with me. She didn't tell me she was dying nor did anyone else for that matter because I was in a fairly serious condition myself at the time. She simply asked me how I was and hoped I would get better soon and sent me her love. I had no idea that she would die the next day, but *she* knew all right and she wanted to reach out and speak to me for the last time.

When I recovered and went home, I was given this vast collection of my letters, all so neatly bound with green tape, more than six hundred of them altogether, dating from 1925 to 1945, each one in its original envelope with the old stamps still on them. I am awfully lucky to have something like this to refer to in my old age.

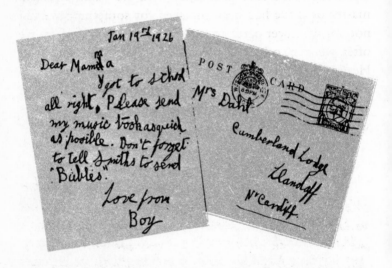

Letter-writing was a serious business at St Peter's. It was as much a lesson in spelling and punctuation as anything else because the Headmaster would patrol the classrooms all through the sessions, peering over our shoulders to read what we were writing and to point out our mistakes. But that, I am quite sure, was not the main reason for his interest. He was there to make sure that we said nothing horrid about his school.

There was no way, therefore, that we could ever complain to our parents about anything during term-time. If we thought the food was lousy or if we hated a certain master or if we had been thrashed for something we did not do, we never dared to say so in our letters. In fact, we often went the other way. In order to please that dangerous Headmaster who was leaning over our shoulders and reading what we had written, we would say splendid things about the school and go on about how lovely the masters were.

. A man called Mr Nichell gave us a fine lecture last knight on birds, he told us how owls owls eat mice they eat the hole mouse shin and all, and then all the shin and bones goes into a sort of little pas parsel in side him and he puts it on the ground, and those are caled pelets, and he showed us some pictures of some witch he has found, and of fotes of other Birds.

Mind you, the Headmaster was a clever fellow. He did not want our parents to think that those letters of ours were censored in this way, and therefore he never allowed us to correct a spelling mistake in the letter itself. If, for example, I had written . . . *last Tuesday knight we had a lecture* . . ., he would say:

'Don't you know how to spell night?'

'Y-yes, sir, k-n-i-g-h-t.'

'That's the other kind of knight, you idiot!'

'Which kind, sir? I . . . I don't understand.'

'The one in shining armour! The man on horseback! How do you spell Tuesday night?'

'I . . . I . . . I'm not quite sure, sir.'

'It's n-i-g-h-t, boy, n-i-g-h-t. Stay in and write it out for me fifty times this afternoon. No, no! Don't change it in the letter! You don't want to make it any messier than it is! It must go as you wrote it!'

Thus, the unsuspecting parents received in this subtle way the impression that your letter had never been seen or censored or corrected by anyone.

St Peter's
Weston-super-mare.

Jan. 27th 1928.

Dear Mama

Thank you very much for the cake etc. I got the book the day before yesterday, quite a nice edition. How are the chicks? hope they'll all live. By the way, you said she would'nt get any.

The Matron

At St Peter's the ground floor was all classrooms. The first floor was all dormitories. On the dormitory floor the Matron ruled supreme. This was her territory. Hers was the only voice of authority up here, and even the eleven- and twelve-year-old boys were terrified of this female ogre, for she ruled with a rod of steel.

The Matron was a large fair-haired woman with a bosom. Her age was probably no more than twenty-eight but it made no difference whether she was twenty-eight or sixty-eight because to us a grown-up was a grown-up and all grown-ups were dangerous creatures at this school.

Once you had climbed to the top of the stairs and set foot on the dormitory floor, you were in the Matron's power, and the source of this power was the unseen but frightening figure of the Headmaster lurking down in the depths of his study below. At any time she liked, the Matron could send you down in your pyjamas and dressing-gown to report to this merciless giant, and whenever this happened you got caned on the spot. The Matron knew this and she relished the whole business.

She could move along that corridor like lightning, and when you least expected it, her head and her bosom would come popping through the dormitory doorway. 'Who threw that sponge?' the dreaded voice would call out. 'It was *you*, Perkins, was it not? Don't lie to me, Perkins!

Don't argue with me! I know perfectly well it was you! Now you can put your dressing-gown on and go downstairs and report to the Headmaster this instant!'

In slow motion and with immense reluctance, little Perkins, aged eight and a half, would get into his dressing-gown and slippers and disappear down the long corridor that led to the back stairs and the Headmaster's private quarters. And the Matron, as we all knew, would follow after him and stand at the top of the stairs listening with a funny look on her face for the *crack . . . crack . . . crack* of the cane that would soon be coming up from below. To me that noise always sounded as though the Headmaster was firing a pistol at the ceiling of his study.

Looking back on it now, there seems little doubt that the Matron disliked small boys very much indeed. She never smiled at us or said anything nice, and when for example the lint stuck to the cut on your kneecap, you were not allowed to take it off yourself bit by bit so that it didn't hurt. She would always whip it off with a flourish, muttering, 'Don't be such a ridiculous little baby!'

'We've got a new matron. Last term, one night in the washing room, having inspected a boy called Ford the KISSED him and —

On one occasion during my first term, I went down to the Matron's room to have some iodine put on a grazed knee and I didn't know you had to knock before you entered. I opened the door and walked right in, and there she was in the centre of the Sick Room floor locked in some kind of an embrace with the Latin master, Mr Victor Corrado. They flew apart as I entered and both their faces went suddenly crimson.

'How *dare* you come in without knocking!' the Matron shouted. 'Here I am trying to get something out of Mr Corrado's eye and in you burst and disturb the whole delicate operation!'

'I'm very sorry, Matron.'

'Go away and come back in five minutes!' she cried, and I shot out of the room like a bullet.

After 'lights out' the Matron would prowl the corridor like a panther trying to catch the sound of a whisper behind a dormitory door, and we soon learnt that her powers of hearing were so phenomenal that it was safer to keep quiet.

Once, after lights out, a brave boy called Wragg tiptoed out of our dormitory and sprinkled castor sugar all over the linoleum floor of the corridor. When Wragg returned and told us that the corridor had been successfully sugared from one end to the other, I began shivering with excitement. I lay there in the dark in my bed waiting and waiting for the Matron to go on the prowl. Nothing happened. Perhaps, I told myself, she is in her room taking another speck of dust out of Mr Victor Corrado's eye.

Suddenly, from far down the corridor came a resounding *crunch*! *Crunch crunch crunch* went the footsteps. It sounded as though a giant was walking on loose gravel.

Then we heard the high-pitched furious voice of the Matron in the distance. 'Who did this?' she was shrieking. 'How *dare* you do this!' She went crunching along the corridor flinging open all the dormitory doors and switching on all the lights. The intensity of her fury was frightening. 'Come along!' she cried out, marching with crunching steps up and down the corridor. 'Own up! I want the name of the filthy little boy who put down the sugar! Own up immediately! Step forward! Confess!'

'Don't own up,' we whispered to Wragg. 'We won't give you away!'

Wragg kept quiet. I didn't blame him for that. Had he owned up, it was certain his fate would have been a terrible and a bloody one.

Soon the Headmaster was summoned from below. The Matron, with steam coming out of her nostrils, cried out to him for help, and now the whole school was herded into the long corridor, where we stood freezing in our pyjamas and bare feet while the culprit or culprits were ordered to step forward.

Nobody stepped forward.

I could see that the Headmaster was getting very angry indeed. His evening had been interrupted. Red splotches were appearing all over his face and flecks of spit were shooting out of his mouth as he talked.

'Very well!' he thundered. 'Every one of you will go at once and get the key to his tuck-box! Hand the keys to Matron, who will keep them for the rest of the term! And all parcels coming from home will be confiscated from now on! I will not tolerate this kind of behaviour!'

We handed in our keys and throughout the remaining six weeks of the term we went very hungry. But all through those six weeks, Arkle continued to feed his frog with slugs through the hole in the lid of his tuck-box. Using an old teapot, he also poured water in through the hole every day to keep the creature moist and happy. I admired Arkle very much for looking after his frog so well. Although he himself was famished, he refused to let his frog go hungry. Ever since then I have tried to be kind to small animals.

Each dormitory had about twenty beds in it. These were smallish narrow beds ranged along the walls on either side. Down the centre of the dormitory stood the basins where you washed your hands and face and did your teeth, always with cold water which stood in large jugs on the floor. Once you had entered the dormitory, you were not allowed to leave it unless you were reporting to the Matron's room with some sickness or injury. Under each bed there was a white chamber-pot, and before getting into bed you were expected to kneel on the floor and empty your bladder into it. All around the dormitory, just before 'lights out', was heard the *tinkle-tinkle* of little boys peeing into their pots. Once you had done this and got into your bed, you were not allowed to get out of it again until next morning. There was, I believe, a lavatory somewhere along the corridor, but only an attack of acute diarrhoea would be accepted as an excuse for visiting it. A journey to the upstairs lavatory automatically classed you as a diarrhoea victim, and a dose of thick white liquid would immediately be forced down your throat by the Matron. This made you constipated for a week.

Thanks for your letter. there are exactly 23 boys with the measles and all the other schools in (boys) in here have got it. Hope Louis hasn't had any thing else wrong

The first miserable homesick night at St Peter's, when I curled up in bed and the lights were put out, I could think of nothing but our house at home and my mother and my sisters. Where were they? I asked myself. In which direction from where I was lying was Llandaff? I began to work it out and it wasn't difficult to do this because I had the Bristol Channel to help me. If I looked out of the dormitory window I could see the Channel itself, and the big city of Cardiff with Llandaff alongside it lay almost directly across the water but slightly to the north. Therefore, if I turned towards the window I would be facing home. I wriggled round in my bed and faced my home and my family.

From then on, during all the time I was at St Peter's, I never went to sleep with my back to my family. Different beds in different dormitories required the working out of new directions, but the Bristol Channel was always my guide and I was always able to draw an imaginary line from my bed to our house over in Wales. Never once did I go to sleep looking away from my family. It was a great comfort to do this.

Do you know that a chap called Ford has got double Pneumonia on top of measles!!!!!! we're all got to be like mice going up to bed.

There was a boy in our dormitory during my first term called Tweedie, who one night started snoring soon after he had gone to sleep.

'Who's that talking?' cried the Matron, bursting in. My own bed was close to the door, and I remember looking up at her from my pillow and seeing her standing there silhouetted against the light from the corridor and thinking how truly frightening she looked. I think it was her enormous bosom that scared me most of all. My eyes were riveted to it, and to me it was like a battering-ram or the bows of an icebreaker or maybe a couple of high-explosive bombs.

'Own up!' she cried. 'Who was talking?'

We lay there in silence. Then Tweedie, who was lying fast asleep on his back with his mouth open, gave another snore.

The Matron stared at Tweedie. 'Snoring is a disgusting habit,' she said. 'Only the lower classes do it. We shall have to teach him a lesson.'

She didn't switch on the light, but she advanced into the room and picked up a cake of soap from the nearest basin. The bare electric bulb in the corridor illuminated the whole dormitory in a pale creamy glow.

None of us dared to sit up in bed, but all eyes were on the Matron now, watching to see what she was going to do next. She always had a pair of scissors hanging by a white tape from her waist, and with this she began shaving thin slivers of soap into the palm of one hand. Then she went over to where the wretched Tweedie lay and very carefully she dropped these little soap-flakes into his open mouth. She had a whole handful of them and I thought she was never going to stop.

What on earth is going to happen? I wondered. Would Tweedie choke? Would he strangle? Might his throat get blocked up completely? Was she going to kill him?

The Matron stepped back a couple of paces and folded her arms across, or rather underneath, her massive chest.

Nothing happened. Tweedie kept right on snoring.

Then suddenly he began to gurgle and white bubbles appeared around his lips. The bubbles grew and grew until in the end his whole face seemed to be smothered in a bubbly foaming white soapy froth. It was a horrific sight. Then all at once, Tweedie gave a great cough and a splutter and he sat up very fast and began clawing at his face with his hands. 'Oh!' he stuttered. 'Oh! Oh! Oh! Oh no!

Wh-wh-what's happening? Wh-wh-what's on my face? Somebody help me!'

The Matron threw him a face flannel and said, 'Wipe it off, Tweedie. And don't ever let me hear you snoring again. Hasn't anyone ever taught you not to go to sleep on your back?'

With that she marched out of the dormitory and slammed the door.

very bad, he got better on Friday but has again got very ill, Ford is still

P.S. We have just been informed that poor little Ford died early this morning.

Homesickness

I was homesick during the whole of my first term at St
Peter's. Homesickness is a bit like seasickness. You don't
know how awful it is till you get it, and when you do, it
hits you right in the top of the stomach and you want
to die. The only comfort is that both homesickness and
seasickness are instantly curable. The first goes away the
moment you walk out of the school grounds and the second
is forgotten as soon as the ship enters port.

I was so devastatingly homesick during my first two
weeks that I set about devising a stunt for getting myself
sent back home, even if it were only a few days. My idea
was that I should all of a sudden develop an attack of acute
appendicitis.

You will probably think it silly that a nine-year-old boy
should imagine he could get away with a trick like that,
but I had sound reasons for trying it on. Only a month
before, my ancient half-sister, who was twelve years older
than me, had actually *had* appendicitis, and for several days
before her operation I was able to observe her behaviour
at close quarters. I noticed that the thing she complained
about most was a severe pain down in the lower right side
of her tummy. As well as this, she kept being sick and
refused to eat and ran a temperature.

You might, by the way, be interested to know that this
sister had her appendix removed not in a fine hospital

operating-room full of bright lights and gowned nurses but on our own nursery table at home by the local doctor and his anaesthetist. In those days it was fairly common

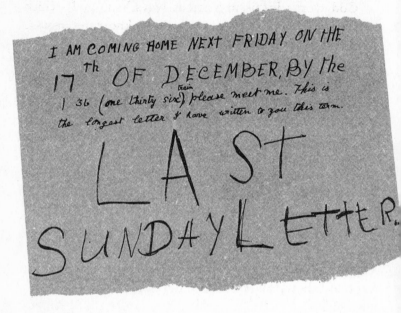

I AM COMING HOME NEXT FRIDAY ON THE 17th OF DECEMBER, BY the 1 36 (one thirty six) train please meet me. This is the longest letter I have written to you this term.

LAST SUNDAY LETTER.

practice for a doctor to arrive at your own house with a bag of instruments, then drape a sterile sheet over the most convenient table and get on with it. On this occasion, I can remember lurking in the corridor outside the nursery while the operation was going on. My other sisters were with me, and we stood there spellbound, listening to the soft medical murmurs coming from behind the locked door and picturing the patient with her stomach sliced open like a lump of beef. We could even smell the sickly fumes of ether filtering through the crack under the door.

The next day, we were allowed to inspect the appendix itself in a glass bottle. It was a longish black wormy-looking thing, and I said, 'Do *I* have one of those inside me, Nanny?'

'Everybody has one,' Nanny answered.

'What's it for?' I asked her.

'God works in his mysterious ways,' she said, which was her stock reply whenever she didn't know the answer.

'What makes it go bad?' I asked her.

'Toothbrush bristles,' she answered, this time with no hesitation at all.

'*Toothbrush* bristles?' I cried. 'How can *toothbrush* bristles make your appendix go bad?'

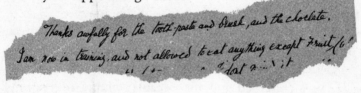

Nanny, who in my eyes was filled with more wisdom than Solomon, replied, 'Whenever a bristle comes out of your toothbrush and you swallow it, it sticks in your appendix and turns it rotten. In the war', she went on, 'the German spies used to sneak boxloads of loose-bristled toothbrushes into our shops and millions of our soldiers got appendicitis.'

'Honestly, Nanny?' I cried. 'Is that honestly true?'

'I never lie to you, child,' she answered. 'So let that be a lesson to you never to use an old toothbrush.'

For years after that, I used to get nervous whenever I found a toothbrush bristle on my tongue.

As I went upstairs and knocked on the brown door after breakfast, I didn't even feel frightened of the Matron.

'Come in!' boomed the voice.

I entered the room clutching my stomach on the right-hand side and staggering pathetically.

'What's the matter with you?' the Matron shouted, and the sheer force of her voice caused that massive bosom to quiver like a gigantic blancmange.

'It hurts, Matron,' I moaned. 'Oh, it hurts so much! Just here!'

'You've been over-eating!' she barked. 'What do you expect if you guzzle currant cake all day long!'

'I haven't eaten a thing for days,' I lied. 'I *couldn't* eat, Matron! I simply *couldn't!*'

'Get on the bed and lower your trousers,' she ordered.

I lay on the bed and she began prodding my tummy violently with her fingers. I was watching her carefully, and when she hit what I guessed was the appendix place, I let out a yelp that rattled the window-panes. 'Ow! Ow! Ow!' I cried out. 'Don't, Matron, don't!' Then I slipped in the clincher. 'I've been sick all morning,' I moaned, 'and now there's nothing left to be sick with, but I still feel sick!'

This was the right move. I saw her hesitate. 'Stay where you are,' she said and she walked quickly from the room. She may have been a foul and beastly woman, but she had had a nurse's training and she didn't want a ruptured appendix on her hands.

Within an hour, the doctor arrived and he went through the same prodding and poking and I did my yelping at what I thought were the proper times. Then he put a thermometer in my mouth.

'Hmm,' he said. 'It reads normal. Let me feel your stomach once more.'

'Owch!' I screamed when he touched the vital spot.

The doctor went away with the Matron. The Matron returned half an hour later and said, 'The Headmaster has telephoned your mother and she's coming to fetch you this afternoon.'

I didn't answer her. I just lay there trying to look very ill, but my heart was singing out with all sorts of wonderful songs of praise and joy.

I was taken home across the Bristol Channel on the paddle-steamer and I felt so wonderful at being away from that dreaded school building that I very nearly forgot I was meant to be ill. That afternoon I had a session with Dr Dunbar at his surgery in Cathedral Road, Cardiff, and I tried the same tricks all over again. But Dr Dunbar was far wiser and more skilful than either the Matron or the school doctor. After he had prodded my stomach and I had done my yelping routine, he said to me, 'Now you can get dressed again and seat yourself on that chair.'

He himself sat down behind his desk and fixed me with a penetrating but not unkindly eye. 'You're faking, aren't you?' he said.

'How do you know?' I blurted out.

'Because your stomach is soft and perfectly normal,' he answered. 'If you had had an inflammation down there, the stomach would have been hard and rigid. It's quite easy to tell.'

I kept silent.

'I expect you're homesick,' he said.

I nodded miserably.

'Everyone is at first,' he said. 'You have to stick it out. And don't blame your mother for sending you away to boarding-school. She insisted you were too young to go, but it was I who persuaded her it was the right thing to do. Life is tough, and the sooner you learn how to cope with it the better for you.'

'What will you tell the school?' I asked him, trembling.

'I'll say you had a very severe infection of the stomach which I am curing with pills,' he answered smiling. 'It will mean that you must stay home for three more days. But promise me you won't try anything like this again. Your mother has enough on her hands without having to rush over to fetch you out of school.'

'I promise,' I said. 'I'll never do it again.'

I'm taking the Calcium, but haven't needed one of the Pills yet.

A drive in the motor-car

Somehow or other I got through the first term at St Peter's, and towards the end of December my mother came over on the paddle-boat to take me and my trunk home for the Christmas holidays.

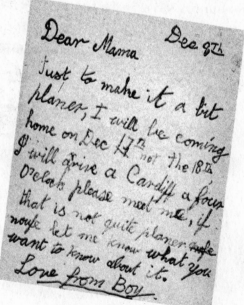

Dear Mama   Dec 9th

Just to make it a bit planer, I will be coming home on Dec 17th not the 18th. I will drive a Cardiff a four o'clock please meet me, if that is not quite planer, let me know what you want to know about it.

Love from Boy

Oh the bliss and the wonder of being with the family once again after all those weeks of fierce discipline! Unless you have been to boarding-school when you are very young, it is absolutely impossible to appreciate the delights of living at home. It is almost *worth* going away because it's so lovely coming back. I could hardly believe that I didn't have to wash in cold water in the mornings or keep silent in the corridors, or say 'Sir' to every grown-up man I met, or use a chamber-pot in the bedroom, or get flicked with wet towels while naked in the changing-room, or eat porridge for breakfast that seemed to be full of little round lumpy grey sheep's-droppings, or walk all day long in perpetual fear of the long yellow cane that lay on top of the corner-cupboard in the Headmaster's study.

The weather was exceptionally mild that Christmas holiday and one amazing morning our whole family got ready to go for our first drive in the first motor-car we had ever

owned. This new motor-car was an enormous long black French automobile called a De Dion-Bouton which had a canvas roof that folded back. The driver was to be that twelve-years-older-than-me half-sister (now aged twenty-one) who had recently had her appendix removed.

She had received two full half-hour lessons in driving from the man who delivered the car, and in that enlightened year of 1925 this was considered quite sufficient. Nobody had to take a driving-test. You were your own judge of competence, and as soon as you felt you were ready to go, off you jolly well went.

As we all climbed into the car, our excitement was so intense we could hardly bear it.

'How fast will it go?' we cried out. 'Will it do fifty miles an hour?'

'It'll do sixty!' the ancient sister answered. Her tone was so confident and cocky it should have scared us to death, but it didn't.

'Oh, let's make it do sixty!' we shouted. 'Will you promise to take us up to sixty?'

'We shall probably go faster than that,' the sister announced, pulling on her driving-gloves and tying a scarf over her head in the approved driving-fashion of the period.

The canvas hood had been folded back because of the mild weather, converting the car into a magnificent open tourer. Up front, there were three bodies in all, the driver behind the wheel, my half-brother (aged eighteen) and one of my sisters (aged twelve). In the back seat there were four more of us, my mother (aged forty), two small sisters (aged eight and five) and myself (aged nine). Our machine possessed one very special feature which I don't think you see on the cars of today. This was a second windscreen in the back solely to keep the breeze off the faces of the back-seat passengers when the hood was down. It had a long centre section and two little end sections that could be angled backwards to deflect the wind.

We were all quivering with fear and joy as the driver let out the clutch and the great long black automobile leaned forward and stole into motion.

'Are you sure you know how to do it?' we shouted. 'Do you know where the brakes are?'

'Be quiet!' snapped the ancient sister. 'I've got to concentrate!'

Down the drive we went and out into the village of Llandaff itself. Fortunately there were very few vehicles on the roads in those days. Occasionally you met a small truck or a delivery-van and now and again a private car, but the danger of colliding with anything else was fairly remote so long as you kept the car on the road.

The splendid black tourer crept slowly through the village with the driver pressing the rubber bulb of the horn every time we passed a human being, whether it was the butcher-boy on his bicycle or just a pedestrian strolling on the pavement. Soon we were entering a countryside of green fields and high hedges with not a soul in sight.

'You didn't think I could do it, did you?' cried the ancient sister, turning round and grinning at us all.

'Now you keep your eyes on the road,' my mother said nervously.

'Go faster!' we shouted. 'Go on! Make her go faster! Put your foot down! We're only doing *fifteen miles an hour!*'

Spurred on by our shouts and taunts, the ancient sister began to increase the speed. The engine roared and the body vibrated. The driver was clutching the steering-wheel as though it were the hair of a drowning man, and we all watched the speedometer needle creeping up to twenty, then twenty-five, then thirty. We were probably doing about thirty-five miles an hour when we came suddenly to a sharpish bend in the road. The ancient sister, never having been faced with a situation like this before, shouted 'Help!' and slammed on the brakes and swung the wheel wildly round. The rear wheels locked and went into a fierce sideways skid, and then, with a marvellous crunch of mudguards and metal, we went crashing into the hedge. The front passengers all shot through the front windscreen and the back passengers all shot through the back windscreen. Glass (there was no Triplex then) flew in all directions and so did we. My brother and one sister landed on the bonnet of the car, someone else was catapulted out on to the road and at least one small sister landed in the middle of the hawthorn hedge. But miraculously nobody was hurt very much except me. My nose had been cut almost clean off my face as I went through the rear windscreen and now it was hanging on only by a single small thread of skin. My mother disentangled herself from the scrimmage and grabbed a handkerchief from her purse. She clapped the dangling nose back into place fast and held it there.

Not a cottage or a person was in sight, let alone a telephone. Some kind of bird started twittering in a tree farther down the road, otherwise all was silent.

My mother was bending over me in the rear seat and saying, 'Lean back and keep your head still.' To the ancient sister she said, 'Can you get this thing going again?'

The sister pressed the starter and to everyone's surprise, the engine fired.

'Back it out of the hedge,' my mother said. 'And hurry.'

The sister had trouble finding reverse gear. The cogs were grinding against one another with a fearful noise of tearing metal.

'I've never actually driven it backwards,' she admitted at last.

Everyone with the exception of the driver, my mother and me was out of the car and standing on the road. The noise of gear-wheels grinding against each other was terrible. It sounded as though a lawn-mower was being driven over hard rocks. The ancient sister was using bad words and going crimson in the face, but then my brother leaned his head over the driver's door and said, 'Don't you have to put your foot on the clutch?'

The harassed driver depressed the clutch-pedal and the gears meshed and one second later the great black beast leapt backwards out of the hedge and careered across the road into the hedge on the other side.

'Try to keep cool,' my mother said. 'Go forward slowly.'

At last the shattered motor-car was driven out of the second hedge and stood sideways across the road, blocking the highway. A man with a horse and cart now appeared on the scene and the man dismounted from his cart and walked across to our car and leaned over the rear door. He had a big drooping moustache and he wore a small black bowler-hat.

'You're in a fair old mess 'ere, ain't you?' he said to my mother.

'Can you drive a motor-car?' my mother asked him.

'Nope,' he said. 'And you're blockin' up the 'ole road. I've got a thousand fresh-laid heggs in this cart and I want to get 'em to market before noon.'

'Get out of the way,' my mother told him. 'Can't you see there's a child in here who's badly injured?'

'One thousand fresh-laid heggs,' the man repeated, staring straight at my mother's hand and the blood-soaked handkerchief and the blood running down her wrist. 'And if I don't get 'em to market by noon today I won't be able to sell 'em till next week. Then they won't be fresh-laid any more, will they? I'll be stuck with one thousand stale ole heggs that nobody wants.'

'I hope they all go rotten,' my mother said. 'Now back that cart out of our way this instant!' And to the children standing on the road she cried out, 'Jump back into the car! We're going to the doctor!'

'There's glass all over the seats!' they shouted.

'Never mind the glass!' my mother said. 'We've got to get this boy to the doctor fast!'

The passengers crawled back into the car. The man with the horse and cart backed off to a safe distance. The ancient sister managed to straighten the vehicle and get it pointed in the right direction, and then at last the once magnificent automobile tottered down the highway and headed for Dr Dunbar's surgery in Cathedral Road, Cardiff.

'I've never driven in a city,' the ancient and trembling sister announced.

'You are about to do so,' my mother said. 'Keep going.'

Proceeding at no more than four miles an hour all the way, we finally made it to Dr Dunbar's house. I was hustled out of the car and in through the front door with my mother still holding the bloodstained handerchief firmly over my wobbling nose.

'Good heavens!' cried Dr Dunbar. 'It's been cut clean off!'

'It hurts,' I moaned.

'He can't go round without a nose for the rest of his life!' the doctor said to my mother.

'It looks as though he may have to,' my mother said.

'Nonsense!' the doctor told her. 'I shall sew it on again.'

'Can you do that?' My mother asked him.

'I can try,' he answered. 'I shall tape it on tight for now and I'll be up at your house with my assistant within the hour.'

Huge strips of sticking-plaster were strapped across my face to hold the nose in position. Then I was led back into the car and we crawled the two miles home to Llandaff.

About an hour later I found myself lying upon that same nursery table my ancient sister had occupied some months before for her appendix operation. Strong hands held me down while a mask stuffed with cotton-wool was clamped over my face. I saw a hand above me holding a bottle with white liquid in it and the liquid was being poured on to the cotton-wool inside the mask. Once again I smelled the sickly stench of chloroform and ether, and a voice was saying, 'Breathe deeply. Take some nice deep breaths.'

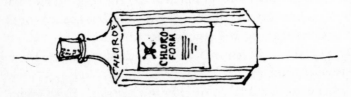

I fought fiercely to get off that table but my shoulders were pinned down by the full weight of a large man. The hand that was holding the bottle above my face kept tilting it farther and farther forward and the white liquid dripped and dripped on to the cotton-wool. Blood-red circles began to appear before my eyes and the circles started to spin round and round until they made a scarlet whirlpool with a deep black hole in the centre, and miles away in the distance a voice was saying, 'That's a good boy. We're nearly there now . . . we're nearly there . . . just close your eyes and go to sleep . . .'

I woke up in my own bed with my anxious mother sitting beside me, holding my hand. 'I didn't think you were ever going to come round,' she said. 'You've been asleep for more than eight hours.'

'Did Dr Dunbar sew my nose on again?' I asked her.

'Yes,' she said.

'Will it stay on?'

'He says it will. How do you feel, my darling?'

'Sick,' I said.

After I had vomited into a small basin, I felt a little better.

'Look under your pillow,' my mother said, smiling.

I turned and lifted a corner of my pillow, and underneath it, on the snow-white sheet, there lay a beautiful golden sovereign with the head of King George V on its uppermost side.

'That's for being brave,' my mother said. 'You did very well. I'm proud of you.'

Captain Hardcastle

We called them masters in those days, not teachers, and at St Peter's the one I feared most of all, apart from the Headmaster, was Captain Hardcastle.

This man was slim and wiry and he played football. On the football field he wore white running shorts and white gymshoes and short white socks. His legs were as hard and thin as ram's legs and the skin around his calves was almost exactly the colour of mutton fat. The hair on his head was not ginger. It was a brilliant dark vermilion, like a ripe orange, and it was plastered back with immense quantities of brilliantine in the same fashion as the Headmaster's. The parting in his hair was a white line straight down the middle of the scalp, so straight it could only have been made with a ruler. On either side of the parting you could see the comb tracks running back through the greasy orange hair like little tramlines.

Captain Hardcastle sported a moustache that was the same colour as his hair, and oh what a moustache it was!

A truly terrifying sight, a thick orange hedge that sprouted and flourished between his nose and his upper lip and ran clear across his face from the middle of one cheek to the middle of the other. But this was not one of those nailbrush moustaches, all short and clipped and bristly. Nor was it long and droopy in the walrus style. Instead, it was curled most splendidly upwards all the way along as though it had had a permanent wave put into it or possibly curling tongs heated in the mornings over a tiny flame of methylated spirits. The only other way he could have achieved this curling effect, we boys decided, was by prolonged upward brushing with a hard toothbrush in front of the looking-glass every morning.

Behind the moustache there lived an inflamed and savage face with a deeply corrugated brow that indicated a very limited intelligence. 'Life is a puzzlement,' the corrugated brow seemed to be saying, 'and the world is a dangerous place. All men are enemies and small boys are insects that will turn and bite you if you don't get them first and squash them hard.'

Captain Hardcastle was never still. His orange head twitched and jerked perpetually from side to side in the most alarming fashion, and each twitch was accompanied by a little grunt that came out of the nostrils. He had been a soldier in the army in the Great War and that, of course, was how he had received his title. But even small insects like us knew that 'Captain' was not a very exalted rank and only a man with little else to boast about would hang on to it in civilian life. It was bad enough to keep calling yourself 'Major' after it was all over, but 'Captain' was the bottoms.

Rumour had it that the constant twitching and jerking and snorting was caused by something called shell-shock, but we were not quite sure what that was. We took it to mean that an explosive object had gone off very close to him with such an enormous bang that it had made him jump high in the air and he hadn't stopped jumping since.

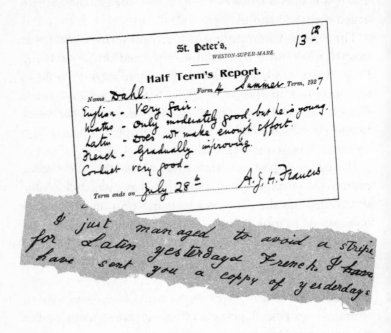

St. Peter's,
WESTON-SUPER-MARE.

Half Term's Report.

Name *Dahl*   Form *4*   *Summer* Term, 192*7*

English — Very fair.

Maths — Only moderately good, but he is young.

Latin — Does not make enough effort.

French — Gradually improving.

Conduct — very good —

Term ends on *July 28th*   A. G. H. Francis

I just managed to avoid a stripe for Latin yesterday. French. I have sent you a coppy of yesterday's

For a reason that I could never properly understand, Captain Hardcastle had it in for me from my very first day at St Peter's. Perhaps it was because he taught Latin and I was no good at it. Perhaps it was because already, at the age of nine, I was very nearly as tall as he was. Or even more likely, it was because I took an instant dislike to his giant orange moustache and he often caught me staring at it with what was probably a little sneer under the nose. I had only to pass within ten feet of him in the corridor and he would glare at me and shout, 'Hold yourself straight, boy! Pull your shoulders back!' or 'Take those hands out of your pockets!' or 'What's so funny, may I ask? What are you smirking at?' or most insulting of all, '*You*, what's-your-name, get on with your work!' I knew, therefore, that it was only a matter of time before the gallant Captain nailed me good and proper.

The crunch came during my second term when I was exactly nine and a half, and it happened during evening Prep. Every weekday evening, the whole school would sit for one hour in the Main Hall, between six and seven o'clock, to do Prep. The master on duty for the week would be in charge of Prep, which meant that he sat high up on a dais at the top end of the Hall and kept order. Some masters read a book while taking Prep and some corrected exercises, but not Captain Hardcastle. He would sit up there on the dais twitching and grunting and never once would he look down at his desk. His small milky-blue eyes would rove the Hall for the full sixty minutes, searching for trouble, and heaven help the boy who caused it.

The rules of Prep were simple but strict. You were forbidden to look up from your work, and you were forbidden to talk. That was all there was to it, but it left you precious little leeway. In extreme circumstances, and I never knew what these were, you could put your hand up and wait until you were asked to speak but you had better be awfully sure that the circumstances were extreme. Only twice during my four years at St Peter's did I see a boy putting up his hand during Prep. The first one went like this:

MASTER. What is it?
BOY. Please sir, may I be excused to go to the lavatory?
MASTER. Certainly not. You should have gone before.

BOY. But sir . . . please sir . . . I didn't want to before . . .
I didn't know . . .

MASTER. Whose fault was that? Get on with your work!

BOY. But sir . . . Oh sir . . . Please sir, let me go!

MASTER. One more word out of you and you'll be in
trouble.

Naturally, the wretched boy dirtied his pants, which
caused a storm later on upstairs with the Matron.

On the second occasion, I remember clearly that it was
a summer term and the boy who put his hand up was called
Braithwaite. I also seem to recollect that the master taking
Prep was our friend Captain Hardcastle, but I wouldn't
swear to it. The dialogue went something like this:

MASTER. Yes, what is it?

BRAITHWAITE. Please sir, a wasp came in through the window and it's stung me on my lip and it's swelling up.

MASTER. A *what*?

BRAITHWAITE. A wasp, sir.

MASTER. Speak up, boy, I can't hear you! A *what* came in
through the window?

BRAITHWAITE. It's hard to speak up, sir, with my lip all
swelling up.

MASTER. With your *what* all swelling up? Are you trying
to be funny?

BRAITHWAITE. No sir, I promise I'm not sir.

MASTER. Talk properly, boy! What's the matter with you?

BRAITHWAITE. I've told you, sir. I've been stung, sir. My
lip is swelling. It's hurting terribly.

MASTER. *Hurting terribly?* What's hurting terribly?

BRAITHWAITE. My lip, sir. It's getting bigger and bigger.

MASTER. What Prep are you doing tonight?

BRAITHWAITE. French verbs, sir. We have to write them out.

MASTER. Do you write with your lip?

BRAITHWAITE. No, sir, I don't sir, but you see . . .

MASTER. All I see is that you are making an infernal noise and disturbing everybody in the room. Now get on with your work.

They were tough, those masters, make no mistake about it, and if you wanted to survive, you had to become pretty tough yourself.

My own turn came, as I said, during my second term and Captain Hardcastle was again taking Prep. You should know that during Prep every boy in the Hall sat at his own small individual wooden desk. These desks had the usual sloping wooden tops with a narrow flat strip at the far end where there was a groove to hold your pen and a small hole in the right-hand side in which the ink-well sat. The pens we used had detachable nibs and it was necessary to dip your nib into the ink-well every six or seven seconds when you were writing. Ball-point pens and felt pens had not then been invented, and fountain-pens were forbidden. The nibs we used were very fragile and most boys kept a supply of new ones in a small box in their trouser pockets.

Prep was in progress. Captain Hardcastle was sitting up on the dais in front of us, stroking his orange moustache, twitching his head and grunting through his nose. His eyes roved the Hall endlessly, searching for mischief. The only noises to be heard were Captain Hardcastle's little snorting grunts and the soft sound of pen-nibs moving over paper. Occasionally there was a *ping* as somebody dipped his nib too violently into his tiny white porcelain ink-well.

Disaster struck when I foolishly stubbed the tip of my

nib into the top of the desk. The nib broke. I knew I hadn't got a spare one in my pocket, but a broken nib was never accepted as an excuse for not finishing Prep. We had been set an essay to write and the subject was 'The Life Story of a Penny' (I still have that essay in my files). I had made a decent start and I was rattling along fine when I broke that nib. There was still another half-hour of Prep to go and I couldn't sit there doing nothing all that time. Nor could I put up my hand and tell Captain Hardcastle I had broken my nib. I simply did not dare. And as a matter of fact, I really *wanted* to finish that essay. I knew exactly what was going to happen to my penny through the next two pages and I couldn't bear to leave it unsaid.

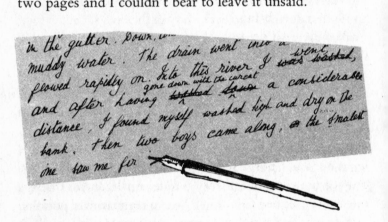

in the gutter. Down, ...
muddy water. The drain went into a
flowed rapidly on. Into this river I went
gone down with the current
and after having travelled down a considerable
distance, I found myself washed high and dry on the
bank. Then two boys came along, & the smallest
one saw me for

I glanced to my right. The boy next to me was called Dobson. He was the same age as me, nine and a half, and a nice fellow. Even now, sixty years later, I can still remember that Dobson's father was a doctor and that he lived, as I had learnt from the label on Dobson's tuck-box, at The Red House, Uxbridge, Middlesex.

Dobson's desk was almost touching mine. I thought I would risk it. I kept my head lowered but watched Captain

Hardcastle very carefully. When I was fairly sure he was looking the other way, I put a hand in front of my mouth and whispered, 'Dobson . . . Dobson . . . Could you lend me a nib?'

Suddenly there was an explosion up on the dais. Captain Hardcastle had leapt to his feet and was pointing at me and shouting, 'You're talking! I saw you talking! Don't try to deny it! I distinctly saw you talking behind your hand!'

I sat there frozen with terror.

Every boy stopped working and looked up.

Captain Hardcastle's face had gone from red to deep purple and he was twitching violently.

'Do you deny you were talking?' he shouted.

'No, sir, no, b-but . . .'

'And do you deny you were trying to cheat? Do you deny you were asking Dobson for help with your work?'

'N-no, sir, I wasn't. I wasn't cheating.'

'Of course you were cheating! Why else, may I ask, would you be speaking to Dobson? I take it you were not inquiring after his health?'

It is worth reminding the reader once again of my age. I was not a self-possessed lad of fourteen. Nor was I twelve or even ten years old. I was nine and a half, and at that age one is ill equipped to tackle a grown-up man with flaming orange hair and a violent temper. One can do little else but stutter.

'I . . . I have broken my nib, sir,' I whispered. 'I . . . I was asking Dobson if he c-could lend me one, sir.'

'You are lying!' cried Captain Hardcastle, and there was triumph in his voice. 'I always knew you were a liar! *And* a cheat as well!'

'All I w-wanted was a nib, sir.'

'I'd shut up if I were you!' thundered the voice on the

dais. 'You'll only get yourself into deeper trouble! I am giving you a Stripe!'

These were words of doom. A Stripe! *I am giving you a Stripe!* All around, I could feel a kind of sympathy reaching out to me from every boy in the school, but nobody moved or made a sound.

Here I must explain the system of Stars and Stripes that we had at St Peter's. For exceptionally good work, you could be awarded a Quarter-Star, and a red dot was made with crayon beside your name on the notice-board. If you got four Quarter-Stars, a red line was drawn through the four dots indicating that you had completed your Star.

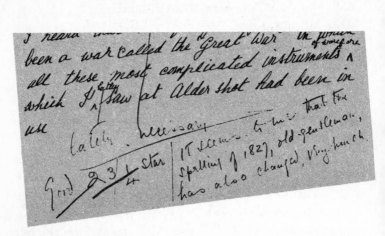

For exceptionally poor work or bad behaviour, you were given a Stripe, and that automatically meant a thrashing from the Headmaster.

Every master had a book of Quarter-Stars and a book of Stripes, and these had to be filled in and signed and torn out exactly like cheques from a cheque book. The Quarter-Stars were pink, the Stripes were a fiendish, blue-green colour. The boy who received a Star or a Stripe would pocket it until the following morning after prayers, when the Headmaster would call upon anyone who had been given one or the other to come forward in front of the whole school and hand it in. Stripes were considered so dreadful that they were not given very often. In any one week it was unusual for more than two or three boys to receive Stripes.

And now Captain Hardcastle was giving one to me.

'Come here,' he ordered.

I got up from my desk and walked to the dais. He already had his book of Stripes on the desk and was filling one out. He was using red ink, and along the line where it said *Reason*, he wrote, *Talking in Prep, trying to cheat and lying.* He signed it and tore it out of the book. Then, taking plenty of time, he filled in the counterfoil. He picked up the terrible piece of green-blue paper and waved it in my direction but he didn't look up. I took it out of his hand

and walked back to my desk. The eyes of the whole school followed my progress.

For the remainder of Prep I sat at my desk and did nothing. Having no nib, I was unable to write another word about 'The Life Story of a Penny', but I was made to finish it the next afternoon instead of playing games.

The following morning, as soon as prayers were over, the Headmaster called for Quarter-Stars and Stripes. I was the only boy to go up. The assistant masters were sitting on very upright chairs on either side of the Headmaster, and I caught a glimpse of Captain Hardcastle, arms folded across his chest, head twitching, the milky-blue eyes watching me intently, the look of triumph still glimmering on his face. I handed in my Stripe. The Headmaster took it and read the writing. 'Come and see me in my study', he said, 'as soon as this is over.'

Five minutes later, walking on my toes and trembling terribly, I passed through the green baize door and entered the sacred precincts where the Headmaster lived. I knocked on his study door.

'Enter!'

I turned the knob and went into this large square room with bookshelves and easy chairs and the gigantic desk topped in red leather straddling the far corner. The Headmaster was sitting behind the desk holding my Stripe in his fingers. 'What have you got to say for yourself?' he asked me, and the white shark's teeth flashed dangerously between his lips.

'I didn't lie, sir,' I said. 'I promise I didn't. And I wasn't trying to cheat.'

'Captain Hardcastle says you were doing both,' the Headmaster said. 'Are you calling Captain Hardcastle a liar?'

'No, sir. Oh no, sir.'

'I wouldn't if I were you.'

'I had broken my nib, sir, and I was asking Dobson if he could lend me another.'

'That is not what Captain Hardcastle says. He says you were asking for help with your essay.'

'Oh no, sir, I wasn't. I was a long way away from Captain Hardcastle and I was only whispering. I don't think he could have heard what I said, sir.'

'So you *are* calling him a liar.'

'Oh no, sir! No, sir! I would never do that!'

It was impossible for me to win against the Headmaster. What I would like to have said was, 'Yes, sir, if you really want to know, sir, I *am* calling Captain Hardcastle a liar because that's what he is!', but it was out of the question. I did, however, have one trump card left to play, or I thought I did.

'You could ask Dobson, sir,' I whispered.

'*Ask Dobson?*' he cried. 'Why should I ask Dobson?'

'He would tell you what I said, sir.'

'Captain Hardcastle is an officer and a gentleman,' the Headmaster said. 'He has told me what happened. I hardly think I want to go round asking some silly little boy if Captain Hardcastle is speaking the truth.'

I kept silent.

'For talking in Prep,' the Headmaster went on, 'for trying to cheat and for lying, I am going to give you six strokes of the cane.'

He rose from his desk and crossed over to the corner-cupboard on the opposite side of the study. He reached up and took from the top of it three very thin yellow canes, each with the bent-over handle at one end. For a few seconds, he held them in his hands, examining them with some care, then he selected one and replaced the other two on top of the cupboard.

'Bend over.'

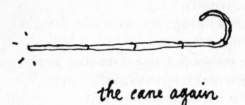

the cane again

I was frightened of that cane. There is no small boy in the world who wouldn't be. It wasn't simply an instrument for beating you. It was a weapon for wounding. It lacerated the skin. It caused severe black and scarlet bruising that took three weeks to disappear, and all the time during those three weeks, you could feel your heart beating along the wounds.

I tried once more, my voice slightly hysterical now. 'I didn't do it, sir! I swear I'm telling the truth!'

'Be quiet and bend over! Over there! And touch your toes!'

Very slowly, I bent over. Then I shut my eyes and braced myself for the first stroke.

Crack! It was like a rifle shot! With a very hard stroke of the cane on one's buttocks, the time-lag before you feel any pain is about four seconds. Thus, the experienced caner will always pause between strokes to allow the agony to reach its peak.

So for a few seconds after the first *crack* I felt virtually nothing. Then suddenly came the frightful searing agonizing unbearable burning across the buttocks, and as it reached its highest and most excruciating point, the second *crack* came down. I clutched hold of my ankles as tight as

I could and I bit into my lower lip. I was determined not to make a sound, for that would only give the executioner greater satisfaction.

Crack! . . . Five seconds pause.

Crack! . . . Another pause.

Crack! . . . And another pause.

I was counting the strokes, and as the sixth one hit me, I knew I was going to survive in silence.

'That will do,' the voice behind me said.

I straightened up and clutched my backside as hard as I possibly could with both hands. This is always the instinctive and automatic reaction. The pain is so frightful you try to grab hold of it and tear it away, and the tighter you squeeze, the more it helps.

I did not look at the Headmaster as I hopped across the thick red carpet towards the door. The door was closed and nobody was about to open it for me, so for a couple of seconds I had to let go of my bottom with one hand to turn the door-knob. Then I was out and hopping around in the hallway of the private sanctum.

Directly across the hall from the Headmaster's study was the assistant masters' Common Room. They were all in there now waiting to spread out to their respective classrooms, but what I couldn't help noticing, even in my agony, was that *this door was open*.

Why was it open?

Had it been left that way on purpose so that they could all hear more clearly the sound of the cane from across the hall?

Of course it had. And I felt quite sure that it was Captain Hardcastle who had opened it. I pictured him standing in there among his colleagues snorting with satisfaction at every stinging stroke.

Small boys can be very comradely when a member of their community has got into trouble, and even more so when they feel an injustice has been done. When I returned to the classroom, I was surrounded on all sides by sympathetic faces and voices, but one particular incident has always stayed with me. A boy of my own age called Highton was so violently incensed by the whole affair that he said to me before lunch that day, '*You* don't have a father. I do. I am going to write to my father and tell him what has happened and he'll do something about it.'

'He couldn't do anything,' I said.

'Oh yes he could,' Highton said. 'And what's more he will. My father won't let them get away with this.'

'Where is he now?'

'He's in Greece,' Highton said. 'In Athens. But that won't make any difference.'

Then and there, little Highton sat down and wrote to the father he admired so much, but of course nothing came of it. It was nevertheless a touching and generous gesture from one small boy to another and I have never forgotten it.

Little Ellis and the boil

During my third term at St Peter's, I got flu and was put to bed in the Sick Room, where the dreaded Matron reigned supreme. In the next bed to mine was a seven-year-old boy called Ellis, whom I liked a lot. Ellis was there because he had an immense and angry-looking boil on the inside of his thigh. I saw it. It was as big as a plum and about the same colour.

One morning, in came the doctor to examine us, and sailing along beside him was the Matron. Her mountainous bosom was enclosed in a starched white envelope, and because of this she somehow reminded me of a painting I had once seen of a four-masted schooner in full canvas running before the wind.

'What's his temperature today?' the doctor asked, pointing at me.

'Just over a hundred, doctor,' the Matron told him.

'He's been up here long enough,' the doctor said. 'Send him back to school tomorrow.' Then he turned to Ellis. 'Take off your pyjama trousers,' he said. He was a very small doctor, with steel-rimmed spectacles and a bald head. He frightened the life out of me.

Ellis removed his pyjama trousers. The doctor bent forward and looked at the boil. 'Hmmm,' he said. 'That's a nasty one, isn't it? We're going to have to do something about that, aren't we, Ellis?'

'What are you going to do?' Ellis asked, trembling.

'Nothing for you to worry about,' the doctor said. 'Just lie back and take no notice of me.'

St Peters
Jan. 25th

Mrs Dahl
Cumber

Roald has a very mild attack of flu with several other boys he has only a very slight temperature if he continues well I shant be writing again but if his temp goes up I will let you know.

M. Francis

Little Ellis lay back with his head on the pillow. The doctor had put his bag on the floor at the end of Ellis's bed, and now he knelt down on the floor and opened the bag. Ellis, even when he lifted his head from the pillow, couldn't see what the doctor was doing there. He was hidden by the end of the bed. But I saw everything. I saw him take out a sort of scalpel which had a long steel handle and a small pointed blade. He crouched below the end of Ellis's bed, holding the scalpel in his right hand.

'Give me a large towel, Matron,' he said.

The Matron handed him a towel.

Still crouching low and hidden from little Ellis's view by the end of the bed, the doctor unfolded the towel and spread it over the palm of his left hand. In his right hand he held the scalpel.

Ellis was frightened and suspicious. He started raising himself up on his elbows to get a better look. 'Lie down, Ellis,' the doctor said, and even as he spoke, he bounced up from the end of the bed like a jack-in-the-box and flung the outspread towel straight into Ellis's face. Almost in the same second, he thrust his right arm forward and plunged the point of the scalpel deep into the centre of the enormous boil. He gave the blade a quick twist and then withdrew it again before the wretched boy had had time to disentangle his head from the towel.

Ellis screamed. He never saw the scalpel going in and he never saw it coming out, but he felt it all right and he screamed like a stuck pig. I can see him now struggling to get the towel off his head, and when he emerged the tears were streaming down his cheeks and his huge brown eyes were staring at the doctor with a look of utter and total outrage.

'Don't make such a fuss about nothing,' the Matron said.

'Put a dressing on it, Matron,' the doctor said, 'with plenty of mag sulph paste.' And he marched out of the room.

I couldn't really blame the doctor. I thought he handled things rather cleverly. Pain was something we were expected to endure. Anaesthetics and pain-killing injections were not much used in those days. Dentists, in particular, never bothered with them. But I doubt very much if you would be entirely happy today if a doctor threw a towel in your face and jumped on you with a knife.

the wart on my thum has come off beautifly, but the one on my knee has'nt even turned into a blister.
You meant me to learn singing did'nt you.

Goat's tobacco

When I was about nine, the ancient half-sister got engaged to be married. The man of her choice was a young English doctor and that summer he came with us to Norway.

Manly lover and ancient half-sister (in background)

Romance was floating in the air like moondust and the two lovers, for some reason we younger ones could never understand, did not seem to be very keen on us tagging along with them. They went out in the boat alone. They climbed the rocks alone. They even had breakfast alone. We resented this. As a family we had always done everything together and we didn't see why the ancient half-sister should suddenly decide to do things differently even if she had become engaged. We were inclined to blame the male lover for disrupting the calm of our family life, and it was inevitable that he would have to suffer for it sooner or later.

The male lover was a great pipe-smoker. The disgusting smelly pipe was never out of his mouth except when he was eating or swimming. We even began to wonder whether he removed it when he was kissing his betrothed. He gripped the stem of the pipe in the most manly fashion between his strong white teeth and kept it there while talking to you. This annoyed us. Surely it was more polite to take it out and speak properly.

One day, we all went in our little motor-boat to an island we had never been to before, and for once the ancient half-sister and the manly lover decided to come with us. We chose this particular island because we saw some goats on it. They were climbing about on the rocks and we thought it would be fun to go and visit them. But when we landed, we found that the goats were totally wild and we couldn't get near them. So we gave up trying to make friends with them and simply sat around on the smooth rocks in our bathing costumes, enjoying the lovely sun.

The manly lover was filling his pipe. I happened to be watching him as he very carefully packed the tobacco into the bowl from a yellow oilskin pouch. He had just finished doing this and was about to light up when the ancient half-sister called on him to come swimming. So he put down the pipe and off he went.

I stared at the pipe that was lying there on the rocks. About twelve inches away from it, I saw a little heap of dried goat's droppings, each one small and round like a pale brown berry, and at that point, an interesting idea began to sprout in my mind. I picked up the pipe and knocked all the tobacco out of it. I then took the goat's droppings and teased them with my fingers until they were nicely shredded. Very gently I poured these shredded droppings into the bowl of the pipe, packing them down with my thumb just as the manly lover always did it. When that was done, I placed a thin layer of real tobacco over the top. The entire family was watching me as I did this. Nobody said a word, but I could sense a glow of approval all round. I replaced the pipe on the rock, and all of us sat back to await the return of the victim. The whole lot of us were in this together now, even my mother. I had drawn them into the plot simply by letting them see what I was doing. It was a silent, rather dangerous family conspiracy.

Back came the manly lover, dripping wet from the sea, chest out, strong and virile, healthy and sunburnt. 'Great swim!' he announced to the world. 'Splendid water! Terrific stuff!' He towelled himself vigorously, making the muscles of his biceps ripple, then he sat down on the rocks and reached for his pipe.

Nine pairs of eyes watched him intently. Nobody giggled to give the game away. We were trembling with anticipation, and a good deal of the suspense was caused by the fact that none of us knew just what was going to happen.

The manly lover put the pipe between his strong white teeth and struck a match. He held the flame over the bowl and sucked. The tobacco ignited and glowed, and the lover's head was enveloped in clouds of blue smoke. 'Ah-h-h,' he said, blowing smoke through his nostrils. 'There's nothing like a good pipe after a bracing swim.'

Still we waited. We could hardly bear the suspense. The sister who was seven couldn't bear it at all. 'What *sort* of tobacco do you put in that thing?' she asked with superb innocence.

'Navy Cut,' the male lover answered. 'Player's Navy Cut. It's the best there is. These Norwegians use all sorts of disgusting scented tobaccos, but I wouldn't touch them.'

'I didn't know they had different tastes,' the small sister went on.

'Of course they do,' the manly lover said. 'All tobaccos are different to the discriminating pipe-smoker. Navy Cut is clean and unadulterated. It's a man's smoke.' The man seemed to go out of his way to use long words like discriminating and unadulterated. We hadn't the foggiest what they meant.

The ancient half-sister, fresh from her swim and now clothed in a towel bathrobe, came and sat herself close to her manly lover. Then the two of them started giving each other those silly little glances and soppy smiles that made us all feel sick. They were far too occupied with one another to notice the awful tension that had settled over our group. They didn't even notice that every face in the crowd was turned towards them. They had sunk once again into their lovers' world where little children did not exist.

The sea was calm, the sun was shining and it was a beautiful day.

Then all of a sudden, the manly lover let out a piercing scream and his whole body shot four feet into the air. His pipe flew out of his mouth and went clattering over the rocks, and the second scream he gave was so shrill and loud that all the seagulls on the island rose up in alarm. His features were twisted like those of a person undergoing severe torture, and his skin had turned the colour of snow. He began spluttering and choking and spewing and hawking and acting generally like a man with some serious internal injury. He was completely speechless.

We stared at him, enthralled.

The ancient half-sister, who must have thought she was about to lose her future husband for ever, was pawing at him and thumping him on the back and crying, 'Darling! Darling! What's happening to you? Where does it hurt? Get the boat! Start the engine! We must rush him to a hospital quickly!' She seemed to have forgotten that there wasn't a hospital within fifty miles.

'I've been poisoned!' spluttered the manly lover. 'It's got into my lungs! It's in my chest! My chest is on fire! My stomach's going up in flames!'

'Help me get him into the boat! Quick!' cried the ancient half-sister, gripping him under the armpits. 'Don't just sit there staring! Come and help!'

'No, no, no!' cried the now not-so-manly lover. 'Leave me alone! I need air! Give me air!' He lay back and breathed in deep draughts of splendid Norwegian ocean air, and in another minute or so, he was sitting up again and was on the way to recovery.

'What in the world came over you?' asked the ancient half-sister, clasping his hands tenderly in hers.

'I can't imagine,' he murmured. 'I simply can't imagine.' His face was as still and white as virgin snow and his hands were trembling. 'There must be a reason for it,' he added. 'There's got to be a reason.'

'I know the reason!' shouted the seven-year-old sister, screaming with laughter. 'I know what it was!'

'What was it?' snapped the ancient one. 'What have you been up to? Tell me at once!'

'It's his pipe!' shouted the small sister, still convulsed with laughter.

'What's wrong with my pipe?' said the manly lover.

'You've been smoking goat's tobacco!' cried the small sister.

It took a few moments for the full meaning of these words to dawn upon the two lovers, but when it did, and when the terrible anger began to show itself on the manly lover's face, and when he started to rise slowly and menacingly to his feet, we all sprang up and ran for our lives and jumped off the rocks into the deep water.

Repton and Shell,

1929—36

(age 13—20)

THE PRIORY HOUSE,
REPTON,
DERBY.

Dear Mama
Thanks awfully for the parcel
and your letters. We had a great supper
last night. We fried the sausages and poured
hieny beans over them. then we had force &
cream. Those biscuits are awfully good.
Last night we had a heavy snowfall, and
there is about _____ of snow on the ground.
Macdonald & I _____ _____ Tobogganing

photography at Repton

On ship to Newfoundland
1933

Getting dressed for the big school

When I was twelve, my mother said to me, 'I've entered you for Marlborough and Repton. Which would you like to go to?'

Both were famous Public Schools, but that was all I knew about them. 'Repton,' I said. 'I'll go to Repton.' It was an easier word to say than Marlborough.

'Very well,' my mother said. 'You shall go to Repton.'

We were living in Kent then, in a place called Bexley. Repton was up in the Midlands, near Derby, and some 140 miles away to the north. That was of no consequence. There were plenty of trains. Nobody was taken to school by car in those days. We were put on the train.

alfhild, me, asta, Else
and dogs. Tenby.

I was exactly thirteen in September 1929 when the time came for me to go to Repton. On the day of my departure, I had first of all to get dressed for the part. I had been to

London with my mother the week before to buy the school clothes, and I remember how shocked I was when I saw the outfit I was expected to wear.

'I can't possibly go about in *those!*' I cried. 'Nobody wears things like that!'

'Are you sure you haven't made a mistake?' my mother said to the shop assistant.

'If he's going to Repton, madam, he must wear these clothes,' the assistant said firmly.

And now this amazing fancy-dress was all laid out on my bed waiting to be put on. 'Put it on,' my mother said. 'Hurry up or you'll miss the train.'

'I'll look like a complete idiot,' I said. My mother went out of the room and left me to it. With immense reluctance, I began to dress myself.

First there was a white shirt with a detachable white collar. This collar was unlike any other collar I had seen. It was as stiff as a piece of perspex. At the front, the stiff points of the collar were bent over to make a pair of wings, and the whole thing was so tall that the points of the wings, as I discovered later, rubbed against the underneath of my chin. It was known as a butterfly collar.

To attach the butterfly collar to the shirt you needed a back stud and a front stud. I had never been through this rigmarole before. I must do this properly, I told myself. So first I put the back stud into the back of the collar-band of the shirt. Then I tried to attach the back of the collar to the back stud, but the collar was so stiff I couldn't get the stud through the slit. I decided to soften it with spit. I put the edge of the collar into my mouth and sucked the starch away. It worked. The stud went through the slit and the back of the collar was now attached to the back of the shirt.

I inserted the front stud into one side of the front of the

shirt and slipped the shirt over my head. With the help of a mirror, I now set about pushing the top of the front stud through the first of the two slits in the front of the collar. It wouldn't go. The slit was so small and stiff and starchy that nothing would go through it. I took the shirt off and put both the front slits of the collar into my mouth and chewed them until they were soft. The starch didn't taste of anything. I put the shirt back on again and at last I was able to get the front stud through the collar-slits.

Around the collar but underneath the butterfly wings, I tied a black tie, using an ordinary tie-knot.

Dear Mama

Thanks for your letter.
I mean half a dozen Van Heusen
Collars. not Shirts.

Love from
Roald.

Then came the trousers and the braces. The trousers were black with thin pinstriped grey lines running down them. I buttoned the braces on to the trousers, six buttons in all, then I put on the trousers and adjusted the braces to the correct length by sliding two brass clips up and down.

I put on a brand new pair of black shoes and laced them up.

Now for the waistcoat. This was also black and it had twelve buttons down the front and two little waistcoat pockets on either side, one above the other. I put it on and did up the buttons, starting at the top and working down.

I was glad I didn't have to chew each of those button-holes to get the buttons through them.

All this was bad enough for a boy who had never before worn anything more elaborate than a pair of shorts and a blazer. But the jacket put the lid on it. It wasn't actually a jacket, it was a sort of tail-coat, and it was without a doubt the most ridiculous garment I had ever seen. Like the waistcoat, it was jet black and made of a heavy serge-like material. In the front it was cut away so that the two sides met only at one point, about halfway down the waistcoat. Here there was a single button and this had to be done up.

From the button downwards, the lines of the coat separated and curved away behind the legs of the wearer and came together again at the backs of the knees, forming a pair of 'tails'. These tails were separated by a slit and when you walked about they flapped against your legs. I put the thing on and did up the front button. Feeling like an undertaker's apprentice in a funeral parlour, I crept downstairs.

My sisters shrieked with laughter when I appeared. 'He can't go out in *those*!' they cried. 'He'll be arrested by the police!'

'Put your hat on,' my mother said, handing me a stiff wide-brimmed straw-hat with a blue and black band around it. I put it on and did my best to look dignified. The sisters fell all over the room laughing.

the hat-band being something like this:___ the white stripes are realy blue, and the bit filled in is black.

My mother got me out of the house before I lost my nerve completely and together we walked through the village to Bexley station. My mother was going to accompany me to London and see me on to the Derby train, but she had been told that on no account should she travel farther than that. I had only a small suitcase to carry. My trunk had been sent on ahead labelled 'Luggage in Advance'.

'Nobody's taking the slightest notice of you,' my mother said as we walked through Bexley High Street.

And curiously enough nobody was.

'I have learnt one thing about England,' my mother went on. 'It is a country where men love to wear uniforms and eccentric clothes. Two hundred years ago their clothes were even more eccentric then they are today. You can consider yourself lucky you don't have to wear a wig on your head and ruffles on your sleeves.'

'I still feel an ass,' I said.

'Everyone who looks at you', my mother said, 'knows that you are going away to a Public School. All English Public Schools have their own different crazy uniforms. People will be thinking how lucky you are to be going to one of those famous places.'

We took the train from Bexley to Charing Cross and then went by taxi to Euston Station. At Euston, I was put on the train for Derby with a lot of other boys who all wore the same ridiculous clothes as me, and away I went.

Beagling, Repton 1930.

Boazers

At Repton, prefects were never called prefects. They were called Boazers, and they had the power of life and death over us junior boys. They could summon us down in our pyjamas at night-time and thrash us for leaving just one football sock on the floor of the changing-room when it should have been hung up on a peg. A Boazer could thrash us for a hundred and one other piddling little misdemeanours – for burning his toast at tea-time, for failing to dust his study properly, for failing to get his study fire burning in spite of spending half your pocket money on fire-lighters, for being late at roll-call, for talking in evening Prep, for forgetting to change into house-shoes at six o'clock. The list was endless.

'Four with the dressing-gown on or three with it off?' the Boazer would say to you in the changing-room late at night.

Others in the dormitory had told you what to answer to this question. 'Four with it on,' you mumbled, trembling.

This Boazer was famous for the speed of his strokes. Most of them paused between each stroke to prolong the operation, but Williamson, the great footballer, cricketer and athlete, always delivered his strokes in a series of swift back and forth movements without any pause between them at all. Four strokes would rain down upon your bottom so fast that it was all over in four seconds.

A ritual took place in the dormitory after each beating. The victim was required to stand in the middle of the room and lower his pyjama trousers so that the damage could be inspected. Half a dozen experts would crowd round you and express their opinions in highly professional language.

'*What* a super job.'

'He's got *every single* one in the same place!'

'Crikey! Nobody could tell you had more than *one*, except for the mess!'

'Boy, that Williamson's got a *terrific* eye!'

'*Of course* he's got a terrific eye! Why d'you think he's a Cricket Teamer?'

'There's no wet blood though! If you had had just one more he'd have got some blood out!'

'Through a *dressing-gown*, too! It's pretty amazing, isn't it!'

'Most Boazers couldn't get a result like that *without* a dressing-gown!'

'You must have tremendously thin skin! Even Williamson couldn't have done that to *ordinary* skin!'

'Did he use the long one or the short one?'

'Hang *on*! Don't pull them up yet! I've *got* to see this again!'

And I would stand there, slightly bemused by this cool clinical approach. Once, I was still standing in the middle of the dormitory with my pyjama trousers around my knees when Williamson came through the door. 'What on earth do you think you're doing?' he said, knowing very well exactly what I was doing.

'N-nothing,' I stammered. 'N-nothing at all.'

'Pull those pyjamas up and get into bed immediately!' he ordered, but I noticed that as he turned away to go out of the door, he craned his head ever so slightly to one side to catch a glimpse of my bare bottom and his own handiwork. I was certain I detected a little glimmer of pride around the edges of his mouth before he closed the door behind him.

The Headmaster

and again!

The Headmaster, while I was at Repton, struck me as being a rather shoddy bandy-legged little fellow with a big bald head and lots of energy but not much charm. Mind you, I never did know him well because in all those months and years I was at the school, I doubt whether he addressed more than six sentences to me altogether. So perhaps it was wrong of me to form a judgement like that.

What is so interesting about this Headmaster is that he became a famous person later on. At the end of my third year, he was suddenly appointed Bishop of Chester and off he went to live in a palace by the River Dee. I remember at the time trying to puzzle out how on earth a person could suddenly leap from being a schoolmaster to becoming a Bishop all in one jump, but there were bigger puzzles to come.

From Chester, he was soon promoted again to become Bishop of London, and from there, after not all that many years, he bounced up the ladder once more to get the top job of them all, Archbishop of Canterbury! And not long after that it was he himself who had the task of crowning our present Queen in Westminster Abbey with half the world watching him on television. Well, well, well! And this was the man who used to deliver the most vicious beatings to the boys under his care!

By now I am sure you will be wondering why I lay so

much emphasis upon school beatings in these pages. The answer is that I cannot help it. All through my school life I was appalled by the fact that masters and senior boys were allowed literally to wound other boys, and sometimes quite severely. I couldn't get over it. I never have got over it. It would, of course, be unfair to suggest that *all* masters were constantly beating the daylights out of *all* the boys in those days. They weren't. Only a few did so, but that was quite enough to leave a lasting impression of horror upon me. It left another more physical impression upon me as well. Even today, whenever I have to sit for any length of time on a hard bench or chair, I begin to feel my heart beating along the old lines that the cane made on my bottom some fifty-five years ago.

There is nothing wrong with a few quick sharp tickles on the rump. They probably do a naughty boy a lot of good. But this Headmaster we were talking about wasn't just tickling you when he took out his cane to deliver a flogging. He never flogged me, thank goodness, but I was given a vivid description of one of these ceremonies by my best friend at Repton, whose name was Michael. Michael was ordered to take down his trousers and kneel on the Headmaster's sofa with the top half of his body hanging over one end of the sofa. The great man then gave him one terrific crack. After that, there was a pause. The cane was put down and the Headmaster began filling his pipe from a tin of tobacco. He also started to lecture the kneeling boy about sin and wrongdoing. Soon, the cane was picked up again and a second tremendous crack was administered upon the trembling buttocks. Then the pipe-filling business and the lecture went on for maybe another thirty seconds. Then came the third crack of the cane. Then the instrument of torture was put once more upon the table and a box of matches was produced. A match was struck and applied to the pipe. The pipe failed to light properly. A fourth stroke was delivered, with the lecture continuing. This slow and fearsome process went on until ten terrible strokes had been delivered, and all the time, over the pipe-lighting and the match-striking, the lecture on evil and wrongdoing and sinning and misdeeds and malpractice went on without a stop. It even went on as the strokes were being administered. At the end of it all, a basin, a sponge and a small clean towel were produced by the Headmaster, and the victim was told to wash away the blood before pulling up his trousers.

Do you wonder then that this man's behaviour used to puzzle me tremendously? He was an ordinary clergyman at that time as well as being Headmaster, and I would sit in the dim light of the school chapel and listen to him preaching about the Lamb of God and about Mercy and Forgiveness and all the rest of it and my young mind would become totally confused. I knew very well that only the night before this preacher had shown neither Forgiveness nor Mercy in flogging some small boy who had broken the rules.

So what was it all about? I used to ask myself.

Did they preach one thing and practise another, these men of God?

And if someone had told me at the time that this flogging clergyman was one day to become the Archbishop of Canterbury, I would never have believed it.

It was all this, I think, that made me begin to have doubts about religion and even about God. If this person, I kept telling myself, was one of God's chosen salesmen on earth, then there must be something very wrong about the whole business.

Chocolates

Every now and again, a plain grey cardboard box was dished out to each boy in our House, and this, believe it or not, was a present from the great chocolate manufacturers, Cadbury. Inside the box there were twelve bars of chocolate, all of different shapes, all with different fillings and all with numbers from one to twelve stamped on the chocolate underneath. Eleven of these bars were new inventions from the factory. The twelfth was the 'control' bar, one that we all knew well, usually a Cadbury's Coffee Cream bar. Also in the box was a sheet of paper with the numbers one to twelve on it as well as two blank columns, one for giving marks to each chocolate from nought to ten, and the other for comments.

All we were required to do in return for this splendid gift was to taste very carefully each bar of chocolate, give it marks and make an intelligent comment on why we liked it or disliked it.

It was a clever stunt. Cadbury's were using some of the greatest chocolate-bar experts in the world to test out their new inventions. We were of a sensible age, between thirteen and eighteen, and we knew intimately every chocolate bar in existence, from the Milk Flake to the Lemon Marshmallow. Quite obviously our opinions on anything new would be valuable. All of us entered into this game with great gusto, sitting in our studies and nibbling each bar with the air of connoisseurs, giving our marks and making our comments. 'Too subtle for the common palate,' was one note that I remember writing down.

For me, the importance of all this was that I began to realize that the large chocolate companies actually did possess inventing rooms and they took their inventing very seriously. I used to picture a long white room like a laboratory with pots of chocolate and fudge and all sorts of other delicious fillings bubbling away on the stoves, while men and women in white coats moved between the bubbling pots, tasting and mixing and concocting their wonderful new inventions. I used to imagine myself working in one of these labs and suddenly I would come up with something so absolutely unbearably delicious that I would grab it in my hand and go rushing out of the lab and along the corridor and right into the office of the great Mr Cadbury himself. 'I've got it, sir!' I would shout, putting the chocolate in front of him. 'It's fantastic! It's fabulous! It's marvellous! It's irresistible!'

Slowly, the great man would pick up my newly invented chocolate and he would take a small bite. He would roll it round his mouth. Then all at once, he would leap up from his chair, crying, 'You've got it! You've done it! It's a miracle!' He would slap me on the back and shout, 'We'll sell it by the million! We'll sweep the world with this one! How on earth did you do it? Your salary is doubled!'

It was lovely dreaming those dreams, and I have no doubt at all that, thirty-five years later, when I was looking for a plot for my second book for children, I remembered those little cardboard boxes and the newly-invented chocolates inside them, and I began to write a book called *Charlie and the Chocolate Factory*.

Saturday, first I broke it in half, and only half came out, then the other bit came out, it was my dog tooth, and it was a very bad one, I am glad it came out. Will, you please send me a few sweets because we had none, last week, I am sorry my writing is so untidy, but I have not much time on week days.

Corkers

There were about thirty or more masters at Repton and most of them were amazingly dull and totally colourless and completely uninterested in boys. But Corkers, an eccentric old bachelor, was neither dull nor colourless. Corkers was a charmer, a vast ungainly man with drooping bloodhound cheeks and filthy clothes. He wore creaseless flannel trousers and a brown tweed jacket with patches all over it and bits of dried food on the lapels. He was meant to teach us mathematics, but in truth he taught us nothing at all and that was the way he meant it to be. His lessons consisted of an endless series of distractions all invented by him so that the subject of mathematics would never have to be discussed. He would come lumbering into the classroom and sit down at his desk and glare at the class. We would wait expectantly, wondering what was coming next.

'Let's have a look at the crossword puzzle in today's *Times*,' he would say, fishing a crumpled newspaper out of his jacket pocket. 'That'll be a lot more fun than fiddling around with figures. I hate figures. Figures are probably the dreariest things on this earth.'

'Then why do you teach mathematics, sir?' somebody asked him.

'I don't,' he said, smiling slyly. 'I only *pretend* to teach it.'

Corkers would proceed to draw the framework of the

crossword on the blackboard and we would all spend the rest of the lesson trying to solve it while he read out the clues. We enjoyed that.

The only time I can remember him vaguely touching upon mathematics was when he whisked a square of tissue-paper out of his pocket and waved it around. 'Look at this,' he said. 'This tissue-paper is one-hundredth of an inch thick. I fold it once, making it double. I fold it again, making it four thicknesses. Now then, I will give a large bar of Cadbury's Fruit and Nut Milk Chocolate to any boy who can tell me, to the nearest twelve inches, how thick it will be if I fold it fifty times.'

We all stuck up our hands and started guessing. 'Twenty-four inches, sir' . . . 'Three feet, sir' . . . 'Five yards, sir' . . . 'Three inches, sir.'

'You're not very clever, are you,' Corkers said. 'The answer is the distance from the earth to the sun. That's how thick it would be.' We were enthralled by this piece of intelligence and asked him to prove it on the blackboard, which he did.

Another time, he brought a two-foot-long grass-snake into class and insisted that every boy should handle it in order to cure us for ever, as he said, of a fear of snakes. This caused quite a commotion.

I cannot remember all the other thousands of splendid things that old Corkers cooked up to keep his class happy, but there was one that I shall never forget which was repeated at intervals of about three weeks throughout each term. He would be talking to us about this or that when suddenly he would stop in mid-sentence and a look of intense pain would cloud his ancient countenance. Then his head would come up and his great nose would begin to sniff the air and he would cry aloud, 'By God! This is too much! This is going too far! This is intolerable!'

Thanks awfully for the Tablets. I took some a few times and the indigestion has stopped now, they are jolly good

We knew exactly what was coming next, but we always played along with him. 'What's the matter, sir? What's happened? Are you all right, sir? Are you feeling ill?'

Up went the great nose once again, and the head would move slowly from side to side and the nose would sniff the air delicately as though searching for a leak of gas or the smell of something burning. 'This is not to be tolerated!' he would cry. 'This is *unbearable*!'

'But what's the *matter*, sir?'

'I'll tell you what's the matter,' Corkers would shout. 'Somebody's *farted*!'

'Oh no, sir!' . . . 'Not me, sir!' . . . 'Nor me, sir!' . . . 'It's none of us, sir!'

At this point, he would rise majestically to his feet and call out at the top of his voice, '*Use door as fan! Open all windows!*'

This was the signal for frantic activity and everyone in the class would leap to his feet. It was a well-rehearsed operation and each of us knew exactly what he had to do. Four boys would man the door and begin swinging it back and forth at great speed. The rest would start clambering about on the gigantic windows which occupied one whole wall of the room, flinging the lower ones open, using a long pole with a hook on the end to open the top ones, and leaning out to gulp the fresh air in mock distress. While this was going on, Corkers himself would march serenely out of the room, muttering, 'It's the cabbage that does it! All they give you is disgusting cabbage and Brussels sprouts and you go off like fire-crackers!' And that was the last we saw of Corkers for the day.

School dinners !

Fagging

I spent two long years as a Fag at Repton, which meant I
was the servant of the studyholder in whose study I had
my little desk. If the studyholder happened to be a House
Boazer, so much the worse for me because Boazers were
a dangerous breed. During my second term, I was unfortu-
nate enough to be put into the study of the Head of the
House, a supercilious and obnoxious seventeen-year-old
called Carleton. Carleton always looked at you right down

I dont think that I've told you what we do everyday sort of thing: the
First bell goes at quarter-past seven, and the fag who is in water in
each bedder, gets up and fills the cans with hot water, and closes
the windows. then if he want to get into bed again. the Second
bell goes at half past seven, and everyone must be down for prayers
by quarter to eight. then we h
to an hour   of m
H

the length of his nose, and even if you were as tall as him,
which I happened to be, he would tilt his head back and
still manage to look at you down the length of his nose.
Carleton had three Fags in his study and all of us were
terrified of him, especially on Sunday mornings, because
Sunday was study-cleaning time. All the Fags in all the
studies had to take off their jackets, roll up their sleeves,
fetch buckets and floor-cloths and get down to cleaning
out their studyholder's study. And when I say cleaning

out, I mean practically sterilizing the place. We scrubbed the floor and washed the windows and polished the grate and dusted the ledges and wiped the picture-frames and carefully tidied away all the hockey-sticks and cricket-bats and umbrellas.

All that Sunday morning we had been slogging away cleaning Carleton's study, and then, just before lunch Carleton himself strode into the room and said, 'You've had long enough.'

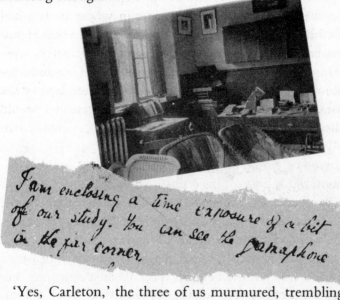

I am enclosing a time exposure of a bit of our study. You can see the Damaphone in the far corner

'Yes, Carleton,' the three of us murmured, trembling. We stood back, breathless from our exertions, compelled as always to wait and watch the dreadful Carleton while he performed the ritual of inspection. First of all, he would go to the drawer of his desk and take out a pure-white cotton glove which he slid with much ceremony on to his right hand. Then, taking as much care and time as a surgeon in an operating theatre, he would move slowly round the study, running his white-gloved fingers along all the ledges, along the tops of the picture-frames, over the surfaces of the desks, and even over the bars of the fire-grate. Every few seconds, he would hold those white fingers up close to his face, searching for traces of dust, and we three Fags would stand there watching him, hardly daring to breathe, waiting for the dreaded moment when the great man would stop and shout, 'Ha! What's this I see?' A look of triumph would light up his face as he held up a white finger which had on it the tiniest smudge of grey dust, and he would stare at us with his slightly popping pale blue eyes and say, 'You haven't cleaned it have you? You haven't bothered to clean my study properly.'

To the three of us Fags who had been slaving away for the whole of the morning, these words were simply not true. 'We've cleaned every bit of it, Carleton,' we would answer. 'Every little bit.'

'In that case why has my finger got dust on it?' Carleton would say, tilting his head back and gazing at us down the length of his nose. 'This *is* dust, isn't it?'

We would step forward and peer at the white-gloved forefinger and at the tiny smidgin of dust that lay on it, and we would remain silent. I longed to point out to him that it was an actual impossibility to clean a much-used room to the point where no speck of dust remained, but that would have been suicide.

'Do any of you dispute the fact that this is dust?' Carleton would say, still holding up his finger. 'If I am wrong, do tell me.'

'It isn't *much* dust, Carleton.'

'I didn't ask you whether it was *much* dust or *not much* dust,' Carleton would say. 'I simply asked you whether or not it was dust. Might it, for example, be iron filings or face powder instead?'

'No, Carleton.'

'Or crushed diamonds, maybe?'

'No, Carleton.'

'Then what is it?'

'It's . . . it's dust, Carleton.'

'Thank you,' Carleton would say. 'At last you have admitted that you failed to clean my study properly. I shall therefore see all three of you in the changing-room tonight after prayers.'

> *You seem to have been doing a lot of painting; but when you paint the lav. don't paint the seat, leaving it wet and sticky, or some unfortunate person who has not noticed it, will adhere to it, and unless his bottom is cut off ~~unless he chooses~~ to go about with the seat ~~bed~~ sticking behind him always, he will be doomed to stay where he is*

The rules and rituals of fagging at Repton were so complicated that I could fill a whole book with them. A House Boazer, for example, could make any Fag in the House do his bidding. He could stand anywhere he wanted to in the building, in the corridor, in the changing-room, in the yard, and yell 'Fa-a-ag!' at the top of his voice and every Fag in the place would have to drop what he was doing and run flat out to the source of the noise. There was always a mad stampede when the call of 'Fa-a-ag!' echoed through the House because the last boy to arrive would invariably be chosen for whatever menial or unpleasant task the Boazer had in mind.

During my first term, I was in the changing-room one day just before lunch scraping the mud from the soles of my studyholder's football boots when I heard the famous shout of 'Fa-a-ag!' far away at the other end of the House.

I dropped everything and ran. But I got there last, and the Boazer who had done the shouting, a massive athlete called Wilberforce, said, 'Dahl, come here.'

The other Fags melted away with the speed of light and I crept forward to receive my orders. 'Go and heat my seat in the bogs,' Wilberforce said. 'I want it *warm*.'

I hadn't the faintest idea what any of this meant, but I already knew better than to ask questions of a Boazer. I hurried away and found a fellow Fag who told me the meaning of this curious order. It meant that the Boazer wished to use the lavatory but that he wanted the seat warmed for him before he sat down. The six House lavatories, none with doors, were situated in an unheated outhouse and on a cold day in winter you could get frostbite out there if you stayed too long. This particular day was icy-cold, and I went out through the snow into the outhouse and entered number one lavatory, which I knew was reserved for Boazers only. I wiped the frost off the seat with my handkerchief, then I lowered my trousers and sat

down. I was there a full fifteen minutes in the freezing cold before Wilberforce arrived on the scene.

'Have you got the ice off it?' he asked.

'Yes, Wilberforce.'

'Is it *warm*?'

'It's as warm as I can get it, Wilberforce,' I said.

'We shall soon find out,' he said. 'You can get off now.'

I got off the lavatory seat and pulled up my trousers. Wilberforce lowered his own trousers and sat down. 'Very good,' he said. 'Very good indeed.' He was like a winetaster sampling an old claret. 'I shall put you on my list,' he added.

I stood there doing up my fly-buttons and not knowing what on earth he meant.

'Some Fags have cold bottoms,' he said, 'and some have hot ones. I only use hot-bottomed Fags to heat my bog-seat. I won't forget you.'

He didn't. From then on, all through that winter, I became Wilberforce's favourite bog-seat warmer, and I used always to keep a paperback book in the pocket of my tail-coat to while away the long bog-warming sessions. I must have read the entire works of Dickens sitting on that Boazer's bog during my first winter at Repton.

Games and photography

It was always a surprise to me that I was good at games. It was an even greater surprise that I was exceptionally good at two of them. One of these was called fives, the other was squash-racquets.

Fives, which many of you will know nothing about, was taken seriously at Repton and we had a dozen massive glass-roofed fives courts kept always in perfect condition. We played the game of *Eton*-fives, which is always played by four people, two on each side, and basically it consists of hitting a small, hard, white, leather-covered ball with your gloved hands. The Americans have something like it which they call handball, but Eton-fives is far more complicated because the court has all manner of ledges and buttresses built into it which help to make it a subtle and crafty game.

Fives is possibly the fastest ball-game on earth, far faster than squash, and the little ball ricochets around the court at such a speed that sometimes you can hardly see it. You need a swift eye, strong wrists and a very quick pair of hands to play fives well, and it was a game I took to right from the beginning. You may find it hard to believe, but I became so good at it that I won both the junior and the senior school fives in the same year when I was fifteen. Soon I bore the splendid title 'Captain of Fives', and I would travel with my team to other schools like Shrewsbury and

Uppingham to play matches. I loved it. It was a game without physical contact, and the quickness of the eye and the dancing of the feet were all that mattered.

A Captain of any game at Repton was an important person. He was the one who selected the members of the team for matches. He and only he could award 'colours' to others. He would award school 'colours' by walking up to the chosen boy after a match and shaking him by the hand and saying, 'Graggers on your teamer!' These were magic words. They entitled the new teamer to all manner of privileges including a different-coloured hat-band on his straw-hat and fancy braid around the edges of his blazer and different-coloured games clothes, and all sorts of other advertisements that made the teamer gloriously conspicuous among his fellows.

Fives Team
Priory House

A Captain of any game, whether it was football, cricket, fives or squash, had many other duties. It was he who pinned the notice on the school notice-board on match days announcing the team. It was he who arranged fixtures by letter with other schools. It was he and only he who had it in his power to invite this master or that to play against him and his team on certain afternoons. All these responsibilities were given to me when I became Captain of Fives. Then came the snag. It was more or less taken for granted that a Captain would be made a Boazer in recognition of his talents – if not a School Boazer then certainly a House Boazer. But the authorities did not like me. I was not to be trusted. I did not like rules. I was unpredictable. I was therefore not Boazer material. There was no way they would agree to make me a House Boazer, let alone a School Boazer. Some people are born to wield power and to exercise authority. I was not one of them. I was in full agreement with my Housemaster when he explained this to me. I would have made a rotten Boazer. I would have let down the whole principle of Boazerdom by refusing to beat the Fags. I was probably the only Captain of any game who has never become a Boazer at Repton. I was certainly the only unBoazered Double Captain, because I was also Captain of squash-racquets. And to pile glory upon glory, I was in the school football team as well.

A boy who is good at games is usually treated with great civility by the masters at an English Public School. In much the same way, the ancient Greeks revered their athletes and made statues of them in marble. Athletes were the demigods, the chosen few. They could perform glamorous feats beyond the reach of ordinary mortals. Even today, fine footballers and baseball players and runners and all other great sportsmen are much admired by the general public and advertisers use them to sell breakfast cereals.

This never happened to me, and if you really want to know, I'm awfully glad it didn't.

But because I loved playing games, life for me at Repton was not totally without pleasure. Games-playing at school is always fun if you happen to be good at it, and it is hell if you are not. I was one of the lucky ones, and all those afternoons on the playing-fields and in the fives courts and in the squash courts made the otherwise grey and melancholy days pass a lot more quickly.

There was one other thing that gave me great pleasure at this school and that was photography. I was the only boy who practised it seriously, and it was not quite so simple a business fifty years ago as it is today. I made myself a little dark-room in a corner of the music building, and in there I loaded my glass plates and developed my negatives and enlarged them.

Our Arts Master was a shy retiring man called Arthur Norris who kept himself well apart from the rest of the staff. Arthur Norris and I became close friends and during my last year he organized an exhibition of my photographs. He gave the whole of the Art School over to this project and helped me to get my enlargements framed. The exhibition was rather a success, and masters who had hardly ever spoken to me over the past four years would come up and say things like, 'It's quite extraordinary' . . . 'We didn't know we had an artist in our midst' . . . 'Are they for sale?'

Arthur Norris would give me tea and cakes in his flat and would talk to me about painters like Cézanne and Manet and Matisse, and I have a feeling that it was there, having tea with the gentle soft-spoken Mr Norris in his flat on Sunday afternoons that my great love of painters and their work began.

After leaving school, I continued for a long time with photography and I became quite good at it. Today, given a 35mm camera and a built-in exposure-meter, anyone can be an expert photographer, but it was not so easy fifty years ago. I used glass plates instead of film, and each of these had to be loaded into its separate container in the dark-room before I set out to take pictures. I usually carried with me six loaded plates, which allowed me only six exposures, so that clicking the shutter even once was a serious business that had to be carefully thought out before-hand.

You may not believe it, but when I was eighteen I used to win prizes and medals from the Royal Photographic Society in London, and from other places like the Photographic Society of Holland. I even got a lovely big bronze medal from the Egyptian Photographic Society in Cairo,

and I still have the photograph that won it. It is a picture of one of the so-called Seven Wonders of the World, the Arch of Ctesiphon in Iraq. This is the largest unsupported arch on earth and I took the photograph while I was training out there for the RAF in 1940. I was flying over the desert solo in an old Hawker Hart biplane and I had my camera round my neck. When I spotted the huge arch standing alone in a sea of sand, I dropped one wing and hung in my straps and let go of the stick while I took aim and clicked the shutter. It came out fine.

Goodbye school

During my last year at Repton, my mother said to me, 'Would you like to go to Oxford or Cambridge when you leave school?' In those days it was not difficult to get into either of these great universities so long as you could pay.

'No, thank you,' I said. 'I want to go straight from school to work for a company that will send me to wonderful faraway places like Africa or China.'

You must remember that there was virtually no air travel in the early 1930s. Africa was two weeks away from England by boat and it took you about five weeks to get to China. These were distant and magic lands and nobody went to them just for a holiday. You went there to work. Nowadays you can go anywhere in the world in a few hours and nothing is fabulous any more. But it was a very different matter in 1934.

So during my last term I applied for a job only to those companies that would be sure to send me abroad. They were the Shell Company (Eastern Staff), Imperial Chemicals (Eastern Staff) and a Finnish lumber company whose name I have forgotten.

I was accepted by Imperial Chemicals and by the Finnish lumber company, but for some reason I wanted most of all to get into the Shell Company. When the day came for me to go up to London for this interview, my Housemaster told me it was ridiculous for me even to try. 'The Eastern

Staff of Shell are the *crème de la crème*,' he said. 'There will be at least one hundred applicants and about five vacancies. Nobody has a hope unless he's been Head of the School or Head of the House, and you aren't even a *House* Prefect!'

My Housemaster was right about the applicants. There were one hundred and seven boys waiting to be interviewed when I arrived at the Head Office of the Shell Company in London. And there were seven places to be filled. Please don't ask me how I got one of those places. I don't know myself. But get it I did, and when I told my Housemaster the good news on my return to school, he didn't congratulate me or shake me warmly by the hand. He turned away muttering, 'All I can say is I'm damned glad I don't own any shares in Shell.'

I didn't care any longer what my Housemaster thought. I was all set. I had a career. It was lovely. I was to leave school for ever in July 1934 and join the Shell Company two months later in September when I would be exactly eighteen. I was to be an Eastern Staff Trainee at a salary of five pounds a week.

That summer, for the first time in my life, I did not accompany the family to Norway. I somehow felt the need for a special kind of last fling before I became a businessman. So while still at school during my last term, I signed up to spend August with something called 'The Public Schools' Exploring Society'. The leader of this outfit was a man who had gone with Captain Scott on his last expedition to the South Pole, and he was taking a party of senior schoolboys to explore the interior of Newfoundland during the summer holidays. It sounded like fun.

Without the slightest regret I said goodbye to Repton for ever and rode back to Kent on my motorbike. This splendid machine was a 500 cc Ariel which I had bought the year before for eighteen pounds, and during my last term at Repton I kept it secretly in a garage along the Willington road about two miles away. On Sundays I used to walk to the garage and disguise myself in helmet, goggles, old raincoat and rubber waders and ride all over Derbyshire. It was fun to go roaring through Repton itself with nobody knowing who you were, swishing past the masters walking in the street and circling around the

got the job with Shell!

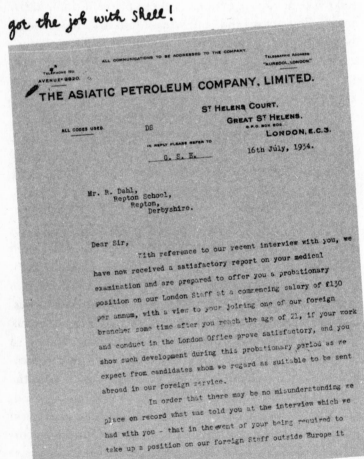

ALL COMMUNICATIONS TO BE ADDRESSED TO THE COMPANY.

TELEGRAPHIC ADDRESS:
"AUREOOL, LONDON."

TELEPHONE NO.
AVENUE: 8820.

THE ASIATIC PETROLEUM COMPANY, LIMITED.

ALL CODES USED.

DS

ST HELENS COURT,
GREAT ST HELENS,
G.P.O. BOX 202.
LONDON, E.C.3.

IN REPLY PLEASE REFER TO

G. S. E.

16th July, 1934.

Mr. R. Dahl,
    Repton School,
      Repton,
        Derbyshire.

Dear Sir,

    With reference to our recent interview with you, we have now received a satisfactory report on your medical examination and are prepared to offer you a probationary position on our London Staff at a commencing salary of £130 per annum, with a view to your joining one of our foreign branches some time after you reach the age of 21, if your work and conduct in the London Office prove satisfactory, and you show such development during this probationary period as we expect from candidates whom we regard as suitable to be sent abroad in our foreign service.

    In order that there may be no misunderstanding we place on record what was told you at the interview which we had with you - that in the event of your being required to take up a position on our foreign Staff outside Europe it dangerous supercilious School Boazers out for their Sunday strolls. I tremble to think what would have happened to me had I been caught, but I wasn't caught. So on the last day of term I zoomed joyfully away and left school behind me for ever and ever. I was not quite eighteen.

I had only two days at home before I was off to New-foundland with the Public Schools' Explorers. Our ship sailed from Liverpool at the beginning of August and took

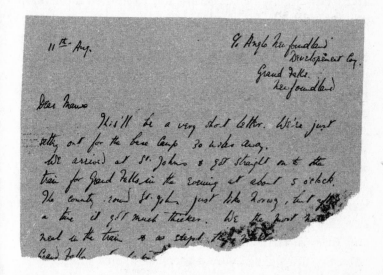

six days to reach St John's. There were about thirty boys of my own age on the expedition as well as four experienced adult leaders. But Newfoundland, as I soon found out, was not much of a country. For three weeks we trudged all over that desolate land with enormous loads on our backs. We carried tents and groundsheets and sleeping-bags and saucepans and food and axes and everything else one needs in the interior of an unmapped, uninhabitable and inhospitable country. My own load, I know, weighed exactly one hundred and fourteen pounds, and someone else always had to help me hoist the rucksack on to my back in the mornings. We lived on pemmican and lentils, and the twelve of us who went separately on what was called the Long March from the north to the south of the island and back again suffered a good deal from lack of food. I can remember very clearly how we experimented with eating boiled lichen and reindeer moss to supplement our diet. But it *was* a genuine adventure and I returned home hard and fit and ready for anything.

There followed two years of intensive training with the Shell Company in England. We were seven trainees in that year's group and each one of us was being carefully prepared to uphold the majesty of the Shell Company in one or another remote tropical country. We spent weeks at the huge Shell Haven Refinery with a special instructor who taught us all about fuel oil and diesel oil and gas oil and lubricating oil and kerosene and gasoline.

After that we spent months at the Head Office in London learning how the great company functioned from the inside. I was still living in Bexley, Kent, with my mother and three sisters, and every morning, six days a week, Saturdays included, I would dress neatly in a sombre grey suit, have breakfast at seven forty-five and then, with a brown trilby on my head and a furled umbrella in my hand, I would board the eight-fifteen train to London together with a swarm of other equally sombre-suited businessmen. I found it easy to fall into their pattern. We were all very serious and dignified gents taking the train to our offices in the City of London where each of us, so we thought, was engaged in high finance and other enormously important matters. Most of my companions wore hard bowler hats, and a few like me wore soft trilbys, but not one of us on that train in the year of 1934 went bareheaded. It wasn't done. And none of us, even on the sunniest days, went without his furled umbrella. The umbrella was our badge of office. We felt naked without it. Also it was a sign of respectability. Road-menders and plumbers never went to work with umbrellas. Business-men did.

the Businessman

I enjoyed it, I really did. I began to realize how simple life could be if one had a regular routine to follow with fixed hours and a fixed salary and very little original thinking to do. The life of a writer is absolute hell compared with the life of a businessman. The writer has to force himself to work. He has to make his own hours and if he doesn't go to his desk at all there is nobody to scold him. If he is a writer of fiction he lives in a world of fear. Each new day demands new ideas and he can never be sure whether he is going to come up with them or not. Two hours of writing fiction leaves this particular writer absolutely drained. For those two hours he has been miles away, he has been somewhere else, in a different place with totally different people, and the effort of swimming back into normal surroundings is very great. It is almost a shock. The writer walks out of his workroom in a daze. He wants a drink. He needs it. It happens to be a fact that nearly every writer of fiction in the world drinks more whisky than is good for him. He does it to give himself faith, hope and courage. A person is a fool to become a writer. His only compensation is absolute freedom. He has no master except his own soul, and that, I am sure, is why he does it.

The Shell Company did us proud. After twelve months at Head Office, we trainees were all sent away to various Shell branches in England to study salesmanship. I went to Somerset and spent several glorious weeks selling kerosene to old ladies in remote villages. My kerosene motor-tanker had a tap at the back and when I rolled into Shepton Mallet or Midsomer Norton or Peasedown St John or Hinton Blewett or Temple Cloud or Chew Magna or Huish Champflower, the old girls and the young maidens would hear the roar of my motor and would come out of their cottages with jugs and buckets to buy a gallon of kerosene for their lamps and their heaters. It is fun for a young man to do that sort of thing. Nobody gets a nervous breakdown or a heart attack from selling kerosene to gentle country folk from the back of a tanker in Somerset on a fine summer's day.

Then suddenly, in 1936, I was summoned back to Head Office in London. One of the Directors wished to see me. 'We are sending you to Egypt,' he said. 'It will be a three-year tour, then six months' leave. Be ready to go in one week's time.'

'Oh, but sir!' I cried out. 'Not *Egypt*! I really don't want to go to *Egypt*!'

The great man reeled back in his chair as though I had slapped him in the face with a plate of poached eggs. 'Egypt', he said slowly, 'is one of our finest and most important areas. We are doing you a *favour* in sending you there instead of to some mosquito-ridden place in the swamps!'

I kept silent.

'May I ask why you do not wish to go to Egypt?' he said.

I knew perfectly well why, but I didn't know how to put it. What I wanted was jungles and lions and elephants and tall coconut palms swaying on silvery beaches, and Egypt had none of that. Egypt was desert country. It was bare and sandy and full of tombs and relics and Egyptians and I didn't fancy it at all.

'What is wrong with Egypt?' the Director asked me again.

'It's . . . it's . . . it's', I stammered, 'it's too *dusty*, sir.'

The man stared at me. 'Too *what*?' he cried.

'Dusty,' I said.

'*Dusty!*' he shouted. 'Too *dusty*! I've never heard such rubbish!'

There was a long silence. I was expecting him to tell me to fetch my hat and coat and leave the building for ever. But he didn't do that. He was an awfully nice man and his name was Mr Godber. He gave a deep sigh and rubbed a hand over his eyes and said, 'Very well then, if that's the way you want it. Redfearn will go to Egypt instead of you and you will have to take the next posting that comes up, dusty or not. Do you understand?'

'Yes, sir, I realize that.'

'If the next vacancy happens to be Siberia,' he said, 'you'll have to take it.'

'I quite understand, sir,' I said. 'And thank you very much.'

Within a week Mr Godber summoned me again to his office. 'You're going to East Africa,' he said.

'Hooray!' I shouted, jumping up and down. 'That's marvellous, sir! That's wonderful! How terrific!'

The great man smiled. 'It's quite dusty there too,' he said.

'Lions!' I cried. 'And elephants and giraffes and coconuts everywhere!'

'Your boat leaves from London Docks in six days,' he said. 'You get off at Mombasa. Your salary will be five hundred pounds per annum and your tour is for three years.'

I was twenty years old. I was off to East Africa where I would walk about in khaki shorts every day and wear a topi on my head! I was ecstatic. I rushed home and told my mother. 'And I'll be gone for three years,' I said.

I was her only son and we were very close. Most mothers, faced with a situation like this, would have shown a certain amount of distress. Three years is a long time and Africa was far away. There would be no visits in between. But my mother did not allow even the tiniest bit of what she must have felt to disturb my joy. 'Oh, well done *you*!' she cried. 'It's wonderful news! And it's just where you wanted to go, isn't it!'

The whole family came down to London Docks to see me off on the boat. It was a tremendous thing in those days for a young man to be going off to Africa to work. The journey alone would take two weeks, sailing through the Bay of Biscay, past Gibraltar, across the Mediterranean, through the Suez Canal and the Red Sea, calling in at Aden and arriving finally at Mombasa. What a prospect that was!

I was off to the land of palm-trees and coconuts and coral reefs and lions and elephants and deadly snakes, and a white hunter who had lived ten years in Mwanza had told me that if a black mamba bit you, you died within the hour writhing in agony and foaming at the mouth. I couldn't wait.

mama, 1936

Although I didn't know it at the time, I was sailing away for a good deal longer than three years because the Second World War was to come along in the middle of it all. But before that happened, I got my African adventure all right. I got the roasting heat and the crocodiles and the snakes and the long safaris up-country, selling Shell oil to the men who ran the diamond mines and the sisal plantations. I learned about an extraordinary machine called a decorticator (a name I have always loved) which shredded the big leathery sisal leaves into fibre. I learned to speak Swahili and to shake the scorpions out of my mosquito boots in the mornings. I learned what it was like to get malaria and to run a temperature of 105°F for three days, and when the rainy seasons came and the water poured down in solid sheets and flooded the little dirt roads, I learned how to spend nights in the back of a stifling station-wagon with all the windows closed against marauders from the jungle. Above all, I learned how to look after myself in a way that no young person can ever do by staying in civilization.

When the big war broke out in 1939, I was in Dar es Salaam, and from there I went up to Nairobi to join the RAF. Six months later, I was a fighter pilot flying Hurricanes all round the Mediterranean. I flew in the Western Desert of Libya, in Greece, in Palestine, in Syria, in Iraq and in Egypt. I shot down some German planes and I got shot down myself, crashing in a burst of flames and crawling out and getting rescued by brave soldiers crawling on their bellies over the sand. I spent six months in hospital in Alexandria, and when I came out, I flew again.

But all that is another story. It has nothing to do with childhood or school or Gobstoppers or dead mice or Boazers or summer holidays among the islands of Norway. It is a different tale altogether, and if all goes well, I may have a shot at telling it one of these days.

Love from
Boy

ROALD DAHL SAYS

'I think probably kindness is my number one attribute in a human being. I'll put it before any of the things like courage or bravery or generosity or anything else. If you're kind, that's it.'

'I am totally convinced that most grown-ups have completely forgotten what it is like to be a child between the ages of five and ten . . . I can remember exactly what it was like. I am certain I can.'

'When I first thought about writing the book *Charlie and the Chocolate Factory*, I never originally meant to have children in it at all!'

'If I had my way, I would remove January from the calendar altogether and have an extra July instead.'

'You can write about anything for children as long as you've got humour.'

Roald Dahl's
PUFFIN PASSPORT

Autograph	*Roald Dahl*
Birthday	13 September, 1916
Colour of eyes	Blue-grey
Colour of hair	Greyish
Special virtue	Never satisfied with what I've done.
Special vice	Drinking
Favourite colour	Yellow
Favourite food	Caviar

Favourite music — Beethoven

Favourite personality — My wife and children

Favourite sound — Piano

Favourite TV programme — News

Favourite smell — Bacon frying

Favourite book when young — "Mr. Midshipman Easy"

If I wasn't an author I'd like to be — A Doctor

My most frightening moment — In a Hurricane, 1941, RAF

My funniest moment — Being born

Motto

My candle burns at both ends
It will not last the night
But ah my foes and oh my friends
It gives a lovely light.

A DAY IN THE LIFE OF
Roald Dahl

Roald Dahl had a very strict daily routine. He would eat breakfast in bed and open his post. At 10.30 a.m. he would walk through the garden to his writing hut and work until 12 p.m. when he went back to the house for lunch – typically, a gin and tonic followed by Norwegian prawns with mayonnaise and lettuce. At the end of every meal, Roald and his family had a chocolate bar chosen from a red plastic box.

After a snooze, he would take a flask of tea back to the writing hut and work from 4 p.m. till 6 p.m. He would be back at the house at exactly six o'clock, ready for his dinner.

He always wrote in pencil and only ever used a very particular kind of yellow pencil with a rubber on the end. Before he started writing, Roald made sure he had six sharpened pencils in a jar by his side. They lasted for two hours before needing to be resharpened.

Roald was *very* particular about the kind of paper he used as well. He wrote all of his books on American yellow legal pads, which were sent to him from New York. He wrote and rewrote until he was sure that every word was just right. A lot of yellow paper was thrown away. Once a month, when his large wastepaper basket was full to overflowing, he made a bonfire just outside his writing hut (where one of the white walls was soon streaked with black soot).

Once Roald had finished writing a book, he gave the pile of yellow scribbled paper to Wendy, his secretary, and she turned it into a neat printed manuscript to send to his publisher.

Roald Dahl's
WRITING HUT

Roald Dahl wrote his books in a brick hut, which was built especially for him, on the edge of the orchard at Gipsy House. It was painted white with a yellow front door.

His writing hut was full of gadgets: a chair with a hole cut out of the back (to prevent pressure on his damaged spine), a writing board of exactly the right thickness, tilted at exactly the right angle, and an old suitcase filled with logs for a footrest. His legs were tucked up in a green sleeping bag. He also rigged up a rickety old electric fire on two parallel wires on the ceiling and would pull it towards him if his fingers got cold. Roald wouldn't allow anyone else inside the hut, so it was never cleaned or dusted!

The only thing in the hut that was cleaned regularly was the writing board, which Roald Dahl had designed and made himself. It was covered in green felt and Roald used an old clothes brush to sweep off the bits of rubber from all his rubbings-out. He simply swept them on to the floor and that was where they stayed!

The hut still stands exactly as Roald left it, with everything set up ready for writing. His cigarette ends are in the ashtray and the wastepaper basket is almost full. It's as if he had just popped out for a bit.

Roald Dahl's

WRITING TIPS

'A story idea is liable to come flitting into the mind at any moment of the day, and if I don't make a note of it at once, right then and there, it will be gone forever. So I must find a pencil, a pen, a crayon, a lipstick, anything that will write, and scribble a few words that will later on remind me of the idea. Then, as soon as I get the chance, I go straight to my hut and write the idea down in an old red-coloured school exercise book.'

Can you guess which book came from this idea?

What about a chocolate factory
That makes fantastic and marvellous
Things — with a crazy man running it?

Charlie and the Chocolate Factory

The reason I collect good ideas is because plots themselves are very difficult indeed to come by. Every month they get scarcer and scarcer. Any good story must start with a strong plot that gathers momentum all the way to the end. My main preoccupation when I am writing a story is a constant unholy terror of boring the reader. Consequently, as I write my stories I always try to create situations that will cause my reader to:

1. Laugh (actual loud belly laughs)

2. Squirm

3. Become enthralled

4. Become TENSE and EXCITED and say, "Read on! Please read on! Don't stop!"

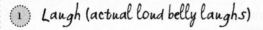

All good books have to have a mixture of extremely nasty people – which are always fun – and some nice people. In every book or story there has to be somebody you can loathe. The fouler and more filthy a person is, the more fun it is to watch him getting scrunched.

Roald Dahl's
FAVOURITE THINGS

There was a table in the writing hut on which Roald Dahl kept his collection of special things. And they're all still there.

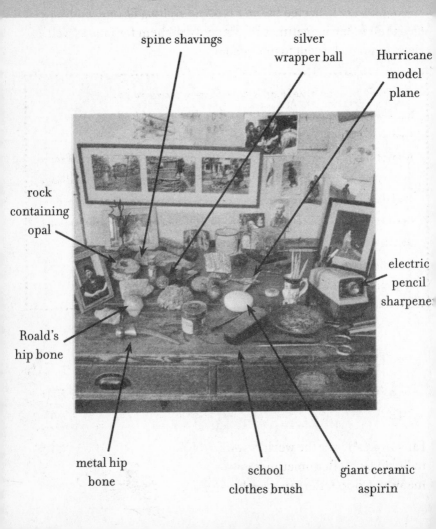

spine shavings

silver
wrapper ball

Hurricane
model
plane

rock
containing
opal

electric
pencil
sharpene

Roald's
hip bone

metal hip
bone

school
clothes brush

giant ceramic
aspirin

Roald Dahl's POEMS

Roald Dahl loved writing poems as well as stories. He often made them up in the bath.

His poems are collected in *Dirty Beasts*, *Revolting Rhymes* and *Rhyme Stew*, but sometimes he would write them for fans as well. Here's a poem he sent to one school:

My teacher wasn't half as nice as yours seems to be.

His name was Mister Unsworth and he taught us history,

And when you didn't know a date he'd get you by the ear

And start to twist while you sat there quite paralysed with fear.

He'd twist and twist and twist your ear and twist it more and more,

Until at last the ear came off and landed on the floor.

Our class was full of one-eared boys, I'm certain there were eight,

Who'd had them twisted off because they didn't know a date.

So let us now praise teachers who today are all so fine

And yours in particular is totally divine.

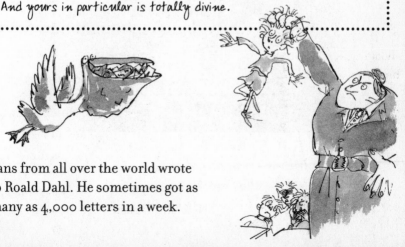

Fans from all over the world wrote to Roald Dahl. He sometimes got as many as 4,000 letters in a week.

GOBBLEFUNK

Roald Dahl loved playing around with words and inventing new ones. In *The BFG* he gave this strange language an even stranger name – Gobblefunk!

BABBLEMENT

A babblement is a nice gossipy conversation.

BOOTBOGGLER

An idiot or foolish person.

CHATBAG

A chatbag is someone who talks a lot.

ELECTRIC FIZZCOCKLER

A crazy Chinese sweet that gives you an electric shock.

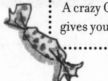

FROBSCOTTLE

The BFG's favourite drink. It's pale green and fizzy, and makes him whizzpop!

GLUBBAGE

Put it in the bin, it means rubbish.

HIPSWITCH

Means doing something very quickly.

MINT JUJUBE

One of Willy Wonka's creations, this sweet turns your teeth green.

ROTSOME

When something starts rotting and going a bit manky.

PINK-SPOTTED SCRUNCH

A venomous creature that can eat a person in one bite!

SCRUMDIDDLYUMPTIOUS

Delicious and lovely.

TELLY-TELLY BUNKUM BOX

The BFG's word for television!

WONKA-VITE

Willy Wonka invented this formula to make people instantly look younger.

THERE'S MORE TO ROALD DAHL THAN GREAT STORIES . . .

Did you know that 10% of author royalties* from this book go to help the work of the Roald Dahl charities?

Roald Dahl's Marvellous Children's Charity exists to make life better for seriously ill children because it believes that every child has the right to a marvellous life.

ROALD DAHL'S *Marvellous* Children's Charity

This marvellous charity helps thousands of children each year living with serious conditions of the blood and the brain – causes important to Roald Dahl in his lifetime – whether by providing nurses, equipment or toys for today's children in the UK, or helping tomorrow's children everywhere through pioneering research.

Can you do something marvellous to help others? Find out how at **www.marvellouschildrenscharity.org**

The Roald Dahl Museum and Story Centre, based in Great Missenden just outside London, is in the Buckinghamshire village where Roald Dahl lived and wrote. At the heart of the Museum, created to inspire a love of reading and writing, is his unique archive of letters and manuscripts. As well as two fun-packed biographical galleries, the Museum boasts an interactive Story Centre. It is a place for the family, teachers and their pupils to explore the exciting world of creativity and literacy.

THE ROALD DAHL MUSEUM AND STORY CENTRE

Find out more at **www.roalddahlmuseum.org**